GOLDEN PLAGUE

Ila Monroe

PADMORE PUBLISHING GROUP

GOLDEN PLAGUE © Ila Monroe. All rights reserved. Printed in the United States of America. No part of this publication may be reproduced or transmitted in any form or by any means, electronic or mechanical, including photocopy, recording, or any information storage and retrieval system, without permission in writing from the publisher. For more information, please go to: www.padmorepublishing.com

Cover design: Viviana Longueira / Gum LLC
© Cover: Padmore Publishing Group
Translation: Simon Breden / ComTranslations

This book is a work of fiction. Names, characters, places and incidents are products of the author's imagination or are used fictitiously. Any resemblance to actual events, locales or persons, living or dead, is entirely coincidental.

Library of Congress cataloging in publication data

ISBN: 978-1-939866-00-4 (ebook)
ISBN: 978-1-939866-02-8 (paperback)

Part of the proceeds from the sale of this book will be donated to the Cystic Fibrosis Foundation in the United States.

GOLDEN PLAGUE

GOLDEN PLAGUE • ILA MONROE

> "If I am to live in fear,
> I would rather die smiling
> with my memories alive."
>
> -Ruben Blades
> (Adán García song)

GOLDEN PLAGUE • ILA MONROE

To Sarah López, RIP
an angel now in heaven

TABLE OF CONTENTS

PROLOGUE: London 11

PART 1: Definition Of The Problem 16

PART 2: Lab Rats 45

PART 3: Changes In The Variables 84

PART 4: In The Eyepiece 118

PART 5: Data Analysis 144

PART 6: Relationship Between Variables 170

PART 7: Null Hypothesis 212

PART 8: The Resistance 326

LONDON

Miguel could not speak or read any English even though he had been living in London for three months. The label for the medications that he took daily behind his boss' back were in Spanish because his mother would send them to him straight from Puerto Rico in a sealed package. The second it arrived in his London mailbox, he would stash it in a suitcase beneath the bed so that his roommate would not see.

He shared an apartment with Paco Beltrán, who was eighteen just like him, but that was where the similarities ended. Paco came from Barcelona, the cradle of Catalan modernist architecture, although he was not the least bit interested in modernism, architecture or the arts. His fortes were sciences and languages. As well as Spanish, he was fluent in French and English having travelled the world with his parents. Being the son of an ambassador had its perks.

The day they met, amongst the thousands of details they talked about, Paco told Miguel:

"I have three homes: one in Spain, one in France, and now the one you and I share in England."

This was not the case with Miguel, as this was his first time outside his home country, on a quest for more time.

"Life is short, mom, you know that better than anyone. Let me have one last little getaway," he told his mother before the departure of his flight from San Juan to London.

Back in his home country, he would spend his days shacked up between the four walls of his house in the mountains, or prisoner to the depressing and unwelcoming hospital room that greeted him at least three times a year. His occasional excursions were either to school when he was not sick or doctor's appointments in San Juan, the capital of the Caribbean Island he called home. Today was the twelfth week anniversary of his first ever departure from Puerto Rico.

He woke up at dawn, not just out of habit nor to make some coffee, but because of the freezing cold of London's winter nights. That cold would work its way between the blankets and not let him sleep, forcing him to curl up into a little ball. Even with the heating on at full blast, Miguel felt the cold creep up his toes at about five am, making him get out of bed and jump into the shower to give himself a nice warm bath.

This morning is colder than ever, he thought. *Not even twenty minutes under the shower will be enough. I'll wait at least thirty minutes to let my bones thaw out.*

"Paco, get up", he yelled at his roommate the moment he stepped out of the bathroom, now fully dressed for the day.

The only time he made the mistake of setting foot outside the bathroom wrapped only in a towel to get dressed in his room, he immediately felt his balls seize up with the cold and so he had learnt never to attempt that again.

Likewise, Paco no longer bothered to set his alarm clock. Miguel was always awake before he was, so what was the point? Every time Miguel complained about having to wake him up every day, Paco would reply without the least embarrassment:

"I can't use the bathroom anyway, so I'm better off getting another half hour of sleep rather than torture myself by standing around outside the door holding my pee in."

This had actually happened to him once, and Miguel would not let him in, even though he almost caved the door in begging him to open up.

"Close the curtain you moron! What do you think, that I want to see you butt naked?" Paco shouted at him from his room that morning.

Nothing doing. Miguel remained in the refuge of the bathroom. This was why Paco had never seen his new friend naked, not even in briefs. Today would be the first time, at the end of the afternoon.

The roommates left their apartment after having breakfast and ready to accomplish their daily routine. They arrived at the laboratory very early. At once, Miguel thought:

It's ironic that the job I got is at a research lab when all I've tried to do all my life is get away from doctors and medications.

Even though the stench of chemicals and detergent revived his hatred of anything laboratory and hospital related, he had accepted the job because they promised good pay and guaranteed that they would only test the effects of certain organic dyes.

"Hey, look, we're not the first ones in," Miguel heard Paco say, noticing that Dr. Fowler was already there.

The rest of the staff arrived almost an hour later. They were six in total. Miguel only knew their names. He had never spoken to them, not even to Dr. Francis Fowler, who was his immediate superior. Paco acted as his translator.

So that they would not use the language barrier against him, Miguel made a special effort from the outset to do his job perfectly. Every day he would put on his gloves and mask and run the disinfectant drenched cloth over the tabletops, chairs and equipment. He ran the vacuum cleaner over the floors three or four times until there was not even the tiniest dust particle remaining and he cleaned the air filter every day even though not enough time had passed for it to become dirty again. Everything sparkled once he finished his meticulous work. He would do the exact same thing back at his own apartment.

That morning, his instructions for the day's work were the same as usual, but for the first time he had to repeat it at six in the evening while the rest of the staff went out for dinner.

"But what about me?" he complained to Paco when he broke the news to him.

"Don't worry, Doctor Fowler says we'll bring you some food," said Paco when they went out to find a place to eat.

The entire staff was excited about getting to eat at one of the area's many restaurants that only opened at night.

"There's no end to the working day today, Miguel. I'll bring you something delicious. See you later!" said Paco as he departed while his friend donned the gloves to begin his rounds.

An hour later, his voice trembling as he tore the mask off his face, Miguel screamed:

"It's going to kill us; it's going to kill us!"

He ran headlong towards the glass door that connected the laboratory to the main hallway of the building. Beads of sweat started to form on his forehead as if they were sent to rescue the runaway nerves all over his face. He could feel his face trembling, but the worst part was his cheeks that shook with the intensity of the chattering of his teeth. He suddenly came to a dead stop and leaned against the wall almost at the corner of a junction in the corridor. Although he had only run for a bare thirty seconds, he suddenly felt that he could not breathe, that his lungs tightened, and that his throat went dry.

At the end of the corridor he heard two doors open at once and saw through clouded eyes a group of men walking calmly towards him. Slowly, they came closer. They were all dressed in white, just like him, except for the tallest member of the group. This man was dressed in a grey jacket and trousers, the same dark grey that seemed to be enveloping everything around him. In an instant, Miguel sensed that the walls were beginning to disappear, to melt in front of him forming a large puddle on the floor. He had nowhere to hold on to, except for the floor, so he let himself drop.

Paco was the first one to see him sprawled on the floor as if he had jumped from a skyscraper.

"What's the matter?" he shouted in alarm as he carefully drew closer to his friend's pale face, seeing that his eyes were still open.

"Take me to the hospital," Miguel replied closing his eyes without looking at the rest of his coworkers who were gathering around him.

When he felt that Paco was beginning to stand up, Miguel grabbed his arm to stop him, and said:

"Take us all to the hospital," and he briefly opened his eyes to fix his stare on the man in the grey suit.

"What do you mean all of us?" Paco insisted.

But Miguel was no longer responsive.

PART 1
Definition Of The Problem

Chapter 1

Sam Cosgrove crossed a checkpoint manned by two private security guards before being granted entry to the house where his brother Josh lived, in a secluded part of Chicago inhabited mostly by high flying executives. The house was within a gated community that bordered on the ridiculous and the paranoid. Now he lived in this walled palace as his brother's house guest, who had insisted he abandon his hometown of London to come and be by his side. Sam parked outside the house marveling that Josh Cosgrove's home was more beautiful than his wife, more elegant than his associates, and more refined than his lovers. *And that is the way Josh wants it*, he thought as he checked to see if any lights were on in the second floor.

As he stepped out of the car and faced the entrance to the Cosgrove mansion, he could not help but shake his head while contemplating the imposing alabaster of its façade. *A house whiter than the souls that live in it*, he mused.

After that brief reflection, he proceeded to open the trunk of the car, from which he produced a small cloth package and a metal box. He had a key to the French doors to Josh's office which opened out to the patio, and he headed towards them.

As he drew nearer, he could make out through the windows that his brother was in the office. He was chatting on the phone, perched on a black carved mahogany desk which had "cost him an arm and a leg" as he liked to remind him. While his brother continued his conversation, the light in one of the bedrooms on the second floor went out. Sam did not think twice about it. He climbed a stone staircase that connected the patio to the upper balcony and in less than a minute was standing before the double doors to the master bedroom. He could make out the room through the translucent curtains, but there was only one thing in there he was interested in and it lay on the bed.

Sam opened the door cautiously, slipped into the room, and advanced firmly towards the edge of the bed. He nudged the mattress with his knee and gave a hushed whistle:

"Psst."

Josh's wife opened her eyes slowly and looked around in a sleepy daze. It did not matter at what point she realized she was in trouble, since there was no longer anything she could do about it. A second later Sam covered her mouth, pressing down with his left hand, and immobilized her by resting his entire body on top of hers.

Sam saw the fear and hate mixed with anger in her eyes; he was surprised at how much the reaction pleased him.

"Don't be silly and don't try to scream. Josh is in his office and he might hear you."

She lay still, but even so the man's hand remained over her mouth.

"I'm going to start now", he announced.

With his free hand, Sam lifted the hem of her nightgown and caressed the skin beneath her lace panties, enjoying himself. He delved deeper until he reached her pubis and he ran two fingers through her tuft. Eventually he tired of toying with her, and forcefully pushed his fingers inside her.

The woman's eyes rolled into the back of her head, and her groan was audible even though Sam's hand was still pressing against her mouth.

"You like this?" he asked, staring fixedly at her.

She struggled a little beneath him. She closed her eyes and shook her head hard from side to side, but not enough to shake loose the hand that was gagging her.

"Oh no you don't, don't stop looking at me. Open your eyes" he begged intensely as he pressed his forehead against hers. "Look at me!" he ordered when he realized that he had not convinced her the first time.

As soon as she opened her eyes, he pulled his head away to be able to see her better, and almost tenderly said:

"Why don't you answer me? Not sure? I only wanted to know if you liked it," and he removed his hand from her mouth.

She tried to close her eyes, but stopped when she felt the brusque movement between her legs intensifying.

"Do you like it or not?" Sam spat at her through clenched teeth, his hand still deep in her panties and roving freely.

"Yes," she murmured in tears.

"Now that's what I wanted to hear. You responding to me," he told her.

Sam stopped moving his hand all of a sudden, and released the feminine body. He hopped up from the bed, and watched the woman begin to cry inconsolably.

"Don't worry. I had never been in your room before, and I never will again. I was just curious," he told her, and winked as he backed out through the balcony door.

At the bottom of the stairs he found his belongings just as he had left them before ascending to the balcony. He collected them and crossed the patio towards Josh's office. When his brother saw him arriving, he signaled him to come in, not because he required permission to enter, but because he was longing to see the contents of the metal box Sam had brought with him.

"How are you?" they greeted each other putting their hands on each other's shoulders.

"It all went smoothly, eh? I'm proud of you, Sam. You have no idea how excited I am."

"You asked me to protect some little Petri dishes with my life, and that's exactly what I did."

"That's why I made you my chief of security. I knew you could protect my interests and those of the pharmaceutical company better than any stranger."

"I think it's great you have such a high opinion of me," nodded Sam, running the fingers of his right hand across his lips and slipping a tiny note of cynicism into his words.

For a second he drifted away from the conversation with his brother and listened to the sounds of the household. Josh's wife was coming down the stairs, her high heels signaling her intent to go out. He counted her steps. *One, two, three, four, five*. The door to the hallway opened and closed, and a car engine fired up and gunned down the avenue. Sam laughed inwardly.

"Let's see. Put the briefcase here, on the desk," Josh requested.

A dozen Petri dishes, circles full of knowledge, made of ultrafine glass were deposited in a special tray that Josh lovingly placed on the desk. They sat there, admired as if they were works of art by two grown men who as children would play at breaking glass containers for fun. Bottles, test tubes, milk bottles, windows... no glass was safe from the hands of the Cosgrove brothers when they were kids. Now they handled each Petri dish with the delicacy usually shown by museum curators when they hold articles of antique fine porcelain in their hands. But no museum artifact was as valuable as the contents of those Petri dishes, and their owners knew it.

"I'm turning in for the night, I'll leave you to savor your victory," said Sam with unusual formality, apparently getting carried away with the petulant atmosphere of the room.

"Won't you join me?" asked Josh as he moved towards the bar with a gesture indicating he was going to pour himself a drink.

"When have I ever joined you?" he replied and left the way he had entered.

By the back door to the house, as if that door were his personal entry and exit, his secret doorway.

———

Josh's slap in the face made his cheek pop like a chewing gum bubble. A burning sensation rushed to his face, his skin felt hot and he could not hold back the tears that welled in his eyes.

"I told you not to touch them! I told you not to touch them! Can't you see they're dangerous? Is that so hard to understand?" Josh Cosgrove yelled as if possessed, turning his back on his son Dean after striking him.

It was not the first time his father had mistreated him, but lately it had become more and more common. For any little thing he would hit him, pull his hair, pinch him, kick him, push him onto the bed, shove him against the wall, punch him in the stomach, and whip his back with a belt.

"Get out of here!" he yelled again, noticing that Dean was still in the office.

As the boy left, Josh Cosgrove removed his jacket and tie and rolled up his shirt sleeves and then pulled on a pair of rubber gloves and a mask over his face. When he finished getting ready, he sat down on a chair before the desk to minutely examine the twelve Petri dishes one-by-one and ensure that no harm had come to them. Everything looked normal, so he removed the gloves and mask and threw them in the trash.

"Clarita, Clarita, come here immediately," he called for the maid impatiently, "Take responsibility for that boy this minute. I don't ever want him in my office, is that clear? NEVER. I don't know how else to explain this," and without pausing, added, "Where is his mother?"

Clarita shrugged her shoulders in response, although she knew very well where Mrs. Cosgrove was. The lady of the house would surely get her punishment even though she had not been at the scene of the crime. It wouldn't matter at what time she arrived; she would be beaten until she fainted, as always happened whenever her son forgot the rules set by his father.

"All you have to do is bring that boy up. It's all I ask of you and you can't even do that right," the husband shouted at his wife the moment he heard the clip-clop of her high heel shoes tapping on the marble floors.

Josh never called Dean his "son", as if he were not his. As if somehow he were the exclusive responsibility of his wife, or worse, the product of his wife and some unknown lover. But Dean was his heir and he was sure of this because his wife did not have it in her to find a lover, not even out of revenge, and besides, he had ordered a paternity test at the pharmaceutical lab just to be sure.

"Mom, I didn't even touch them, seriously," erupted Dean when he saw his mother come through the door to his room, which was decorated in Western style.

The woman fixed her stare on an Indian amulet that hung from the wall, which her son had made four years previously when he was a Boy Scout. She herself had taken him to pick out the materials in the handcrafts shop, but had never found out how he had made it. His team leader had helped him. What she did remember was when Dean made her cover her eyes to hang the amulet around her neck on his return from the weekly meeting, as usual drenched to the bone in mud. She was standing in the kitchen. Josh, of course, had not yet arrived back home from the office. Suddenly her son rushed in like the clouds being carried by a high wind. Dean was eight years old when this happened.

"This will protect you from all evil," Dean told her as he dangled from her shoulders.

However, he weighed quite a bit more than a little boy, and his mother felt a sharp snap in her spine.

"Get off, get off, I can't carry you anymore!" she said pushing Dean away and attempting to extricate herself from him.

The amulet did not survive the push. The string that was holding it snapped and fell to the floor between the mother and her son. The boy's happy face transformed into shock and his freckles, up to then barely noticeable, suddenly sprouted, victims of the change in his skin tone. His face said it all… the moment was gone.

Since that day, her relationship with Dean had been tense and worsened day by day. Every attempt to get closer to her son was rejected with an internal violence only expressed by his eyes. The boy would flee from her arms now that he was entering adolescence and she had no clue how to retain him, much less when she had to discipline him to protect him from his own father.

"You know that your father doesn't like people touching his things," began today's sermon.

It was a similar version to the usual one.

"Why does he leave them lying around then?" replied Dean, noting that his mother had already taken sides in the matter.

He had never understood his mother. *Why does she cover up the abuse we both receive day after day under my father's yoke? Why is she still taking sides with the villain?*

"That doesn't mean you have permission to touch them, Dean. Why do you insist on behaving like a little boy, acting out the whole time? You're twelve years old now. You know better. Your father's things are very delicate."

"They're not delicate. He's a control freak. It's as if we lived in a glass house! 'Don't touch this, don't touch that'. Always the same old, same old," said the angry little boy.

"Dean, you can do whatever you want on the second floor, but the first floor is your father's territory, particularly his office. Why can't you just…?"

The boy interrupted her:

"Mom, are you listening to yourself? I can't be on the first floor of my own home?"

"Don't be so dramatic, Dean, it doesn't suit you. What I'm telling you is to leave your father in peace, and he will leave us in peace."

"You mean ignore us."

"I mean, in peace," replied his mother bitterly. "The more invisible we are to him, the better."

"Then you and me may as well go and live someplace else. Problem solved."

"Ok, and who is going to pay for the house, food and your wonderful school? Why do you think your father works so much? He has a sensitive job, Dean. It's up to him that the company goes well. It's a huge responsibility. Who knows what's in those Petri dishes you were playing with! The cure for cancer maybe, and you're sticking your nose where it's not welcome."

"Some cure, yeah right! I don't think so because he told me they were dangerous."

"Dangerous?" asked the mother with an expression of concern, now gripping her son by the shoulders.

Dean shook himself free, sharply pulled away from his mother, and from the other side of the room yelled:

"Yes, dangerous!"

"If he told you they were dangerous, then they must be," said his mother in a soothing voice, turning to look right at her son.

"Aw, mom, you always take his side. How dangerous can they be when I heard him tell Uncle

Sam that they would be the salvation of MagMell Laboratories?"

With that, the boy decided the conversation was over. He went into his en-suite bathroom, but left the door open. He stood in front of the toilet, pulled down his pants and briefs to his ankles, and calmly began to urinate. Needing no further provocation, his mother left his room.

Chapter 2

Ten minutes before the agreed time, Valeria Loperena arrived at the foyer of MagMell Laboratories' offices. The marketing and PR agency which she worked for had won the contract to represent them, the victors of a long campaign between five agencies fighting over the account. This triumph would give Valeria her first shot at working for a pharmaceutical company, alongside her best friend Mercedes.

Merci, as she affectionately dubbed her, was the Marketing Manager in charge of launching the company's new product, so together they would select the most appropriate marketing campaign. As part of the promotion, they would prepare television, radio and written press ads, in particular aimed at health magazines and those directed towards the target market of women between twenty-five and sixty-five who were more likely to pay attention to illness prevention topics.

They would not be buying billboard space because those were not appropriate to the pharmaceutical industry. Instead they would be preparing information leaflets. There would be one task entirely new to Valeria: she could not forget to add the awful list of specifications that always accompanied the ads, as required by the FDA. The small print explaining the side effects of all medications sold in the United States. *The one that tells consumers watching TV ads of perfectly healthy people that taking the medication could perforate their liver and that pregnant women cannot take any medication, absolutely none, while they are carrying due to the risk of giving birth to a monster*, she thought as she made a mental note not to forget the specifications.

When she got to the forty floor building that housed the main offices of MagMell, Valeria took some time to open the solid glass door to the foyer. She became entranced with the vision of an impressive sculpted bronze map of the world. The sculpture floated on immense glass sheets, representing the global presence of the pharmaceutical company. A shining blue dot on the city of London indicated where it had all started.

Once inside the foyer, Valeria skirted around the sculpture and slid her high heel shoes over a soft beige carpet adorned with a thick blue stripe, symbolizing the company's color scheme. She followed the path indicated by the carpet, and arrived at the reception area where she was signed into the guestbook after giving the name of the person she had come to visit. Then she sat down on one of the three enormous beige sofas that formed a perfect square in front of a digital wall that displayed several messages and ads of company products. One of them caught her eye.

In the first scene, a colossal boat resting on a river of purest white clouds was waiting for some patients. All were dressed in white robes and came walking across a verdant plain that converged with the exits to hundreds of hospitals visible in the distance. The patients were strolling slowly, unhurried, and one-by-one climbed onto the great boat. Once it was full of people, the boat glided up along the river of clouds and headed towards a majestic floating structure where the patients were greeted with coffers full of multicolored pills and medications in potion bottles.

In the next scene, the patients jumped off the boat and began to guzzle the treasures. Feeling restored, they joined forces, turned the boat around, all pushing at once, making the noises and grimaces characteristic of rowing crews, until they guided the boat back to the plain.

In the final scene, all the patients rushed off the boat across the verdant plain where they were greeted by friends and family. A soothing voice and a single phrase emerged from the screen:

HEAVEN CAN WAIT

Finally the company logo and tagline appeared:

MagMell Laboratories
Giving you the fullest of lives… here on earth.

That ad is genius! So effective! she thought, catching its meaning. It was a direct reference to the phrase Mag Mell, which in Celtic tradition symbolized a mythical heaven.

She glanced over at the reception desk to see if she was being called, but the receptionist was deep in a telephone conversation.

That campaign must have won an award! Valeria exclaimed to herself, again remembering the ad she had just seen, and suddenly she was assailed with doubts and thoughts of inferiority. *Why has a new agency been called on for this product if they already have a wonderfully creative one?*

All of these ideas and questions danced around her head for a few moments, but before she could dwell on it any longer the receptionist called her over and told her she was expected in the meeting room on the twenty-sixth floor.

She took the elevator on the left and hit the button for her floor. Inside the elevator stood an elegantly dressed man with a tailored suit and shiny shoes, who was reading a newspaper and remained absorbed in it as she entered. Since he did not even look up, she held back her good morning greetings. *If he wants to be rude, then so be it.*

A few seconds later the elevator stopped, two floors below her destination. The man behind her began to walk to the doors and stopped just off her shoulder. He lowered his paper and folded it at his side. He slowly turned his head, as if he were looking into

Valeria's ear, dipped his chin and with a penetrating stare spoke in a husky voice:

"Good morning, Miss Loperena."

She swiveled her head so abruptly than she could have seriously twisted her neck and been stiff for months. The man on the elevator was Mr. Josh Cosgrove, President and General Manager of MagMell Laboratories, and the person she would be meeting imminently.

"I didn't recognize you, Mr. Cosgrove. Sorry I didn't say hello," she managed to stammer before he left the elevator.

I already started on the wrong foot, she scolded herself as she ascended the last two floors to her destination. Mercedes was waiting for her at the elevator doors, so Valeria relaxed when she saw her friend. She immediately told her about the greeting incident.

"Don't worry about it, Vale. He loves doing that sort of thing. Going unnoticed. He does it to feel more powerful. You have no idea how often I'm concentrating in my office working on the computer and I suddenly discover him just sitting there in front of me. I swear I don't know how he does it, but you can't hear his footsteps, you can barely tell he's breathing, until he's right beside you. It's horrible," she said, trying to briefly explain the habits of her boss, Josh Cosgrove.

Mercedes introduced Valeria to her personal assistant, who was waiting for them in the middle of the corridor and who signaled that the meeting room was now ready.

"Thanks, Claire", and they headed towards Mercedes' office.

"Go on, sit down. We have a few minutes before the meeting begins. Would you like a coffee?"

"No thanks, I'm good."

"I'm so excited that we're going to work together on this project," said Mercedes.

"Me too, although I've got to say I'm a little on edge. It's the first time I've worked with a pharmaceutical company."

"That's exactly why Mr. Cosgrove picked you. He wants a fresh marketing campaign, something different from the norm, from what we're used to. The agencies we hire for the rest of our products are good, but we want something more modern for this one, something out of the ordinary for the pharmaceutical industry. That's where you come in."

"Ok, enough flattery. I guess that once I have all the details and get to know the product I'll get over my nerves. You know the ones I always get when we start a new campaign. Like an actor waiting to take the stage. You may have done it a million times, but you can't help but feel nervous."

Standing at 5'9" and with a considerable bust, Valeria oozed sensuality, but she tried to ignore this fact. She wore a touch of make-up, neither too little nor too much. A healthy dose of mascara to highlight her eyes, some foundation to light up her skin and a dark eyeliner but only applied to her upper eyelid to make her eyes seem even bigger. Her mouth loathed rouge. She preferred natural tones and clear lipgloss that gave her lips the effect of being constantly moist.

While they waited to be told that Mr. Cosgrove was ready to meet them, Valeria and Mercedes caught up on their private lives.

"I don't like any of Gabriela's friends, and they're only twelve years old", Mercedes complained as they began their conversation. "Marianne likes to act like she's older, Isabel has no common sense, Camille has no personality, Patrice is super bossy, Olivia is dumb, extra dumb; Dinorah is a mass of insecurities and as for Gabriela, my dearest Gabriela, she's naïve to the nth degree. They make a hell of a group."

"I see you think very highly of them! An excellent opinion of your daughter's best friends!"

"I can't help but notice what's blindingly obvious! They're seven girls in total, too many to be real friends, but no matter how I explain it, my advice falls on deaf ears. The cloying mother whose opinion is no longer wanted."

"Merci, you're much too involved in Gabriela's life. Leave her alone," Valeria mischievously scolded her.

Valeria and Mercedes had been friends since childhood. Their parents were Puerto Rican immigrants who arrived to the United States in the fifties and, by chance the girls were enrolled in the same academy to take Spanish lessons on Saturday afternoons so that they could practice the language of their grandparents. Ever since they met, they became inseparable at school, in the neighborhood and at the ballroom dancing classes. But suddenly they drifted apart at the age of eighteen. They followed different paths when they went to college. Now, as adults, they were seeing each other more than ever because they lived and worked in Chicago, the same town they grew up in.

"How can I not try to protect her from her own ignorance?" asked Mercedes as she added two sachets of artificial sweetener to the unsolicited double espresso her personal assistant had served her.

Having drunk her coffee, she added:

"They're only twelve years old, and they think they're masters of the universe. I wasn't like that at their age."

"Oh no?" interjected Valeria. "Are you forgetting how we would go into the shops and stir everyone up, going through all the shop windows looking for hats that would make us look like socialites? That shopkeeper, do you remember her? The one who always begged us not to touch anything and then would spend ages putting everything back in place after we'd been there. It was a miracle she kept her job for so long. We really took advantage of her good grace!"

"That was just the harmless mischief of extremely bored little girls," Mercedes said defending herself and giggling at those divine memories.

"Can you bring me the product portfolio?" Mercedes replied to her personal assistant when she asked if she needed anything else. "We were simply very, very bored," she continued addressing Valeria.

"And what do you think is wrong with your daughter and her friends? I don't suppose you expect them to be reading philosophy and literature at their age. They're having fun the only way they know how."

"I'm telling you she's going to get in trouble. They are too silly for the world we live in, Vale, and it will be all your fault for convincing me I'm a busybody."

She laughed explosively, as they both followed with their eyes the steady footsteps of a strange man who walked right by them. The man, who was over six feet tall, impeccably dressed, with cold, grey, impassive eyes, finally perched on the corner of the desk, after having briefly flirted with the notion of sitting on Mercedes' personal assistant's chair only to put it back where it was and then continue on his way to the end of the corridor.

"I guess he wanted some privacy. We scared him off with our malevolent laughter," they joked to each other while continuing to muse on why the man had changed his mind about sitting opposite them.

"He can watch us better from the corner," was the conclusion they arrived at, playing with the idea that the stranger was interested in one of them.

How right they were. They were the only reason that Sam Cosgrove was sniffing around there.

———

The conversation between Valeria and Mercedes went on unhindered for several more minutes. Even though they changed the subject several times, invariably the conversation returned to Mercedes' daughter.

"All it took for Gabriela was a few seconds in front of a mirror to suddenly yell: 'This blouse is for old women! Look at it!' I thought it was a pretty standard blouse, but my daughter described it as the most awful piece of clothing in the whole world."

"And what did you say?"

"I said: 'well, it's definitely not for old women because that fuchsia pink tone is for young people's clothes'. Obviously Gabriela ignored the 'obsolete' opinions of her mother and fled the store's changing room like a startled horse to look for other options. She came back with five different possibilities, all the same damn pink color."

Mercedes could not stop telling her story even faced with the incredulous expression of her friend, Valeria, who was about to suggest that perhaps they ought to talk about the marketing campaign and the new product from MagMell Labs.

"'All my life I've loved pink', Gabriela tells me every time she gets dressed to go out. In every single last photo she comes out wearing some pink tone. 'You're a genuine pink lady out of time', I tell her when I buy her anything in another color, but she always turns it down without the slightest consideration just because it isn't pink."

"Don't you think that choosing to always dress in pink is an expression of her individuality?" suggested Valeria, standing up to accept the offer of another coffee from the personal assistant since Mr. Cosgrove was being unavoidably delayed. "I'll help myself, thanks," she told the personal assistant.

"No, I don't think so," went on Mercedes, as she pointed her friend towards the coffee pot. "Do you know what she says every time I criticize her for dressing in the same color all the time? 'I love pink.

Why do you insist on making me wear other colors? Valeria always wears blue and you never say anything to her. Just because you don't like pink doesn't mean that I can't like it. I love pink, I love it and I love it!"

"How many times are we going to have the same conversation, Merci? You've gone over it a hundred times. Don't you think you're too involved in her life? Aren't you tired of her telling you so," Valeria ploughed on to prevent the imminent interruption of her childhood friend. "Of course Gabriela has to have her own personality. With her actions she is screaming at you that she doesn't want to be like you," she lectured.

However, she immediately swapped her serious expression for a smile and said:

"If you weren't on top of her every minute of every day, our little breakfasts would be so much more fun,"

Mercedes did not notice Valeria's attempt to lighten the mood.

"But it makes me mad! She doesn't listen to anything I tell her. The only thing we agree on is that Dean Cosgrove 'is hot'. Can you imagine? Dean and Gabriela?"

They had already discussed Gabriela's obsession with her boss's son.

"But how is she going to listen to you if you don't get off her back?" said Valeria in defense of Gabriela.

"Whose side are you on anyway?" Mercedes said challenging her.

"Isn't it obvious?" she replied mischievously.

She immediately realized it was time to stop before the argument escalated to the point of no return, and in an attempt to change the subject she added:

"Merci, it's time for you to find another hobby."

Big mistake. Mercedes launched into a ten minute monologue of sententious statements, all of them witness to her lack of time for hobbies.

"Being there for my daughter is my obligation, my responsibility, my reason for living. If I don't take this role seriously, then who will? My daughter will be lost amongst human faults, with no path to follow, no starting point, lost in an inhospitable world full of diversions and wolves."

"Forget it," said Valeria, "you're acting as if I had insulted your mother or something. Next time I'll follow my own advice and keep my opinions to myself. Like they say, I should be seen and not heard."

She placed her napkin on the desk as she finished speaking. The conversation had turned her stomach, and she could not finish her coffee.

It was not Valeria's intention to push her best friend away, but Gabriela's upbringing had always been a sore point between them. Valeria had always been there for her best friend, but as Gabriela got older, the gap had widened between them on this subject and become an unfathomable chasm. Only time would prove one of the two right. Or neither of them.

Chapter 3

After the unexpected argument with Mercedes, Valeria wondered if she had done the right thing participating in the proposal to win the MagMell Laboratories account. Starting that very morning the two friends would be working together at all times, and Valeria was not sure that they would be able to set aside their personal matters. With every passing day Mercedes was becoming angrier, more impenetrable, and at that point Valeria found it improbable that they would agree on anything. All this even though new projects always filled her with a positive spirit and new energies and helped her to recharge her batteries. This was what she most loved about her work, the lack of superfluous monotony and the fact that every month, or sometimes more often, a new project came along that just blew her away. New challenges and innovative ideas to come up with.

But now, even though she and Mercedes had always got along, she had unwelcome nightmares just thinking that due to her job they might end up tearing each other's hair out for weeks on end in a senseless struggle simply for neither to admit that the other was right. *But it's done now*, she concluded. Her new clients were already waiting for her.

The personal assistant interrupted them to announce that they were expected. Valeria leaped out of her chair.

"Girl, you just got up as if an Italian had just pinched your butt." Mercedes was still seated, mocking her friend. She spun in her seat and grabbed some folders from a filing cabinet. Once she had collected them all, she slowly stood up and walked towards the door.

"Easy," she told Valeria, who followed her down the corridor to the meeting room, slowing down with every step to match Mercedes' pace, but with the constant urge to overtake her and finally arrive.

"Why is it that you're so reasonable all of a sudden when a while ago you were acting like a girl having a hissy fit?"

Mercedes just smiled. Inside the conference room stood a large oval table, twelve chairs, a large projection screen, a podium and a sideboard with a coffee pot, milk, cream, three jugs of water, a dozen glasses and a tray with an assortment of petit fours. The room was bordered by wall to wall windows with views over the river, the LaSalle Street bridge and a wall of buildings on the horizon that gave the meeting room a sense of magnitude.

The spectacular view of the city of Chicago with its glass skyscrapers, spheres and spires that reflected the sun and admirably bordered the flow of the majestic river, could never cease to impress tourists and reinvigorate its inhabitants. The breeze that travelled down the channels made of streets and buildings between Lake Michigan and the other side of the city not only picked up all skirts, coats and scarves, but also the spirits of the people who had chosen this great city as the starting point for their lives.

Mr. Cosgrove was standing at the other side of the conference room taking in the view, while he chatted to another much taller man. Even at this distance, Valeria could appreciate that Mr. Cosgrove's presence imposed itself over that of everyone else present. He had thick white hair, cropped quite short, receding slightly on his forehead, which gave him a regal air. He was of slim build, and the dark jacket he wore framed the width of his shoulders. You could say that Mr. Cosgrove was athletic, that he looked after his body and that age had not fazed him the slightest.

"Here they are! The dynamic duo," Josh Cosgrove interrupted the hubbub of the gathering. "Ladies and gentlemen, I'd like to introduce you to

Mercedes Mojena, our Marketing Manager, and Valeria Loperena, Creative Manager of C2 Marketing. They will both be entrusted with the launch of VANCON."

A brief round of applause punctuated the introductions, which made both women simultaneously perform a slight bow in thanks for the gesture. They were the only women present, amongst a sea of men, nine in total, including Mr. Cosgrove and his brother Sam Cosgrove, the tall man in the corner who was visiting the Chicago offices for the first time.

"Sam is in charge of the security division in London, but for a few months he'll be working out of the North America offices," explained his older brother.

The rest of the men were introduced one by one. Some were doctors from the research and development division of the pharmaceutical company, others were executives from the legal department and finally there were two representatives from the ad agency who were part of Valeria's working team.

"We're going to have to forgive Dr. Berry. She won't be able to make it to this our first meeting. Instead we have her assistant Dr. Paves in her place," Josh Cosgrove said completing the introductions.

"Well, at least there is a female doctor," Valeria whispered to Mercedes, "I was beginning to think I could sue them for discrimination."

They both laughed, but their smiles froze after seeing all the doctors had sat down and Mr. Cosgrove was preparing to speak.

Why so many doctors invited to a meeting? thought Valeria as a feeling came over her that she had got herself into a mess. She was about to be bombarded with a medical lecture and she had not studied for something like that; her thing was the creative arts. She would now probably have to study more than ever to have any understanding of the needs of this client, who now required her help. But that was how she made a living, with precisely this kind of challenge, and this was certainly a nice juicy challenge.

She kept mulling things over in her head.

Why is there a representative from the security department? What kind of security are we talking about? She chewed on these thoughts while she observed Sam Cosgrove.

His face was familiar but she could not put her finger on where she had seen or met him before. *Sam Cosgrove is extremely attractive and virile, but not as much as my James,* she thought, *but certainly a distraction at a meeting where I need to keep my wits about me.*

"It's the man who ran away from the desk outside my office, remember?" Mercedes whispered in her ear, rolling her chair closer to her friend.

It was obvious that Mercedes had also been watching the mysterious man and had remembered where they had seen him.

"Now we'll have the chance to meet him," replied Valeria with a mischievous smile.

He's perfect for Merci, if only she could be tempted this time. Considering all the men she works with, it's a miracle she hasn't had a partner for so long, she mused. But Mercedes had a phobia about men.

"They're all cheats and liars," she said whenever the topic came up during one of their breakfasts.

"Not all of them. You had a good one beside you and you cast him aside like a banana skin," Valeria reminded her. "I still can't believe that you never told him he was going to be a father. That's a crime, everyone has the right to know."

"I've told you a million times. He was too young to take on that responsibility. What are you thinking in that dreamer's head of yours? That he was going to ask for my hand in marriage?"

"You could have given him a chance."

"Yeah, how? Long distance? Or did you also want me to adopt him once he told his parents he was moving out of their house. He was a kid."

"A beautiful kid who offered you love. The only love you've ever known, because look at how after all that you've become a bitter old spinster."

"Hold it right there, Valeria, otherwise we're going to end up disagreeing and there is no way you can win," she ordered her lifting her arms as if challenging her friend to fist fight.

Their conversations always ended in laughter just at the thought of a physical contest taking place between them, which was totally unlikely since Mercedes' musculature from her daily gym workouts would leave her best friend prone on the floor with a single blow.

"Miss Loperena's credentials are certainly impressive," Mr. Cosgrove was saying.

Upon hearing her name, Valeria had no choice but to pay attention and set aside her thoughts about Mercedes and their conversations about men.

"For four consecutive years C2 Marketing has won the prestigious Clio award, and in terms of personal achievements, Miss Loperena has won many other awards, in particular the Hispanic Creative Marketing Award when she directed the Latin market division here in Chicago and the agency offices in San Juan, Puerto Rico. Now we have the privilege of having her work for us carrying out the most important product launch of the last six years."

Stress, stress... now I definitely have to make it work, thought Valeria.

Her credentials made her one of those people who always get it right. It was a difficult standard to maintain. However, Valeria loved this kind of challenge. She loved the feeling of her adrenalin boiling inside her. The way it sparked her brain, which was always wanting to provide ideas at all times, even at three o'clock in the morning. Her best tool for making ideas flow was to take a bath in hot water. In the bathtub, the ideas would flow from her like water. She had taken many notes on that damp notepad she always kept within reach on the toilet seat. It was not the toilet seat that inspired her, like other people who used the porcelain throne as a writing desk. For her it was the bathtub.

"I'm going to hand you over to Dr. Parker who will explain in detail the background and how necessary this product is as part of a strategy of prevention in such a fearsome situation," went on Mr. Cosgrove.

In response, the doctor wearing the most serious expression stood up to take over the meeting. Dr. Parker began outlining the alarming statistics related to the MRSA bacterial infections that had taken place in the years since the discovery that staphylococcus aureus was resistant to most well-known antibiotics.

"It is resistant to meticillin, an antibiotic related to penicillin, which is the one most commonly used in cases of human infection,", he said as the giant screen lit up with the projected images showing case after case studying the bacteria and proving it to be resistant to the antibiotic antistaphylococcal beta-lactam, and to medications based on sulphates, tetracyclines and clindamycin.

"Only one antibiotic remains capable of fighting it, and that is Vancomycin," he concluded. "All other antibiotics that could fight it are at the design stage."

"MagMell Laboratories has no antibiotics of this kind in development, but our competitors do," interjected Josh Cosgrove.

What had most struck Valeria of the whole presentation were the statistics Dr. Parker presented from the CDC (Centers for Disease Control and Prevention) which indicated that MRSA infections were responsible for more deaths a year than those caused by breast cancer and AIDS combined.

"How can that be?" Valeria asked out loud.

She had heard and read hundreds of reports on MRSA, the 'superbug' as the press had dubbed it, but had never thought it was the greatest epidemic since AIDS. At least that's not how the government described it.

"When AIDS appeared in the eighties, there was a big fuss," Valeria began explaining to the gathering. "Massive campaigns were launched for prevention. All hospitals and doctors were alerted. Hundreds of documentaries and ads were filmed warning the community. Anyway, a big joint effort between the government, doctors, pharmaceuticals, the press, and the community to try to halt the spread of the disease as soon as possible. Why isn't this happening now with MRSA?" concluded Valeria.

As she was preparing to go on, she noticed that Mr. Cosgrove was speaking directly to her.

"That is part of our frustration, Miss Loperena. We do not perceive that the government, or specifically the CDC, are giving this the priority it deserves since the majority of the cases are being found within the "controlled" environment of a hospital," Josh explained. "As you go on reading about this epidemic, because here at MagMell Laboratories we consider it an epidemic, you will see the critical importance of the campaign you will create for us, not just because it should emphasize the significance of our product, but because it must make the public, doctors, and the government aware that they need to act now."

"Miss Loperena", added Dr. Parker, "we will provide you with all this information for you to study," signaling towards three, two-inch thick binders sitting before him. "If you have any doubts, just feel free to call me; I will answer them for you at once."

"Thank you Dr. Parker. I think after reading all that I will be able to apply for the position of Head of Research and Development once you retire."

Everyone laughed spontaneously. Everyone except Sam Cosgrove.

"Seriously", went on Valeria taking on a more formal tone of voice. "Thank you for your kind offer, as it is very likely I will need your help to understand some of the terminology of such a delicate and technical subject."

"Well, that woman didn't impress me at all," Sam Cosgrove told his brother without hesitation when his office door was shut.

"You didn't like her because she's livelier than we're used to. However, she's perfect for the campaign. You'll see, we'll get exactly what we want."

Seeing that his brother was not convinced, he added:

"She's quite skillful, but the best part is that she likes teamwork and listening to the client's suggestions, instead of imposing her own. I carefully read up on her profile before I picked her. Listen to what she said at an NBC interview." He read from a sheet inside the folder labeled with Valeria Loperena's name. "The most important thing is to get into the client's head, to turn into them for a couple of months, breathe like them, walk like them. It's the only way you can satisfy their needs."

"When she says client, she might mean the consumer, Josh, not us. You shouldn't think she's going to be easy to manipulate."

"Trust me," Josh replied, and they both left the office.

After their tremendously successful meeting, Mercedes and Valeria went for lunch at an intimate little Italian place on the corner of Clark Street. They felt like planning the task ahead, but at a more relaxed venue, to try to fit together science and everyday reality.

"This is a really interesting issue, but we have to adapt it to a language the consumer can understand;

that they will be able to process, but at the same time will make them take action. If not, we'll have wasted our efforts. We need to connect emotionally," began Valeria.

"We could use real life cases," suggested Mercedes.

"Put the families of people who have died as a result of MRSA infection on screen? Are you sure? It's a bit depressing for the first phase…"

"It's a question of getting people to identify and help them understand that this could happen to them, to their children, to their neighbors. Not that it could happen to them, rather that it is already happening and that's it," Mercedes emphasized.

"Yes, it's not a bad idea, but we have to be careful. We don't want to cause panic. There has to be a balance between taking action and people running scared and looting pharmacies across the nation," Valeria concluded while calling the waiter to take their order.

Once the waiter arrived, Valeria had no trouble ordering what she wanted: a dish of spaghetti with garlic pan-fried shrimp.

"Talking about diseases has made me hungry. Is that crazy, or what?" Valeria asked.

"Me too."

And they laughed heartily, scolding each other for dealing with such a serious issue so irreverently.

"If people could hear us, they'd call us insolent."

They laughed again, just thinking about the opinions of the serious doctors who that morning had served them a cocktail of medications and statistics.

Insolent indeed. A couple of little girls in the spectacular bodies of grown women, thought the man who was listening in on their conversation thanks to his earpiece.

Sam stopped the recorder when, over an hour later, Valeria and Mercedes said goodbye to the waiter and left the restaurant on their way back to the central offices of MagMell Laboratories.

PART 2
Lab Rats

Chapter 4

One week before Valeria's meeting at MagMell Laboratories, an ambulance was on its way to the A&E department at St Mary's Hospital along the ramp on South Wharf Road in the city of London. The paramedics briefed the waiting doctors and nurses the moment it pulled into the Emergency room.

"He's seriously ill," announced Paco, pointing at Miguel as the ambulance doors opened.

The boy stepped aside to give room to the paramedics, who were carrying his friend on a gurney. A second later they were lost from view behind the doors to the emergency room. That was when Paco allowed them to help him into a wheelchair.

Paco did not have the same symptoms as Miguel, but he had noticed a small red swelling on his shoulder, in the same spot he had scratched himself a few nights ago as he slept. He knew precisely what it was, but he could not say anything until the man in the grey suit, Sam Cosgrove, arrived.

Sam is in the next ambulance, so he'll arrive soon, he reassured himself at the same time as he wondered why Miguel was so ill.

Just then a curtain slid aside and a nurse with short blonde hair walked out. *She's beautiful!* he thought, becoming momentarily distracted.

He turned back towards the open curtain, stood up from the wheelchair and moved closer to see if Miguel was the person on the bed. It was him. All of his clothes had been removed, except for his underwear. The doctors were carefully inspecting every inch of his body. There was no swelling on his chest, but he had one on his knee. The swelling looked like an insect bite or a swollen boil. From where he was standing he could not tell if it was festering.

Paco observed Miguel's body. He was thin and did not have much in the way of muscles. *And he is seriously pale!,* he thought. It was not what he expected from someone who had lived in the tropics his whole life.

I wonder if Ana has ever seen him naked, he mused. *Will they get a chance to see each other again?,* he went on, but he paused his thoughts on his friend's girlfriend when he noticed a slight twitch in Miguel's legs. A mask was feeding him oxygen since he was still having trouble breathing, and Paco could hear one of the nurses saying he was running a high fever.

Just then, another nurse arrived with a tray, removed the oxygen mask and ran a swab into his nose to take a sample. Miguel was unconscious, but even so his face registered the discomfort of having someone rummaging around in his nostril. Tests would also be run with tissue samples taken earlier. The other lab employees were being placed on other beds, but still no sign of Dr. Francis Fowler and Sam Cosgrove.

What's keeping them? wondered Paco, scared that the doctors would start asking him questions and that he would not have a clue what to say. *Please let them get here, please let them get here,* he silently begged.

When the door to A&E swung open, he looked up hopefully, but instead of Francis or Sam, a man staggered in with a bloodied hand asking for help. He was followed by two police officers dressed in double breasted jackets and the typical bobbies' helmet. The doctors reported an incident where several people had been infected by a potentially contagious condition meaning that a representative of the Health Protection Agency would be on his way.

While all of this was going on, Paco mentally journeyed back to his first day of work. They had been warned from the start. Just like Dr. Fowler and everybody else, they had signed a confidentiality agreement, everyone except for Miguel.

"He won't be working directly with the substances, so he doesn't need to know," had explained Sam Cosgrove, the man in charge of the laboratory, on that first day they met three months ago.

Every day since the second week of November they went to work, including weekends and Christmas.

"We need results soon," Sam had explained with great intensity.

After much insistence, trial and error, and analysis, at last the tedious process was completed and all the test results were submitted. Today was the last day on the job. Their only remaining task was to close the lab until further notice.

His introspective mood was interrupted when he heard what the supervisor was saying at the nurse's station:

"The last ambulance with the infected patients had an accident in transit. Get ready to receive injured people."

What next? Paco wondered, and the panic began to grip his expression.

He waited until no one was watching and began to walk towards the street as nonchalantly as possible to avoid being noticed. None of the nurses realized that he was leaving the emergency room except for the one with the short blonde hair who shouted just as the door was closing behind him:

"Hey, you can't leave!"

But he was already running full tilt towards London Street.

"Wilton Crescent, please," he instructed the taxi driver to head towards his parent's apartment as he jumped in the car opposite Paddington Tube Station.

His parents would not be home, so he would not have to confront them just yet. The maid would open the door for him. However, Paco changed his mind, and leaned forward to give the cabbie a different destination address.

———

Forty minutes before Paco fled the hospital, the ambulance that was carrying Dr. Fowler and Sam Cosgrove advanced along a dark street on the other side of town. The driver stopped at a junction for a moment when the traffic lights turned red. That was when he got the surprise of a lifetime.

One of the ambulance passengers punched him in the jaw on the right side of his face, leaving him stunned for a few seconds, long enough for the man to wheel him around in his seat and finish him off with a second stronger punch to the other side of the face. It was the second blow that knocked the driver out, but it did not stop the rain of punches that followed.

Dr. Francis Fowler watched the scene unfold in front him in a bewildered state, cooped up in the claustrophobic rear of the ambulance. Instead of charging to the driver's rescue, he waited motionless for Sam Cosgrove to finish what he had started. Once the ambulance driver was unconscious, bereft of pulse and breath, Sam turned to Francis who was still frozen with panic. He, Dr. Francis Fowler, with a degree in Pharmacology and Toxicology from Imperial College London, was not used to violence. In fact, he loathed violence. He had been a victim of bullies his whole childhood and adolescence, who had targeted him for being short and a know-it-all.

"It's not your fault that you're the smartest boy in the classroom," his mother used to tell him every afternoon when he got back from school.

His classmates did not share this view, and they proceeded to punish him on a daily basis for his high grades and for participating in class until he stopped doing it. He went on getting high grades, but in silence. When the teachers noticed the change, they stopped announcing test results in class, but the damage had already been done. Francis continued to be the target of punches and insults until he graduated from high school.

Once in college, he concentrated on his medical studies and kept his distance from social life. His group of friends consisted of the occasional girl with whom he would enjoy brief relationships, and a couple of old work colleagues who he would meet up with once in a blue moon. His mother had died two years before, so now he lived alone in his childhood home. Absolutely no one was going to miss him if Sam Cosgrove managed to get his way.

I've got to get out of here right now, ran his feverish thoughts.

He quickly rolled over the chair towards the ambulance door, but before he could get there, Sam blocked his path. Just like when he was a boy, there was no escape. He blamed the slow reflexes he inherited from his mother and which now prevented him from saving himself.

"Don't even think about it," said Sam, poking Francis hard in the middle of the forehead with his index finger, pushing his head against the wall of the ambulance.

They were now seated and facing each other, so close that it felt like the walls of the vehicle were caving inwards making the cabin narrower.

"What are you going to do?" asked Francis, fearing the worst.

"Follow instructions, and obey protocol," Sam answered coolly.

"But Sam, you're getting ahead of yourself here. There is still no reason for a police investigation."

"Yes, but if we all arrive at the hospital there will be," said Sam with his enormous hands gripping the doctor's slim shoulders, practically shattering them with no effort.

Francis tried to persuade him.

"You haven't been exposed. You don't need to go to the hospital."

"But with you, that makes six," he said lifting the small man out of his seat.

"One person more or less, what's the difference?" begged the doctor.

"The others aren't microbiologists like you. They won't raise any eyebrows," Sam said firmly, tiring of having to explain himself.

"You don't think that five laboratory employees won't cause alarm?" the doctor said while trying to reason with him.

"Who said they were laboratory employees? They all know what they have to say. Case closed, but the authorities won't believe you."

With that said, he grabbed the sides of his head with both hands and began bashing him against the walls, the seats, and the floor of the ambulance. Fists flew and kicks connected. The ambulance rocked like a weeping baby's cradle. Until Francis stopped breathing and lay motionless beside the body of the driver who had died only three minutes before him.

There is only one thing left to do to conclude this mission, thought Sam.

He had to simulate a car accident for the ambulance and that both victims had died due to injuries sustained. He knew what to do. It would not be the first time that an ambulance had had an accident in transit with fatal consequences thanks to him, although it would be his first time doing so in London.

"Nothing to worry about. This is my home town. I know it back to front. It'll be a piece of cake," he concluded out loud, as he drove the ambulance at full throttle towards the platform.

Paco Beltrán fled St. Mary's hospital and headed towards his own apartment in the taxi he had originally hailed to take him to his parent's home. He never thought he would be going back to his place so upset. He had no idea how to process the day's events. He did not know what to do. He tried to contact Dr. Fowler, but all in vain. *Is everything ok? Have they escaped the accident unscathed? Why has everything gone so wrong?*

"We took every imaginable precaution," Paco said to himself out loud.

He had no idea how it had happened, but they had obviously got contaminated in the lab. Even so, he still could not believe it, because the previous night they were feeling great and both even arrived home in high spirits and with their arms full of vegetables and shellfish. They were planning to make a paella, a typical Spanish dish that would fill their stomachs and warm their hearts with fond memories. Neither of them would have admitted it at the time, but they were clearly suffering from a serious case of homesickness. Paco missed his home country and Miguel his Spanish girlfriend.

Paco recalled how last night they had divided up the cooking tasks as if they were two experienced chefs in perfect synch, and had started chopping up the vegetables together. Suddenly, Miguel got serious, looked Paco right in the eye and asked him:

"Is the substance they're running tests on dangerous?"

Paco looked up and put down the knife before answering:

"Not dangerous exactly, but delicate enough to be taking all these precautions."

"So why the big mystery?" insisted Miguel.

"Because the company that hired us also made us sign a confidentiality agreement. They don't want us discussing it."

"Is it illegal?"

"No." Paco replied.

He burst out laughing at Miguel's stricken expression; he was looking at the front door as if the police were suddenly going to burst through and arrest them both.

"It's not illegal," Paco reassured him. "It's normal for companies to require a confidentiality agreement to protect their intellectual property and prevent their competitors from stealing their ideas and commercializing products first."

"Why do I have to clean everything, over and over? Gloves, masks. I mean, I don't know much about all this stuff, but I have to admit that I'm not at all comfortable. It reminds me of a hospital…" and he stopped himself from going on.

Before his friend could ask him why he knew so much about hospitals, he quickly changed the subject:

"You know, like those movies where guys dressed like astronauts come along and quarantine everyone."

When Miguel saw Paco move to the other side of the kitchen, trying to hide the fact that he was swallowing hard, he realized that he had hit the jackpot.

"Could we get infected?" he asked in an incredulous tone, trying to convince himself that this was not a real possibility since twelve weeks had already gone by since they had been on the job and no one had remotely suggested that he was in danger of being infected with an unknown substance.

"I didn't say that," Paco replied.

His eyes betrayed insecurity and uncertainty.

"Of course you didn't say that. That's why I'm asking you! How could you not tell me? Don't you think I deserve to know?"

"Miguel, you have nothing to worry about. You aren't in direct contact with the bacteria."

"It's a bacteria?" he screamed slightly louder than you would to hail a taxi. "They told me they were testing a chemical on different materials!"

"I didn't say anything," Paco repeated.

Paco certainly did not manage to say anything else, because Miguel jumped on him and began hitting him over the head repeatedly with an open palm. An astonished Paco did not even have time to shield himself from the first blows, so the part of his head just above the ear that received the punishment was ringing like a church bell.

"What's your problem? I'm not your boss, or your dad. I am not responsible for you. Why are you hitting me?" Paco shouted, at last managing to get away from Miguel.

"Because you… because you…"

He had no idea how to finish the sentence. He wanted to say because you are my friend, but now that felt like a fantasy. In truth, they had only known each other for a few weeks. Even though they treated each other like brothers from the moment they met, as if they had known each other their entire lives; now he was wondering if they really were friends.

Paco noticed the uneasy expression in his eyes, and decided to comfort him as best he could.

"Listen, Miguel. You have nothing to be afraid of. The bacterium is called MRSA. Maybe you've heard of it on the news."

"Of course I know what MRSA is…" he stopped himself when his wrath almost made him disclose the following: *every time I go to the hospital it's what my doctors are most scared of.*

He did not want to confess his situation to Paco. He had promised himself that no one else would know. But the circumstances had changed. How did he end up in this lion's den, rubbing elbows with the very bacterium that could prematurely kill his dreams?

Paco went on, oblivious to the fact that Miguel was not listening.

"We've been very careful. The bacterium is contained in a controlled environment. We have taken every possible precaution. We use air-based disinfectants to ensure a sterile working environment and that's why you're constantly decontaminating the equipment and the work surfaces. Do you think any of us want to get infected?"

Miguel listened in silence. He had lost the will to fight.

"I'm young too, and maybe you think I don't know what I'm talking about, but medicine has been my passion since I was a little boy and every summer since I was fifteen I have volunteered at benchmark labs in every city I've lived in."

Miguel did not react to his companion's explanations.

"It was hard to persuade my parents to let me work, but since they thought that their son playing scientist was a passing hobby, they let me. I have been exposed to many situations like the one we're in now, with contagious substances, and nothing has ever happened. I can assure you that Dr. Fowler is an expert in handling MRSA. He is recognized in the scientific field for his work on studying the bacterium ever since its high resistance was noted over a decade ago. And the same goes for the rest of his team; they've been with him for years. They are all experts. The only newcomers to MRSA are you and me."

For some reason, none of this consoled Miguel in the least. Paco could tell by his expression, so he felt obliged to go on.

"This project is under the auspices of a world renown pharmaceutical company. I promise you. You have nothing to worry about," he said offering his hand to lift him from the kitchen floor where he had remained since the open palmed attack.

"Come on, let's make that paella. I'm seriously hungry now," Paco concluded.

But the shrimp, cod, onions and tomatoes remained where they were. Without looking at his roommate, Miguel picked up his backpack and left the apartment to take shelter amongst the shadows of the trees in Hyde Park. Still unnerved by what had happened, Paco threw himself on his bed without eating, and fell asleep leaving all the ingredients out. When Miguel came home several hours later, the stink of shellfish hit him so hard that he threw it all straight in the trash. The craving was gone and the desire to feel that his beautiful girlfriend was closer thanks to the food. Right then he decided that the next day would be his last so that he could get paid and leave London for good. Unfortunately, that was not what happened.

Chapter 5

He could not hear any footsteps in the corridor, and a sinister silence cut through the air. He could only make out a barely audible female voice; not the murmur of a single woman, but of several chatting. One of them left the group, her steps could be heard tapping on the white vinyl floor. She seemed to be coming closer. She stopped outside the door to his room. A second later she was inside. She did not knock to ask permission to enter, nor did she close the door behind her. She did not even say good evening or look at him even though his eyes were open and he was staring straight at her. She completely ignored him and went straight to check on the bag of saline solution intravenously connected to his right arm.

"Why aren't you asleep, young man?" the nurse asked him at last.

Miguel clearly did not understand because she spoke to him in English, but he guessed by her tone of voice that he was being told off. He instinctively closed his eyes to prevent the woman from continuing to talk to him.

Twelve hours had passed since he arrived at the hospital after the accident at the lab, and Miguel had begun to recover consciousness an hour ago. The doctors were administering antibiotics intravenously so they would take effect as soon as possible. He had a severe MRSA infection and the doctors were treating it aggressively although without much hope of saving him because MRSA infections are not easy to cure. In some cases they eat up the body a little at a time, in others they attack the patient mercilessly and take over all the organs with unstoppable speed until it's far too late to stop.

All of this was what Miguel assumed the doctors were saying as they slowly spoke to him, practically spelling out every letter, as if that would help to get their message across. But it was impossible. He would have given anything right now to have paid attention in those English classes back in school, or to have made more of an effort with those movies his mom watched on cable TV. All of his Puerto Rican friends spoke perfect English, but he had not cared. He had never shown an interest in anything that was not immediate, or that he could not use and take advantage of instantly. At least not until he met Ana. Thanks to her he began to look towards the future. His love of tomorrow began when he met her.

The first time he saw her, he had been taking a stroll to stretch his legs in his own room at the San Juan Presbyterian Hospital. He was numb from having been in bed too long, and worse still he was bored. His friends had sent him a book of logic puzzles, crosswords and Sudoku to kill time, but he had already completed most of them. He had also filled a whole sketchpad, but his mom had promised to buy him a new one that very day.

"It's a shame that I don't have it now, because I've had a great idea for a mural," he said out loud to himself as he walked around his room.

He was thinking of the colors he would use.

"Chartreuse green, turquoise blue, some splashes of orange, red and yellow. Really bright, with a modern air, something along the lines of a Joan Miró."

"Are you talking to yourself?" he was interrupted by the sweet melodious voice of a girl who was poking her head around the door to his room.

"Uh… no," he said, a little ashamed. "I was just thinking out loud."

"Isn't that the same thing?" asked the girl with a mischievous smile.

They both laughed and Miguel refused to leave things at that.

"Well, I just wouldn't want you to think I'm nuts. You don't have to be crazy to be here, but it helps... you know, like the joke?"

He just wanted to keep talking to the girl so she would not leave. She was the first person his age he had seen working at the hospital, and since his friends only visited on the occasional weekend, he was longing to continue the conversation.

"I'm not familiar with that joke. Are you sure it's a joke and not that you're actually here because you really are crazy?" the girl asked, and she laughed with such open honesty that Miguel could not help but laugh with her.

"I swear it's a joke, listen..."

Miguel told her the joke, and others from his repertoire. He had never had such a captive audience. All of his friends knew his jokes by heart; he had been telling them for years although normally not one after another. Now he felt like a stand-up comedian with a single spectator. For as long as Ana was having fun, there was no reason to stop, so he kept going until he could not dig out another file from the joke category in the department of memories in his head.

"Those are all the ones I know," he confessed.

"Oh, what a shame," she replied.

"You obviously like jokes."

"I like anything that makes me laugh," said Ana.

"So how come you work at a hospital?"

"I don't, I'm a volunteer. I only come here a few afternoons."

"But still, why do you come to a hospital when they're so depressing?" Miguel said repeating his question.

He could not read this girl. What was a young and cheerful girl doing in the pestilent environment of the sick?

"I keep my dad company. He's a doctor. Besides, I come here to make the patients laugh. It makes me happy. It warms my heart."

"Well then, mission accomplished. You made me laugh. You warmed my heart," Miguel assured her.

He stared intensely into her eyes, wanting to connect her heart to his and fuse them forever.

"What are you in for?" asked Ana, interrupting the brief silence.

Ah, reality. The magic would be broken for sure. Now she'll just look at me with pity, thought Miguel.

"I'm sick," was all he managed to stammer out.

"Really? No way? I would have figured that out on my own," said Ana mockingly, taking a step towards him.

"Why do you need more details?" he replied, looking down at the row of buttons on his pajamas, as if he were going to begin counting them one at a time.

"Because I'm nosy. Because I like to know everything about the people I meet. And you are today's victim."

"What else would you like to know about me?," Miguel replied shyly, not knowing if he would be able to answer her questions.

He was not sure he knew himself very well, so he doubted his ability to offer interesting information in a way that a curious girl could genuinely get to know him.

"How long have you been sick?" was Ana's first question.

It certainly was not what Miguel was hoping for.

"Couldn't you ask me what my favorite color is?" he replied, offering her a question he would rather answer.

"Why? Are you scared of talking about your illness?" Ana challenged him, now playing with the hem of Miguel's pajama sleeve.

She had stealthily drawn close to him and was beside him in the corner of the room next to the window. There was no view from the window. Its only function was to let natural light into the room. However, the same light that was so appreciated when a person who has been locked up longs to see the light of day, now felt like an intruder lighting up feelings that he did not wish to be revealed.

"I'm not scared of anything. Not even of dying," was his stung reply, moving Ana aside so that he could return to the middle of the room.

As he gently touched her shoulders to move her aside, he felt his hands sticking to her youthful skin through the thin film of her blouse. He quickly removed his hands noticing how they trembled, fearing they would give away his nerves and prove his anxiety.

"Wow, how brave! I want to be like you when I grow up," said Ana giggling, trying to hide how captivated she was by the back of Miguel's erect neck.

Her gaze traveled the length of his manly back to the point where his pajama shirt hung over his trousers. She could take her time over the examination, because Miguel was standing with his arms crossed trying to hide his face from her, so he had no idea she was looking him up and down.

Believe me, you don't want to be me, thought Miguel, but he kept it to himself.

He got back into bed and slid his legs under the sheets. He was silent and thoughtful for a moment. The truth was he was not afraid of dying. He often thought that the sooner it happened, the better. But there were days when his thoughts would drift and would align themselves into a sequence of happy moments. He would imagine himself rolling around on the beach with a beautiful brunette with a homely laugh. It was always the same girl. He could not see her face, but he knew she was beautiful. He would describe her to himself: her skin is white like the foam from the waves that caress her feet, and her hands are smooth like the clouds she tries to touch stretching her arms into the air. He could feel that he loved her, and that she loved him, and they played joyfully together dreaming of having three boys and two girls once they got married. But the dream always ended there... the thoughts of marriage brought him back down to earth. He could never marry. It would be too selfish of him.

"Let's see," he heard the girl's voice again, now bringing a chair close to the bed and sitting down. "You have an incurable disease. The prognosis is you will die young, since no one survives it beyond thirty-five. Am I warm?"

Miguel did not look at her. He was motionless, stiff as a statue. He had been so lively just a few minutes before as he barraged her with jokes. Now he was still, static, waiting for her to uncover all of his secrets.

"You undergo therapy to expectorate your chest twice a day and you take enzymes to help you digest your meals. Getting warmer?"

Miguel still did not answer as if he were listening to a sermon delivered by his parish church preacher.

"You have to take a load of antibiotics every day. You see? I know all of this just from keeping my ear to the wall," Ana finished with a laugh, referring to the punch line from one of Miguel's jokes.

But the boy did not find it funny. The girl had obviously read his file at the nurse's station. She already knew everything that he did not want to reveal.

"If you already know everything, why are you asking me? What do you want? To turn me into today's experiment? No, I get it. You picked the most pathetic case of all on this floor and decided to make him your project. Let's see if I can make this guy laugh?" Miguel fired off.

He brusquely cast aside the sheet that was covering him, and sat up on the edge of the bed.

"Are you annoyed?" Ana asked him playfully.

As if the charming boy she had just met had not just had a fit of anger, she moved her chair to come even closer to the bed.

Ana had seen him before. She spied on him when he walked up and down the hospital corridor, hidden from his view by the nurse station. She thought he was really cute. A little thin maybe, but with very handsome features. All the nurses said so: "What a handsome boy! It's such a shame he's so ill!" Ana always ignored the second comment, and enjoyed looking at him. There had been plenty of opportunities to visit him, but for some reason she never dared. She picked other patients, some of whom she had visited many times, to avoid his room. Something about him attracted her intensely, and she preferred not to explore those feelings rather than find out why she felt the way she did.

Today, for some inexplicable reason, she had woken up full of desires to set her fears aside. She dressed for school and between her classes planned an excuse to gain entrance to his room. She could always use the same line she used on other patients:

"I've come to bring you some magazines and books to keep you busy."

Or she could ask him if he wanted to reply to the satisfaction questionnaire regarding the cafeteria meals that she had designed herself so that the hospital administration could keep track of the tastes and preferences of the patients. Not that they paid her questionnaires the slightest attention, but it helped her to start a conversation with the patients and made her feel useful if maybe her suggestions were kept in mind. However, none of these options felt appropriate as an icebreaker with Miguel.

Little by little she learnt all of his personal details. She read his file every chance she got and ran her finger over his name, longing to do the same thing to his lips. Miguel had the most perfect lips she had ever seen in her life, which she went and admired every time she overheard the nurses saying he was asleep. Those were the only times she would go into his room, because she knew he was exhausted. She would change the water in his jug, and watch him sleep, hoping he would wake up. She wanted to kiss him before he was discharged.

Now that she had him sitting on the edge of the bed in front of her with an annoyed expression, she lost a little hope of kissing him. She had not planned to anger him. She had imagined the moment differently. Her fantasy involved edging closer to him as they smiled and he would have kissed her on the mouth, which she would have responded to unhesitatingly. Now she could not see how that was going to happen. It would have to wait for another opportunity.

She stood up from the chair and went to him to say goodbye. She did not want to leave him in this state. He looked at the floor and dangled his feet that were hanging as low as his thoughts. Ana lifted his face with the tips of her fingers, holding him by the chin. He brushed her hand away, but met her gaze. Almost whispering, Ana said:

"Don't be angry with me. I'd feel really bad if I made you angry. It wasn't my intention."

She did not even realize she had done it until afterwards, but she touched her lips against his, begging forgiveness.

When she tried to pull away, Miguel took her shoulders and pressed her close, preventing her from moving away. He looked at her lips, but his face did not move. He opened his mouth, but did not move his lips closer to hers. He was asking for permission to kiss her again with his gestures. She nodded, and received only tenderness with each kiss. She felt like a porcelain doll caressed by the most loving of owners. Her lips responded passionately to the honesty of his attentions.

Once they separated, they could not look each other in the eyes. A tear rolled down Miguel's cheek. So handsome, so tender, Ana could never have imagined it. Now that she had witnessed it, her desire was to stay close to him.

"I will visit you every day," she promised as she left.

How many days will that be? Miguel wondered as he watched her leave.

Many, few, only time could tell, but months had passed since that first kiss and keeping that promise to speak every day, and now he found himself in a hospital again, but this time in London. Today, just like always, Ana was expecting his call and if he could not find a way to communicate with her, she would not receive it. Miguel knew he had to find a way to express that he needed to make a phone call. But his eyes were closing. He was physically exhausted. The skin inflammation around the infected blister, the coughing and constant effort to breathe did not let him sleep properly, so he drifted in and out of sleep every few hours. He had not slept well since he had arrived at the hospital.

Chapter 6

As he entered his apartment, Paco felt an irrepressible anxiety. He looked out of the windows at least three times in a row; he repeatedly opened the doors to the rooms and the kitchen drawers. Fifteen minutes later, after conducting a thorough search of his home that even an armed bomb disposal squad would have been proud of, he became completely convinced that he was making too much of it all; that all the precautions were unnecessary and that if he really was being pursued then he would have plenty of time to escape.

If the ambulance carrying Sam and Dr. Fowler had an accident, who knows what condition they're in. They could be dead, he considered as he went into his room.

When he remembered the two men, his mind immediately travelled to that last day of work. His intentions that morning had been to confront Dr. Fowler alone at some point and ask him a few questions that had occurred to him after his argument with Miguel: why had they been picked to help out at the lab instead of more experienced personnel? How could a legitimate pharmaceutical company allow two young men who had not even graduated college to work on such a critical project as was being undertaken at the lab? Why had the lab installations been housed in a virtually abandoned building instead of any one of the ultramodern facilities that pharmaceuticals all around the world worked out of?

However, he never got a chance to ask his questions. Sam Cosgrove was also at the lab, and what Paco had overheard surreptitiously remained recorded in his mind like magnetic tape.

"Sam, would you like to see?"

Dr. Francis Fowler gently slid the high-resolution microscope sample to show the investor the morphology of the MRSA bacterium that was being studied at his cytology laboratory. The same bacterium that terrorized doctors and nurses, but most of all hospital administrators, once its presence became known in post-op patients.

"Don't they just look like gold coins?" purred Dr. Fowler with an almost affectionate tone, as if he were talking about a pet. Sam Cosgrove observed the tiny yellow circles on the digital screen, which now looked like harmless cells frolicking merrily, but when joined together would mercilessly eat the skin and organs of a weakened human being and invade the host without much effort when it was most vulnerable: in an operating room.

"Yes, that's just what they look like. Gold coins," said Sam still looking at the screen that was offering him a unique view of the fascinating germ. "The same coins that are going to make me rich and you…"

"…famous," Dr. Fowler finished the sentence. "That's all I want, to be famous. Famous for eradicating this fascinating bacterium."

"Even if innocents die in the process?" asked Sam, turning to look him right in the eye.

"Even if innocents die in the process."

Paco pushed the mental image away. Perhaps instead of a couple of hours he had only minutes to get away. The sooner he collected his things, the better.

He immediately decided to quickly collect some of his personal items and a few of Miguel's too. He could always find a way of giving them back to him later, or drop them off with the doorman in the building's lobby. He scanned his room until he found his backpack, and he filled it with shirts, underwear, socks and two pairs of jeans. Another pair of shoes, plus the ones he was wearing, would be plenty for the time being. Everything else he would just have to say goodbye to. He would have the rest of his life to buy more clothes.

Then he went into Miguel's room. He did not know where to begin. He opened the closet but could not find any bags or suitcases.

"Where the hell has he put it?" he asked furiously, struggling to understand how finding a simple suitcase in Miguel's room was so difficult.

He looked next to the bed, nothing. Then in their shared bathroom…

"Aha!" he said out loud.

He found a black case. It was a little small but it was all there was. Since he thought it was empty he pulled far too hard and ended up hitting himself in the thigh when he tried to lift it.

"Motherfucker!" he swore under his breath.

The case seemed to weigh a ton, or at least that's what he thought. When he opened it, he realized that it contained a strange machine with a series of tubes coming out of both ends and a navy blue waistcoat.

"What the hell?"

He yanked on it as gently as he could, and left the bathroom back to Miguel's room. Under the bed he found another large suitcase, also very heavy.

"What is this? Was he all packed and ready to go?" he asked himself in surprise, extracting the suitcase by force and placing it on the bed.

When at last he was able to open it, he was knocked off his feet. At first sight, it was not what he was expecting. There were dozens of medicine bottles, dietary supplements, folders and papers instead of clothes, shoes and books. He looked at the medicine labels: expectorants or drugs to aid to expectorate, antibiotics, pancreatic enzyme supplements.

"Miguel must have taken a load of pills before every meal!" he said out loud, still shocked.

Paco went on rummaging and also found nutritional supplements and vitamins.

How could he be so thin when he was taking these things that have so many calories? Thousands of questions surged to the front of his mind as he searched for answers in some folders he found beneath the medications. One of them contained prescriptions and handwritten notes from his mother on how to use the respiratory therapy machine.

"That was the thing in the bathroom," Paco realized, remembering the heavy bag he had tried to lift thinking it was empty.

According to the instructions, Miguel had to undergo therapy twice a day. The machine helped him to separate the phlegm from the walls of his lungs and spit it out. After each session he had to cough for a while to get rid of all that phlegm in his lungs.

When did he do that? I never heard a thing, he wondered to himself. *He must have snuck away while I was sleeping. That was why he didn't let me into the bathroom.*

The more he thought about it, a strangling knot formed in his throat.

He remembered hearing Miguel coughing violently in the bathroom early one morning. He had told him he was throwing up and that he had indigestion. Now Paco realized that after each therapy he had to cough a lot to loosen the phlegm... he did not do it while he was in the apartment; he had to hide. Like he did that day he had a coughing fit in his room. Paco walked over, knocked on his closed door and asked:

"Are you ok?"

"It's the damned cold," his friend replied.

It's terrible! thought Paco upon remembering all these details. *Why didn't he ever tell me? Why was he hiding it from me? Why was he so ashamed of it?*

He went on searching, and found another handwritten note with numbered steps for his daily morning routine:

1. Use the aerosol inhaler
2. Use the ventilator to clear out respiratory system
3. Expectorate with waistcoat
4. Eat a hearty breakfast, lots of calories
5. Take all medications, antibiotics, enzymes
6. Go to school...

It was a note that Miguel's mother wrote him when he was little so that he could follow the steps on his own. It was wrinkled and stained.

Paco began to figure the whole thing out. Miguel was suffering from some lung condition. He rummaged through the folder and came up with the answer. The letter confirmed Miguel's participation in a clinical study for sufferers of cystic fibrosis at Imperial College London.

Attached to the letter, he found a copy of a timetable of the days and hours he had to be present for tests. Paco now understood why Miguel's work shift was several hours in the morning and then a long gap until he came back at three in the afternoon. At the time Paco thought it had something to do with the convenience of cleaning all the instruments and surfaces of the laboratory at the beginning and end of each working day, but now he realized there was a dual purpose to it. In the middle of the day, his friend was a guinea pig in a rather important genetic study. He had a terminal illness and instead of waiting patiently for the inevitable end, he became a volunteer for an innovative research project in the hope that they would find a cure.

Paco could not disguise his amazement. He shook his head from side to side and laughed to himself. *Miguel has completely fooled me! Who would have thought that beneath that little mousy exterior roared a brave lion!* he reflected and in his heart he felt pride, admiration and concern for his friend.

In the last folder he found several letters, some handwritten; some barely started, others already finished. None of them were sealed in an envelope. They were loose sheets and open so anyone who found them could read them. Maybe he had not got round to buying the envelopes and write the addresses. Even so, irrespective of whether they were private or not, Paco read them. They were farewell lyrics for his friends. The one for this mother was full of sad phrases and many regrets.

Reading only the first lines, Paco understood that when Miguel called his mother half asleep in the early hours of the morning, he felt guilt and sadness. Many of the letters carried messages of love, tribulations of a soul in pain, a young man and a dreamer seeking relief. On one specific sheet, with borders decorated with colorful drawings, there was a longer message in comparison to the rest, which was addressed to Ana. This one was entitled: All I Want.

I want you to be happy to see me in heaven
without coughing or the ventilator;
Skipping and carried on four winds
full of health and courage.
I want you not to cry at night
for the brief time the creator gave us,
for I will always be grateful to Him
for having put you in my path.

*I want you to go after your dreams
beautiful girl;
To have a home for yourself
and to be a good wife.
I want to see you from high above
surrounded by grandchildren
and enjoying your life, full to the brim
of love and joyous happiness.*

*I want you not to worry about me.
My burden is almost gone.
I will be free. I will be happy.
I already want to sing songs in heaven
and the angels to take me on their
wings.
I want to be at peace.*

This I promise you.

Paco could not contain the tears any longer, which he bravely held in during the laboratory accident. Miguel had written that letter the day before, when Paco told him they were working on the bacteria. A mixture of remorse, pain, desperation and anxiety hit Paco from all sides, tore down his defenses and left him gasping. He had no choice but to fall back onto the carpet and cry like a little child. He held his chest as if this could stop the piercing pain that seemed to be cracking his sternum. He let the tears run freely down his face and made no effort to clean them away, drenching the carpet beneath him

Little by little his sadness began to harden and to transform into anger. He remembered Dr. Francis Fowler and the greedy look in his eyes when he spoke of how his studies of MRSA would earn him worldwide recognition; maybe even a Nobel Prize. And Sam Cosgrove, hurrying them to complete the experiment. Maybe the infection had happened because he was in a rush.

"Miguel and the others are victims of men without scruples," he growled as he suddenly picked himself off the floor.

He collected Miguel's folders and stored them in the backpack that he had left in the room beside all the food he found in the kitchen. He also stuffed away a knife for cutting bread and a set of utensils including a butter knife.

At the hospital, he arrived at the conclusion that he would not continue to be toyed with by his bosses and that he would not obey their orders. When he saw that Miguel was ill, he concluded that it was not the time to trust in anyone or anything. One single thought was running through his head as he looked at the prone body of his friend.

"What a coincidence that we would be infected the same day that the project ends! No sir, they are not taking me for a ride again," said Paco out loud.

As he prepared to close the suitcase, he heard the buzzer. The call was coming from the building's lobby, and the doorman's voice told him:

"There's a man on his way up to your apartment. I couldn't stop him."

Paco ran out of his room, suitcase in hand, and picked up the travel bag he left in the middle of the dining room. With his backpack, suitcase and the other case he was carrying too much, so he left his bag of clothes in preference of Miguel's suitcase, who he believed needed it more than he did. He had plenty of cash on him because his father was always giving him five-hundred euro bills. The antibiotic bottles he took from the laboratory were safely stored in the inside pocket of his coat.

He tried to open the emergency window, but it was hermetically sealed. *How is it possible that it's sealed if it's an emergency exit?* he screamed inwardly. That was when his nerves betrayed him. He did not know where to run, where to hide, or what to do. He was paralyzed in the middle of the room and his head swung violently from side to side looking for a way out. But there was none except the front door that connected to the same corridor where a stranger was nearing his apartment.

"He might come up the stairs," he said under his breath as he moved swiftly towards the door. "Or the elevator, which stops on other floors because people will be coming back from work," he concluded, gripping the door handle before opening.

"And if he's coming, he'll have to go through me!" he said, this time out loud to give himself courage. "I am stronger, tougher, faster and cleverer."

At last he convinced himself. He hung the backpack from his shoulder and released Miguel's suitcase. He had to risk it, rather than simply stand there.

He took his coat, scarf and hat, opened the door and listened for steps in the corridor. He only heard the usual noise from the neighbor's radio. The floor was a large "T" with the elevators in the middle and the corridors and stairwells on all three sides. Instead of running to the nearest stairwell, Paco ran for the elevators. He turned ninety degrees in the corridor facing the elevators and headed towards the next set of emergency stairs. This stairwell connected to the lobby and out onto the main street, so he reasoned that strangers and passers-by would protect him from his visitor.

Just as he turned in front of the elevators, he heard one of the elevators arriving. If it was the elevator on the right, the man would not see him because the wall obscured part of the corridor from sight. But if it was the one on the left, he would see him right away and run right after him. The elevator doors opened. The man was holding a gun in his right hand.

Chapter 7

Miguel was battling it out with all his might. He did not want to close his eyes. Before he met Ana, there were times he would go to bed early in the hope of never opening them again. At that time, he did not want to live through another day of his illness. He fought every day with his mother, but mainly with God because it was all so unfair.

He did not realize when he was younger that he had a terminal illness. His mother never told him directly, nor did any of his family members; uncles or cousins. Little by little he came to understand that his situation was not normal thanks to his constant visits to the doctor.

When he was twelve, his mother confessed to him the reason for so many medications and so much time spent at the hospital, and that was when he really understood the impact of it all. Years later, an internet search answered all of his questions, although today he still wondered if it was for better or for worse. *Isn't it better to live without knowing when you are going to die?* If he had not known, he would have avoided the intense fear of catching a cold every time someone sneezed next to him.

That same year, when he was fifteen, was the worst of all. All his friends would invite him out and he would not be able to go. His immune system was weaker than ever. Any infection could annihilate him. That was when he decided that he would not go on tormenting himself. He wanted dawn to arrive, but to no longer be there to see it. He prayed for God to correct his mistake and take him away in the middle of the night. But it never happened. Every morning he opened his eyes again and had to face the nightmare.

Now that he was in London, he was praying for the opposite. He was praying for God to grant him a miracle so that he could open his eyes and see Ana again.

"Promise me that you're going to live," Ana begged him with her tender voice, now lodged in his memory.

That was how they said goodbye every day when they spoke on the phone.

"I promise," Miguel always said before hanging up.

Remembering that promise made the boy surge back into consciousness.

"Nurse... Nurse...," he called out anxiously in Spanish, forgetting in his rush to press the button to alert the nurse station.

A janitor who was walking by heard him, and hearing his own language piqued his curiosity.

"What's wrong young man?" said the fifty-something man who walked into his room in Spanish.

"Oh, at last, someone who speaks Spanish!" said Miguel, greatly relieved. "You have no idea how bad this has been for me, I don't speak a word of English. Do you?"

"Enough," he replied. "I've lived in London for a few years now with my daughter."

As they got to know each other, he discovered that the man was from Mexico, and Miguel told him he was from Puerto Rico.

"A beautiful island, Puerto Rico. I visited when I was a boy and I started chasing a Puerto Rican girl around, but she dumped me for a yank that lived on the island and ran a refreshment bottling factory. Then, when I went back to my country, I heard that the yank dumped her, as they say around here, when the head office sent him back to the Carolinas; no idea if it was North or South."

"Listen," Miguel interrupted to prevent the man from telling him his whole life story and not giving him a chance to ask for the favor he needed.

"What can I do for you?" asked the janitor, guessing his intentions.

"I lost my cell phone on my way here and I need to speak to my girlfriend who lives in Spain to tell her where I am. And with my mother who lives in Puerto Rico, so she knows I'm ill."

"Don't you have any family in London?" he inquired, taken by surprise by the request.

It would be a problem to make international phone calls to distant relatives. Loved ones who would take hours to arrive.

"If you're in a rush, which is what it sounds like from your tone of voice, it's better to call a nearby relative," said the old man with a sweet tone. "even if the one who's further away is closer to your heart."

"I have an uncle, but I want to call my girlfriend or my mother first," Miguel insisted.

"I understand. But wouldn't it be best if your uncle came and helped you? It's not that I don't want to help, but it would be good if you had someone familiar here to keep you company. Don't you think?"

"You're right, but I'm just so scared I won't be able to say goodbye."

"Hey, kid. You'll have plenty of time. These doctors are amazing. You'll see, you'll be out of here in no time."

At once he went out to speak with the nurses about Miguel's needs.

"Nurse Betty, I know how you can get in touch with his family. The boy has an Uncle here in London. Let him call him," the janitor said, now acting as Miguel's lawyer.

"Why don't you just get hold of the telephone number and let us call him?" the nurse replied; but the man did not back down.

"Because the kid is obstinate. He wants to say goodbye himself. He thinks he's going to die. He won't give me his uncle's number until he's spoken to his girlfriend or his mother."

"They haven't brought me a phone yet," complained Miguel to the janitor the moment he woke up after falling asleep for an hour. A troublesome cough interrupted his speech.

"They've issued the authorization, kid. You have to be a little patient. You'll see, the technician will be here in a moment to activate the service," the janitor said, trying to calm him down.

Miguel struggled to understand what the janitor was saying because this time he visited him wearing a mask over his face.

"They gave it to me just in case," the janitor explained when he realized the boy was looking right at the mask.

"Can you get me a pen and paper?" he managed to ask after a coughing fit.

He covered his mouth with one hand in an attempt to stop the phlegm that was surging up his throat.

"Are you going to write a letter?" the janitor asked him, as he looked to one side to give Miguel some privacy as he coughed it all up.

"Yes," he replied more with a nod of his head than with his voice.

The phlegm was still not letting him speak.

"For your mom and your girlfriend?"

"Yes, to them too," Miguel answered when he finally got his voice back.

"What do you mean, too? How many letters are you going to write?"

"As many as I have to. Can you get me plenty of paper?"

"You're pretty demanding all of a sudden," the janitor smiled to try to lighten the mood feeling he now knew the kid well enough to be a little less formal around him.

"Life gives you lemons, you make lemonade. If you can't help me with the telephone, maybe the paper will be easier," Miguel stated without much energy, but recovering some of his sense of humor and changing the tone of voice he used on the poor man who was doing everything in his power to help him.

"I don't know why you are putting all your energy into saying goodbye instead of concentrating on getting better."

"Believe me I'm trying to get better, but this is like fighting alone against an army of a million soldiers attacking you on all sides."

"Then concentrate on killing them with the help of those antibiotics running through your veins. Take the enemy by surprise. Then use that positive energy to squash that negative effect. We'll see who's stronger!" advised the janitor.

In his eleven years working in a hospital, he had seen a couple of miracles, or the power of the mind as the more skeptical would describe an unexpected cure.

"I'm trying. I really am," said Miguel, as he faded out of consciousness again.

The janitor rushed out of the room in a big hurry, and collected two reams of paper and a couple of pens he borrowed from the hospital administrator's office on the first floor. When he went up to Miguel's room, he found he was still sleeping, but his face expressed anxiety and pain.

"He's not doing well," said Nurse Betty when she saw the janitor scrutinizing Miguel.

"What's wrong with him? I didn't dare ask him so he wouldn't have to think about it," asked the janitor, adjusting the straps of his mask.

"He's got an invasive infection of the MRSA bug, which has rapidly attacked all his vital organs," explained the nurse.

The janitor opened his eyes wide in visible shock. He had read about MRSA in the newspapers. Some students had caught the bug in the locker room shower of the athletics department of their college. It had been covered by all the papers and news broadcasts throughout the country and around the world. They were football players. Kids with a bright future ahead of them, but a bad roll of the die had put their lives in danger. He listened as the nurse continued her explanation.

"Usually we can contain the bacteria when it is lodged in the skin, but six percent of cases go quickly because they have other conditions which means their immune systems are compromised. This happens to patients who catch the bacterium during an operation, for instance, or who are undergoing chemotherapy."

"Miguel has cancer?" the janitor interrupted.

"No, he suffers from cystic fibrosis, a genetic illness that means his lungs don't have the capacity to appropriately dispose of phlegm. MRSA advances quickly in this kind of patient, causing lethal pneumonia."

"That's why he won't stop coughing," nodded the janitor.

"Yes, and that's why I gave you the mask, white coat and gloves. Always wear them when you come to see him and as I showed you. This is why we have him isolated. I'm not supposed to let anyone visit him, but since you are the only person who can communicate with him, I am making an exception. But I don't want you near other isolated patients."

"Are there more patients with MRSA here?"

"Yes, in rooms 1221 and 1222. They are Miguel's work colleagues," explained the nurse.

"Are they as sick as he is?"

"No, they're much better, but we have them under observation. They could get worse at any moment. We are also treating them with intravenous antibiotics."

"So how long…?" began the janitor, but he was unable to finish the sentence.

The nurse's expression was now tense and her brow had furrowed.

"Since when do you ask so many questions?" she asked, leaving him standing there without another word.

While Nurse Betty was leaving, Miguel emitted a small groan, so small that the janitor nearly missed it.

"Mommy, forgive me," said Miguel in a state of waking unconsciousness, with past events running through his mind seeming as real to him as if he were living them.

He was remembering one of his last visits to his doctor in Puerto Rico. At this particular appointment, the doctor explained to him the details of a clinical trial taking place at Imperial College London, and that it was a real opportunity for Miguel and many other patients like him to improve his quality of life and find a possible cure. It was an experiment that involved manipulating the gene that triggered cystic fibrosis.

"Latin Americans have a 1 in 46 chance of being carriers of the gene. Black people have a 1 in 65 chance. However, people descended from European roots, particularly from Northern Europe have a 1 in 29 chance. That's why there are so many cases of cystic fibrosis in England."

Miguel did not wait for the doctor to finish his explanation. He lunged for his mother, took her by the hand, and dragged her into a corner of the examination room.

"Mom, I'm going to London. I can't stay here... I'll die if I don't go."

"Don't worry, angel. Calm down," his mother told him, seeing him so upset.

"Mommy, you know I have always handled this situation as calmly as possible. But I want to fight this and if you don't give me your permission then I'll have to go without your approval."

"I don't have the money to send you," she lamented.

"I know, but we have to turn over every rock, mom. Can't we call Uncle Roberto in Chicago, or

Uncle Alberto in London? Maybe they can help with the cash."

The doctor interrupted their conversation.

"You have nothing to worry about. I already obtained funds for travel, accommodation and meals for three months, which is how long the study will last."

"Doctor, you know perfectly well I have no way of paying you for it," said Miguel, concerned.

"Oh, that's not an issue. These funds come from the Alternate Assistance Foundation. They designate funds for these purposes," he said placing a friendly hand on his shoulder. "You only need to convince your mother now, because you can't go without her permission. You need her to sign a release and authorization form, because you'll have to go to London several weeks before you're eighteen. Don't think for a second you're in charge yet...," said the doctor teasing his patient and pulling him to his chest to give him a hug and several affectionate pats on the back.

Even though his mother knew it was for the best, it did not stop her from crying inconsolably as her son finished packing his suitcase. All that was left for Miguel to pack were the last medications. When he closed his suitcase, his mother finally snapped and wrenched it from his hands.

"Don't go, darling. What if that study goes all wrong and you don't have enough time to come home? I would die just thinking I couldn't be with you if you fall ill," she said tearfully, unable to stop her weeping.

"Uncle Alberto can look after me while I get better."

But his mother wrapped her arms around him and prevented him from moving.

"Mommy, don't be so sad. I'll be fine. Please let me go. Give me a kiss," he said as he picked up his suitcase and the bag containing the respiratory therapy machine.

He tenderly pushed her aside, but his mother would not release his face as she covered his cheeks with kiss after kiss, barely pausing to breathe between each one.

"Ok, that's enough Mom. I'm leaving," as he walked out of the door before she could stop him again.

Now he was the one who could not breathe. The tears strangled his breathing and ran down his cheeks where only a few seconds earlier his mother planted her warm kisses.

Miguel opened his eyes, startled. He tried to sit up in the hospital bed, but a stabbing pain in his chest left him reeling. The image of his mother crying was engraved in his mind. He looked around to confirm that he was alone in the darkened London hospital room. Seeing that he was, he spotted the reams of paper and the pens that the janitor left on his bedside table. He carefully opened one of the packages and produced several sheets from within.

He would not write to his mother or to Ana yet. He had a more important letter to write.

"Someone needs to know about this. They don't get to kill me for fun," he said in a low voice as he began to write a letter addressed to the London Daily newspaper as quickly as his exhaustion allowed him.

PART 3
Changes In The Variables

Chapter 8

As she returned home after her second meeting at MagMell Laboratories, Valeria Loperena forced herself to stop thinking about MRSA and she placed her briefcase beside the hall table, unaware of the microphone that was placed imperceptibly in its lining. She was planning on coming back for her briefcase after dinner, but she had something urgent to do first. She threw herself on the enormous curved sofa she bought for when all her friends came over and she sifted through the mail for anything received from a far-off place. No. Nothing.

She had not heard from James for three weeks. She called him on his cell phone every day; nothing. She wrote him e-mails and they also went unanswered. Her only chance to hear from him were mailed letters, assuming that wherever he was he did not have access to the Internet.

He must have gone somewhere really remote. The whole world is wrapped in satellite waves so there's virtually no reason to be cut off, Valeria thought to herself when she did not find the tiniest clue in the mail as to James' whereabouts.

She found it hard to understand why he had not called once, not even from his cell phone. In the modern world, these prevented anyone from having a reason for disappearing for days on end without giving explanations or coming up with excuses for coming home late. *Who knows how many times I've interrupted his trysts with a lover with the incessant vibrations of my phone calls, similar to those from an impatient wife who is expecting her husband every day between six and seven at night?* But Valeria was not James' wife, not yet.

"No one can find a hiding place in the world nowadays. There are ways of tracking people, of finding them when they use their cell phones", she argued with James in her thoughts.

But she knew very well what was going on. *He obviously lost his phone. Or "lost" it on purpose?*

She refused to torment herself over the issue any longer. She had work to do. That was why she brought her briefcase, even though when she started going out with James she promised not to bring homework. But it was inevitable. In reality, her mind was always at work. It was the curse of creative people who are always drawing inspiration from any little thing; they are always sketching, cutting out photographs, newspaper and magazine articles, and scribbling ideas on any scrap of paper they find lying around. Valeria was trying to work as little as possible outside of office hours, but today was not one of those days. Today would be an exception to the rule. She had to dedicate some time to the MagMell labs campaign because she was backed up with work and to an extent she had never before experienced in her career.

Lately she found herself distracted at all hours of the day. Her thoughts always turned to James. She would discover him in the Amazonian jungle, half-drowned face down on the banks of the river. Or half-naked in the burning desert sands of the Sahara, delirious with dehydration, begging for help from the mirages that arose in his path. Her favorite was finding him in Africa in a majestic Safari, surrounded by hungry lions, or having to pay off the Somali militia to free him from jail for taking pictures of civilian arrests. Her thoughts felt like episodes from any of the seven films from the *Road to...* series with Bing Crosby and Bob Hope, but devoid of all comedy. Sitting at her office desk she would imagine convoluted scenarios where the heroine would always save her defenseless loved one.

Her dear James, who never spoke of what he did to earn a living, nor why he did it. Valeria thought that after six months together they would begin to share the day-to-day details of their jobs, but he remained an enigma.

The first time Valeria discovered that James' job required constant travelling was after three months during which they were totally inseparable. They had only been drawn apart by her office working hours. That day she found him sitting on the sofa of her apartment, waiting to tell her that he was off on an important assignment. He had already prepared a rucksack containing a change of clothes and provisions.

"Don't keep asking, you know I'm not going to tell you," was his reply when she asked where he was going.

"But what do you do for a living? It's a perfectly ordinary question at any bar conversation or party around town. What's the big mystery?" Valeria asked, but even then she did not get an answer.

When he came back a week later, he finally replied. He was a photographer for the EFE agency, but an extremely strict confidentiality agreement prevented him from revealing the destinations of his assignments. The next time that he went abroad he called her every day that he was away so she had no cause for concern.

Since then, many assignments had interrupted their romantic evenings, some longer than others, but none lasted more than ten days. During many of those periods, James did not get in touch with her every single day that he was away, but a couple of days without talking to him were not going to kill her. Besides, he warned her from the start: "don't try to tie me down, because I will run a mile." This was the first time she had not heard for him for such a long time.

Early the following morning, Valeria left home in a rush as she was already late for her appointment with Mercedes. She paused at the door facing the stairs to adjust her scarf and hat. *Damn cold, making me wear layer after layer after layer of clothes. What a pain!*

With the same grit and determination of a bull that has just been stuck with the point of a lance, she attacked the snow with her feet and ducked away from the snowflakes falling on her face. She made her way along the pavement until she reached the door of the Intelligentsia Coffebar.

"I was starting to think you had stood me up," said Mercedes by way of greeting when Valeria at last arrived at the table after battling her way through the heavy snow that, unluckily for her, started to fall the moment she crossed the first street.

"Don't make such a big deal, Merci."

Valeria removed her coat as quickly as she could without getting tied up in her scarf, which was what usually happened to her, and she immediately sat down so that her friend would calm down.

"I don't know what you're complaining about, you've been waiting for a whole fifteen minutes warming your little tush while I was out freezing in the snow," Valeria answered, absolutely livid.

"Well, someone is in a foul mood! Come on, let's get a coffee, an extra-large one."

The first sip of the coffee had the required effect. It got rid of the chills running cruelly along their skins, and reduced the pressure invading every artery. Now the women could have a civilized conversation. They would have to raise their voices a little, because at this time, the coffebar was packed with people running off to work. A steady hemorrhage of trench coats flowed in and out of the main chamber of the coffee house, all purchasing the energy that they needed to continue on their treks along the city streets. What a difference fifteen minutes can make! Only a few minutes earlier Mercedes had been practically alone in the joint.

"I haven't heard from James in three weeks," Valeria began, staring intensely at the edge of her coffee cup seeking her boyfriend's whereabouts in her drink.

"I knew something was up with you!" Mercedes interrupted, trying in vain to make eye contact.

But Valeria's mind was no longer there. She was with James, but he was in the arms of an exotic dancer...

Her small dancer's hands were coquettishly running blue silk handkerchiefs along James' virile features. The aroma of the woman's body, mixed with the sweat from the dancing was intoxicating the man's pleasure saturated senses, as he allowed himself to be pampered. After a few moments, she pointed him towards a corner of the room surrounded by curtains, carpets and all kinds of colorful cushions. She asked him to sit with a seductive wave of her delicate arms. And when her prey was comfortable and absorbed in the fullness of her breasts adorned with muslin, ribbons and gold chains, she began to dance exclusively for him.

The rhythm of her swaying hips, first to one side, then to another, dizzied him like the waves when they beat against the sides of a row boat. There was no way to escape except to concentrate on the dancer's waist and direct a mesmerized gaze towards it as if nothing else existed. All of a sudden the woman's pelvis began to convulse, making the belly vibrate uncontrollably. James suddenly leapt up, nauseous. His chest was drenched in sweat. Disoriented he stumbled towards the exit, but his legs failed him and he collapsed on the carpet in front of the door to the room.

"I'm going! I'll see you on Friday!" blurted Valeria, coming out of her trance. "Where shall we meet? I'm told Carnivale is fashionable again. We could eat there and go over the ideas for the leaflets. Do you want to go?" she went on breathlessly as she stood up and instinctively slipped her honey colored coat back on. "We could have the beef stew or the Galician pie," she added, listing her favorite dishes on the menu.

"I guess so, why not?" replied Mercedes, beginning to worry about how weird her friend was acting. "Valeria," she paused, "are you ok?"

"Of course I am, girl, nothing to worry about. See you Friday..." she replied shouting, already at the door.

After the first restorative sip, neither of them had finished their coffees.

Valeria had no idea where she was headed, but definitely not towards her office. She was practically running along the pavement, in a state of emotional desperation. The pressing of bodies slowed her pace down, and she had to push between the forest of arms and legs to make her way. She could not find a way out. Finally she plunged down an emptier tunnel and turned right, not looking in what direction she was going. But she did not care, because the canyons of buildings surrounded her and protected her. She felt safe there, far from the bustle and far from the misery of her thoughts. Far from James.

Where is he? Where is he, really? and *Why am I so worried?* Thousands of questions vied for Valeria's attention. Since when did she worry about the fate of people who showed no concern for her? James had promised nothing, and refused to define their relationship. That had been her idea. She spoke of him as her boyfriend, because she did not want to go around explaining herself to anyone who asked. It was easier to call him her "boyfriend" than her lover, her friend, or her acquaintance.

But today's feelings were different. She had a bad feeling that was going to affect her whole day. She had been waking up with this bad feeling for weeks. Something dark was looming closer and she could feel it in every pore of her body, as if she were a witch all of a sudden and could predict an uncertain future. And the worst part was... she did not believe in that kind of stuff; however, her reason betrayed her. No rationale was good enough. It was all feelings and premonitions.

At last she spun around, stepped out of the tunnel, arrived at an intersection and hailed a cab. She could not resolve something that had not happened yet. *I must be patient, and wait. I will wait for James. I will wait for the dark future. Meanwhile, I will keep myself busy with work.*

"Mind if we share the taxi?" she heard a man's rasping voice interrupting her thoughts, making her heart skip a beat.

When she turned to look, she saw Sam Cosgrove smiling at her.

Chapter 9

James opened his eyes. A stabbing pain just above his eyelids – right where the cranium makes room for the eyeball – prevented him from fully opening them. Out of the corner of his eye he glimpsed that he was in a multicolored room, the same one he had entered with the exotic dancer. He was no longer on the floor. Someone had moved him, or he had moved by himself, who could say. Now he was lying on the orange, red, yellow and blue cushions that decorated the corner beneath the window.

He seemed to be alone, at least in this room. He heard nothing from the rest of the house, but he was not totally sure that he was alone. The inhabitants of this region, for some reason unknown to him, muttered instead of talking out loud. They never raised their voices, not even when a sandstorm was incoming. They would all run in an astonishing silence and seek refuge from the deadly sands. Seeing the sandstorms so often had made them immune to fear. Why shout and become alarmed if the result would be exactly the same? They hid, they survived and they would go on surviving until the next assault of wind, sand and solitude.

Likewise, James had to survive. He had to get out of this desert country he came to following Sam and Josh Cosgrove's trail. In all probability his cameras had already been sold on the black market. Maybe the dancer had put his Nokia in one of her drawers to take pictures of her next family reunion. Those digital cameras were so easy to use that even an octogenarian Egyptian, heretofore unexposed to any form of technology, could take a picture of his grandchildren and see it at once. Instant gratification.

"*Bugger!!!* If those damned cameras were not so attractive, maybe I'd still have them," James shouted as he stood up amongst the multicolored cushions.

He lost the cell phone the moment he set foot in the room for the first time. The dancer took it from him as a sign that it was time for relaxation. James figured that for as long as he could see the cell phone, he had no problem with the woman taking it from him. But obviously he lost sight not only of his phone, his cameras and his wallet, but also of the woman who tricked him. He had been sure not to eat or drink anything,so it was a mystery to him how she managed to make him pass out.

He searched under the cushions in case he could find the cell phone or his cameras, but found nothing. Not a trace. There were no clues or trails he could follow to solve the puzzle of the theft or the whereabouts of the woman.

Not wasting any more time on feeling sorry for himself, he went in search of the exit, a task complicated by the fact that all the rooms looked alike and the building was a maze of doors and corridors. He knew how to reach civilization if he were lost deep in a forest by obeying the S.U.R.V.I.V.A.L. acronym invented by the US army, and how to get out of trouble if he were poisoned with cyanide in case someone were trying to get rid of him for good. But here he found himself incessantly opening doors, with no idea of the sort of labyrinth in which he found himself.

He had now twice ended up back in the room where his little odyssey had begun. It seemed incomprehensible to him that he could not find a way out. He felt as if he was in the middle of a forest on a thick bed of fallen leaves, branches, and roots that prevented him from seeing where he was going and forced him to walk in circles. But how could he advance in circles in a structure made out of mud, sand and salt? The only thought that occurred to him was that it was all premeditated. That it had been built this way on purpose. It was a real life labyrinth.

James continued to touch the walls and open doors until he noticed an almost imperceptible change. Now the floor was made of earth and there was no ceiling, just the black sky. However, he was still locked in on all sides. He heard noises and began to hurry towards them, but he could not tell exactly where the sounds were coming from. The walls absorbed the sound.

Suddenly, he ran into two men walking along the earth floor corridor towards him. They ignored his pleas for help. They did not understand English, or at least acted like they did not. Even though he stopped the men, grabbing their shoulders and speaking right into their faces, they pushed away from him and continued on their way speaking words unintelligible to James, in hurried tones and with annoyed expressions.

James thought of following them to see if he could find a way out, but he realized that they must have come from a nearby door and his chance was lost. He decided not to go through any more doors. At least now he was on the outside and could see the sky, even though its darkness did not offer much help because it was the darkness of the night sky where you can only glimpse a single star.

He made up his mind to find the exit by following the earth path, but it was a cold night. *Who would have thought, being in the middle of a desert?* But that was what the nights were like in the Sahara, frozen like a stiffened corpse half-buried in the snow. At least the dancer had not taken his shoes or his light jacket.

James weighed his alternatives. He could go on marching through a freezing night in the hope of finding a way out of the maze, or he could hide out in one of the rooms to wait for dawn and try to find a helpful soul.

He did not think about it much, because the cold was already in his bones; he could no longer feel his nose, his legs, and his eyelids felt like lead weights. He had to find a roof to protect him. He had to open a door and remain beside it so as not to lose the earth path.

He entered a dark room. There were carpets on the floor and sheets and cushions covered every corner. A family of four: father, mother and two small children were sleeping. He drew closer to the smallest child, sharing part of his sheets. He would have to get up before dawn and before the owner of the house could slit his throat on suspicion of being a pervert. Meanwhile, he would be protected from the inclemency of the elements for a few hours.

———

James fell asleep well beyond the first light of the morning. When at last he stirred beneath the sheets, the day was half done. He felt a cramp in his legs and his back suffered some kind of spasm or musculoskeletal pain. He struggled to his feet from the iron embrace of the floor. His right forearm was so numb that he felt like it had been anaesthetized. His throat was dry from inhaling cold night air, instead of the moisture that covers leaves with dew. He had to urgently find water and a bathroom, unless he wanted to leave a little "gift" for his unwitting hosts.

He looked around. He was in a living room, dining room and kitchen: an all-in-one. There was no furniture as such, just carpets on the floor and a small table in a corner at knee level with a virtually industrial scale tea urn, sugar in a large container, and enough plates and glasses for four people. A boy with large, dark and expressive eyes, like those of an owl, observed him, gripping the corner of the wall where the room ended and the corridor began. He was sitting on the floor just like James, but he had no trouble standing up and running away down the corridor.

In the time it took James to get to his feet, the child went to fetch his mother who was now coming closer and speaking her language at the high-speed that people speak when they are nervous or upset. She grabbed him by the waist and pushed him towards the door, but he released himself from her hands easily as the woman was no more than five foot tall and was delicate and frail. Her aggression was more expressed by the lines of her face than by her fists.

James tried to calm her down by speaking very gently and walking slowly towards the cups and the tea urn. He picked up a glass and served himself tea, still looking at the woman and then the door. He was afraid someone would hear her and rush to her aid if she was asking for help. But the woman fell silent the moment James began to drink the tea. She held his arm to prevent him from drinking more, and with her other hand took three sugar lumps and put them in the glass. She gave him instructions with her hands and mouth to drink. She seemed indignant that he had taken her tea without sugar. Perhaps even more than she had been about finding him in her house without permission.

Next she spoke to the boy while James drank the tea. Before his mother had finished issuing her instructions, the boy ran off down the corridor again. This time he returned with bread and something that looked like a canteen full of water. The woman whipped them from his small hands and chucked them at James' waist so quickly that he barely had the reflexes to grab them both with his free hand. He gave the cup to the woman, who was now forcing him backwards towards the door. She opened it and with the phrase "Ale, ale..." slammed the door on him.

The narrow earth path was now full with the voices of people going about their business. Neighbors were leaning against the walls chatting and in the distance he heard what he thought were the wheels of a cart. He headed in that direction, until he found a square in the middle of the walls, the largest space he had found so far. He barely had the time to admire the space when he saw the young woman who seduced him with her dance heading right for him. He waited calmly for her to recognize him and turn and run, but to his surprise she kept on coming, even looking at him and speaking with her eyes. *Oh no. I'm not falling for that again*, thought James. The only reason he went with her was because she had been in the company of two elderly women and he did not think he was in any danger. She had offered him information on Sam Cosgrove in a badly pronounced statement, but it was all a trick to get him out of Cairo and steal his possessions. He had never felt so stupid. Now he would be more careful.

When the woman stopped in front of him, she brusquely grabbed his hand and put a paper in it.

"It's from Bakran-Al-Kali," she spoke in the rasping voice of someone who has memorized a sentence in a language she does not speak.

Bakran was his contact in Cairo. Why didn't he deliver this in person?

"Dear James: apologies for the abrupt way I had to get you out of the city. You are in Bawiti, a village in the Bahariya Oasis, just three hundred kilometers from Cairo. The girl who has given you this letter is one of my nieces and the two old women are my great-aunts. Some way to introduce you to them! You have been staying at their home for three weeks. I believe you have been semi-unconscious due to the tea sweetened with barbiturates that you have been drip fed while you slept. It seems they didn't want to argue with you! I don't blame them... the point is that someone has put a price on your head and there is an assassin out hunting you down in the capital. What kind of trouble have you got yourself into this time, Nancy boy? The price is so high that I was tempted to turn you in myself... The cloth salesman at the bazaar sold you out at once. You have no idea everything I

have done to make it look like you fled to Sudan. You owe me one. Well, more than one, but I will settle for you taking me to London. Follow the instructions on the next page, which will bring you to me. For a safe return, mate."

The young woman was still standing there, waiting. When James began to fold the letter up again to put it in his pocket, the girl gestured for him to follow her. He immediately discarded the doubts he held just a few seconds earlier. No one else called him *Nancy boy*, so the letter was from Bakran.

Bawiti was certainly a labyrinth of alleys and buildings.

"No wonder I was so lost," he said out loud, although he knew the woman would not understand him.

The girl calmly walked on. Every step in the sand beneath his feet told James that soon they would cease to see brown walls and blue doors. Sure enough, five minutes later they left the last alley towards a frontier of sand and palm trees and a cloudless sky.

For some strange reason he felt more lost now than when he was inside the labyrinth. The immensity of the desert rendered him speechless. However, the feeling of freedom was intoxicating. So much so that he believed he could cross the desert to Cairo running only on the adrenalin currently pumping through his veins.

He had lost three weeks of his life and had not even realized it. Aside from a numb body, there were no signs of having lost so much time. The women must have bathed him and shaved him. *Who knows what else they've done!* He felt as vulnerable as a three year old child. He had always been in control of his actions and movements, and suddenly he discovered that he had been at the mercy of two old women and a twenty year old girl. Too vulnerable. *This is really embarrassing...* he would never tell his bosses, or Valeria.

Chapter 10

Valeria met James only six months earlier. His direct, but sweet expression and his deliberate voice immediately won her over. She loved those things about him. She had never felt so attracted to a stranger, but this was not a man like all the others she had met before.

For starters, he had a spectacular British accent that lured her like a magnet simply because she had to pay more attention than usual to not miss a single word. If she lost concentration for a moment, and focused on his captivating brown eyes, or the curve of his chin adorned with the shadow of a short beard that gave him a mysterious air, then she would not understand a word of what he was saying. Asking him to repeat what he said was not an option. She did not want him to think that she was a Latina who had just arrived in the country.

They met over a simple and brief question:

"Excuse me. Could you tell me, if you would be so kind, where the Principal's office is?"

This was the first sentence that this magnificent man had spoken to her and which stopped her cold on the pavement in front of a school. She was sure that was what he said. She concentrated on each one of his words. When she heard him say, "if you would be so kind", it took all her effort not to faint then and there, but she stayed alert with all senses ready for the rest of the sentence. They were both blocking the entrance to a school and were knocked by the backpack or shoulder of every inconsiderate pre-adolescent hurrying inside, as it was almost time to be in class.

Valeria had never been inside that particular school or indeed any other since she finished high school, but that day she was doing Mercedes a favor. It was the first day of Gabriela's new school year and

Mercedes was at a meeting with her new boss, Josh Cosgrove. She was summoned to the office at seven in the morning.

"You know what this means," she informed Valeria when she called the previous night to ask her to take Gabriela to school. "Not only will I miss taking Gabriela on her first day, but I will have to battle it out with this guy who is obviously planning on coming in and imposing his style. When they call you in at seven in the morning, it's a declaration of intent."

"Yes, I know," said Valeria. "Whoever can't or doesn't want to work early in the morning is better off staying at home. And if you don't like it, you can just look for another job."

Valeria had already gone through something similar when her old boss retired and a guy from central offices arrived to take over. He would arrange meetings at seven in the morning or at eight at night. It was a war for the survival of the fittest. Whoever could keep up, could keep their job. Thank God they transferred him a year later and now she was head of the Chicago offices, and she had much more common sense than her predecessors. She tried to keep her employees motivated and happy even though from time to time a project would require working into the night.

"Don't worry about Gabriela, Merci. I'll take her. What time do you want me to pick her up?"

Valeria arrived punctually at Mercedes' house the following day.

"Heeeeelloooooo...," Gabriela welcomed her, stretching out the standard greeting word as if it were a song.

"Heeeeelloooooo...," Valeria replied, following her lead and trying to sound cool.

"So what's up? What's new with your life? Ready for the seventh grade?" asked Valeria the moment the girl closed the car door.

"I think so. They say it's harder than sixth and eighth, so we'll see."

"Are you still in class with your friends? With your *Pandilla*?"

"I don't know yet. I'll find out today. What's this about a *Pandilla*?" Gabriela asked, shrugging her shoulders.

"You just punctured my cool aura. When a teenager doesn't know what an adult is talking about, it just makes the generation gap wider. I hate you now!" Valeria said, laughing hard.

"Don't feel so bad. I just wasn't sure what you were talking about,"

"Ok, I forgive you. *La Pandilla* was a Spanish band who sang boleros and pop songs when I was a little girl. My aunt brought me a live album from Spain when she visited, and I fell in love for the first time when I saw the cover. They were three boys and one girl. I liked the one named Rubén; he wasn't the most handsome, but he had the voice of an angel."

"That's hilarious!" nodded Gabriela.

She was speaking with her mouth full of cereal, sitting in the passenger seat with her feet on the dashboard.

"You think you are the only ones who fall in love with singers?" Valeria said as she ran her hand through Gabriela's hair in an effort to comb it.

"No, obviously. But it's funny the way you tell it. Tell me more."

"Well, if you want the whole story, then there were times I would fantasize that Rubén sang only for me. Other times I was the girl in the group and we would sing in a different country every week and all the boys in the world were in love with me, including Rubén and the rest of the *Pandilla*."

"*Pandilla* means gang, right?" asked Gabriela.

"Exactly."

"I love that name. I'm going to tell my friends. From now on we can call ourselves the *Pandilla*.

Olivia suggested Sexy Babes but I think our mothers would kill us if they found out."

She was so deep in conversation that Valeria drove right past the turn-off to Gabriela's school. Now they would have to take a different route.

"Sorry, Gabriela. I'm going to make you late to your first day of school."

"Don't worry. It's not like I'm in the first grade. I can explain it to the teacher."

But they arrived in time, just in time, but in time nonetheless. They parked one block away to avoid traffic and ran the rest of the way. Gabriela insisted that she could go alone, but Valeria, knowing Mercedes, was not going to run the risk of something happening to Gabriela. Mercedes would hold it over her head for the rest of her life. The unexpected bonus that made this decision the correct one was meeting the enigmatic British man who asked her for directions at the school.

"To be honest, I don't know where the Principal's office is," Valeria replied, "It's the first time I've set foot in this school, so I really can't help you."

She tried to be as polite as possible and accompany her reply with a smile.

"Ah, is it your daughter's first day too?" the man asked, leaving her mute for a few seconds.

His smile made her lose her concentration.

"No... it's my first day. She's studied at this school for two years now."

When she realized that the man was giving her a strange look, she realized he probably thought she was a bad mother who never took her daughter to school. He probably took his son to school every day. Him or his wife.

"Oh no, she's not my daughter. She's my best friend's daughter. She couldn't bring her today and I'm doing her a favor."

"Same as me!" he replied.

Of course, Valeria thought, *he's bringing his girlfriend's son.*

"He's my nephew, but today really is his first day at this school, so I need to find the Principal's office," explained the man looking her right in the eye.

"Well, let's ask my friend's daughter," said Valeria, abruptly looking away from his face.

She looked everywhere, except at the man whose presence was shattering her sanity.

"There she is. She hasn't gone into class yet."

"Don't worry, I can find the office on my own," said the man, misinterpreting her discomfort.

"It's no trouble," insisted Valeria, this time with a smile, unable to resist the pull of his charming allure.

They arrived together at the door to Gabriela's classroom, as she chatted to one of her friends in the corridor.

"Gabriela, excuse me."

"Valeria, what are you doing here?"

"Gabriela, I'd like to introduce you to… I'm sorry, what did you say your name was?" Valeria spoke with a formality she was not used to, perhaps under the influence of the British accent of the man she was about to introduce.

"James… James Penton," said the man, laughing suddenly, but Valeria totally missed the James Bond reference and ploughed on.

"Mr. Penton is looking for the Principal's office. It's his nephew's first day…"

Gabriela didn't let her finish her sentence.

"End of the corridor on the right. See you…" she said turning abruptly and entering the classroom.

"I'm sorry. Looks like she's in a hurry," said Valeria a little embarrassed.

"Looks like it."

They all laughed, including the boy who was with them.

"You see, I told you Dean. Life here in America is really fast paced," James told his nephew.

"I can tell. We'd better hurry," Dean replied. He was almost as handsome as his uncle, but his hair was blonde instead of brown like James', giving him a mischievous air.

"If you have the time, maybe we could go for a cup of coffee," he dared to say to Valeria even though he knew he was imposing.

However, Valeria was not the kind of woman you could allow to get away. *Maybe she's married or she has a boyfriend waiting for her at home*, thought James, *but I'd rather go for it now than regret not doing anything later. If she says yes, great. If she says no, then she can give me her reasons for not accepting the invitation.*

Valeria did not know what to say. She actually had a meeting with a client who was expecting an overdue presentation. This particular client had requested so many changes that the campaign was already two months behind schedule. On the other hand, this was a once in a lifetime opportunity. *How often does an Indiana Jones type man walk up to a girl like me, particularly on the steps to a school?*

She was no longer a girl for starters, but that's how she saw herself in her mind's eye every time that she let her imagination run wild. Her creativity knew no bounds. She used this to her advantage as Creative Manager of C2 Marketing, the agency she had worked at for fifteen years. The same imagination that helped her fill up her lonely days creating alternate universes for her life. *But fantasizing doesn't pay the rent, nor does it help you hold down a job if you don't show up to client meetings. I'll have to take a rain check on that coffee,* Valeria concluded her internal debate.

"Ok. I'll wait for you across the street," Valeria replied to James, who had been waiting the whole time for her answer to his invitation. "I've got to make a few work calls and we can go for coffee when you're done."

She wandered down the corridor uncertain how she ended up replying the exact opposite to what she decided was the best course of action. Now she would have to manage the situation and run some damage control. She had to call the client to let him know that she would not arrive at his office in time to make the presentation.

"Yes, tomorrow, without fail. I will be there tomorrow," she said, hanging up the phone after explaining to the client that she was going to have a coffee with the man of her dreams.

That was what she would have liked to say if she were being honest, but the client probably would not have accepted that as an excuse, so she virtually gave no explanation. She simply informed him that she could not make it and offered another date for the meeting.

But tomorrow came and went and Valeria did not keep that appointment either; nor the day after, nor the day after that. She did not go to work for three days. After the coffee, there was no escape. James Penton had taken over her days, her appointments, and her commitments. A packed agenda was thrown out the window. There was only one meeting place, the bed in her apartment. Meeting after meeting. One after another, with some breaks for food, which they would prepare in their underwear in the kitchen. Afterwards, they would go on working on getting to know one another, comfortably, informally, with no prior commitments or schedules or anyone else waiting for them or rushing them. No start or end time either. A two person meeting.

When there was no choice but to go back to reality, return to her real job, the one that turns people into slaves of money and schedules, Valeria refused to say goodbye to James. She wandered in circles around the apartment, and James laughed inwardly.

"I'll be here when you get back," he promised.

And she believed him.

At last she went to the office. As the elevator doors opened, she felt a piercing embarrassment that her coworkers would be able to read all over her face, her skin and her pores, precisely what she had been up to for the past three consecutive days.

"I was sick," she decided would be a good enough excuse for her absence.

She was not really lying either when you analyzed the way that this extraordinary event had affected her heart and mind. *I'm sick*, this was the best statement, she concluded. *Love sic*k... and she mocked herself for not having a single excuse in her head.

"It's best I tell them that I *am* sick. They'll leave me alone and they might even let me go early. If I say I *was* sick that means that I'm better now."

She began to cough violently, but instead of phlegm from her lungs, where there was none, she spat from the pit of her stomach.

"You're not well!" the receptionist told her as she walked past her desk.

I passed the first hurdle. That gossipy receptionist will tell everyone. Now all I have to do is get to my office, 'spreading germs' down the whole corridor full of PAs and office workers. Her office did not have glass walls, so she would be able to close the door for some privacy, and no one would notice she was only coughing when she had visitors. Her office was one of the few private ones in the marketing agency because all the others that were not corner offices had glass walls to encourage creativity and communication. 'Open plan' was usually the ad agencies' motto, and they designed the offices so that ideas would flow, so that creativity could surge forth in the corridors and at the writing desks; not just in the offices or meeting rooms.

When she went back to her apartment, James was waiting for her... that night they went for a walk. They went to the Navy Pier and spent several hours enjoying the "Earth Globes" exhibition, compiling work by many artists.

"Why is it so hard for people to live in harmony and not hurt one another... to live in a community?"

James said when they stopped to look at an interpretation of the Earth with children holding hands while carrying the planet. It was the first time he spoke to Valeria about his passions. James was a lover of nature, a staunch supporter of justice… a free spirit with a social conscience, just like her. Soul mates now cruelly separated.

Chapter 11

Valeria! James screamed alarmed in his thoughts. By now she had probably had him declared dead, or at least missing. *Have I lost her forever?* he thought and a strange knot formed in his throat.

"I think I'm dehydrated," he told the Egyptian girl who was showing him the way in Bawiti.

He wanted another cup of tea.

"Either that or I'm addicted to the tea in this country," he said out loud, trying to laugh and dislodge Valeria from his thoughts.

He had to call her as soon as he met with Bakran. He already tried to get the young dancer to return his cell phone, but to no avail. He did not even ask for the cameras; they would be her payment for saving his life.

The call would have to wait because he would not see Bakran until he arrived in Cairo. Even though he was trained to be level headed, he was worried that Valeria would not be sitting patiently on the sofa waiting for him. *A woman that alive has probably already forgotten all about me. I have to call her immediately to try to save this relationship.*

Ever since he met her, his life had been turned upside down. Now that he was with Valeria no assignment was enough of a challenge or exciting enough, much less when only a month before meeting her he had decided to retire at the end of the year. He accepted this assignment because it was a personal matter, an old unsettled score that he wanted to resolve so he could retire in peace. *However, no assignment should jeopardize my relationship with such a stunning woman.*

Valeria was not the first woman that invited him to her apartment the same day they met, but it was the first time that he did not want to leave her only a week after meeting. Before her, his life consisted of whiling away the day between assignments and taking advantage of fleeting pleasures with whoever happened to cross his path. His job did not encourage long term commitments, and he had not wanted one until now. However, even though it was the perfect lifestyle for him, it just was not gratifying anymore.

He would spend the time it took to return to Cairo to put his thoughts in order. He would find the right words to convince Valeria that even though they were far apart, she was the most important thing in his life. He had to find a way to balance his life in line with hers. He would turn down future assignments as soon as this one was completed. He had to complete his investigation soon… he was anxious to begin a new adventure by Valeria's side.

After begging for a cup of tea with gestures and getting nowhere, James resigned himself to drink the water from the canteen he had been given, because the thirst was killing him.

"Maybe I'm addicted to barbiturates and I'm associating needing them with tea?" James asked himself, thinking it was odd he would want tea at all hours of the day instead of water.

However, the barbiturates could not possibly be harming him. He felt fine, alert, and not drugged.

He followed Bakran's instructions and found the man described in the letter. He was a tourist guide who would drive him to Cairo in a Jeep. After the formalities were over, the man began reducing the air pressure of the Jeep's tires and to issue an explanation that James had not requested.

"It's so we can cross the desert on sand. This is normal here. Tourists and foreigners are forever changing the wheels until they hear that the secret is to not have them too full of air. Once I saw a busload of tourists arriving in Cairo with two destroyed tires, it was practically running on the rims, the whole thing was tilted to one side. It was hilarious," the man explained, demonstrating with his hands how the bus was leaning since it had no tires left on one side.

Egypt is a legendary and fantastical country, where your imagination runs wild with stories of pharaohs, slaves and pyramids as if they were fantasy tales until you see the country in person, drenched in endless sand dunes. *An unparalleled feast for the eyes*, thought James. And here he was, in the middle of the desert, the wind in his face, his eyes protected by large glasses, on his way back to Cairo to say farewell to the magnificent country as quickly as he possibly could.

Once he got to Cairo and as his car fought through the traffic of seventeen million inhabitants, he allowed himself briefly to be carried away with each exotic image that crossed his path, and a thin smile appeared on his lips. Finally the Jeep stopped in a dirty alleyway and the guide told him to hurry as he showed him a decrepit old door that marked his destination.

However, James did not have to enter the pestilent building. Bakran emerged through the door and greeted him with a drawn face, forcing a professional tone, as if they were meeting for the first time.

"You're still in danger, Nancy boy. We have to hurry," he whispered in his ear while he made sure that no one on the street could see or hear them.

They quick stepped to a navy blue car, which they boarded immediately, carrying no suitcases or bags.

After ten minutes on the packed roads of the growing city, they drove into a modern hotel's underground parking lot,and changed cars. This time it was white, like most of the cars in the city.

"What happened? Why did everything go wrong?" asked James the first chance he got.

"The man in the bazaar is to blame. He gave you away without hesitation. He offered information in exchange for money. It would seem that what you gave him wasn't enough for his liking and he tried to double his money by offering information to the highest bidder. Are you getting stingy in your old age, Nancy boy?"

"What do you think? Of course not. I paid him more than enough."

"You were unlucky. We were running surveillance on one of the buyers who went back to the bazaar the next day to say they had changed their minds and were cancelling the order. They found another supplier."

"Which of the two buyers?" asked James.

"Sam Cosgrove."

The reply provoked a long silence, which Bakran eventually broke to continue his explanation:

"I'm guessing that the seller, so he wouldn't come away empty handed, told him there was a man spying on them and he could give them information in exchange for some money. I'm telling you, us people from the Middle East don't have a reputation as merchants for nothing. We've earned that one. Thousands of years of experience... since Ancient Mesopotamia. Not even the British can touch our commercial maturity..."

"Would you like me to bow down before you now, or can you wait until we get to the airport," James interrupted making gestures of reverence with both arms. "Get it while you can, because when we get to London I'm throwing you to the lions... you'll be at my mercy..." he went on, trying to suppress a smile.

"I'm not going to London with you," said Bakran, and his expression turned serious again.

"Wasn't that your only condition?"

"Some other time. I have some unfinished business," his friend replied, handing him a sheet of paper that said: In case of emergency, please take me to the British Embassy, Ahmed Ragheb Street No.7, Garden City. "Put this in your pocket."

James read it slowly, folded it and put it in his pocket. He hoped he would not need to take refuge at the embassy, but it would be his ideal destination if someone found his body shot to pieces or stabbed in any old corner of Cairo.

"What a shame you're not coming with me, I was hoping you were going to be my bodyguard," James went on.

"That's why I'm not going. I'll be watching my own back. My wife has forbidden me to go on another trip and I'm more scared of her than any of the hired thugs we've chased around the world. Besides, thanks to you I have a baby factory. Every one of my children should be named after the city I was visiting with you just before procreating them. When I spend any time away from my wife, I lose all track of time and contraceptives, so I'd better halt the production line and look after the family. Otherwise I'll have children living under my roof my whole life."

With that they said goodbye, after a tight hug and firm pats on the back with both palms.

"Shukran," said James, in thanks.

"Ma'a salama," he heard Bakran's farewell.

Can an adventurer like Bakran settle down forever? Can I? wondered James as he made his way through the throngs of people at the busy Cairo International Airport. He had already gone through the hassle of the queue for the security checks, and he was walking around the terminal looking for the gate for his flight to London. Apparently it was the last departure, because the numbers kept ticking by and he still could not see it. There was barely anyone left on this side of the terminal. *Maybe it's one of the less popular flights, or not many people want to travel from Egypt to London*, he thought.

In any case, for the time being he could sit down at his leisure in any seat that he wanted, because most of them were empty. He double checked his ticket to verify that he was at the correct gate, and looked at the screen, but his flight was still not announced and the airline attendants were nowhere to be found. Just as he was about to go and check if his flight had been cancelled, two men came up behind him. One of them threatened him with a gun jabbed into his side. *Unless he's faking it and all he's poking me with are his fingers*, James reasoned.

"Come with us," said one of the Egyptians.

"I think you've got the wrong man," James stated, trying to start a conversation with them to buy time.

The gun was real; he was sure of that now.

"No, we are sure that it is you we want. We lost you for a while, but we found you again."

"You certainly took your time getting here," said the other man while they walked down the terminal corridor.

"You've been waiting for me at the airport this whole time?" asked James with a smile.

"We can be very patient if we're well paid."

"Someone is paying you to make sure I leave Cairo safely?"

"No, someone is paying us so you never leave Cairo alive."

A smile appeared on the faces of both men.

James looked around while he spoke to the men, who were forcing him towards a door labeled: 'employees only'.

Two against one... no sweat. His reaction was like lightning. As soon as they closed the door of the employee's room behind them, James hit the one carrying the gun, lashing out with his elbow and connecting firmly on the nose, making him drop the weapon and collapse to the ground.

The other thug reacted quickly and tried to punch him in the face, but he missed as James nimbly ducked the fist. Then, he tried to kick him but James grabbed his leg and a second later the other man was also on the ground. However, it was not over yet. The man kicked him in the stomach, winding him. With the strength of a mule, he got up from the floor while James was still gasping for breath, his body folded forward but his eyes fixed on his target, his face tense, and his arms ready for action. As the man came closer, James grabbed his head behind the neck with both hands. They were so close that their foreheads were almost touching and he could smell the other man's bad breath over his face. Before James could avoid it, the man head butted him in the mouth and a trickle of blood made its way down his chin from the split lip. He did not let it distract him and he brought his knee up powerfully into his opponent's groin, and followed it up with a punch in the stomach.

Unfortunately, he was a big guy and James' attacks did not leave him stunned long enough to get away. Before he could turn, the man reached for the gun on the floor and took aim, threatening to shoot.

Damn it! He's good and he seems to have the reflexes of a mongoose, thought James sensing he was cornered.

For a few seconds they stood face to face, until James got tired of playing chicken. He came closer to the man in the tiny room, and the man tensed up, as if not understanding what was going on, or not wanting to understand since his enemy's actions were so unlikely. However, it was happening. James, unarmed, was advancing threateningly. When the thug tried to shoot, James grabbed the gun and twisted his arm, making his whole body turn until he managed to disarm him and deliver a swift blow to the head with the butt of the gun. His reflexes did not turn out to be so good. The man fell unconscious to the floor.

James stood there for a moment, his legs apart and arms out and his chest heaving, breathing heavily, tired and astonished to still be alive. Suddenly, unthinkingly, pushed by the adrenalin pumping through his body, he left the room, closing and locking the door behind him while he dragged one of the food vending stalls in the corridor until it was obstructing the door. Not one person had noticed the commotion.

Returning to the terminal, he checked his flight status on the airport monitors and saw that it was finally there. He then wiped his mouth and spat the blood flowing from his split lip into a trash can. *Occupational hazards*, he thought.

"Passengers for flight 714 to London, please proceed to gate number 23. This flight is now ready for boarding."

Once on the plane, having walked up and down the aisle checking thoroughly for anyone suspicious, James mentally reviewed the incidents that had taken place in Cairo since his arrival three weeks ago until he and Bakran had parted.

"Wait! I almost forgot to give back your credentials," his partner told him before leaving, handing over his NCIA agent documentation, his driving license and British passport. He remembered how he had contacted Bakran the moment he arrived in the city as they often worked together on international assignments. Bakran had watched all of Sam Cosgrove's movements, expeditions, lunches and dinners. The day James arrived at the Egyptian capital, his colleague told him to go to bazaar Khan el-Khalili. It was where Sam and Josh Cosgrove's trail led.

The transaction the Cosgrove brothers carried out in the bazaar was not for souvenirs, spices, pipes or coffee. The Cosgroves ordered forty thousand yards of cotton knit from one of the representatives of a prestigious textile factory in Tanta, a city north of Cairo that specialized in manufacturing.

"They bought industrial quantities of fabrics? Since when do the presidents of pharmaceuticals travel half-way around the world to order textiles in exorbitant quantities? Could they be buying textiles for a third party, a business associate? Why have Josh and Sam taken the trouble to come in person?" James asked breathlessly. "None of this makes any sense."

His boss' orders had been pretty explicit.

"I want you to follow Sam Cosgrove's trail. We have connected him to a clandestine laboratory in Paddington where several people were infected with MRSA. One of the MRSA victims at St. Mary's positively identified him as responsible. The man told one of the nurses that the infection had not been accidental."

"Has Sam deliberately infected those people with MRSA? Is he running a legitimate investigation for MagMell Labs? And if so, why use an external lab when all around the world he has research and development laboratories specifically designed for working with viruses and bacteria? Is he working behind his brother's back? Is he working on something to bring Josh down?" James asked his colleague.

"It doesn't make sense. But something is going on, and we're going to be the ones to break the case wide open. Of course, as long as Sam doesn't manage to get to you first. It's obvious that he already knows you're on his tail. And it's not the first time he has known that someone is after him."

Both agents remembered the months lost by the agency chasing down inconclusive clues that linked Sam Cosgrove to violent incidents. Nothing conclusive enough to be able to arrest him. His superiors never wanted James to work on the investigations due to an apparent conflict of interests.

"Why does it matter that Sam Cosgrove is my sister's husband's brother?" he repeated the tongue twister over and over. "To me he's a lowlife like any other," he insisted to his boss. "This suspect has proved to be more slippery than a squid. How can I convince you that no one is better suited than me to make a case against him? Besides, I really hate the guy."

The check-mate came when he said to his boss:

"Sam is one of those people in every family. A bad seed; poisonous. I would do anything to get rid of him if I had the chance."

His boss gave him the chance.

"What will you tell your sister when she finds out you're responsible for landing her brother-in-law in jail?" was the last thing he asked James before issuing him his official orders.

"She will probably kick me out of her life like a traitor and that will be the end of family reunions and cocktails parties with friends and family."

However, James did not care about that. That was the Cosgrove's milieu, not something that he, James Penton, was comfortable with. The only relationship he wanted to maintain from the Cosgrove's side of the family was with his nephew Dean. He would need to find a way to see him. At school, perhaps.

"What if Josh is also involved?" he suddenly thought. "No, it can't be," he concluded. "Josh's reputation is spotless."

PART 4
In The Eyepiece

Chapter 12

It took Miguel over an hour to finish his letters. He gestured to the nightshift nurse that he needed some envelopes. At first it was difficult. He tried to pronounce the word in English with no real idea what he was saying. In fact he was just saying "envelope" in Spanish as if he were pronouncing it in English, imitating the sing-song voices British people used when they spoke. But it did not work.

"It would seem that the English word is nothing like the Spanish word," Miguel concluded.

That was when he resorted to mimics as he pretended to fold the letter and put it in an invisible envelope. Finally the woman understood what he wanted. Half an hour later she returned with twenty mustard color manila envelopes. It was not what he had in mind; he imagined traditional white envelopes, but these would have to do. *At least I can save myself the trouble of folding the letters.*

Miguel took his time writing the letters; in many ways it was the same message repeated many times for the editors of the most important newspapers of the city. A surge of energy ran through his body when he found the ream of paper, and he felt no pain, discomfort or fatigue until he had finished his mission. Now all he had to do to complete his plan was wait for dawn. The janitor would not deny him this last favor. Miguel trusted him. He could tell he was a good man. *How else can you explain the way he's helping a total stranger? When I tell him what I want him to do for me, there's no way he'll turn me down.*

He finished writing at about three in the morning, and he settled back to get a good night's sleep and wake up in time to see the janitor when he came through his room during his next shift.

He did not wake up until past eleven in the morning. *Has the janitor already been to my room?* A strange panic gripped him, but it passed when he thought that the man would not go home without at least saying goodbye. *Unless he has been forbidden from visiting me.* Just as another panic attack was about to begin, the janitor stuck his head around the door.

"Kid! I thought I was going to have to go home without seeing you."

"Has your shift ended?"

"No, but the head nurse told me you need a lot of rest, so she's planning on banning all visits to you until further notice."

"No… No. I need you to do one last thing for me."

"Miguel, can't it wait until you get better?"

"No. This can't wait."

And he showed him the twenty manila envelopes.

"You want to say goodbye to that many people by letter?"

"No, I don't know these people."

"You're delirious!" said the janitor in worried tones.

"This is serious," said Miguel, and he closed his eyes for a moment as if to avoid wasting words. "I need you to take a photograph of me and print twenty copies to put in those envelopes."

"You want me to take a picture of you?"

"Yes. Do you have a digital camera?"

"No, I don't," said the man, a little ashamed.

Miguel's anxious face sank.

"But my daughter does!" added the janitor, and new hope invaded Miguel's expression, completely transforming him.

"Can you go and get it and take a photo of me this afternoon? We can have the copies in an hour."

"But what's your rush? If you want to send a snapshot to your groupies, it would be better if you wait until you look better. Right now you don't look very handsome, to be honest..."

Before he could finish his sentence, Miguel pressed his lips, grabbed the man firmly by the collar and looking into his eyes said:

"This is very, very important. Can you help me, or not?"

Of course he helped. Two hours later, Miguel was slipping a photograph of himself into each one of the envelopes, which he sealed using a damp cloth he placed by his side. It was the way his mother had taught him. The first reason for this system was that anything that came near her son's mouth had to be clean and disinfected, as she liked to remind him every time they sat down to eat. Secondly, and perhaps most importantly, because her mother had taken an intense dislike to sealing envelopes with her tongue.

It all began when Miguel told her about the spam e-mail he received about a man who had cockroach eggs growing on his tongue after having licked the glue on an envelope to seal it. His mother immediately changed her habits. Miguel smiled to himself on remembering this incident. When he finished with all the envelopes, he counted them again and placed them on his bedside table.

Now he needed rest. Tomorrow he would have to be fully alert to field any questions the journalists and police officers might have for him. The janitor also promised to lend him a cell phone since his room telephone still had not been installed.

"Finally!" said an ecstatic Miguel when he heard his girlfriend's voice on the other end of the receiver. "They took forever to give me a phone."

"Where are you?" was the first question.

"In the hospital," and a sigh escaped his throat. "I wish I were in Barcelona with you!"

"What happened?" interrupted the girl.

"I have a chest infection, but I'm being treated with intravenous antibiotics," he told a half-truth, leaving out the bacteria that had caused the infection.

Why scare her unduly if telling her he had a chest infection was already bad enough? Ana knew all the possible complications that could aggravate his condition. He did not have to go into medical explanations with her.

Will I die this time? he asked himself, but nothing in his tone of voice told his girlfriend that he was nervous. Rather than nervous, this time he was scared. *Death is mysterious, unpredictable, and you never know when it's going to sweep you away or spare you.* However, Miguel steered his thoughts away from death and focused on his reason for living.

"Do you know I love you with all my heart?" he told Ana after a few seconds of silence. He had left her stunned on the other end of the line when he told her he had caught a chest infection.

"Are you saying goodbye?" and he could hear his girlfriend's voice breaking as she asked the question.

She cried in silence so that he would not hear, but it was obvious. She could not hide it. She was disconsolate, worried and mentally planning how to get to London as quickly as possible.

"Goodbye? Me? I tell you I love you every time we speak," Miguel soothed her, but his voice was so weak that it gave away the seriousness of his condition.

"Promise me," Ana stammered.

Tears drowned her words.

"Hey, take it easy. Don't worry so much about me, my love."

At that, he stopped. He could not promise her he would be fine, not this time.

They both fell silent. Suddenly, and at the same time, as if their minds were connected, they allowed themselves to be carried back on the current of memories to the moment they were alone in Dr. Martinez's examination room in Puerto Rico. It was the last time they had been physically together, hours before Ana returned home to her parents in Barcelona.

The doctor went for lunch, but before leaving he told them with a mischievous glint in his eyes that he would be back in an hour. Miguel almost strangled him when he winked before closing the door. *What's he doing? Now he thinks he's a matchmaker, some kind of wingless cupid?* Miguel simply prayed that Ana had not seen the wink so she would not think it was all a set up.

He did not have the same intentions as his dirty minded doctor. He was convinced that he would behave like a decent gentleman even though his hormones were in full revolt and were sparking unease in his privates and making him break out in a cold sweat all over his body.

He was quite close to Ana, both sitting on the sofa of the doctor's office. *Isn't it in bad taste to have a sofa in an examination room?* Miguel wondered as he tried to avoid rubbing his leg against Ana's uncovered knees. *Shouldn't sofas be banned to avoid sexual harassment suits? Apparently the good doctor isn't up to date with the latest regulations on professional ethics,* he went on musing, looking all around the office to avoid looking right at Ana, who was looking at him intensely as if trying to figure out what was wrong with him.

In fact the doctor was up to date with ethics regulations, but simply preferred to have a sofa for his naps whenever a patient did not turn up to his appointment. He had solved his problem by placing two chairs before his desk where he would seat his patients. The sofa was only for his personal use. However, today he had invited over the two youngsters to sit down on it to try to make them feel at home.

It was the first time the doctor had met Ana in person, although he knew everything about her from Miguel's perspective. Since he felt like he was meeting his surrogate son's girlfriend, he reconverted his office into a living room and offered them juice and biscuits. All of this before he had the idea that maybe he should leave them alone for a little while, because Ana would be going back to Barcelona soon, and who knew if they would have as good a chance to declare their feelings again.

Miguel could not control his nerves. His hands were shaking, his heart was racing, he had a frog in his throat, his mouth was damp, his eyes... kept making the mistake of ending up caught in the depths of Ana's chestnut eyes which spoke to him between blinks: *what are you waiting for?*

Miguel bit his lips. He felt like an idiot before this beautiful woman who was inviting him with her eyes to obey his instincts. His face had turned red while hers remained calm. Natural laws in all their splendor.

Ana could guess his thoughts, saw how nervous he was, and offered him a sweet and flirty smile. Miguel felt his temperature rise. He was thirsty. It was a thirst that only his girlfriend's lips could quench. And he kissed her. At last he caressed her, covered her in a thousand kisses, each one savoring the taste of her, her nectar and the gentleness of her moist lips. When he reached the point he could not go on, when he was about ready to eat her up, he pulled his face away from hers. Suddenly he realized that he was lying on top of her, pressing his hips against her welcoming feminine pelvis. *How did I get here? I can't explain it. I've lost consciousness, I've lost control. We almost made love.*

Miguel bit his lip again, but this time he resisted. He sat up on the other end of the sofa, giving Ana room to sit back up again. Once they were both calmer and their heartbeats had returned to normal, Miguel broke the embarrassing silence:

"Well, at least if we had done it, I wouldn't have got you pregnant."

Ana did not answer. She just looked at him with an expression as if to say she could not believe that this was what he had to say about the most passionate moment of their relationship.

Miguel, realizing this, but now even more embarrassed than before, tried to make amends:

"Because I'm sterile. Did you already know that?"

"I wasn't sure if you were, but I guessed as much. I also read up online, you know. I've studied everything, absolutely everything about your illness. So you have no way of scaring me off. I will be with you forever. Until death do us part."

She came closer to give him another hug and a kiss.

Now on the telephone, she in Barcelona and he in London, they both laughed like children at the memories. Instead of tears, now laughter filled their hearts. Their hearts were full of joy; the joy of knowing they were loved.

The following day, the janitor waited for the perfect moment to slip into Miguel's room, unseen by nurses, doctors or visitors in the adjacent corridors. He had to see Miguel one last time, even if it was off limits. He had made a promise.

He slowly pushed his cleaning cart forward, and stored it in the maintenance room on the same floor. Before closing the door, he looked both ways and advanced towards the isolated room at the end of the corridor. Everything was clear. The family visiting hours had not yet begun and the nurses were doing their first rounds with patients on the other side of their station. It was easy. He slipped into the room without anyone seeing him.

Not even Miguel saw him, because he was not there.

Have they moved him? the janitor asked himself. However, when he saw the manila envelopes on the bedside table, he decided this could not be the case. He quickly grabbed them, stuffed them under his white coat and left as quickly as he had come, heading towards the maintenance room. Once there he removed the white coat and mask, and placed the envelopes in a bag inside the cleaning cart. Then he proceeded to remove the gloves and throw them in the trash. He would address all the envelopes at home and mail them that afternoon. Twenty envelopes for twenty recipients.

As he was exiting the main doors of the hospital, with the bag full of envelopes under his arm, he thought of Miguel and the empty room.

"I will come and see him tomorrow. They must be running some additional tests on him," he said, and he went on his way towards Paddington station.

On the other side of London, two men were exchanging insults.

"They were all supposed to die the same day, Sam. You have to fix this, right now."

The speaker threw a hard bound book inches over Sam's head, swearing at the top of his voice.

"The idea was to infect the staff with MRSA just as they were completing the lab project. Then you were supposed to take each one to different safe houses in Lincolnshire where they would each take their sweet time dying, depending on the effects of the bacteria. This would ensure that they would say nothing, they would just become statistics in the argument that there are increasing numbers of cases in the community."

Obviously, the staff had no idea this was the plan. They did know that in case of accident or infections, they would be taken outside London. Sam Cosgrove had assured them that he would take personal responsibility for seeing them back to full health with a barrage of antibiotics set aside in case of emergency. A private doctor and nurse would tend to them in the comfort of a country cottage. So that they would not worry in the slightest about their health, he even allowed Dr. Fowler to store a dose of antibiotics in the laboratory just for them.

But nothing took place as planned, because when they found Miguel on the floor, one of the employees panicked and immediately called the emergency services who arrived before the private ambulance Sam had contracted. The emergency services sent not one, but two ambulances, so Sam was left with no choice but to allow the staff to board them. Everyone except Dr. Fowler. Before they left, he told the technicians to follow protocol. They already knew what that meant and what it implied, and that for giving a fictitious story he would deposit one hundred and fifty thousand euros into their personal accounts when they left the hospital. A little bonus for lying.

"It's no use, Sam. The plan is in ruins. Now it's just a contagion in a laboratory. What are you going to do about it? Well?", the man asked and then added: "What are you prepared to do?"

It was the sign Sam Cosgrove needed to immediately wrap the pending issue up, so he said goodbye, jumped in his car and drove off towards St. Mary's hospital. He would have to inject more MRSA bacteria in the employee's drips.

Chapter 13

Paco ran down the apartment building corridor and away from the elevator as quickly as his legs would carry him. As he ran for the door to the emergency stairs, he used the handle of his butter knife to break each one of the light bulbs that lit up the corridor. He then heard the elevator doors grind open before he could take out the last light bulb. As soon as the glow began to fade, that half-light that remains like a residue of the switched off light, Paco heard the footfalls of the man entering the corridor and a voice saying:

"Kid, I know you're there. Don't be afraid. I'm a friend of Sam Cosgrove and I am here to help you."

Paco did not answer when he realized that the man lowered his arm and hid the gun close to his thigh. Not only did he hold his tongue, he held his breath. The man spoke again.

"I have a very strong antibiotic with me which will cure you right away."

Of course. A gun shaped "antibiotic" that will get me out of the way nice and quickly and solve all of Sam Cosgrove's problems, thought Paco taking care to be as still as a tiger stalking its prey.

The man drew closer and when he stopped, the far off glow of the last light bulb briefly lit his face. It was enough for Paco to see that he had a deep scar on his face that ran from the left eye to his jaw. He could also see that now he carried the gun openly with his finger on the trigger.

Typical, thought the youngster. *Do they slash their faces on purpose so that they conform to the requisite stereotype? To make people more scared of them?*

Paco bolted. He ran down the stairs as if his life depended on it, as indeed it did. When he opened the door to the lobby, he ran towards the outdoor patio of the building. As he entered, he looked back and saw the man crossing the patio, making his way through the snow. He could not tell if he was still armed, but he was not about to wait until he was next to him to find out, so he quickly opened his backpack and produced the bread knife.

The man was virtually on top of him now, only ten paces away. He was over a foot taller than Paco, with thick arms twice the size of those of the youngster. Paco felt his legs sink into the snow. His impotence was so evident that he felt ashamed. What could he do armed only with a simple kitchen knife against the monster bearing down on him? He had to act brave, he decided, *because villains are like dogs: they can smell the fear*.

The man walked calmly towards him with his hands in his pockets and a thin smile drawn on his lips, as if this were all a game to him. *Sam Cosgrove sure knows how to pick 'em*, thought Paco. *He looks like a bounty hunter who kills for pleasure*. However, instead of making him more afraid, the thought assured him it was now or never and so he started to run again. Every nerve in his body stood on alert for any reaction.

"I am faster, I am smarter," he repeated the mantra over and over to himself, just as he had when he left the apartment.

When he got to the other end of the patio, he stopped and turned to strike back, knife in hand and he waited for the man to catch up, who was running towards him as quickly as his heavy set legs allowed. Just as the man jumped him, Paco dodged like an experienced bullfighter, a movement he had practiced a million times since childhood when he played at bullfighting with his friends. He was always the bullfighter and his neighbor Manolo, who was a little fatter, was always the bull. Now this man, who was inviting him to play with his sardonic smile, would see exactly what he was up against.

"You want to play? Where'd you hide your gun?" Paco asked.

The man did not reply, he just smiled. They repeated the game twice.

"Olé," exclaimed the boy every time he dodged the man, who always brushed past him, slipping a little in the fallen snow.

Third time's a charm. The man lunged with all his strength, now annoyed like a mule, but still could not catch Paco.

When the boy looked around, he saw the man slipped as he tried to turn, his body snapping forward and back. In an effort to produce the gun from his pocket, he waved his arms to try to keep on balance, but it only made matters worse. His feet slid on the ice uncontrollably, making his arms and legs look like scissors cutting nothing but air. Paco began to obey the impulse to help him, but realized in time that this was not a game. A few seconds later the man was down. Paco moved over quickly and began kicking his hand first to make him release the gun, and then in the stomach, legs and back, everywhere he could, venting his fury. The man did not even flinch, he simply went stiff.

Paco then put the knife to his throat and held it there, pressing the skin as hard as he could without cutting it. Adrenaline was pumping through his body, his heart was pounding in his chest, his breathing made his shoulders heave up and down. He wanted to kill the man.

As he pressed down harder on his enemy's throat, he noticed that his dark eyes were not blinking and were in fact beginning to glaze over. He was bleeding heavily from an injury to the head which was staining the snow a deep purplish red. The man had hit himself on the edge of the brick wall of the patio when he fell over. He had breathed his last sigh.

Paco was paralyzed, staring at him. *That could have been me in that pool of blood*, he thought, and he quickly staggered to his feet. He tried to get away from the man, but he tripped over the motionless body and fell over with his hands buried in the red snow. Horrified, he stood up as quickly as possible, and cleaned his hands on the man's coat. The body was already turning as cold as the snow. Once on his feet, he lowered his head and tried to scream, but nothing came out. In that patio, staring at the floor strewn with snow, mud and blood, Paco witnessed the death of a human being for the first time.

He had nothing left to do in that place. He put the knife away in his backpack, collected his things, and headed out of the patio. He went into the shadows and followed the footprints that his attacker had left just a few minutes ago, looking in both directions around the black and damp skeletal tree trunks that dotted the edge of the patio.

———

Miguel's manila envelope had been waiting for days to be opened at the offices of the London Daily. It was lost in a sea of letters from readers, flyers, press releases from marketing agencies, packages and samples of new products that arrived daily at every magazine and newspaper office around the world. A simple manila envelope was easily mixed up with many others. It did not matter how important its contents were, even in life or death circumstances such as transcendental premises and proposals for exclusive interviews, they would invariably be lost in the blizzard of correspondence.

Anyone in possession of urgent news had to get straight in contact with the editor of the publication. However, it was usually best to get in touch with the journalist who covered the beat because if not he would have to face a busy PA, or in a worst case scenario, a receptionist who would merely take a message. Even so, a phone call was more likely to be taken into account than a letter, particularly if there was no return address on the envelope.

However, today it would be Miguel's manila envelope's turn to be opened. It was the job of one of the London Daily personal assistants to discard or archive correspondence to maintain some kind of control over the chaos of the office.

"My desk is basically the editor's trash can," she complained every time someone left an envelope or communique on it.

This was all in spite of the fact that they received much less post now in the age of internet.

The first thing the PA did was to remove the correspondence from its envelope and classify it according to the newspaper sections. Since she was in charge of everything that arrived without an addressee, she had to scan each letter or press release to see which journalist or editor should receive it. If the subject matter was of interest to her, she would read the whole thing. Unfortunately, that was the exception to the rule. Most people only wrote to complain. *It takes all sorts*, she thought as she went through the letters, one at a time.

She was already half way through the pile of letters she had determined to sort through that morning when the front page news editor interrupted her. He had an envelope in his hand. *Another one?* the woman complained inwardly.

"Adela, see if you can read this one, they sent it to me in Spanish."

"Throw it out. Whoever thought of sending a letter in Spanish to the biggest newspaper in England has got to be an idiot. We shouldn't waste a precious second of our time on it," she replied mischievously, imitating the hoarse voice of the General Manager of the newspaper.

"That's what I thought, but the phrase URGENTE/EMERGENCIA caught my eye, it's handwritten on the envelope. Even though I don't speak any Spanish, I'd have to be an idiot to not understand it," and he dropped it on her desk.

The word urgent was indeed pretty much the same in English and Spanish. The only difference was an extra e in Spanish.

"What's urgent for you is not what's urgent for a bored reader sitting at home with nothing better to do than write to a newspaper to make themselves feel important..." the woman started to say, but it was too late.

The editor had locked himself in his office and she, now annoyed, had one more letter to read.

Her first impulse was to throw the envelope violently in the trash, but instead she released it again on her pile of work to pick up the phone which had started to ring on her desk. It was her best friend, asking her out to lunch. She did not think twice about it, and bored by the task she had been assigned, she stood up, collected her briefcase and left. Miguel's letter remained unread, yet again.

An hour later, after a quick lunch where the PA caught up on her best friend's life and news, who happened to be a nun with the airs of a rebel, Miguel's envelope at last received the attention it deserved.

"The other papers must have done what we almost did," the PA told the front page news editor when she finished reading the letter. "Since it arrived in Spanish and worse still, handwritten, they probably threw it in the trash. I haven't seen anything published about this story and you know I read all the papers, national, international and the internet editions," the PA explained, clearly excited.

"Adela, how can you be sure this isn't some story to waste our time?"

"Obviously you doubt me because I'm just an ordinary PA..."

"Hey, I find that a little offensive. That's not what I'm saying at all. But you've got to admit it, Adela, it sounds pretty outlandish."

"Of course. But you're the ones who investigate important stories every day, however outlandish they sound. What do you call it? Hunch, lead, gut feeling. This is my gut feeling. I understand it's hard to believe because what you're hearing is my version of what this kid has written, but how about if I translate it word for word?"

"Ok. Go ahead."

Dear Editors,

My name is Miguel Ramírez. I came to London three months ago to take part in a clinical study on genetic therapy for cystic fibrosis patients, which is currently being undertaken at Imperial College, because I am a sufferer of this condition. At the same time that I was taking part in the study, I worked at a private research laboratory to earn some money (this lab has nothing to do with Imperial College).

At first I did not know what this laboratory was working on, but a few days ago I found out they were studying the MRSA bacterium.

At this, the editor interrupted her.

"What's the story, Adela? We already published an article about that clinical study and everyone is studying MRSA all over the world. That bacteria is the flavor of the week."

"Be patient, here comes the good part," Adela replied, and she read on.

At the moment all the employees, including myself, are at St. Mary's hospital with severe infections caused by the bacteria. We have no idea how it happened. We were extremely careful. I do not know if the pharmaceutical that contracted us is aware of what has happened, but none of their representatives have come to visit me and I have been in the hospital for three days now. At no point was I informed that we would be working with that bacteria, nor did they identify themselves as a pharmaceutical, because we were not working at official facilities but instead at a clandestine laboratory. I found out about this the same day I discovered about the MRSA, because a work colleague told me. He told me it had to remain a secret.

As you can see, I am scared. My life is in danger and I think it is fair that an investigation be conducted. I think my colleagues have all already spoken to the police. Today will be my chance, because at first I didn't get a chance because I don't speak English, but I have an interpreter now. The press must know what is happening. Please, get in touch with me at room 1220.

*Yours sincerely,
Miguel Ramírez*

The editor was silent, mulling things over.

"Adela, I don't know what to think. We definitely need to cover this story because several people have been infected. But what catches my attention about this is the 'clandestine laboratory' he's talking about."

"I knew this would smell funny to you... I knew it," she said exhilarated, not quite believing that she was helping to develop a story.

"Call Paul Claron and tell him I want to see him," the editor requested.

In two seconds flat, Adela returned to reality, from future reporter to merely a PA. She picked up the phone on her boss' desk and called the reporter. She had called him so often since arriving at the London Daily that she knew his number by heart.

"Unless this pharmaceutical is holding on to a huge time bomb, a cure for all ills, why else would they keep their identity a secret?" said the editor. "This could be the scoop of the week."

He could already see the headline: Pharmaceutical in search of a cure infects employees. He loved big stories about pharmaceuticals screwing up. Fraud, money laundering, open wars to develop medications even when their benefits have not been proven. It was a red-hot story, that was for sure.

The editor went on pondering. Three days ago the body of Dr. Francis Fowler had been found in an ambulance on the other side of London, in Bromley. It had appeared on page three of the newspaper. Dr. Fowler, MRSA expert, found dead in traffic accident. It had never been clarified what he was doing in the ambulance. It was a private ambulance. Apparently the driver had been called directly, and he had also died in the accident, so there were no leads to chase down on that end either.

"Could our doctor have something to do with this clandestine lab?" said the editor out loud. "Too much of a coincidence to have been just three days ago."

And so it was that with no fuss and a simple letter, Miguel got what he wanted. He set the ball rolling.

Chapter 14

Paco spent a whole two weeks secluded away in the home of a little old lady and her son, who had granted him asylum in the countryside. Although it was not a small house, the young man felt like a caged tiger. He already knew every corner of the house and even discovered a centuries old well in the basement for watering the sheep. In the old days, the livestock lived in the foundations of the houses and humans on the upper floors. *How lucky that they have their own stable now!* thought Paco, although maybe the company of animals would have done him some good.

After taking his regular dose of antibiotics, he left his room to speak to the old lady, since he had nothing better to do. However, when he went into the living room, he found her sound asleep in her arm chair. The man and his son were practicing reading from a book about dinosaurs, so Paco took three steps back so as to not interrupt them. Boredom pushed him back to his room to seek solace in Miguel's letters and e-mails, which he had stashed in his backpack before fleeing the apartment.

Miguel had printed all of his correspondence with Ana, perhaps to remove the computer trail and to protect his privacy. Or maybe for more romantic reasons: to store the proof of his love for Ana. This reason made Paco feel like a criminal, an intruder, reading every letter and every verse. But he could not help it. It was intoxicating.

Ana and Miguel spoke of poetry in their letters:

"I love it when you write me poems. You never answered my question: when did you start writing them, and why? Come on, please tell me and write me one while you're at it. It's been a while since you've written me a poem. I'm going to try my hand at some verse. Don't you dare laugh, even if you think it's awful.

> I can't just tell you that I love you
> because a lovesick beat
> gives my secret away.
> My life is yours
> yours is my inspiration
> yours is my joy
> yours is my heart"
> –Ana

"Ana, my love. Poetry and lyrics are fleeting moments that speak of longings or hopes, of desires, of loss, of pain and absurdity. That's why I started to write poetry. To express myself. In my little world, my little twelve-year-old world, poetry became my everything. I couldn't understand the poetic measures, and I had no teachers. However, I did know what I was feeling, and I could describe what I saw. My poetry, if you can call it that, is a tool to uncover my feelings. You can't lie when you write poetry. All of my thoughts and fears are exposed, right there to be seen.

The last thing your poem caused was laughter. I wanted to get on a plane so I could see you at once. So I could hug you, and cover you in kisses. Thank you for writing it. Thank you for loving me."

They spoke about their plans for the future via internet.

"Ana, I will be going to London soon so that I can be closer to you. My Uncle found me a job and my family will give me some money. Dr. Martinez is going to call one of his friends in Barcelona to let me stay with him when I finish the study at Imperial College while they sort out my work permit. I dream of working at a record label. Do you think I will be lucky in Spain?"

"Of course! Even more if you're married to a Spaniard as clever as I am."

"Who's talking about getting married? Ana, focus, I'm talking about work."

"To find a job in Spain you're going to need me... you need to marry a Spaniard, and even then it's an uphill battle. You have no choice, you're going to have to marry me. You're mine. I am claiming you as my property."

They also discussed the risks of taking part in the clinical trial:

"*Ana, there is a salsa song called Adán García by Rubén Blades which says: 'If I am to live in fear, I would rather die smiling with my memories alive.' It's my motto. I don't want to live in fear... I want to do everything I can to beat this sickness. I want to be with you.*"

"So do I, but sometimes I think you are putting yourself in harm's way. You promised me you were going to last until you're thirty-five years old at least."

"*I'm doing everything I can. This study is my best hope. It's tangible, it's achievable, it's promising... that's what all the reports say. Have a little faith.*"

"You didn't go into this study because you're backing out of our agreement, right? You haven't forgotten?"

"*You mean to get married next year and have a fifteen year marriage?*"

"What other pact could I possibly be talking about?"

"*Of course I haven't forgotten, Ana, I dream about it every day. Who knows if the doctors on the study can change my fuses, maybe they can replace the defective genes, give me a lung transplant and you'll have to put up with me for fifty-five years instead of just fifteen. Maybe you'll regret it."*

"*I'm going to kiss you every night, even when I'm a senile old lady and you're a decrepit old man. You're not getting away from me.*"

They spoke of love.

Ana and Miguel offered themselves just as they were, in their own words. Now Paco was the keeper of their memories, swimming in their passions and their dreams. He lived out their adolescent love as if it were his own, and he felt that his heart was swelling with the words of a girl he had never set eyes on. He could taste the love, a fleeting love which longs to be real and he wanted to feel that for himself one day: to be loved, desired.

The following day, as the sun pierced the fog and expelled the night, Paco heard laughter and festivities coming from the kitchen. He dressed quickly and headed towards the room where all the sounds of joy were coming from. The old lady and her son were hugging a tall young man who laughed nonstop with the most contagious laugh that Paco had ever heard. He smiled too, not knowing why, caught up by the show.

Suddenly they all noticed his presence. When they realized they had awoken him with all the noise, the old lady and her son apologized profusely and introduced him to Armand. The young man was the six year old boy's brother, who was just back home from visiting his aunt for a few weeks. He sported spiky dyed blonde hair and the athletic physique of someone used to playing a lot of sports. Armand was like an alien crash landed in this house full of humble farmers.

The two teenagers immediately fell to talking and realized that they had thousands of things in common.

Both loved outdoor sports, and they talked for hours about all kinds of activities. Horseback riding, motor boating, the joyous sensation of climbing mountains, of water skiing and ordinary skiing, and of one thing that neither had yet had the chance to do: fly a biplane in the mountains. They spoke of all the fun things they would do on their summer holidays. They talked about the kinds of things that boys talk about.

"Do you have a girlfriend?" Paco asked Armand when they ran out of extreme sports to discuss, and dusk gave way to night.

"Yeah, lots. You?"

"No. I used to, but we broke up in the fall."

"If you like I'll introduce you to some of my girlfriends," Armand smiled, nudging his shoulder as if to say, 'go on, I dare you'.

However, Paco was not interested in the invitation, although he did think of one girl. The mental image of Ana formed clearly in his mind, along with her words: "You're mine. I am claiming you as my property" which she had written to Miguel. Right now, she was the only girl he was interested in.

Paco and Armand both looked out of the window. The house was being beaten by gales of wind. Snow pounded the earth. Armand's father turned his coat and scarf into a kind of makeshift shelter as he stumbled back to the house from the barn, trying to hide from the inclemency of the weather and the frozen gusts of wind that whipped around the mountains and fields.

Armand spoke first.

"No girls today, it'll have to be some other day, today we're snowed in. You'll have to wait," and he curled up, holding his legs.

They sat on the carpet on the floor in Armand's room, and began to throw a small rubber ball to each other, which would bounce against the walls, the lamp, the desk or the bed whenever they could not catch it. Paco told him about his job at the laboratory and how much he loved science and running experiments. Then it was Armand's turn to ask questions. He was not familiar with matters of sciences.

After a long inquisition about Petri dishes and microscopes, Armand interrupted.

"Who is Miguel?" he asked after Paco inadvertently mentioned his name during one of his explanations.

"He was my roommate. We worked together at the lab."

Without revealing any details about what had happened at the lab, he told him about Miguel. He told him about Ana. He read several poems and letters.

"That girl sounds amazing," said Armand.

"Yes…" but Paco said no more.

"Do you know what she looks like? Don't you have a photo of her?" insisted Armand.

"No," Paco lied.

He did not want to share the photo of Ana. She kept him company at night. Ana's beautiful brown eyes gave him hope, they had become his guide. He had made up his mind. He would not sleep easy again until he met her in person. He had a good reason, a purpose… to return her correspondence, to return her photo. He would give her all the love messages that she had written to someone else, to his friend Miguel.

PART 5
Data Analysis

Chapter 15

Walk on…, my whole life walking on, sang Valeria's radio alarm clock, playing the number one hit from the Latino station that she listened to in an attempt to not forget how to speak Spanish. But today, Valeria was not listening. A heavy dream prevented her from hearing the radio, the dripping leak from her faucet or the bustle of the city several floors below.

She could, however, hear the noise of her anxious footfalls as they noisily hit the tarmac of the street she was walking on. She was walking fast and straight for the Plaza España, which is where she found herself in her dream. She had been told that James was begging there, living in old cardboard boxes. When she got to the square, she ran into a multitude celebrating the patron saint's festivities. The jubilation was such that she could not tell women from men and the children were tied to their parent's waists with colorful ribbons to avoid getting lost.

Valeria caught up to the people, grabbed them by the shoulders and spun them around to be able to look at their faces. They were all identical, all white skinned and dark haired, but none of them were James. She got up on tip toe and tried to look over the sea of heads. *There he is!* she exclaimed to herself when she saw a poorly dressed man sitting at the feet of the statues of Don Quixote and Sancho Panza, playing a Spanish guitar with no strings.

She ran for him, pushing everyone that she bumped into in her rush to get to the monument dedicated to Miguel de Cervantes. "I'm almost there… I know I'm going to find you", she heard a far-off voice saying, but it was not Valeria speaking. It was a man's voice, a singer's voice, a masculine voice backed by a guitar, it was Valeria's radio which woke her up at long last and brought her back to the reality that she had to race to get up and get dressed in time for her presentation at MagMell.

"Did you bring your laptop? Do you need a projector or something?" asked Mercedes, checking that Valeria had everything she needed for the presentation.

"Yes. My team sent me a message to say that they arrived fifteen minutes ago. They should be setting the projector up in the conference room as we speak. Can you ask Claire if she saw them arrive?"

Mercedes called her PA.

"Yes, everything is under control. I already asked them and they are going to be ready to start at ten on the dot."

"Thank you, Claire. Alert us five minutes before it's time, alright?"

Mercedes was always prepared for her meetings, but she did not feel she was in control of this one. Valeria had sent her a summary of the presentation, and her first instinct was that it was an appropriate campaign, quite aggressive but not falling in the mistake of prompting a crisis or unnecessarily scaring people about an outbreak. However, she had a feeling it would not all go as planned. The fact that both Josh and Sam Cosgrove would be present made her hair stand on end.

"I don't understand what Sam Cosgrove does here. Can you explain it to me? I had to share a taxi with him the other day…"

"Why?"

"I don't know. I was about to get in a taxi and he was just standing there asking if we could share it, and I'm telling you it was not pleasant. I don't think we spoke five words to each other, because the guy doesn't talk, and worst of all, he just kept looking me over as if he could see through my clothes until I said to him: have you lost something?"

"No! You said that? What did he say?" Mercedes exclaimed.

"What do you think? Nothing. He smiled at me like nothing had happened and he patted me condescendingly on the thigh just before he got off the taxi."

"It's now five to ten," Claire announced over the phone.

"Thank you," Mercedes replied.

Both friends stood up with their coffee mugs in hand and a folder under their arms, and headed towards the conference room.

Twenty minutes later, once the formalities were over, Valeria had her audience eating out of the palm of her hand.

"What we want is action, we want the consumer to demand a strategy of prevention from their doctors. We want the consumer to take control of the issue, and for doctors to ask for help, like a grassroots intervention – a coalition, a combined front coming from below, from the masses, to get the government and hospitals to see that they must take action."

"The first phase of the campaign," she went on, "will be to print information leaflets to be handed out in schools, universities, athletics departments, gyms and pediatrician's offices."

"And t-shirts…" interrupted Josh Cosgrove with his potent voice. He was sitting opposite Valeria with both elbows on the table, one hand holding his chin and his whole body leaning forward.

Like a predator eyeing his prey, thought Valeria, but she immediately set her thoughts aside. It was not the time to be carried away by her imaginings.

Valeria paused her presentation, looked Mr. Cosgrove in the eye, prepared to respond, but decided to ignore his comments and went on with her presentation as it was planned.

"The campaign will also include a message to be disseminated through mass media, digital publications and healthcare publications with a two page spread for the first three months, then reduced to a one page ad for at least three additional months. We will monitor internet impact of the ads and we will rotate them depending on efficacy. This will be combined, of course, with the visits of Sales Representatives to each medical office to present the vaccine," and she directed these last few words to the Executive Director for Planning, in charge of the vaccines division, who nodded. "We should begin with pediatricians and then move on to general practitioners…"

But she was unable to finish the sentence because Josh Cosgrove interrupted again, but this time with an edge to his voice, like a father telling off his five year old daughter.

"I said that I want t-shirts we can give out to patients."

He looked at her defiantly with his serpent eyes, and then scanned the rest of the faces gathered around the conference room table.

"Mr. Cosgrove, if you will excuse me. I do not believe that t-shirts are the most effective means," Valeria went on, choosing to ignore the fact that she had practically been given an order.

Mercedes sank lower in her chair. She was cringing.

"Ms. Loperena, can we make t-shirts? Yes, or no?" Cosgrove insisted.

"Who is going to want to wear a t-shirt about a disease?" Valeria asked at the same time that she chided herself, knowing full well that she should have shut her mouth several minutes ago, even though it would have been going against her nature.

"That is what I contracted you for, to find a way," replied Josh with a merciless expression, and he stood up to issue his final order.

"By next week I want to see how you incorporate t-shirts into the campaign. Everything else is fine by me. You can leave it with Mercedes who will pass it on to me. I will review it on the plane on the way to London. I will see you next week."

He left the room in great strides, without looking back. He was inscrutable in his tailored iron grey suit, like a suit of armor; he was impenetrable.

This man is a warrior and he didn't contract me to make suggestions but to follow orders, concluded Valeria.

The problem was that Valeria was the one used to giving the orders... it was a clash of the titans... and this time it looked like she was going to lose... with a client like this, you could only worship them and smile. Valeria would struggle to accept this.

"If he wants a turd on a plate, that's what we'll give him. The most creative turd he has ever seen," Valeria told her team once the MagMell Laboratories staff had all left the room so that the agency people could collect their materials and presentation equipment.

"What is it with him and his t-shirts?" Valeria asked Mercedes once she was done with her staff and had gone to her friend's office.

"I have no clue. He has never been so involved with a campaign until now. It's the first time he's come to a meeting with an ad agency. That's usually up to my department. Once the campaign is fully polished and we have agreed on all the preliminary changes, that's when he usually weighs in. I don't understand why he's so insistent on t-shirts," replied a disconcerted Mercedes.

"Merci, t-shirts usually only appeal to a young market, and they are not going to put on a t-shirt advertising a vaccine... can't you find out if this idea is absolutely essential?"

"I can tell you that right now. If you don't present something with t-shirts next time around, you run the risk of losing the account."

"He's that inflexible?" Valeria asked, uncomfortable, because she had rarely found herself in a situation where the client was trying to trample all over her instead of working together.

"When he gets an idea into his head, yes. This isn't a democracy like you have in your agency where almost everyone has the right to voice an opinion. In this place there is a chain of command with Josh Cosgrove at the very top... and whoever doesn't like that..."

"Yes, I know," Valeria interrupted, disappointed with the situation.

"You know that this means starting over. Another slogan, another heading, another idea to tie the whole campaign together to make it coherent. Otherwise it'll just be a mess... a bunch of separate ideas, without a central body to govern them. If that's what he wants, he should say so right now, because then it's me who quits."

"Think it over, Vale. I know you could run an educational campaign like you want to, with a t-shirt as an added element. The ideas you presented today are very good. It's just a question of adapting them."

"Well, I guess we could make a website with a catchy phrase instead of the name of the medication, and the t-shirt could be an ad for the site address, something with an attractive design to make people go online to look for more info about the vaccine."

"See? The ideas are flowing already. I'm sure you'll have no problem."

"Let me see what I can come up with. This doesn't mean that I don't think your boss is a..."

"Don't waste your breath," Mercedes interrupted before she could finish her sentence. "Every adjective you're thinking of I have used at least a zillion times in the past six months."

They parted with a kiss on the cheek as the elevator doors opened to carry Valeria back down to her long walks along Lake Michigan to stimulate her senses, the glasses of wine in front of the fireplace with piles of papers about MRSA accompanying her every sip, and a relaxing bath in warm water where the protective walls built during the day could be dissolved by the soap. All in search of inspiration. In search of one great idea.

Once inside the elevator, a digital display in the upper corner summarized the headlines of the day, the time, the current temperature of 28 degrees Fahrenheit and that snow was expected later that afternoon. "It's very cold for walking around the city. So cold that we'll probably find at least one dog stuck to a fire hydrant with its hind leg in the air," Valeria laughed at the presenter's joke.

She called her office and asked her PA to send her briefcase and binder containing everything she had on MRSA, to her apartment. She was going to lock herself up all afternoon if necessary. Josh Cosgrove had publicly called her out. Now it was up to her to prove what she was made of.

Josh Cosgrove is seriously mistaken. He doesn't know that I know more about the pharmaceutical market than he thinks and whatever I don't know I can easily find out. I will leave no stone unturned to find my answers, Valeria told herself as she remembered the year that she spent as a journalist specializing in the pharmaceutical industry.

This had happened just after graduating from college, when she still was not sure what she wanted to do with her life. Her degree in marketing allowed her to work on several possible fronts, and her first chance came in the form of an offer from a specialized magazine where her International Marketing professor worked. But it was a short-term job because the news just did not interest her. Her boss criticized her because she placed a lot of emphasis on large pharmaceutical takeovers of small innovative industries instead of new medication product launches.

"Product launches get into the news anyway. They send out a press release to all the media outlets," she replied to her boss, who could not understand why she was so attracted to the psychology behind the purchases and large industry takeovers.

"The excitement is to make the story interesting for the readers," he kept telling her.

But this was not the kind of challenge that Valeria sought to fulfill herself. So it was that she made the wisest decision of her life: she quit the magazine.

It took her over six months to find a job in the competitive world of Chicago marketing agencies, where the psychology behind purchases was the order of the day. However, once she got it, her career skyrocketed, and it was as exciting as she had hoped it would be.

Now she was facing perhaps the biggest challenge an ad agent can face. She had to work shoulder to shoulder with a difficult and demanding client, someone used to making all the decisions with little input from employees, suppliers or agents. Even though this was her first campaign with a pharmaceutical, it was not the first time that she had to face a client with an ego the size of Tutankhamen, or rather Ramses II, the Great. In the end, Valeria used their egotistic traits against them: she would inflate their egos to stratospheric levels and then impose her opinions in the most subtle way possible. And she never once had to use her feminine charms to get it done. That would have been too low. It was more a game of chess between two professionals, both with their pieces, or egos, to protect.

What Valeria did not yet realize was that in the case of Josh Cosgrove, it was more than just ego.

Josh was listening in on the conversation that Sam was holding with an FDA employee (U.S. Food and Drug Administration) in Silver Springs, Maryland. The younger of the Cosgrove brothers first contacted him months ago, after spying on him for a few weeks in an attempt to discover the places he frequented. Their first conversation took place in a gym the man used to go to every evening, since he did not have a wife waiting for him. Today Sam was communicating directly with him via Josh's private home phone.

"You got some news for us?" Sam asked, trying without much success to seem polite.

"Yes, the vaccine is about to receive final approval. It passed the efficacy tests and the clinical study reviews. I made sure that nothing went wrong. It wasn't hard, since this product only has one indication. I mean that it only has one use. If you had requested approval for more uses, it would have been trickier."

What an idiot, thought Josh Cosgrove impatiently. Sam seemed to read his brother's mind, and said to the FDA man:

"You would be in the presence of a miracle if we had found a vaccine that could prevent more than one disease. No, this one only prevents MRSA contagion."

It was impossible to ignore the sarcasm oozing from his voice, even on the other end of the line.

"I'm sorry, Mr. Cosgrove, it's just the standard explanation for medications. I just got ahead of myself. I'm a little nervous, you see. You know, I've never done anything like this before."

Josh gestured to him to calm down, so Sam returned to the patient tone of voice that was so difficult for him to maintain.

"There's no need to be nervous. I'm not asking you to do anything illegal, nor to ignore agency protocols, nothing like that. I just need to speed up the process as much as possible, so that citizens can benefit from this."

"Yes, yes, I understand. The employees I picked are used to the FDA culture. They're fairly new employees, they joined after the last PDUFA review in 2007."

"What's that?" Sam asked Josh, covering the mouthpiece so that the man on the line would not hear him.

"The Prescription Drug User Fee Act," he replied in hushed tones. "It's an act that Congress approved so that pharmaceuticals would pay a charge in exchange for application reviews for new medications. I'll explain later."

And he signaled him to go on with the conversation.

"Let me know when you have more news," Sam concluded, trying to be affable.

"Yes, don't worry. Count on me. In terms of…" the man stopped because he could not figure out how to ask his question. In the meantime, his brow began to sweat, and his hands shook.

"You will receive your payment in person in the gym the day after tomorrow as agreed," replied Sam, returning to his more sinister forceful voice.

No more Mr. Nice Guy. He punched the receiver into the phone so as not to hear another second of the feeble voice of a man selling his integrity for cash.

"What is this goddamn PUDF, or PUTAS, or whatever the hell it was?" asked Sam as soon as he calmed down after his outburst.

"PDUFA. It's a government act that did us a huge favor, since what it basically told FDA employees was that 'we want you to review applications for new medications quicker, because if we don't, we leave the population bereft of medications that could save their lives.' Thanks to this act the performance evaluations of employees are effectively measured according to how many applications they approve in a year. They have to meet deadlines established as reasonable by the PDUFA so that the medication can receive the FDA stamp of approval. In other words, the more medications an employee approves, the better their evaluation will be. Pharmaceuticals don't have to wait so long anymore…"

"In other words, we make them spread for us, just like PUTAS," Sam interrupted, very pleased with his little joke that the PDUFA sounded a little like the Spanish word for whores. "What do you think of that as an incentive!" he said grabbing his groin.

"Why must you always be so vulgar, Sam?"

"And why must you always be so hoity-toity and polite, my lord. That's your role to play out. The lead. Leave me my supporting role, the lowlife, because I like it. I don't even need to act, because I grew up with the best of them. You should be able to play it just as well as me, you grew up on the same block. If you hadn't married that first wife of yours, the old trout that gave you all that money and power when you were nineteen... I bet you didn't think it was coarse the way I got her out of your life?"

Josh began applauding from the other side of the room.

"It's a good thing you don't want to be an actor, because after that little monologue I wouldn't be surprised if you stopped being a thug to become a thespian," Josh told his brother in the most ironic tone he could muster as he blew smoke from his cigarette.

"Don't worry. As long as you keep paying me well, you'll have me on your side. I prefer this lifestyle where I get dressed up in Armani for the cocktail parties, but I go to work in jeans, t-shirt and gloves."

He raised his glass of whiskey on the rocks in a toast to thin air, then downed it in one gulp.

Chapter 16

Valeria had been sitting on the floor in front of her sofa in her living room for five hours. She went over the papers, read news stories, searched online, scribbled in her ruled notepad and read women's fashion magazines. Inspiration sometimes came from the unlikeliest of places and the fashion magazines contained many designer t-shirts. *Perhaps I can draw some inspiration from one of these t-shirts which artists love so much for the humble sum of one-hundred and twenty-five dollars each*, she thought as she paused on a DKNY ad. Maybe this would provide the solution to the problem raised by Josh Cosgrove's blasted t-shirts.

For now, however, it had been a fruitless search. All the technical information on MRSA was killing her creativity. So she decided to focus on the educational campaign to find a hook to attract doctors and think later about creatively engaging younger people.

She stood up from the floor, her back numb from the second vertebrae to her coccyx, so she resembled the Hunchback of Chicago as she hobbled towards the kitchen in search of a bottle of wine.

Thank God James isn't here lying on the couch the way he always does on Saturdays so we can catch up on the week, Valeria said to herself to dress up her melancholic thoughts in positive terms every time James came to mind. *I'd better go to the gym tomorrow, even though it's Sunday. Otherwise, this posture will be my new sexy if I keep on using the floor as my desk.*

She uncorked a bottle of Merlot Blue Pyrenees which an Australian client had given her, and she leaned back on the work surface to read three sheets she had brought with her from the floor. They were part of a twenty-page report drafted by the MagMell marketing department. The sheets were a copy of a memo written by Mercedes in 2002 when Josh Cosgrove made it to the company presidency and was running MagMell from London. The memo was a tiny part of the report that aimed to summarize the US pharmaceutical market for the new boss, who had to quickly get up to speed on the North American market since he had mainly been in charge of managing the business in England and Europe.

The document contained detailed statistics, income reports sorted by product categories, expenses related to R+D, and marketing and ad expenses amongst other matters critical to management. Unlike all the other reports, Mercedes' memo spoke of the future rather than the past.

"Of the over five-hundred drugs currently in development in the pharmaceutical industry, only five are antibiotics. No one wants to focus on the antibiotics business because it is expensive and risky. They prefer the statins market for cholesterol reduction and hypertension inhibitors or blockers. This is currently the most profitable market in the field of pharmaceutics. But there is a niche that could represent a business opportunity for MagMell which other pharmaceuticals are moving away from: vaccines.

Last year in the United States, there were periods where stocks of eight of the eleven infant vaccines were exhausted, including influenza which is historically the most devastating infectious disease on the planet. This statistic does not include other countries around the world where medications are not accessible and where the lack of vaccines is not quantifiable, a fact that is clearly against the best interests of the population.

This is an opportunity for MagMell to acquire small medication manufacturing companies and specialize them in the task of vaccine production. In this way, we can manufacture our own vaccines, we can be sub-contracted by other pharmaceuticals and even acquire patents which other pharmaceuticals may be willing to sell."

Was her friend Mercedes responsible for the change in strategy that had taken place at MagMell? Had Josh Cosgrove taken her evaluation of the industry seriously?

"Impressive," said Valeria. "I knew Mercedes hid her claws well."

She burst into laughter thinking how her friend had survived at MagMell by acting as if butter wouldn't melt in her mouth, at least according to what she had seen in the conference room meetings. *Is Merci the brains of the outfit?* She would have to find out… and soon.

―――

That night, for a change, another nightmare interrupted Valeria's sleep and subjected her to a utopia of pure imagination. This time it was 'James of Arabia', dressed in white linen jacket and trousers, his hair dyed ash blonde and his skin burnished in the sun. He rode a two humped camel of the kind that is rarely seen in the deserts of Arabia, and was being pursued by a dozen horseback riders wearing purple turbans on their heads and wielding large scimitars. She observed all the action sitting on a sand dune, with a parasol and a glass of lemonade in hand.

"This way, James," she said as she showed him the way with a delicate flick of her hand. "Lower those swords, I can't see what's going on!" she instructed the Bedouins who were chasing James.

When she saw that the Arab men were not paying attention, and neither was James, she stood up, closed her parasol and screamed:

"Do whatever you want."

She opened her eyes and woke up. For a few seconds she thought of turning on the light, but she fell asleep again since it was four hours until dawn and it was still not time to get out of bed.

Very early on Monday, Valeria called Mercedes' PA to see if she was expected to be in the office during the morning.

"Mercedes never misses work," was the PA's reply.

Valeria knew this very well, but since she had not been able to get in touch with Merci over the entire weekend, she was beginning to wonder if she had taken a brief vacation without telling her.

After several hours in her office taking calls and issuing instructions to her team for the toothpaste campaign that had to go to production that week, she called Mercedes on her cell phone.

"I'm in the middle of a meeting, I'll call you later," she replied in an agitated voice before she could even say hello.

"Are you in the office?" Valeria managed to say before she hung up on her.

"Yes," she replied, ending the call.

Two seconds later, Valeria picked up her leather briefcase and her navy blue coat and headed towards the car park to get her car, but when she saw the jammed rainy streets, she turned on her heel and hailed a taxi. *Better to arrive safe and sound.* She hated driving in winter. When a taxi pulled up, she ran out into the cold rain, jumped in the car and slammed the passenger door as hard as she could.

"234 LaSalle," she ordered. "And fast."

The taxi driver complied, and suddenly accelerated making Valeria's head snap backwards and bump against the seat. *That's what you get for being in such a hurry*, thought the driver, smiling.

When she arrived at the Marketing Department offices at MagMell, Valeria tried to interrupt Mercedes by waving at her, but she was hunched over reading a document and her black lank hair cascaded over her shoulder and did not allow her to see to the side, so she did not notice that Valeria had been observing her for a few seconds.

"Psst!" she whistled from the door.

Mercedes jumped abruptly in her seat, making Valeria laugh out loud as she took a seat opposite her friend.

"Glad to see my whistles still startle you," she smiled at her, and Mercedes forced a smile although her body, her face, her arms and her legs were tense like the ropes for hanging out the laundry.

"I wasn't expecting you," was the only thing she managed to say.

"Well, I called you all weekend and couldn't get hold of you," Valeria returned, enjoying herself, then immediately asked: "Are you sleeping with Josh Cosgrove? Did you spend the weekend with him in London?"

"Whaaaaaat?" replied Mercedes with a squeal that bounced off the walls and the picture frames.

She was used to men making indecent proposals all the time, like flies buzzing around food, but for her friend to assume that she would accept them was beyond the pale, so she screamed at her:

"Are you crazy? How dare you ask me that?"

"Well, I found this memo which was a couple of years old in which you outlined a strategic plan for the company which, if I am not mistaken, is the current plan, so you must have some influence over Josh Cosgrove to get him to follow your lead," replied Valeria with alarming calmness.

"You are such a sadist, Valeria. I forget sometimes."

"Not a sadist, a realist…"

"But it's not reality. Show me that memo," and she tore it from her hands.

Mercedes read the document carefully. She remembered it well. It was what a young Mercedes had written, the ambassador of great opportunities and altruistic dreams, who thought that pharmaceuticals had the gift of curing the sick. The Mercedes that existed before she was forced to struggle with the incongruence that, at the end of the day, it was all just a business; that everything revolved around making money and that if she did not get on the boat, she would be out of work. Being responsible for a little girl, her dear daughter Gabriela, this was not a luxury she could allow herself at the time.

So she adapted. Even though it felt unfair. Even though she was never one hundred percent in agreement. If the government, the supposed protector, did not intervene, then why should she take the bull by the horns? So she stopped dreaming that pharmaceuticals only want what is best for patients and she got used to the idea that the more medications were sold, the better her paycheck would be. And she ignored everything else, at least apparently.

Back with Valeria, she left young Mercedes behind and explained the meaning of the memo she had written all those years ago.

"Vale, the pharmaceutical industry, just like any industry, has to constantly adapt to the requirements of the market, I don't need to explain that to you. What you should know is that, just like miniskirts and capris go in and out of fashion, the same goes for medications."

"What are you saying? That vaccines are back in fashion? I never realized they had gone out of fashion. Aren't all children supposed to be vaccinated?" Valeria asked, more intrigued than ever.

"No, they have never stopped being relevant, if that's what you mean, but they have stopped being individually lucrative. Nowadays other medications are fashionable, because they are new. When vaccines were discovered, there were millions of people to vaccinate and the market was huge. Now it's just newborns, or at least here in the States. That's why nowadays only four large pharmaceuticals make vaccines."

Valeria listened carefully to Mercedes' cold and calculating tone as she explained herself. It was the same tone she used when she tried to justify her decisions regarding Gabriela's upbringing. Everything was coldly calculated, with no room for error. As if she had a dual personality. Warm and affable over breakfast, when Valeria would share her problems and insecurities, when she encouraged her to excel in her presentations. Where was that Mercedes now? It was as if she wore armor to work and to deal with her family.

"Is this why it's more and more common for vaccines to run out?" asked Valeria, redirecting her thoughts to the matter at hand.

"Exactly. The pharmaceuticals can't fulfill the demand. Several biotech companies have appeared to cover some needs, but they aren't enough."

"This scarcity doesn't always get reported in the press, right?"

"Sometimes it does. But mostly, no."

"Is it a government and pharmaceutical company cover up?"

"I can't tell you exactly what the government's role is in all this. The thing is that there is no centralized system for doctors to express their needs, so when stocks of a particular vaccine are low, they have to call the pharmaceuticals themselves. The government gets notified indirectly, and when it confirms the reports it doesn't do much about it except to ask for pharmaceuticals to produce more," said Mercedes, to which Valeria replied:

"And doctors have no choice but to sit back and wait for the pharmaceuticals to provide them. Patients just have to wait. 'Come back next month, I may have received the polio vaccine by then'. What does all this mean, Merci?"

"That the situation could turn critical. Can you imagine an outbreak of influenza in our times due to a lack of vaccines? A lot of specialists have proposed the possibility that a large scale epidemic could occur very soon. The way I see it, they're not far off. This MRSA thing is the same deal. The government isn't addressing the issue as quickly as it needs to. The Centre for Disease Control is passing the buck to the people by talking about prevention and the importance of washing your hands, which only caused hand disinfectant sales to skyrocket, but it hasn't stopped it spreading in hospitals. The newspapers run a story one day but forget about it the next. No one is making a joint effort because private interests are in control. Hospitals hide their MRSA death statistics. In fact, they don't even have to hide them because no one requests them."

After coming down from her pulpit, so to speak, Mercedes suddenly fell silent. Valeria too. The old youthful Mercedes was back. The armor broke down, destroyed by her anger. Her ideals surged back, along with an innocent longing to be rescued, which could be glimpsed in her words, thoughts and feelings.

"This is the anger I wrote that memo with years ago, Vale. I wanted something to be done about it and this was before MRSA. But no one listened. Josh Cosgrove tossed it in the trash."

"So how do you explain the vaccine against MRSA?" asked Valeria.

"That's new, Vale. The project is not even a year old. For five years they ignored my suggestions and then all of a sudden everything changed. A one-hundred eighty degree turn. Josh bought up a medication manufacturer in Puerto Rico with three plants in different towns around the Island, and contracts to produce medications on behalf of the biggest pharmaceuticals. He managed to get authorization to produce vaccines on a worldwide scale. He never told us, not even informally, nor did he inform us about the clinical studies regarding MRSA being conducted in London until the results were complete."

"But, doesn't it always work like that?"

"No. All the vice-presidents and directors attend meetings where everything in the pipeline is discussed to draft projections, sometimes up to two years in advance. I never heard about the change in policy on vaccines until I was told to start planning their distribution. It was incredible, unheard of. Mr. Cosgrove claimed that since he was based in London and only visited our offices every so often, it was the General Manager's responsibility to inform us, and he was blamed for everything and fired. That was when Josh decided to run the office from the States. Do you remember that meeting on Gabriela's first day of school?"

"Of course I remember," replied Valeria, thinking *how could I forget. It was the day I met James.*

"During that meeting we were told about the purpose of the new plans, and that was why I could barely leave the office for four months. I started to think I would be spending Christmas day with Josh and company."

"But looking at this in a positive light, they're finally working on what you thought was best. They're making sure that vaccines are available," it was Valeria's turn to comfort her friend.

"I guess," was Mercedes' reply, as if not sure whether to be happy or not.

"And you have me by your side helping you out," Valeria went on, now in more cheerful tones, trying to lighten the mood.

"That's why I asked you to come forward for the account, because between the two of us we could give this the right spin, the importance that it needs. But I need to be honest with you, Vale. I don't know, maybe I was too hard on you because of all these blows and disappointments, but I can't shake the feeling that without this launch, the pharmaceutical is in real danger."

"Of course, Merci, don't think for a second that Josh is doing this to save the world. He is only in it for the money."

"I know that. I have no doubt about that, because it's not something that he even bothers to hide."

"What do you mean?"

"That he's making every effort to hide something, and I can't figure out what it is."

"Well use your charms, darling," said Valeria in her best sultry voice.

"Why must you always assume I'm going to use sex to get what I want? You don't. It's always been our code of conduct. Why are you trying to brand me? I don't sleep around, I only did that once. A youthful mistake, but something neither you nor my mother will ever forgive me for."

"I do forgive you. And your mother thinks it was the best thing that ever happened to you because it brought you Gabriela. You've got it the wrong way around, Merci. You're the one who can't forgive yourself. You're the one who always gets defensive. I said that thing about your charms as a joke!"

The silence that followed this attack stifled the office.

How could the conversation have taken such a dramatic turn? Unfinished business between them. The past has a habit of getting in the way of the present. Lives that have intertwined for so long were now becoming an obstacle along the new path.

"It was only a joke, Merci. Jeez! I didn't mean to say that. I didn't mean to imply that you sleep with men to gain a professional advantage. I know you don't sleep around. I was only trying to make a joke," Valeria apologized when she realized what she had done.

She got up from her chair, went around the desk and stood in front of her friend, and stroked her hair. When she perceived that Mercedes did not move a muscle of her body, she leaned over and gave her a tight hug, to melt away her defenses and reclaim their friendship.

At the same time that Valeria and Mercedes were arguing, the Cosgrove brothers were speaking in hushed tones.

"When did you stop listening in on their conversations?" asked Josh.

"Yesterday. I disconnected all the equipment."

"Why?"

"Because they are the dullest chicks I have ever seen in my life. Neither of them has a boyfriend, or a husband, or a lover, or a friend to visit them. Neither of them talks on the phone, only to their mothers every other day and, what's worse, in Spanish. They go to bed before it gets dark. What can I say? There's nothing on tape, so that's that."

"Alright, calm down. All I wanted to know was if they were sharing company secrets with their partners."

"Those two are dry wells begging for water," the younger brother mocked the women, and still sporting his cynical smile, added: "would you like me to quench their thirst?"

"Sam, for God's sake. They're my employees. I told you not to dare touch a hair on their heads."

Just then the telephone rang.

"We'll talk about this later," Sam said to his brother before placing the receiver to his ear and answering the telephone in serious tones.

"Mr. Cosgrove?" asked a timid voice on the other end of the line.

"You have news for me?" Sam went straight to the heart of the matter to avoid wasting time on pleasantries.

"Yes. Good news. The vaccine's approval is final. You will receive official confirmation this week. I thought you would want to know today."

"That's what I'm paying you for," he replied rudely, annoyed by the fastidious tone with which the man conducted his conversations.

Sam would have much preferred to say: "Isn't the substantial payout from the pharmaceutical to the FDA enough? That thing they call the PDUFA funds to make it sound official rather than looking like a bribe? The one that we pay to get our approval application for new medications reviewed? That's the fund that pays your salary, you moron! Don't you realize your job depends on the pharmaceuticals? That without them you are less than nothing? The least you can do is approve our medications." But he held his tongue remembering the warning Josh had given him. They needed the man for future projects. They had to keep him on their side.

"Anything else?" Sam said, trying to imitate the voice Josh adopted when speaking to a subordinate.

The man went on:

"Yes, a question. Are you sure that the vaccine is safe? Forgive my cautiousness."

"I don't deal with that."

It's not my kind of security, Sam thought of saying, but instead asked:

"Why?"

"No, because you know that our focus is to prove the efficacy of the medication or vaccine, that it does what you say it does, which in this case is MRSA prevention. But in terms of safety, the testing hasn't been conclusive, because we depart from the premise that it is safe because otherwise the company wouldn't have sought approval. We are assuming that the pharmaceutical is ensuring compliance with health and safety regulations which are in everyone's best interests. Otherwise, they would be liable for lawsuits and things like that."

"Yes, we know that," Sam replied cuttingly, but when he was about to hang up he heard the man go on.

"I just wanted to make sure because we didn't run many safety tests at our offices. There's no time for extensive testing of all products. So please ensure that your clinical trial demonstrates satisfactorily that it is a safe product to avoid future problems. It's my duty to tell you this."

"Too kind," replied Sam Cosgrove before hanging up and gritting his teeth. He turned to his brother and said, "I feel like sticking my arms down the telephone line and wringing this pathetic little excuse for a man's neck. He's a government stooge, a pawn in the FDA who now, after selling his soul, wants to make himself feel better by giving us moral advice."

―――

Valeria entered the MagMell Laboratories elevator, the same one she had used so often for the past weeks, but this time she was leaving in a terrible emotional state. Her conversation with Mercedes had ended on a sour note. They were not angry at each other, but it all left an uncomfortable sensation. Valeria should never have insinuated that Merci used her sexuality in her favor. However, she had been vile, and had not realized she would unintentionally hurt her friend.

When she returned to her office, she called a meeting with all her creative personnel, editors, graphic artists and writers. She was completely stuck on the t-shirts and the focus for young people.

Does this mean that I'm getting old, that I have become a relic totally out of step with the tastes and preferences of the up and coming generations? Does this mean I can no longer relate to anyone below the age of twenty-two? I refuse to think that's true, Valeria reasoned while her staff gathered.

What she really needed was more time to come up with a campaign. She had to spend less time thinking about Mercedes and Josh Cosgrove, but above all, she had to devote less time to James, even in dreams. The hours of the day were full of professional preoccupations. The nighttime was spent immersed in constant nightmares where James faced unimaginable peril. She still had no news as to his whereabouts and she was no longer worried, but desperate, anxious and furious like a wild animal. It was time to get away. To focus on herself and on the assigned task. It was time to go to San Juan, Puerto Rico.

The first thing I will do when I get to Puerto Rico will be to drink a nice cold Piña Colada under the warm sun and lie down in a hammock between two palm trees beside the beach. I'll recharge my batteries; I will be Valeria again, with renewed energies. How I miss those months that I came up with whole campaigns amongst the cobblestones and historic plazas of Old San Juan. I'll relive those times. I will let the Caribbean wind whisper new ideas in my ears, she thought as she placed all the documents she needed in her briefcase.

"I won't even take my cell phone. If they want to talk to me, they can leave a message at the office or at my apartment, like old times. I'll return calls as necessary," she announced to her PA.

As she boarded the three-hundred seat plane to San Juan, the telephone in her apartment began to ring. "Hello, you have contacted Valeria Loperena. Please leave a message."

"Valeria... Valeria... It's James."

But there was no one home to hear it.

PART 6
Relationship Between The Variables

Chapter 17

Valeria made herself comfortable in seat 18C, an aisle seat on the Boeing 737 that would arrive at her destination in five hours. She preferred aisle seats to have easy access to the restrooms, and they also made her feel freer, as if she had more room, even if she had to tuck in her feet and elbows when the refreshment carts made their way along the plane.

Just as she was fastening her seatbelt, she spotted Gabriela and Mercedes boarding the plane. They had not seen her yet, but Valeria could recognize them clearly. They were looking for their seats. Valeria removed her seatbelt, stood up and called out to them:

"Gaby, Merci!"

Two expressions of amazement looked back at her.

"What are you doing here?" Mercedes asked when she got to the aisle, dodging seats, bags and passengers.

"I'm going to San Juan to recharge my batteries. Didn't they tell you at the office? I left you a message."

"I didn't go to the office. I'll explain why in a moment," Mercedes replied, opening her eyes wide and signaling not to ask any more questions. "Let me find our seats. We'll speak after takeoff."

Half an hour later, after the fasten seatbelts sign was switched off, Mercedes stood up, signaled to Valeria, and left Gabriela listening to music on her iPod, with her eyes tightly shut, as if praying. *Maybe she is*, she thought as she left her daughter.

The two friends moved to the rear of the airplane, right in front of the flight attendant's station, but they could barely talk. Every so often they had to let people through on their way to the restrooms. One of the flight attendants, seeing their dilemma, offered them two empty seats a few rows in front.

Once they had sat down and put their seatbelts on, the conversation began properly, or rather Mercedes was finally able to reply to the questions Valeria had asked her in the aisle.

"Why are you going to Puerto Rico?", but a woman with a small child had crossed between them and she had not been able to answer. "Doesn't Gabriela have classes?" which was when the flight attendant had moved them.

Now Mercedes was able to calmly answer the first question, which in turn answered the second one.

"My Aunt Lourdes' son died. Gabriela is devastated. He was her favorite cousin, even though they didn't see each other often and they weren't the same age. Every time we visited Puerto Rico over the summer they would play together. He was always very attentive to Gaby, even though they only saw each other once a year. He wrote her e-mails and sent poems and drawings in the mail the rest of the time."

Mercedes stopped abruptly. A lump was forming in her throat.

"Just listen to me," she went on, "I'm already referring to him in the past tense when he's only been dead a couple of days. He went straight to heaven, for sure."

The tears began to roll down her cheeks. Valeria fell silent out of respect.

"That boy was an angel, Vale. You have no idea," Mercedes sobbed inconsolably.

"Who was he, Merci? You have a lot of cousins and nephews and they're all charming."

"The one who had cystic fibrosis."

"Miguel?" asked Valeria in a state of shock.

"Yes, Miguel. Do you remember him?"

"How can I forget him, he was always so affectionate. I really held on to the memory of him, particularly when you told me about his illness. I thought a lot about him even months after that great vacation in Puerto Rico. My last vacation, by the way. How long ago was this?"

"Three years ago, Vale."

"That long?! How can time fly so quickly? Are you going to the funeral?"

"Yes, they bury him tomorrow. They're bringing him back from London."

"What do you mean, from London?" asked Valeria.

"Miguel was there on a clinical study for cystic fibrosis patients," Mercedes explained, looking at the floor to hold back her tears.

"Was his mom with him?"

"No, he died all on his own. Not even his girlfriend Ana who lived in Spain found out in time to be able to be with him. That's what really hit Gabriela. She cries all the time, Vale. She had a nightmare last night about Miguel being all alone. 'Alone in that hospital. No company. No one to talk to. No one to hug him.' that's what she said when I turned on the light in her room after I heard her crying at three in the morning. I don't know how to console her."

A comforting hug between friends followed.

"It's so sad, Merci! Why did he go on his own if he knew the risks with his illness?"

Mercedes pulled away from the hug to reply.

"His mom couldn't go with him. She works night and day to pay for the medications and medical care. All that treatment is expensive. And that's even after the whole family chipped in to a monthly fund. But Aunt Lourdes never told us that Miguel was going to London. My mom told me that she didn't want to worry us because the study would only last three months. Miguel's doctor had paid all the expenses and guaranteed it was safe. He was a close friend of the family, and they tell me that he's also devastated, he feels totally responsible."

"How's your mom?"

"She's just as bad. She's already in Puerto Rico. She flew back yesterday on the first flight she could get. Do you know what's most ironic about all this?" asked Mercedes.

"What?"

"Wait for it!" Mercedes said, and she squeezed Valeria's forearm before going on, "Miguel didn't die of cystic fibrosis, but of an MRSA infection. Can you believe that?"

"What? What are the chances of us being close to selling a vaccine for MRSA, and a member of your family dying from it?"

"That's just what I was going over last night; I couldn't stop thinking about the injustice of it all. I kept rolling around in bed. I felt like calling the President of the United States, the president of the American Medical Association, the director of the CDC, Josh Cosgrove. All of them! And making them eat shit."

"Merci!"

"Yes, Vale, that's right. Me, the politest of all your friends. Well that's how out-of-control I felt last night. I wanted to curse the whole world. You would have been proud of me," uttered Mercedes defiantly.

"I would never wish something like this on you."

"I know, old friend," she said lowering her guard, "but I couldn't resist the opportunity of making you feel bad for what you said to me yesterday."

"I've felt bad ever since. Just this morning I called you to apologize again, but I couldn't get hold of you. That's why I left a message. Can you forgive me?" Valeria begged.

"I already did."

Right then they saw Gabriella standing up and coming towards them. Her eyes were red and her cheeks drenched in tears. She had been weeping the whole time. Valeria and Mercedes both made a superhuman effort to contain their own tears. Children suffering, mothers suffering, their hearts tightening because of an unfair death.

"How long until we get there?" asked Gabriela, sitting between both women.

"Not long, my dear," replied Mercedes, wiping her daughter's cheeks.

Gabriela sat on her mother's lap as if she were six years old and allowed herself to be comforted. In a couple of hours they would be on the Island of Enchantment to celebrate Miguel's life.

"It's what he would have wanted. Because if anyone loved life, it was this kid who was on the verge of losing his so often. He appreciated life much more than those of us who are healthy and think we're perfect," Mercedes whispered to Gabriela as she tried to convince herself of the same.

Valeria listened to the love between mother and daughter. It was a generous love that had just been reborn. Some die, others are born. That's life: hellos and goodbyes.

While Valeria philosophized, she realized that once she landed in Puerto Rico she would have to kiss goodbye her hours of creativity on a hammock between two palm trees. Goodbye piña colada and fried codfish on Loíza beach. There would be one more and important goodbye to say, a transcendental farewell. She would go straight to the mountains of Naranjito with her friend Mercedes to be welcomed by the cooing of the *coquí*. Once there, she would dream of hummingbirds and royal palm trees. She would see Miguel's soul carried by the wind through the banana plantations. They would say their last goodbyes. A worldly farewell. The only one us humans can give.

The ceremony in the village church was beautiful. Miguel's school friends sang several of his favorite songs and as a tribute they recited a passage from the salsa song Adán García by Rubén Blades. In essence, it summed up the ideals by which their childhood friend had lived his life.

> "If I am to live in fear,
> I would rather die smiling
> with my memories alive."

The burial was difficult for everyone, particularly Gabriela. Valeria took her aside just as the first prayer was concluded. The girl was horrified by the idea of seeing the coffin lowered into the ground, even though she kept telling her that they no longer did that in front of the family. Who could blame her for wanting to run away? Even Valeria could not handle the sadness, and she had only met Miguel once. She could not even begin to imagine the suffering Gabriela, Mercedes and his close family were going through.

They sat together in the chapel. Gabriela kneeled for what seemed to Valeria like an eternity. She was praying the rosary. He grandmother had taught her. Ten beads for each Ave María, five mysteries, each one with an Our Father. Fifty-five prayers in total. Gabriela recited them with such fervor that Valeria could not hide her emotions and she also fell to her knees and prayed in that chapel, like she had done as a child. In spite of the years that had passed since her last prayer, the phrases came to her unhesitatingly. Her memory had miraculously retained them.

Just as Gabriela finished her prayers, Mercedes came into the chapel. It was time to leave.

They arrived at the San Juan airport past one in the morning. In five hours they would be back in Chicago. Valeria thought of staying in Puerto Rico for a couple of days to spend some time creating the campaign, but her friend needed her. What could be more important? If she lost the MagMell account, Mercedes might lose her job for having recommended her, so they needed each other. For that reason, the idea did not disturb Valeria. Losing an account, or losing a job, used to feel like the end of the world. But not anymore. Seeing death up close had the effect of putting thing into perspective.

Before boarding the plane, they decided to eat something at the only cafeteria in the airport terminal that was still open at that hour. Suddenly, Valeria and Mercedes saw Josh Cosgrove walk right past them. Was he arriving, or leaving Puerto Rico? For now it would remain a mystery, because they did not call him or signal to him to find out.

Chapter 18

The temperature difference between Puerto Rico, where they enjoyed a balmy 90 degrees even in February, and the teeth chattering cold that was hitting Chicago at the same time, was a nasty shock to the system.

Why do I have to live in one of the coldest cities in the United States when I could buy myself a little country cottage in Puerto Rico or a beach front apartment and work out of the agency offices in San Juan?, Valeria wondered as she wrapped herself up in her coat and covered her ears with her hat. *Does this feeling mean I'm ready for a change?*

She brushed the thoughts aside, said goodbye to Gabriela and Mercedes and took a cab to her office. She was longing to talk to her creative team about the ideas that had occurred to her on the plane ride home from Puerto Rico while Gabriela and Mercedes were asleep. She felt Miguel's presence while imagining it. He was her driving force, and she thought of herself as his avenger. Her campaign had to alert people of the dangers of an MRSA infection. No more kids should die because of it.

She was the first to arrive at the C2 Advertising offices, since the taxi left her at the door at precisely seven in the morning. She had to wait over an hour for her staff to get there. Every time one of them arrived, she would shove them into the conference room barely giving them enough time to remove their coats or put down their bags and briefcases at their desks. She could not wait to see their reactions to the new project that was awaiting them.

First of all she outlined her ideas so that the creative department could draw up a leaflet.

"Given the cases of football players, soccer players and athletes in general who have caught CA-

MRSA, which is transmitted in the community rather than in hospitals, we need to create a leaflet with measures to be adopted to avoid MRSA in schools, universities and gyms."

She paused for them to take notes.

"We could use photographs of a football team on the cover, or other athletics teams. They are the most exposed for now because they receive injuries during the game and hygiene in the locker rooms isn't always great. Can you take lead on that?"

Valeria directed her question to Lenny, the Production Manager.

"Of course, consider it done. Do you want us to hire models or try to find a football team that has been infected but beaten MRSA?" Lenny replied.

"Oh, great idea! I hadn't thought of that. It would be perfect to have a real life case about survivors. That's what I like, everyone weighing in."

She could tell that the group was motivated because they were talking amongst themselves about the wealth of possibilities. This was what she most loved about her job. She was surrounded by competent people who loved what they did, who were as committed as she was to any idea they felt deserved development. She went on:

"Lenny, in my file you will find the names of affected schools. Get Millie to help you contact their administrations to see if they want to help."

One of the writers raised a hand.

"Yes, Margaret?" said Valeria with a smile, inviting her to speak.

"If we're going to contact the kids who have already been exposed, why don't we use them to give the advice?"

"Yes, yes… kids talking to other kids. That's excellent!" said Valeria. "In fact, when you approach them, Lenny, I want you to run the idea by them to see if they would consider appearing in a commercial. Don't make too many promises, because the TV commercials are for the third phase of the campaign and I don't have Josh Cosgrove's approval yet."

Valeria went on issuing explanations and instructions:

"In terms of the leaflet contents, we could include photos of the students at their desks in school, by their lockers and in the school washrooms. The way to prevent contagion will be clearly explained with visual aids, numbered lists and flow charts, all highlighting the phrase: Wash your hands. Keep your desks and belongings clean. Shower right after a game. Don't put on someone else's clothes. Clean your sports equipment thoroughly... you know, Paul, for kids, but not too childish so that adults can engage with it. Remember the message is also for their parents," she said addressing one of the graphic designers.

"And Margaret, in terms of the texts, try to find strong phrases, something that will stick in the kids' minds. Something that will impress them," she said to the writer, and she gave some more recommendations. "Also, you should provide at least two text boxes with phrases right from the text. I think one of them should say something along the lines of: 'The MRSA bacterium can live for up to ninety day in textiles and for ten days on surfaces.' That fact shocked me. Can you imagine, bacterium on children's desks for up to ten days! That's a long time for a bacterium to penetrate any kid's body through a bruise or open wound. If I were a mother, I would be panicking!"

Valeria paused for a few seconds to think about that alarming fact, and then asked her team:

"Can you believe that in the stuff I read it said that doctors can infect their own families with MRSA?"

Expressions of surprise and amazement appeared on her coworkers faces, so Valeria did not delay her explanation.

"Sometimes, doctors leave hospitals and clinics with their work lab coats. The bacterium can survive in fabrics for days, so when they go home and hug their children or their wives, they're putting them at risk. Some hospitals forbid doctors leaving work with their white coats on for this very reason. But some smaller clinics aren't quite so strict. In Europe, some hospitals have even implemented the use of disposable white coats and dividing curtains in rooms made with silver filaments, because apparently silver kills the bacterium. I'm not sure if this practice has been implemented in the United States. If not, I don't know what they're waiting for, they need to be more aggressive with prevention. It should be a priority, don't you think? No one should be able to leave a hospital, be it a patient or doctor, with the chance of infecting another human being."

Everyone in the room erupted into spontaneous applause, with laughter and calls of "Valeria for President…"

"Very funny!!! Back to work… go on, back to your desks. We'll talk about other ideas throughout the afternoon."

Several hours later, the same creative staff gathered again in the conference room to discuss the details of the t-shirt campaign they would prepare for adolescents and college students.

"Ok, put your thinking caps on," Valeria challenged her staff, forcing them to concentrate on what she was going to say next and to imagine the phrase and the images, to shape them and breathe life into them in their minds.

"The phrase U N E X P E C T E D   I N F E C T I O N…" she said it slowly, almost a letter at a time, and she paused for effect at the end so that the listeners could engrave the phrase into their consciousness.

"The two words should be interlaced in an abstract image of a couple…" she paused again, and waited, "bodies intertwined… visually impressive, stunning. The image printed on a modern cut t-shirt," she completed her imaginary picture in their minds.

"On first sight, young people will think it's about HIV. But smaller lettering below the illustration should say… and we don't mean AIDS," Valeria concluded, placing a strong emphasis on the final sentence.

Suddenly the tone of the meeting completely changed. Valeria began to speak hurriedly, as if it were a race against time.

"A rumor will start. Sparking curiosity, intrigue. They'll ask themselves: 'what the hell are they talking about?'" and she gave this a youngster's inflection which made her team smile.

As she spoke, her hands whirled through the air. She was unable to stand still for a single second, crisscrossing with agility amongst her audience's seats.

"We invite them to form Facebook groups. Everyone will try to guess what it's all about. Two days later, via Facebook, we will invite them to a website to take part in a competition. Whoever guesses what the drawing and phrase on the t-shirt is about, will win a prize. Nothing fancy, just an incentive to participate. Automatically, with participation, they will receive information about MRSA and the vaccine, together with the phrase Unexpected Infection."

The listeners in the conference room began to look excited, you could tell by the way their faces lit up and the positions their bodies began to adopt. Valeria continued her explanation:

"We will hold a raffle with different prizes according to the region for all participants who get the right answer. A Jet ski for Chicago and the surrounding areas, for example. And then other appropriate prizes depending on the most popular sports in each city. We could get prizes from sponsors, a kind of co-op, so that the pharmaceutical doesn't have to pay for all the prizes, and to connect the sponsors to the promotion."

"Can I take part?" asked Lenny, unable to contain himself and imitating a twenty year old, and one of the other creative answered playing along.

"You, old dude… you went over the age limit decades ago."

"No, seriously, Valeria, this is the perfect campaign. There's no doubt we're going to mobilize thousands of young people," Lenny went on, now back to his professional voice. "I can already think of a few clients we can invite to contribute towards the prizes."

"But that's not all," Valeria interrupted. "Whichever region has the highest number of subscribed young people, doesn't matter if they get it right or not, we will give them tickets to a concert by a major band which they can redeem via Ticketmaster. I already spoke to their management and they loved the idea."

"Finally," Valeria declared, "the TV campaign will show the euphoria of the young people at the concert. Photos of people modeling the t-shirt. Everyone shouting: 'Don't get infected… you're smarter than that.'"

She stopped for a moment so that everyone could assimilate the information.

"Paul and his team will design the website," she went on, "Lenny, you can go ahead and inform the programmers about the specifications, because they're going to have to program to differentiate between correct and incorrect answers, and then create a sample of signed-up kids. They should also prepare a database to publish all the photos the kids take at the concert with the t-shirts on."

Everyone was trying to absorb all the information they had received. They were used to Valeria's speed, but there was still something that was not clear and their blank faces told her so.

"Oh yeah, I was forgetting the best part..." and she paused to take a deep breath at the same time as she thought of the best way to phrase the next item of news to the team.

"We will give the t-shirts away FREE at concerts around the country. The idea is to get the kids to put the shirts on right there and then... it'll have an amazing impact. Imagine everyone getting changed. The trick is to take pictures during the event which will be published on the interactive campaign site. The ones who put the t-shirt on will also get a password to be able to participate in the competition. We should also film the concerts for the TV commercials. The more kids we can get to put on the t-shirt, the better. The logistics of all this are going to be hell, because we not only need to give out t-shirts and take pictures, but also they need to sign consent forms giving us permission to publish the photos. All of this before the band even stars playing. So ladies and gentlemen, let's get some work done."

She patted them all on the back, affectionately inviting them to head back to their work stations.

All this fun and games with the new campaign was like an injection of pure energy that allowed Valeria to be extremely productive for the rest of the day. That was why she could not find a way to leave work. She wanted to get it done. *One more task, and then I'll go*, she promised herself in vain, but the moment she finished the task at hand, she would begin another one. She left the office extremely late, and once she had done so, the anxiety returned, the urgent need to get back to the apartment to see if James had called.

Imagine her surprise when she heard James' voice amongst her messages! He said that he would arrive in London that night and call again in the morning.

"I don't believe it! Not a single explanation of where he's been this whole time!" exclaimed Valeria out loud.

That night, instead of dreaming of her lover, Valeria had a nightmare about MRSA. She now knew that James was safe and that he was an irresponsible, daring scoundrel. *For that reason I would not grant him a single second of time in my nightmares. He is not fit to appear in my mind at all.*

Perhaps because she went to bed mad at James, the subject of MRSA felt free to take over her brain and sent out hallucinatory waves which ruined her sleep for yet another night. In her nocturnal delirium, she went into the cafeteria of a school similar to the one she went to as a girl. All the children looked at her like she was weird, and called the teachers over to come and see her for themselves. They drew closer little by little, with curious expressions, looking her whole body and face up and down. The occasional child reached out a hand as if to stroke her, but before they could, the teachers would shout:

"Don't touch her!"

"Why are you rejecting me? Why are you treating me like I'm from another planet?" she asked in a begging tone and with a sweet and innocent voice.

When she did not get an answer, Valeria raised her eight-year-old girl's arm and saw that her skin color had changed. She was painted silver. She was a little silver girl. Her mom had poured a bucket of paint on her with silver filaments that morning to protect her from MRSA infection, and she was planning to do it every day from then on.

"I had the weirdest dream of my whole life," she confessed over the phone to Mercedes the next morning. "My mom turned me into a silver girl so that MRSA couldn't get into my body. Am I obsessed with this whole thing or what? This is all your fault, Mercedes. Don't you have MRSA nightmares?"

"What do you think?! The only difference is that my dreams aren't as creative as yours. Changing the subject, did you manage to speak to Josh?"

"Yes, I called him on his cell phone. I asked him where he was and if we could meet. He only replied that he wasn't available. He didn't mention anything about Puerto Rico."

"Nothing?" Mercedes insisted.

"No. He totally evaded the question. So I said to him that he would have to listen to my explanation of the t-shirt campaign over the phone because it was quite complex and we needed to start as soon as possible."

"And he told you he would rather meet face to face," Mercedes tried to guess.

"No, he said that the sooner the better. I explained that you had approved it already, but that we needed his endorsement."

"And then? Keep going, you have me hanging by a thread," she hurried her along.

"He loved it! He said it was even better than he had expected. That it was perfect. He even apologized if he had been stubborn on the subject, but that he knew I wouldn't let him down."

"Are you sure you were speaking to Josh Cosgrove?" Mercedes asked, as incredulous as a spectator fooled by a mediocre magician.

"Seriously, Merci. I could even say that he sounded excited... in the euphoric sense, if that's an adjective that could be used to characterize Mr. Cosgrove's reactions... He was definitely smiling. I could feel it over the phone."

"Congratulations, Vale," she said trying to feel happy for her friend, but an uneasy sensation overcame her. What had caused this change in her boss' attitude?

Lately Cosgrove was not behaving in his usual manner. Before Valeria had appeared on the scene and the MRSA campaign had been initiated, her boss had never shown emotion, he had always been cold and calculating. Numbers, or rather numerical figures related to dollars and cents, were the only things that made him smile, and recently there had not been many smiles because the meetings with Accounting and Finance had been pretty depressing for the last trimesters. Or at least so she had been told, because she was not invited to those meetings and Mercedes had no problem with that particular fact.

After all, if it was only to hear foul language and grown men screaming, it was better not to be invited. She still struggled to understand the fact that professionals should use swearwords to communicate with each other. Too much testosterone in too little space, as if it were break time at school and everyone was protecting their territory. Instead of basketball courts or benches under the trees, they were fighting over whose fault it was that things were going badly within the company. At least they did not resort to their fists, or had not until then.

Will it come to that at some point?, Mercedes wondered after finishing her phone conversation with Valeria.

At the same time that Mercedes was marveling at male ineptitude in MagMell's personnel meetings, Josh Cosgrove was holding a private meeting with his brother where instead of swearwords, the good news was flowing freely.

"Sam, guess who just called me?"

"Who?"

"Miss. Loperena. When I tell you her t-shirt idea, you are not going to believe it. Prepare yourself to receive the bonus of the century."

Chapter 19

That night, James' phone was still switched off, his bank account and credit cards were all untouched and his girlfriend Valeria could only wait in her apartment to hear from him. To wait and see if he would get in touch with her from London as promised in his pathetic voicemail message. Leaning back on the headboard of her bed, with sketches for the MagMell t-shirt on her lap and lying in wait, Valeria fell asleep.

Half an hour later the bedroom phone started to ring, but Valeria was in a deep sleep and thought that it was all part of the action in her nocturnal imagination. On the third ring, she realized that there was no phone in the beautiful valley she was sliding along performing a contemporary dance amongst an enormous field of sunflowers. She woke up disoriented, but alert enough to pick up the phone with her right hand.

"Sweetie?"

"James?"

"Yes my dear, it's me."

"Wait a second. Did you just call me sweetie? Don't you dare sweetie me!" she said to him in the calmest tone of voice that she could muster, although her innermost desire was to scream at the top of her lungs so that all her neighbors could hear her and come and knock on her door to see if she was ok.

"But I always call you sweetie," James replied, as patient as an oyster waiting for its precious pearl to polish itself.

"You could call me sweetie twenty days ago, but not anymore," Valeria replied, getting more worked up.

"Swee... Vale, forgive me. I couldn't call you before..." and he paused in his explanation.

What could he tell her? On the flight back home he had tried to come up with some white lie of the kind his job forced him to come up with to protect an investigation, but he knew Valeria would not fall for it. The silence on the line was becoming unbearable, so he went on.

"I was kidnapped."

Even though they were a thousand miles apart and on different ends of a telephone line, Valeria could have laughed in his face and spat at his feet.

"Oh, of course. That's a good excuse with all the terrorists there are nowadays."

"Valeria, they still kidnap tourists in some parts of the world. It was just my turn this time."

"Well, I didn't receive their ransom note," she said cruelly.

Silence.

"I was kidnapped in Cairo," James tried again after a few seconds in which he made a superhuman effort to maintain his composure because he knew his story sounded ridiculous even though it was true.

"Yes, I get it. In Cairo. The mystical city, Indiana Jones' town. James, why are you bullshitting me? Do you really think I'm going to believe this little story of yours? If you want to break up with me, then be man enough to just come out and say so. It would have been better in person, but I can take it over the phone…"

"Valeria María…" he interrupted using her full name as if he were scolding a small child.

"James Penton," Valeria replied without giving him a chance to respond, but he ignored her and ploughed on with his explanation.

"I am not lying to you. All of my cameras have been stolen, my cell phone too and I was unconscious for days. I will explain everything later. Right now, I need you to take a note of my new phone number before the connection gets cut off."

He gave her the numbers without knowing if she was even writing them down.

"From now on, I will call you every day at seven in the evening," James promised. "If I haven't called by ten past seven, you can call me..."

"No, I will not," she stopped him, indignantly.

"You won't have to," he replied sweetly, and laughed before saying, "It's only in case I get kidnapped again, so you can call the British police and let them know," and he laughed heartily unable to contain himself imagining Valeria's expression on hearing that.

"So you're just looking out for yourself, is that it?" she asked, enraged.

"I can't win with you, can I?" asked James, still giggling.

"No, because..."

Word after word and subtle reproaches mixed with frustration came spewing out of Valeria's mouth. She spoke for a minute without stopping, breathlessly, not realizing that between the lines of her complaints were small vestiges of her torment.

"Valeria María Loperena," James again spoke slowly, giving each syllable emphasis.

Firm and undaunted, he breathed his words into the receiver, as if whispering in her ear:

"I love you..."

Valeria immediately fell silent, but when she reacted at last, the words that sprang to mind and which she spat out mercilessly and drenched in disbelief were:

"What? What kind of a cheap stunt is this? If you think that I..."

"Goodness, Valeria. I love you, I am saying that I love you even today that you are making my life miserable," James interrupted jokingly this time to try to halt her pained reproaches which were breaking his heart.

He wanted to love her, not to make her suffer. His plan was to make her laugh and his purpose was to make her happy.

"Why are you telling me this now?" Valeria started, doubting his honesty since it was the first time he had declared his love.

She did not know what to think or feel.

"I would have preferred to tell you in person instead of over the phone from an airport hundreds of miles away."

"Which airport? Are you coming home?" she asked, forgetting the declaration of love.

Back to business. The iron lady.

"No, I'm in London and I still have a couple of things to do which may take me a couple of days, but I will call you every day, Vale. You won't have to worry anymore."

"I wasn't worried," she lied.

"Of course not. But I was, and I want to hear from you every day. Is that alright with you?"

Valeria hesitated for a second, but finally said.

"Yes… it's ok. But if you forget, I promise I will forget you."

"We'll speak tomorrow, Vale. Remember that I love you," he said by way of farewell.

He hoped he would be able to fulfill his promise to call her every day. It was certainly his intention.

Silence.

"James?" finally Valeria's voice was heard.

"I was beginning to think you weren't going to say goodbye to me," James replied with a child-like little giggle.

"I love you too…" Valeria finally said, and she hung up as quickly as her reflexes allowed.

She felt recharged. Like an eighteen year old girl instead of a fully grown woman. That man had her heart and soul.

I hope this isn't another mistake, she thought.

London greeted James with wet streets and an unforgiving half-light, but the vision was not depressing enough to dent his joy at being back home. For some curious reason, from the moment he set foot inside the offices where he would report to his superior, his mind journeyed back to memories of his childhood, his adolescence when he played soccer on the school team, his university education at Trinity College and his first steps as an NCIA agent, as if he felt the need to review his life until then.

Fifty minutes later, after an intense and not particularly pleasant interrogation in which his boss squashed him like a cockroach caught in a pantry, he headed to his office to draw up his reports on the Sam Cosgrove investigation, which would be his only way out of the dungeon he was cornered in. Detailing the events in writing was the most detested task any investigator had to carry out, and James was no exception, but he understood the importance. The very act of depositing findings onto something as concrete as paper forced him to organize the data, tie up loose ends and see the facts with detachment. This was handy because sometimes all the data whirled around his head like merciless tornados, obscuring sight and sanity.

Halfway through his report, which was accompanied by the enigmatic photos of Sam and Josh at the Cairo bazaar, surrounded by gourds, teapots and fabrics, James summed up the final incident in London which led him to take a plane to the Egyptian city.

He watched himself in his mind's eye during his stakeout of the North Kensington boutique that Josh and Sam had visited. As if he were a member of the criminal underclass, James remained under cover, he waited without being seen, fully alert. The Cosgrove brothers had already been inside for half an hour when he suddenly saw them leave with a woman. Stunned, he hid himself pressed up against the wall of the building, but could still hear their conversation.

"Alice, thanks for all your help," Josh Cosgrove said, and he walked away towards a black car parked in front of the store.

"Yeah, you're a real star," added Sam, sarcastically.

A second later he heard the woman howl in pain, after which she exclaimed:

"If you ever pinch me like that again…"

"You'll what? You weren't complaining last night," Sam Cosgrove roared like a lion tearing its prey apart.

James heard Sam's unmistakable voice as he demanded that the woman should stop talking. He could imagine him looking at her with an insulting stare, maybe even menacing her with an upheld arm. Alice did not speak again.

Sam followed his brother and the chauffer made a slight reverence with his head as he shut the door behind him. James waited a couple of seconds in the alleyway, and then leaped from his hiding place, walking fast on the pavement to get there quickly, calling out:

"Sam! Hey, Sam!"

He stopped a couple of paces from Alice, knowing full well that the Cosgrove brothers would not hear him because the car was already moving down the street. However, he achieved his goal, which had never been to attract Sam's attention.

"That was Sam Cosgrove, right?" he turned to ask Alice directly.

The woman did not answer.

"Such a shame I couldn't catch him! We were best friends at high school but we lost touch," James declared, although of course it was untrue.

Sam was at least three years younger than him.

"Don't you see each other anymore?" asked the woman.

Her full name was Alice Felsen. That was what her clothing store was called, James had noticed.

"Not as much as I would like. Do you know where he's going? Maybe I can go and surprise him!" James asked in jovial tones, as if he were overjoyed at the prospect of catching up with an old friend.

"Maybe, if you're willing to follow him to Cairo," the woman replied.

"Cairo? Cairo in Egypt?"

"Yes. They are on their way to the airport right now."

"Jeez, no. I was thinking more along the lines of getting a coffee round here."

In fact he was willing to follow him to Cairo, but the woman did not need to know that.

"You don't have his number by any chance, do you? I'd like to call him when he gets back from Cairo."

But Alice was no longer comfortable with the conversation. You could read it in her eyes, the way her face had fixed. The last straw was the way she folded her arms across her chest to protect the information she was carrying.

"It's alright, don't worry. I think I have it at home somewhere. Thanks," James said, and he left in great strides towards his car which was parked in the alleyway behind the building. He had to get to the airport soon.

The events of that fateful journey to Cairo were well known. He still couldn't get over the fact that he had lost three weeks of his life.

Three weeks! Do you have any idea of all the stuff I can do in three weeks? he muttered to himself as he drove back to his apartment in London. *I could have seen fifteen soccer matches, read at least three books, caught a couple of bad guys, fathered a child...*

A myriad of possibilities. But he had done none of them. He had been unconscious amongst a sea of colorful cushions with no memory of what he had done. For the time being he was already wondering if there was any chance that he had indeed fathered a child without even knowing it.

He fleetingly remembered the feminine hands that had fed him, shaved his beard and sponged him down. Had some woman taken advantage of him in his state of delirium induced by herbs and teas of wondrous powers? If so, he had no knowledge of it, so he could still say he had been faithful to Valeria.

His days of having a lover in every city were over. Not because of Valeria; he had already made up his mind before even meeting her. An abrupt rush of maturity assaulted him one day when he suddenly just did not feel like sleeping with women he had nothing in common with and with whom he could barely have a conversation, in many cases because they did not even speak English. He was curious about knowing, truly getting to know a woman. He had not been in a serious relationship since his fiancée had broken his heart ten years ago, when she told him she would not marry him. And that was that, not even an explanation.

"We're not compatible, my dear," had been her reason, but she had given no explanations or details.

The following year he heard that his ex had moved to Australia and had married a man twenty years her elder.

"She must have been looking for stability and she didn't have that with you," his fellow agents kept telling him.

But he could not forgive the fact that she had denied him an opportunity, even though he also knew it would not have been a possibility. His work demanded constant travel, the same as it did in the present, and at the time he had not wanted to trade the thrill of being an agent for settling down.

Back then he thought that his girlfriend understood perfectly. He never hid his fascination for what he did, although she, like Valeria, had also believed he was just a photographer, and throughout the six years they were together James thought that she had been fascinated by it too. Obviously, the cold hard reality of finding herself alone for weeks on end made her reconsider right before the wedding. It was an event that marked James' life for a decade.

After this unpleasant incident, his mistrust for women reached extremes. For almost eight months after being dumped, he refused to speak to any member of the opposite sex until his need for a strictly physical affection led him into a series of mostly one-night stands, in some cases lasting a few days but never more than two weeks. He would meet these women at airports, onboard planes, at bars, in hotels or in restaurants in countries that he visited. He always took them to a different hotel room to the one he had booked, or he talked them into going back to their apartments or houses if they were locals. He did not want women touching his belongings or becoming too intimate.

When he met Valeria, he had been celibate for two months in his attempt to give a serious relationship another chance. He had only been in Chicago for about a week, just killing time between assignments, waiting to be called for his next job and longing to get a crack at Sam Cosgrove. He spent his days going to pizza parlors, cafés and gyms. At last he discovered a boxing gym where he could practice his fighting skills and work off his nightly frustrations. He also took his nephew Dean to the cinema or to museums, and offered to take him to his first day of school.

The day he set eyes on Valeria for the first time, unthinkingly, he went back into the old habits he had adopted for years. He could not help it. The attraction was so strong that he ended up back at Valeria's apartment that same afternoon. But that was where the similarities to his previous behavior ended.

Ever since he perceived the intensity in her eyes; that he heard the passion in her voice when she spoke of her work, family and friends; that he observed the way her hands moved with her words as if she were an orchestral conductor, giving instructions to her phrases and ideas about how to arrange themselves in her mind; he was captivated. He wanted to see that woman again. He wanted to get to know her.

It had never been his intention to leave her unless she wanted him to, and he would fight to make sure she had no reason for this. However, the involuntary assault in Cairo had nearly changed his plans and made him lose Valeria in the process. Scared of being alone again, he decided it was time to be honest. On his second call to Chicago he explained to Valeria what had happened during his absence, he confessed he was special agent for the National Crime Investigating Agency (NCIA) and that he was after a criminal guilty of bribery and other more serious felonies. Without giving her any details about Sam Cosgrove, James told her he was a dangerous man, a liar and a cheat. He explained that some Egyptians had kidnapped him to protect him from this bad guy. He assured her that he was in no danger. He asked her to keep his confession strictly confidential. After all these explanations, everything returned to normality. Or at least normality according to James Penton, Valeria's long distance lover by night, full-time detective the rest of the time.

"Sweetie?" James called Valeria on the third day, sitting on the empty bed of his room witnessing the day give way to the night.

He was impatient to wait until seven, the agreed upon hour, so he called her an hour earlier. He wanted to hear her voice and feel that she was close.

"James, I didn't get to tell you what happened to me yesterday! I presented the t-shirt campaign I have been working on, and it was approved."

"I have no doubt that if it's your idea, then it's brilliant."

"You just have no idea how nervous I was about this client. Until yesterday he had been real tough and demanding... I wasn't sure I could keep him happy."

"My love, since when do you get nervous?"

"Apparently since Josh Cosgrove came into my life."

James could feel the blood drain from his face.

"Who did you say? Josh Cosgrove?" he asked as nonchalantly as he could.

"Yes, he's the client I told you about. The President of MagMell Laboratories. A very distinguished and highly regarded man in the pharmaceutical industry..."

"I know very well who he is, Valeria," James interrupted gravely, because the news had struck him like a bucket of cold water.

"Do you know him?"

Do I know him? He's my sister's husband. I'm investigating his brother for bribery and other felonies. This was what he wanted to say, but he preferred not to give her too many details because he knew how important the client was to her and he did not want to pressure her unduly.

"Yes, pretty much," he decided to say.

He needed a drink.

"And you're right. He is a very dry and impatient man. I'm glad to hear he is happy with your work. Do you know where I am right now?" he asked to change the subject.

He raised his phone into the air so that Valeria could hear the noises around him.

"Are you at Archie's?" she asked recognizing the host who was presenting the next karaoke singer.

"Yes, I just arrived. I'm going to see if I can find Vincent. It's his wife's birthday today. I'm absolutely certain they'll make her sing. Vincent says she sings beautifully in the shower, but she's out of tune anywhere else it seems. Today is going to be her baptism by fire. I can't stop smiling just to think of your expression when they made you sing the first time we came here. My head still hurts where you hit me with your handbag."

"It was horrible, I will never forgive you. I told you I hated karaoke. I think it's a horrible way to have fun," Valeria recalled how James had taken her on a surprise weekend trip to London so she could see his favorite spots.

Archie's was on the ground floor of his apartment block. He had rushed there as soon as he heard Josh Cosgrove's name.

"You were very good, my love. You were only a little out of tune on three out of five verses," James laughed uncontrollably.

"Very funny!" Valeria replied, ashamed but laughing.

"I can barely hear you anymore. We'll speak tomorrow, ok? Hello, Hello... Vale? If you can hear me, remember that I love you. Watch your back with the old fox Cosgrove." and he hung up the phone.

The following day, James woke up with a migraine headache. He had drunk more beers than was good for him and now he was paying for it. His whole body was in pain, and when he saw how disheveled he looked in the mirror, he realized that his look was in line with how he felt. Even his underwear was half-off, possibly due to his struggle to get out of his pants the night before. Miraculously he had managed to take them off. Suddenly he remembered the day he regained consciousness in Egypt, and he rushed to find his cell phone.

No, he had not lost any days. In fact, he could have slept for longer because it was only ten in the morning and he had nothing to report to his superiors. However, part of Valeria's conversation from the night before had left an unease in his subconscious, which he wanted to try to get rid of before it could trouble him any further.

He switched on his computer and searched for Alice Felsen's telephone number.

"Alice Felsen designs, how may I help you?"

"Yes, can you put Alice on please?" asked James as if they had been friends forever.

"Alice, it's for you," he heard the shop attendant call out.

"This is Alice," replied the woman with a melodic voice.

"Hello Alice, this is James, I'm Sam's friend. We met a few weeks ago outside your store."

"Oh, yes," but all the friendliness had drained from her voice.

"Do you design t-shirts?" James asked quickly to try to get an honest reply and take her by surprise with the question.

But the woman was silent, and James changed the subject.

"Or rather, Alice, I wanted to order some t-shirts for an activity we're doing at the company I work for. Let's say, fifteen-hundred t-shirts..."

"I don't make t-shirts or shirts or suits or any clothes in large quantities," she replied, annoyed. "My creations are unique and individual pieces. Where did you get that idea from? I can tell you know nothing about fashion or styling. Didn't you see the bohemian look of my shop?"

"Oh, excuse me, Alice. I didn't mean to offend you, it's just that since Sam bought all that Egyptian cotton in Cairo, yard after yard of the stuff, I thought it was for you."

"That has nothing to do with me. I wouldn't let Sam buy me a single yard of fabric. In fact, the next time you see him, please throw a rotten egg at him on my behalf and tell him not to dare show up around here again."

She hung up so hard that James felt the physical impact on his ear.

Questions flew through his mind: *Why does Sam want all that damn fabric? Why did he buy it abroad? Is he trying to do legit work for a while to try to clean his image? Is he in a state of hibernation, what criminals do when they have detectives hot on their trails and following their every footstep? That moment when all of a sudden they become decent human beings with noble jobs and fixed salaries, at least until the investigation file with their name on it grows cold?* Unfortunately his questions would not be answered by magic and Bakran had given him no fresh news for now, so James decided to kill some time and take care of his headache by calling Valeria.

"Sweetie?"

"Hello! Did you have fun last night?"

"I had two beers too many."

"Ha, and your head hurts, right?"

Valeria knew that her man could not hold his drink. She had often seen him dragging his feet, body and head towards the bathroom after a night out drinking.

"It's not an easy age, my love. I used to be able to drink like it was water, but now it has all these disagreeable side effects. It's not like I'm not in shape, right?"

"Oh no, you're in better shape than most kids of twenty," Valeria said to make him feel better, at the same time that she remembered the first time she had seen James undress in front of her, without him knowing she was watching.

That day, four days after they met each other, Valeria was lying on the bed, naked under the sheets. James had gone out properly dressed for the first time since they decided to lock themselves in the apartment with the excuse that it was too hot outside to go to work.

He returned a little while later while she was dozing amongst the sheets. He snuck into the room to not wake her up and loosened his tie before untying the knot. Then he removed his shirt and let it slide silently from his arms. Just as it was about to hit the floor, he caught it in midair and then walked on tiptoe to place it on the chair in the corner.

Valeria watched all this with one eye open, the rest of her head half-buried in the pillow she had her arms wrapped around. Her only visible cheek was blushing. She had seen many men undress before, but none as attractive as James. He carefully unbuckled his belt, used his own feet to quietly remove his shoes and then dropped his socks on the carpet. Only the pants were left. He removed his cell phone from his pocket and laid it on the bedside table. Valeria could see the curve of his broad shoulders, the toned chest muscles, his hardened stomach and the silhouette, that drives women crazy, of the pelvic bone jutting out and forming a triangle pointing the way to…

Once he was naked, James slid under the sheets and that was when he realized that she had been watching the whole time. His muscular arms took her by the waist and pulled her towards him. He rested his face on the pillow, close to hers. They both remained still for a time, looking into each other's eyes and observing every line and every pore of the skin. Until the man's knee slowly nudged between her thighs. He kissed her on the forehead and smiled with his eyes closed. "Let's take it slow this time" he whispered in her ear, and he pressed her against his chest. Valeria's memories were abruptly interrupted by James' voice on the other end of the line.

"Thank God you're my age, but with the beautiful body of a goddess," James told her laughing, although he hesitated before adding, "that's why you get me."

"Very funny, James! Very funny! A real comedian!"

This seemed to have become Valeria's favorite phrase lately. Everything said to her in an ironic tone of voice was responded to with the same phrase stretched out for dramatic purpose: very funny! or rather: veeerrry fuunnyyy! She had copied it from a joke Miguel had told her three years ago in Puerto Rico, and which she remembered when she went to his funeral.

"Hey, I forgot to tell you that the day you left me a message on my machine, remember? When you couldn't get hold of me?" Valeria asked.

"Yes," he replied impetuously, dying to know.

"I didn't reply because I was in Puerto Rico."

"And there I was suffering because I thought you were never going to speak to me again," he said jokingly, although he turned serious when he noticed he needed more information. "Did they offer you the Management post in Puerto Rico again?"

"No, I just went back to work on the MagMell campaign, but I ended up going to the funeral of a cousin of Mercedes…"

"How awful," said James.

But Valeria was at full throttle, telling her story, and did not even realize he had spoken.

"…who died in London because of an MRSA infection. Do you remember I told you that I was working on the MRSA campaign for the pharmaceutical company?"

"No. You told me you were working on a t-shirt campaign," James objected.

"It's the same thing. We're working on a t-shirt campaign to educate young people about MRSA. But that's not what I wanted to tell you about.."

"And what did you want to tell me about, my love?" he asked, laughing to himself and fascinated by the way his girlfriend expressed herself, one issue after another, all organized in her mind, a symphony orchestra playing an endless sonata.

"About the way things go. Miguel, Mercedes' cousin, died because of an MRSA infection, which is the subject of the campaign she and I are working on. Not only that, but he died in London which is where you are, when he used to live in Puerto Rico which is where my family is from."

"You lost me," said James.

"What I mean is that life is full of coincidences. I think that Mercedes and I were destined to experience Miguel's death. It was our destiny to both go to Puerto Rico that weekend, perhaps to inspire us or to put a human face on the consequences of MRSA. Perhaps to pay homage to him in our educational campaign and try to prevent other people dying the way he did. Don't you think it's amazing how everything is connected, in some way? We live in a closed circle and I don't mean the earth."

"No. I'm guessing you mean Mars," he mused.

"James, stop fooling around. This is serious. I am just amazed by the way that everything is interconnected, everything happens for a reason."

"That is a theory we are going to have to go on exploring, Vale. For now, I'm just glad you decided to interconnect yourself with me on that fabulous day, at the same time and in the same place even though it was a place neither of us had been to. In fact, a place neither of us have been back to."

"Are you still making fun of me?"

"No. I'm telling you it's a beautiful way of thinking of things," James replied.

"You can't escape your own destiny."

"Ummmm?" asked James, lost again.

"Nothing, nothing. It's just an old saying my mother used to repeat. It means that what's going to happen to you is going to happen, and there is no getting away from it. But let's talk about that another day. I need to get going."

"Remember that I love you."

"Me too, but today you were so silly that I'm going to have to reconsider," she said laughing, and she suddenly sent him a kiss down the telephone line.

"I'll talk to you tomorrow, Vale."

"Talk to you tomorrow, James."

―――

The following day, James chased down an inconclusive lead that associated Sam Cosgrove with the attempted bribery of a professor at Imperial College to obtain documents related to a clinical study being carried out on the premises of the important London University. However, said professor claimed never to have spoken to the man, only over the phone and that the list of required documents arrived anonymously in the office. A student identified Sam as the man who left the envelope on the professors' desk, but the security cameras did not pick up a single man similar in build, height or weight to Sam. The investigation of this event was a dead end.

The two agents who were on the suspect's trail in Chicago let him know that Sam was currently in the MagMell Laboratories offices and that he turned up for work daily at eight in the morning and clocked off at seven in the evening, always in the company of his brother. He was even sleeping in the guest house of Josh's mansion, or rather he was staying there because judging by the female companions that joined him almost every night, sometimes even in groups of two or three, he was not doing much sleeping. *These are all unequivocal signs that he's in hibernation*, James thought. For the time being he would only be able to arrest him for prostitution if he was selling his body, or for solicitation if the agents could confirm that the girls were pros. But it appeared that they were not.

On the other hand, James had to wait for Sam to return to British soil to make any kind of arrest for the bribery charges because he did not want to have to deal with arguments over jurisdiction. So since he had run out of leads in terms of the attempted bribery, and he was not exactly brimming with ideas, he entertained himself with Valeria's interrelations theory.

Mercedes is marketing a vaccine to fight off the same bacteria that killed her cousin Miguel. Her cousin lived in London, where I'm from, but he's originally from Puerto Rico, where Valeria comes from. He lived in London, where Josh and Sam are from. He lived in London... why was Miguel living in London?

Ideas and questions rushed through his brain.

It was too early in the morning to satiate his curiosity and call Valeria, so he decided to find the paper where the news had first appeared.

"Yes, yes, yes..." he said in excitement when he found the old issue of the paper with the front page headline announcing Miguel's death.

The building doorman had kept all his papers and three weeks of correspondence while he had been in Cairo. James had left the pile on a chair beside the front door, and there it had remained since he had returned home until today. Now it was all spread out over the floor, because he vaguely remembered seeing something in the papers. The fact that Valeria had mentioned it yesterday in her theory of interrelations had made him think of the relation between her working for Josh Cosgrove and him trying to arrest his brother Sam.

What other kind of interrelation can there be to help me with this damn investigation? James thought, as he read the story headline.

DEADLY MRSA INFECTION
A clandestine laboratory could be behind it

A photo of Miguel in his hospital bed accompanied the article.

Sunken eyes, short cropped black hair, greyish skin, prominent cheekbones, weak arms stretched over the white sheet which covered his body up to his chest. He was sitting up on several pillows, looking straight at the camera, with a weak smile on his face but scarce signs of life.

James described Miguel to himself as if he were a corpse in a homicide, the sort of case he occasionally had to fill in for when there were not enough detectives to deal with the crimes on the streets, houses and apartments of the city. Those crimes that agents had become immune to, observing the bodies without emotion, without qualms, without a nagging conscience, describing the victims as if they were mannequins, not thinking that a human being had inhabited that body until a few hours previously.

Suddenly he saw something else in the photo.

"This is a young man on a mission."

He could see it clearly in Miguel's eyes. Even though his body was almost a corpse, there was tenacity in his face, something he needed to communicate before he died, even if it meant spending his last drops of energy. When the photo had been taken he was still Mercedes' cousin, Ana's boyfriend, Paco's friend. Now, by means of the article, he was James' informant.

"What do you want to tell me, Miguel? Why have you crossed my path? Why have our lives interlaced and intertwined?"

James went on reading the news, but there was not much in the way of detail. It said that Miguel had written a letter and sent in his photograph and given notice of the infection of employees at a laboratory where the so called "superbug" was being studied.

> "A total of five employees died of their MRSA infections. The police are investigating who was behind the laboratory, and who financed it."

Another story announced the death of Dr. Francis Fowler in a traffic accident while in an ambulance.

> "It is suspected that Dr. Fowler, expert biologist and specialist on MRSA, was also on his way to the hospital having been infected. It has not been possible to corroborate that Dr. Fowler was the person running the laboratory."

The story was signed by Paul Claron, reporter for the London Daily.

Half an hour later, James was at the legendary newspaper's office. He was waiting to see the editor in charge of the publication, who had agreed to meet with him. They had a truly polite meeting, where the editor allowed him to interview the reporter and to see Miguel's archived letter and photo. They allowed him to listen to recordings of the interviews held with doctors and nurses at the hospital. He explained to James that by the time they had gone to interview the boy and the other employees of the lab the very day they read the letter, they were all already dead. They interviewed close family, but none of them knew any details of the project they had been working on. Miguel's letter was the only reference to a pharmaceutical involvement, but they could not corroborate this information even though the reporter had visited several pharmaceuticals with offices in London. None of them admitted to running a laboratory in Paddington.

"Did you go to MagMell?" James asked instinctively.

"Of course," was the editor's reply. "They were very friendly, but tight-lipped, just like the other pharmaceuticals. They gave us a list of all their laboratories around the world, in case we wanted to continue to investigate."

Amongst the reporter's notes and papers, James found the names of the ambulance drivers who took the victims to St. Mary's. The editor explained that both drivers indicated that a third ambulance had arrived at the scene, and provided the reporter with the address of the laboratory where the employees had been picked up. The London Daily had shared this information with the police.

"True. I got the report this morning," James pointed out. "Did you visit the facilities before informing the police?"

It was the first time that the editor did not reply immediately, but this was an answer in itself.

"Did you find anything worthwhile? Anything we could follow up on?" James asked, practically begging.

"No. After a quick look around, we didn't find anyone or anything to give us any leads, so we reported it to the police. Obviously, the police weren't going to call us to keep us updated, so our reporter is still looking under rocks, although I have to admit it's not his only story. If something turns up, great. If not, then we have other news to report on."

The editor's expression registered a wordless agreement that he wanted to establish between them: scratch my back, and I'll scratch yours.

Once back at the NCIA headquarters, James found out, thanks to his police contacts, that the laboratory had been quarantined to avoid further infections, and was being inspected with help from the NHS. The findings report would take several days to be drawn up. Frustrated, he slammed shut the file on Sam and looked at the clock on the wall. It was time to call Valeria.

"Sweetie?"

James always called her by her pet name when they spoke on the phone.

"Who else, James?" Valeria poked fun at him, laughing happily. "Why do you always say sweetie like it's a question?"

"I'm not asking to find out if it's you. I'm asking to find out if you're sweetie because otherwise you're sour-ie and in that case I'd rather wait for you to be sweetie again."

He laughed at this, almost unable to finish his sentence.

"Veeerry fuuunny!"

"How's your client?" James changed the subject quickly.

"Alright, I think. Sometimes I have nightmares about him or his brother. I dream they're chasing me. Like the time we ran into him in the airport at Puerto Rico. I swear it felt like he was chasing me around."

"What was that?" he asked, taken aback.

"James, Merci and I saw Josh Cosgrove at the Puerto Rico airport," Valeria replied incensed, as if giving a statement at a trial.

She went on:

"He didn't give us any explanation. We just assumed he was visiting the factories the pharmaceutical company owns there, but Merci says she asked his secretary and that he didn't have a trip scheduled in his agenda," she paused.

James asked nothing, he was processing the information.

Valeria gave him more details, James did not even have to ask.

"And Sam, his brother, we see him all the time at the places where we go to have lunch. I'm just being paranoid, right?"

"Definitely. This client of yours is affecting your sanity," James tried to hide the panic he was beginning to feel.

His next destination would be Chicago, Illinois. Back home. Back to Valeria's arms. This time not only to pursue a criminal, but to protect his interests.

The following morning, when the sun was trying in vain to peep through the morning mist, James called Bakran on his cell phone.

"Is there some way of tracking the fabric? Find out where it ended up? Please tell me there is."

This was the last conversation he had with Bakran when they said goodbye at Cairo airport. Now he was speaking to his informant and friend once again, the man who had saved his life and who he trusted more than any of his detective colleagues.

"James. I got hold of the information you asked for," he heard the voice on the other end of the line.

"Bakran, how are you, mate? Did your wife break your balls?"

"Not yet, but she has a good firm grip on them!"

They both laughed.

"What have you got for me?" James asked.

"The fabric's trail leads to Puerto Rico."

"Puerto Rico? Are you sure?"

He could not understand why all of a sudden Puerto Rico kept cropping up all over the place. The interrelations and coincidences, everything happens for a reason.

"Yes, Colossal Mills, a clothing manufacturer. I called and said I was Cosgrove, they confirmed that the fabric had arrived safely, but they would not give me any further details. The person who answered the phone gave me that information, but apparently a supervisor turned up and I hung up before he could realize from my thick Arab accent that I'm not even remotely close to being a Cosgrove."

At least James now had the answer to what Josh Cosgrove had possibly been doing in Puerto Rico, and at least he had not been there to chase his girlfriend Valeria.

Am I being as paranoid as she is? Am I obsessed because I'm getting old, or because I'm in love? he mused, chuckling to himself as he showered.

He only had an hour to hail a cab to take him to the airport. He would not be flying straight to Chicago, as he had originally intended. He would first make a quick stop at San Juan, Puerto Rico. A clothes factory was waiting for him.

PART 7
Null Hypothesis

Chapter 20

San Juan, Puerto Rico. James had always wanted to visit the Caribbean Island, but his wish had never come true. For years Puerto Rico had been a tourist destination favored by Europeans thanks to its beaches and palm trees, the friendliness of its inhabitants and balmy temperatures which averaged 85 degrees year round. Up in the clouds, James was pulled in by curiosity and he leaned towards the window to bear witness to its beauty; the blue seas, the green hills, the old walled town, the new part of town with its modern buildings and its dwellings all piled one on top of the other. A metropolis full of life and framed by natural beauty.

Although he was about to arrive in this paradise, he had no hope whatsoever of enjoying its landscapes. That was what usually happened to him when he visited somewhere with a packed agenda. In addition, he needed his senses to be on full alert so he could pursue his investigation without distractions. *At least I can look out of the window of the taxi when I go from one place to another*, James sighed as he thought about the destination that awaited him.

A few minutes later a beautiful flight attendant asked him if he wanted anything else before landing. She was one of those flight-attendant-stunners that you did not often see any more on planes but were all the rage back in the sixties, with her perfectly arranged hair and make-up applied to every feature to highlight her attributes all at once. So much make-up made it impossible for the passenger to know what to concentrate on; her eyes enlarged with eye shadow, mascara firmly applied, or her lips outlined in crimson red.

"No, thanks," James replied to all her questions.

He made sure that all the questions which had to do with services offered on the flight, and those which never left her mouth but which she expressed with a coquettish smile and batting eyelids, with her hand resting on James' shoulder, all received the same reply.

"No thanks, no thanks, no thanks," he answered over and over.

After the exchange with the flight attendant, James redirected his attention to the notes he had set to one side as he watched Puerto Rico sail by. His notes reminded him of his mission, the reason he was there. He was still chasing the trail of the mysterious fabric the Cosgrove brothers had inexplicably bought; it was an inconclusive puzzle. He had no way of tying together this purchase to the Cosgrove's usual daily business. The case was becoming more and more convoluted. Why had they personally gone to buy fabric when Josh Cosgrove had thousands of employees working for him, not just in the same country but all over the world?

"It makes no sense. None. I hope I find the answer soon, because this is driving me nuts," he reflected, hoping to find a clue on the Island of Enchantment, as Puerto Rico is commonly known.

The taxi driver's first question came hot on the heels of James' destination request.

"Have you been to Puerto Rico before?" said the man in perfect English as he drove his car along the Teodoro Moscoso bridge, crossing the San José lagoon that separates the airport from the capital city. Hundreds of Puerto Rican and United States flags lined the bridge, as if announcing that the Island had two owners: its inhabitants and its financial partners since 1898.

Just as the taxi driver was beginning to embark on an explanation of the political history of the Island, James' phone began to vibrate, so he made a friendly gesture towards the man asking him to pause his monologue for a moment.

"Nancy boy, did you get there?" James heard the coarse voice of his friend.

"Yes, Bakran, you're right on time! I'm on my way to the factory right now. I'm sorry about asking for that last favor... are you sure you got me that appointment? Are they expecting me?"

"Yes, James. Our boss' new PA got you the appointment. She's very pretty, by the way."

"How do you know? Are you in London, you bastard?"

"I got here an hour ago. It was our dear boss' idea. He pulled me out of voluntary retirement. He said he's got something for me here in London. I'll find out soon."

"What retirement is this? Ever since I left Cairo you haven't stopped calling me to see what you can stick your nose in! So now, officially, you can't help me anymore."

"How's that? What if he says you need my help? That you can't live without me!" Bakran said to mortify him, which was one of his specialties.

But he left the joke at that, and in the more serious tones of someone completing a work assignment, he explained:

"I understand that the idea is for me to help you. A clue turned up in Paddington yesterday. Apparently the owners of a small local restaurant saw Sam and several men dressed in lab coats have dinner one night at their place. They say that the diners were working in the building where the clandestine laboratory was based."

"Why wasn't I told? I was still in London yesterday. I could have gone to take a look with you," he demanded, outraged.

"The Puerto Rico thing had already been arranged, James. It was a miracle they agreed to see you. A clothes manufacturer involved in an NCIA investigation in London. How would it have looked if we cancelled? If we give them a chance to think about it, they'll never see us. Besides, be careful, because if you make them too uncomfortable they will call in the local police, maybe even the FBI."

"Don't be so dramatic, they're never going to call the FBI! And why would they call the police? It's not as if I'm going to go in there guns blazing. What are they going to arrest me for, asking questions?" he said as if he were immersed in a conversation with his friend over a coffee table.

"What I mean is that you have absolutely no jurisdiction. To them you're just meddling."

"They're not wrong about that, after all Bakran, what are we doing? We're being opportunistic, we're meddling…"

James stopped mid-sentence because he noticed that the taxi driver was clearly eavesdropping on his conversation.

"Sniffing around and asking questions for the good of all humanity," Bakran finished, not noticing why his friend had not finished his sentence: not because he did not know how, but because he was being careful.

"Veeerry fuuunny!" said James, copying the phrase Valeria used and which he liked so much. "I'll call you later."

The taxi driver gave him an unpleasant look in the rearview mirror. James detected suspicion in his eyes, and little desire to pursue their conversation on the charms of the Island. They drove the rest of the way in complete silence, the kind of silence that makes even the mute uncomfortable. He would have to learn of Puerto Rican history another day.

―――

It took him just under forty-five minutes to get to the t-shirt factory and just as Bakran had told him, they were indeed expecting him. Two men of average height, dark hair and brown eyes, almost identical in weight, posture and expression, met him at the reception area. These were undoubtedly the Canabal brothers: Rodrigo and Manuel. They owned a fourteen thousand square foot warehouse in the town of Manatí. Their warm ear to ear smiles welcomed James, who offered his hand as effusively as they offered theirs.

Unfortunately, this friendly show of courtesy was killed when James showed them his NCIA agent identification. He could immediately tell that the posture and expression of both men became rigid and an unmanageable tension was building in their bodies and trying to escape.

"You do realize that we are under no obligation to do this?" asked Rodrigo, fixing his eyes on the agent with a penetrating stare seeking only one answer: he wanted to know if he could trust him.

"Oh, of course. We are extremely grateful and I want to assure you once again that no one in your company is under investigation. Probably our conversation today will lead to nothing conclusive regarding our suspect, but we want to run down all leads," James assured them in calming tones, in line with the look he gave both men, unblinking and not looking at anything else.

"We are very anxious about letting Mr. Josh Cosgrove down. He is an important client and it is the first time he has placed an order with us. It means a lot to us."

"You don't need to worry at all. Mr. Josh Cosgrove is not under investigation either. It's his brother, Sam Cosgrove. Besides, no one will know that I was here. As you can see, I came alone to try to avoid making too much noise and alarming anyone."

Needing no further explanations, the men gestured down a corridor where the tour of the facilities would begin. The Canabal brothers returned little by little to their roles as welcoming hosts as they narrated to James the history of the factory in the 1950s, when their grandfather built it into the most important clothing manufacturer in the country, boasting million-dollar contracts thanks to the tax exemptions implemented to support manufacturing in

Puerto Rico. They explained that even the US Army uniforms were made on the Island back then.

"But all that is in the past now. Nowadays we just about make ends meet," Rodrigo, the elder of the brothers, concluded.

"What exactly is the nature of Mr. Cosgrove's order? Is it some kind of uniform?" James began his interrogation.

"No, no, no. Nothing like that. He needs t-shirts for a pharmaceutical marketing campaign across several states."

"Why were you chosen for this job by Mr. Cosgrove? Wouldn't it be easier for him to manufacture the t-shirts in the States, closer to where they are going to be used?"

"Labor costs are much more expensive in the States. It's expensive here in Puerto Rico too…" Manuel Canabal began his explanation.

"Same as England and almost everywhere else," his brother Rodrigo interjected.

"Yes, it's happening all over the world, except in places where they have been cleverer than us and they have cornered all the mass employment jobs. Even though we consider them developing nations! I'd like to see how the President and our Governor are going to create jobs to stimulate the economy. That's what I'd like to see. They're going to have to lower the minimum wage or reinstate an industrial incentives program, something like that, or otherwise we're all going to go under," Manuel Canabal fired off as if he were on a stand delivering a speech at a political rally where only his brother and the English agent were the spectators.

"Forgive us, agent Penton," Rodrigo interrupted, smiling, "It's just that talking politics is the national pastime here in Puerto Rico. Didn't you know that?"

"No, but I realized pretty quickly. On the way over, the taxi driver tried to teach me a lesson on the meaning of Commonwealth. Half Puerto Rican, half American…"

"Not exactly, but something like that," said Manuel, managing to contain himself from giving the long version of the explanation, and proceeding instead with the tour of the facilities.

They arrived at the production room. They ran into dozens of operators there, each one sitting before a sewing machine, all in rows arranged like a marching band at an honor parade. Yellow lines painted on the floor marked the routes between rows and cordoned off the work stations. Each operator had a bobbin with different colored string and piles of cut shirts, pants or skirts waiting to go through the machine. On the other end of their work space, a wheeled basket received each finished piece. At the end of the production area, another giant room housed all materials. Enormous rolls of fabric of all possible colors decorated row after row of white scaffolding.

The Canabal brothers headed towards one of the scaffolds and once there, with no distinguishing marks to differentiate the rolls, they located the fabric purchased by Josh and Sam Cosgrove in Cairo. Or rather one of the rolls, as all the rest had already been turned into short-sleeve t-shirts and sent to Chicago to begin the campaign.

"Why did they bring their own fabric? Why not pick one of the ones you already had here?" James asked, caressing the other cotton fabrics with his right hand.

"Mr. Cosgrove said that he had been poorly advised. He didn't want standard cotton used for t-shirts," one of the brothers explained, to which the other one added:

"He didn't know we had good quality fabric here. He had already purchased the fabric when he came to us."

"Did Mr. Cosgrove come alone, or with someone?"

"He came alone."

"Did he mention his brother, Sam Cosgrove, at any point while he was here?"

"No, but at the end of his visit he called him on his cell phone to tell him that he had chosen us for the job and he gave him our address to send on the fabric. We guessed it was his brother because when he hung up he said to us, 'I also work with my brother.'"

"Did Mr. Cosgrove mention how he found out about your factory at any point?"

"He said he had come on a routine visit to the pharmaceutical facilities here in Puerto Rico and that his marketing manager in Chicago, who is also Puerto Rican, had told him about us."

"Why didn't she come?" James asked, knowing they were speaking of Mercedes.

"I didn't ask, but I guess he was just killing two birds with one stone," explained the younger Canabal brother.

"Didn't you think it was unusual for the President of a pharmaceutical to come in person to place an order instead of sending an employee from the marketing department for instance, or even from the ad agency who are more experienced with this type of transaction?"

"No, no we didn't find it unusual. All sorts of people come here. From Presidents of companies to sixteen year old kids who want to try their luck with a run of t-shirts using a logo they designed on their home PCs," said Manuel.

Rodrigo also voiced his opinion:

"Some bosses are more relaxed. Others are impetuous and micro-managers. I think this is the case with Mr. Cosgrove, and let me tell you he came fully prepared. He knew exactly what t-shirt design he wanted, the amount, the sizes, and the type of printing. He had also already acquired the colored inks and his brother Sam sent us those too."

"Why? Is that standard procedure?"

"He said that he had sent them for processing according to the specifications given by the graphic artist, because they have a touch of glitter in the mix. It isn't your standard ink for everyday printing. It's the first time a client brings their own ink. But we were happy to accommodate him."

Something changed in James' expression. His brows furrowed, his eyes narrowed, but he did not allow his hypotheses to run wild in his brain. Not yet. This was not the time if he wanted to go on gathering information. So to avoid alarming the Canabal brothers, who were already looking at him with worried expressions, he said cheerfully:

"Well I never! A t-shirt that glitters. I want one of those…"

Chapter 21

Several hours later, in his hotel room, James was working up his investigation report of the t-shirt factory. Aside from learning a great deal about t-shirt making and printing and the differences between silk screening and digital imprint, he had more questions than answers. He still did not know why Josh and Sam were supervising this marketing project. After giving it much thought, he was also unable to figure out why they bought the fabric in Cairo, except that they did indeed receive bad advice. He also could not figure out why on earth they had not ordered the t-shirts to be made directly in Egypt where labor costs were far cheaper. And on top of it all was the issue of bringing their own ink too.

"I didn't discover anything new, except that apart from the fabric they also bought ink for the t-shirt printing process. Isn't it ridiculous that these guys are buying fabrics and colors?" James vented to Bakran when he called him that evening.

"Yes, but what can I say. It must be the eccentricities of millionaires. This is their pet project and they want it to be perfect. I guess since they don't have any new formulae for medicines, they're considering acquiring a t-shirt business. Or maybe they're going to declare themselves fashion designers at their next press conference."

"I think all of your theories are right on the money," James replied in annoyance, and he followed this up shouting down the line, "And on which of these charges shall we arrest Sam Cosgrove?"

He was not sure at what point the fun turned into anxiety, but it was obvious his mood was going from bad to worse.

"You're obviously in no mood for jokes, Nancy boy, and neither am I really," he conceded, understanding James' frustration.

It was the same disappointment that agents suffer more often than they should, particularly when the cases turned into indecipherable enigmas.

"I also had a terrible day," admitted Bakran. "I had to interrogate a couple of old people and it broke my heart."

"The owners of the restaurant?"

"The very same. I bet you'll never guess why they remembered Sam?"

"Because he was the only one not wearing a lab coat?"

"How did you know?" asked Bakran, astounded.

"Because you told me so, asshole... 'Sam and some men dressed in lab coats', remember?"

"Oh, yes, now I remember. I don't even know what I'm doing or saying anymore. But that wasn't what I meant. The reason was that the waitress who served them, who was also the owner's daughter, died a week later of a MRSA infection."

Silence was inevitable after a statement like that. Another victim. Another reason for the unfortunate detectives to feel guilty. Another reason and source of inspiration to step up the investigation. Bakran went on:

"I guess because of the pain of their daughter's death and the fact they couldn't understand how she caught it, the old couple figured that the people from the lab were carrying the bacteria in their work clothes, or something like that."

"And since that sounds insane, no one paid any attention through official channels until our boss got wind of this, am I right?" James questioned as he thought of the damned bureaucracy and human complexity at work.

"More or less," Bakran went on. "Except he didn't hear about it through police channels, he read it in the papers."

"What?" James replied, unable to contain his disbelief.

"Yes, the same reporter who wrote the story on Miguel on the front page, included Sam's name in the article as one of the members of the party from the lab. Sam made a huge mistake, don't you see?"

"Don't tell me he paid for the restaurant bill on his credit card?"

"No, you and I both know Sam is too clever for that."

"So?"

"Apparently he met the girl later and his number was recorded in her cell phone. The reporter is clearly very resourceful, or he's trying to win an award. In any case, when he heard there had been another death by MRSA he looked into it and has uncovered the story of a lifetime. The men from the lab who went to the restaurant are the same ones who died in the hospital with the boy from the front page. The restaurant owners identified them from the hospital autopsy photos."

"But I didn't see any of this in the papers…" James began to reply, but he realized at once why he knew nothing of the story.

He had asked the doorman to hold his papers while he caught up with the ones he had at home. He also had not looked at the headlines on the internet. A very, very serious mistake. However, he could still make up for the blunder, he comforted himself. A new avenue of investigation had opened up.

During the night, he began to feel betrayed by his instincts. He began to doubt all of his actions from the start of the investigation. Some of his decisions did not seem consistent with the expert detective standards that he held himself to. It seemed that his reflexes had forsaken him, but no one had bothered to tell him. This anxiety wracked his nerves. He turned over and over in bed, drenched in a cold sweat. He could not contain himself. His doubts floated around his brain. He questioned his ability to attain his goals. He distrusted the path he had to follow. Worries, concerns, detailed analyses tried to redirect him away from questioning his skills and towards a closer look at the case. How many people would die of the MRSA outbreak at the clandestine laboratory? Could it be true that it had been no accident, or were these the speculations of someone on death's door who, with nothing to lose, tried to place the blame for his condition before passing away? And was Sam Cosgrove to blame merely because he was their employer, or was he involved in something far worse?

―――

On the next day, James was in such a state of alarm that he got up at five am with the intention of tying up loose ends. Time was not on his side, since everyone was still asleep on the Island of Enchantment. The sun had not yet shown its face and the cockerels had not yet sung in the countryside.

His plan was to get in touch with Miguel's mother and the doctor who had looked after him in Puerto Rico. Perhaps they would have answers if the boy had a chance to speak to them from London and give them any details of the work he was doing at the laboratory. As he killed time with his appetite ruined by the worries of the night, James wandered the streets of San Juan which were gradually waking up with every passing minute. Finally a shop window full of pastries, doughnuts and cakes conquered his senses and made his mouth water. His appetite awoke with only a glance at the delicacies.

In spite of the spectacular breakfast that he devoured in half an hour and the positivity with which he began the morning, James would end the day with two completed interviews but which shed no new light on the matters.

"Miguel never said anything nor gave any details about his job in London," replied the doctor.

"His uncle got him the job," explained his mother.

"Miguel spoke more about his girlfriend Ana than how the clinical studies were going at Imperial College," went on the doctor. "Every so often he would tell us about the exploits of his roommate, a nice Spanish kid that he seemed to get along with very well," he added.

However, neither the doctor nor the mother remembered the name of this Spanish kid.

So, with some useless notes in his hand and dragging his feet, James returned to his hotel room to wait for news from Bakran. In the meantime he called Valeria hoping that some of her positive energy would rub off on him. He wanted to have her close, to feel her breath beside him. He wanted the fire to burn inside him. Fortunately, speaking to her was the right call.

An hour with Valeria on the phone brushed away all his discomfort, it fortified his spirit, and gave him back his confidence which had been slippery and playing hide and seek with him since the previous night. With repressed giggles, she blamed his insecurities on his lack of rest, withdrawal symptoms from the Egyptian tea which still attacked him from time to time, and the lack of physical affection. Particularly that last reason, which Valeria felt she could easily resolve as soon as he got back to the Windy City.

When Bakran called, James was back to his usual self. He was energetic and sure of himself, with renewed desires to swiftly move forward in the forefront of his thoughts, as the back of his mind dwelt on urgently returning to Chicago.

"Nancy boy…"

With no further ado, his companion went on with an explanation of the events of the day.

"The last three floors of the building are totally empty. It looks like they're waiting to be refurbished according to a notice on the door. The first floor is full of private offices although they are only marked with numbers. I have the list of tenants, so I can soon find out what kind of businesses they are running."

"What about the lab?" he inquired, more anxious than curious.

"On the second floor. However, I couldn't see it. They wouldn't let me in, the b…"

"That's the NHS's job," James interrupted.

Bakran did not let him finish, having an anxiety attack of his own.

"Don't give me that, you would have tried to see it if you were here. You would have begged, paid or bartered to get in."

"You know me so well!" he said, resolving not to let stress get the better of him.

He laughed, as he always did when he and Bakran crossed swords.

"I have to admit that although I learned from the master, it never worked for me. I guess the fact I look like I'm from Saudi Arabia doesn't help my pathetic attempts to convince them that I needed to be present."

"Go on," James interrupted to make his colleague focus on talking about the investigation.

But he completely ignored James.

"To cut a long story short, I didn't get to put the astronaut outfit on. I was desperate to get into the sealed area so I could feel like I was in deep space and use my respirator to talk like Darth Vader. But I'm not complaining, because just watching the NHS people suit up was an event in itself. For a while there I thought I was on the film set for E.T."

"Cliché, Bakran, cliché. That's what all boys dream of. To meet an extraterrestrial. That and dressing up like astronauts. You really stray from the point, mate. Get on with it, and tell me what they found in the lab."

James' aggressive tone let his friend know that it was time to get serious.

"Ok, ok. Don't throw a wobbly. The laboratory has definitely been a hot zone at some point."

"They found evidence of the bacteria?"
"No."
"So?"
"So they found several empty Petri dishes in the air conduits. Not just empty, sterilized. Apparently they had an Autoclave in the lab. This is just a guess though, because there is nothing left in the lab, not even a simple magnifying glass."

"An auto what?"

"Impressed, huh? An Autoclave. You don't know what an autoclave is?" he asked in a mocking voice.

"Bloody hell, Bakran! Either get to the point or I swear I will crawl down this telephone and beat you to a pulp," James threatened half-joking, half-serious. "You stretch out these explanations so much you would drive anyone up the wall."

"Easy... As I was explaining..." Bakran enjoyed himself, with airs of superiority.

"As was explained to you, no doubt," replied James, parrying his opponent.

"Are you going to keep interrupting me?"

James was silent this time.

"As I was saying, an Autoclave is similar to a pressure cleaner. It is used to sterilize objects with steam."

"A sterilizer, of course. So, how can the NHS tell the Petri dishes contained MRSA?"

"Because they were identified. They had a label which said so. But this is the interesting part," said Bakran to provoke him with his constant pauses.

"What were the Petri dishes doing in the air conduits?" James guessed, to spoil his little game.

"Aside from that. They found a black marker pen beside the dishes which was used to write MRSA on each label. It wasn't carefully written, it seems they wrote it in a hurry and at an uncomfortable angle."

"As if someone had written it once the dishes were already inside the air conduits?" went on James.

"Precisely!"

"But that makes no sense."

"It also makes no sense to put them in the air conduit because MRSA isn't airborne. It survives on surfaces for a long time, so it infects by contact, not inhalation. It enters the body through a wound and then travels on the blood flow. So if someone was trying to infect the workers, they were using the wrong method."

James was struck by a sudden and vague thought, which seemed highly probable and so he shared it with Bakran at once:

"The Petri dishes were never in the air conduits while they were working in the lab. The way I see it, someone very clever hid them there for us to find. Someone left that evidence there for us."

"That's exactly what I think," Bakran confirmed.

Chapter 22

Many weeks had to go by after the fateful MRSA accident before Paco Beltrán could set foot on Spanish soil. He escaped England alive, but arrived at the port of Barcelona in a terrible state. Since he did not dare take a plane in case someone recognized him, Armand, his new friend from his countryside hideout, drove him to the train station and then went with him as far as France on train, where they said farewell with a long hug. Paco found crossing the Mediterranean by boat a little harrowing. The sea was unsettled, and the temperature freezing. When he arrived at his destination, the kid was shriveled up, weak and fragile. It took all his strength to struggle into a taxi and ask the driver to take him to a cheap hostel where the mattresses were not too soft.

The driver told him he knew the perfect place. It was a hostel run by a friend of his family. He assured him he would be well treated there, and he looked at him in the rearview mirror as he spoke to him.

"You're very pale, kid. Are you feeling alright?"

"Yeah, great," Paco replied, as he lay back across the back seats and a tear dropped out of one of his eyes when he closed them sleepily.

It felt like it only took five minutes to arrive at the hostel, and the driver stepped out of the car and helped the boy up from the seat.

"Would you rather I take you to a doctor?" asked the man, visibly alarmed.

"No, no, don't worry. Can you come and pick me up tomorrow at eight in the morning?" Paco asked, offering the man his payment.

"Yes. But let me come up and introduce you to Maria Fernanda, the owner. She's like my sister, you know?" and he took him by the arm and helped him up the steps.

Once he had seen the room, the woman in charge of the picturesque hostel took his temperature with the palm of her hand and forced him to drink a hot cocoa and at last left him alone. Paco had never received such attention and care, and much less from a stranger.

As soon as he closed the door to his room, he looked in his backpack for Ana's address which he had found on one of the letters to Miguel, and he made a note of it on a piece of paper. He placed it on the bedside table and then turned quickly to the mattress. He lay down, promising himself that he would only rest for an hour, but it was a promise he could not keep.

The following day, a beam of light shone through the gap in the curtains and lit up a corner of the room, as if pointing to a small bookcase. A bronze crucifix was hanging on the adjacent wall, and it glowed as it received the sunlight. Its brilliance made Paco close his eyes for a second as his eyes adjusted to the resplendent morning light, and his numb body slowly responded to his brain's commands to get up.

The thought of meeting Ana at long last was the only thing that made him speed up the process. He got up as quickly as he could, and checked the time on the bedside table clock. It was seven in the morning. He let out a sigh of relief. He would have time to clean himself calmly. That was when he realized he was naked. He did not remember having taken his clothes off, but they were neatly folded on the bedside table and he was in the middle of the room, naked as if he had just made love but not quite that lucky.

Twenty minutes later and reinvigorated by a long stimulating shower, Paco heard with unease slow footfalls coming down the corridor. It seemed that someone was advancing cautiously and trying not to be heard. He put his ear to the door to listen, but the person stopped. Paco held his breath, only to let it all out a few seconds later when the knock on his door thundered in his ear.

"It's Maria Fernanda. Are you ready for breakfast?" he heard with relief the voice of the friendly hostel owner.

But the relief was short lived. *What if it's a trap? Is there a man pointing a gun at the woman's head?* he thought, and he hurriedly put his shoes on.

"I'm just getting dressed," he replied, buying time.

"No rush. I'll leave the tray outside your door."

And so Paco heard the steps of the woman as she moved away. After making sure there was no one in the corridor, and walking on tiptoes looking both ways, he arrived in the entrance hall. He asked at reception for Maria Fernanda. She made him wait a while, so Paco took advantage of this delay to sit down on the ample sofa from which he could see the doorway to the hostel.

"You look better than you did yesterday, kid, but you're still a little pale. Did you sleep well? No more nightmares?" asked the woman when she spotted him on the sofa.

"What nightmares?" replied Paco, unsure if she was joking or serious.

"Don't you remember?" she in turn replied as she placed a hand on his forehead.

"No, not at all."

"You were screaming for a while until I went into your room. You were drenched in sweat and running a high fever, so I did everything I could to reduce your temperature. I couldn't leave you with the soaking clothes, or you would have woken up with pneumonia," the woman explained with the authoritarian voice women tend to employ on their children. "You don't have a fever anymore," she finished saying as she removed her hand from Paco's forehead.

"I really appreciate it. There is no need to explain."

That was when the taxi driver stuck his head around the door, and Paco said goodbye to the woman with a kiss on both cheeks. She followed him to the door and asked him:

"Shall I expect you for dinner tonight?"

"I don't know yet. It depends on how today goes," answered Paco, and he disappeared down the alleyway and boarded the taxi.

The taxi ride was short, but eventful. Paco was unable to control his hands and knees when they began to tremble slightly. He also could not control the tickling sensation running up and down his spine nor the beads of sweat that formed on his forehead. His body was mercilessly betraying him.

When the driver stopped the car and pointed out the destination to him, Paco's heart skipped a few beats. He was about to tell the man to drive him back to the hostel. However, he did the opposite. He opened the door to the car and stopped like a soldier on guard outside the house. With one hand he waved to the driver so he would leave and not give him any excuses to back out.

What would he say to Ana when he saw her? He brought neither words of hope nor consolation. He had no words, period. He would tell her his name, his relationship with Miguel, deliver the letters and that would be that. He would leave her life barely having crossed her path.

"Yes?" asked an old man with a coarse impatient voice.

"Hello. My name is Paco Beltrán and I have brought some documents for Ms. Ana…"

In that moment he realized that he did not know her surname. In his imaginary conversations with her he always called her Ana, just as Miguel did in his letters which never once mentioned his girlfriend's surname. There were no formalities between them, and now that he needed to know her full name, Paco was unable to say it.

"What documents?"

The feminine voice that asked the question took him by surprise. He had not expected to hear her until he had entered the house. However, here was Ana in person, receiving him at the door and looking at him with an expression of who the hell are you knocking on my door with a lame excuse.

Apparently seeing the girl unhinged him, because Paco was only able to offer her a bashful smile. While she waited for a reply, he looked at her features with a dry mouth. Ana was dressed in dark jeans and the typical basic white t-shirt that somehow costs several hundred euros. Her brown hair was held up in a loose ponytail which allowed several locks of hair to delicately frame her face. Her almond eyes boasted long eyelashes and her angular nose had a certain flamenco air... *her little gypsy-girl body... a woman half-way done, as if drawn from a song by Mecano,* he concluded his description.

Paco could feel his legs faltering at Ana's beauty, but that was not the only reason. A weakness overcame his body at that moment. He had to rest in the doorway.

"I'm a friend of Miguel Ramirez. I have some documents from him," was all he was able to say before he rested his head against the doorframe.

That reply was enough for Ana to offer her arm and help him in.

Making contact with the girl's body was the electricity that momentarily sparked his senses back into life. His head was no longer spinning. He was able to free himself from her arms and walk on his own. He stopped in the middle of the living room, not accepting the seat that was offered, and he introduced himself again with his full name.

The old man took the initiative of continuing the conversation by introducing himself as Ana's father, and he forced the kid to sit down. The next stage was a series of questions about his pallor and weakness. That was how Paco found out the man was a doctor, but he did not reply to why he was in such a sickly state. All he said was that he was feeling a little unwell. Ana's father went off in search of his stethoscope and Paco turned his attention back to the girl he had come all this way to meet.

Ana could barely look at him; her glassy eyes sought some way to hide her emotions. She folded her arms when she noticed Paco was looking at her, and turned her gaze even further away towards the windows of the house. With that posture and without saying a word, she indicated to Paco that he was not welcome. Perhaps she regretted having granted him shelter. Perhaps she was offended by his constant stare. Perhaps all she wanted were the document so she could get rid of him at once. Perhaps.

Chapter 23

Ana's father did not take long to return, now playing the role of doctor. Paco felt ashamed because he took his temperature in front of Ana. He sounded his chest with a stethoscope, felt his tonsils, and asked him to cough. He made him feel like a little boy on his first visit to the pediatrician. His diagnostic was a little unlikely though:

"I think you have a twenty-four hour virus."

How can I tell this nice man and his daughter that I have a violent infection and I don't know how much longer I have left to live? In the time it took him to think of how to break the news, Ana's father led him to the dining room and encouraged him to have breakfast. Since he did not want to seem ungrateful, he ate it all. Ana did not seem to have much of an appetite, instead she pushed her food around with her fork. She did not participate in the conversation. She did not ask about Miguel.

When they finished their breakfast, the father shook Paco's hand and kissed his daughter on both cheeks before leaving to his work. Once the father had gone, Ana got up hurriedly, took the dishes into the kitchen, and signaled at Paco to follow her.

They returned to the living room. Two large sofas upholstered in dense fabric dominated the space, along with three windows adorned with thick brocaded curtains. It was a somber room. The chimney was not lit, but the temperature in the house was pleasant. Ana did not give him much of a chance to look around carefully, because once they sat down on one of the sofas she quickly asked her first question.

"What have you come to tell me about Miguel?" she asked in a defiant and cutting tone, challenging him with her question and her expression.

Before their meeting, Paco guessed that Ana would realize that all he wanted to do was kneel before her and say how sorry he was about Miguel's death. However, now sitting face to face, he was not sure if she knew he was dead. He did not know if she had read the story online, just as he had found out one morning with Armand. He had the feeling, unfortunately, that the girl was expecting him to confirm her worst fears: that Miguel had ceased to be and would never come knocking on her door the way he had just done.

The scene was unfolding differently to how he had imagined it when he had arrived at the house that morning. Paco had fantasized with Ana inviting him in, allowing him to embrace her tightly which would give him the confidence to tell her about the terror he felt when he stooped to help Miguel when he found him collapsed on the laboratory corridor floor. That illusion felt distant now.

Feeling a tightness in his chest, he watched a few devastating tears fall down her feminine cheeks, showing a glimpse of her bravery, sadness and a million other feelings all at once, forming a powerful vortex that could not be called melancholy or pity, but rather a still fresh sensation of pure shock.

Ana's unexpected behavior made it all much harder. Paco searched in his heart for the right words to begin his tale. He told her everything in detail. How he had met Miguel, their job at the lab, the accident that landed them all in the hospital, his suspicions that they had been deliberately infected. Paco felt that all of his descriptions were catching in his throat and his eyes were welling with tears as he spoke. As he explained how he escaped from the hospital, he closed his eyes to hide the shame he felt for abandoning Miguel.

Ana sobbed slightly. You could tell from a mile off that she was trying to contain her urge to weep disconsolately, to cry out against the injustice of it all, to trade blows with destiny for being responsible for her suffering. Paco looked at her, confused and overwhelmed by her bravery, for there she was, sitting motionless, crying on the inside and avoiding eye contact with him.

Suddenly, and without warning, the girl stood up and Paco followed suit. They looked at one another for a long time, in silence, the air void of sounds except for their own breathing. With his lungs besieged by a disarming agonizing pain, Paco allowed an avalanche of emotions to cascade from his chest and he begged forgiveness, even though he was not to blame.

Ana came closer, took his hand in hers, and with the other hand briefly caressed his chest. Paco let his hand rest in hers for longer than he could ever have dreamt of. And the girl responded affably, and continued to hold his hand. After a few seconds the atmosphere abruptly changed and was charged with a sudden sense of imprudence. They both felt it. Their bodies shook. They looked each other in the eye timidly, they saw the emotion, and Ana released his hand. She doubted herself, and distrusted him. She wrapped herself in a blanket that was on the sofa, and sat down again, as did he. Separate. All wordlessly. Words were unnecessary.

Petrified on a corner of the sofa, Paco longed to wrap his arms around Ana and protect her forever from the anxiety, but right now he was not capable of protecting himself. Even so, he would have given anything to take her in his arms. Soon this blinding fantasy would end. Soon he would have to go, knowing that he would never see her again. Meanwhile, he would pretend that something unimaginable was happening between them.

Ana observed him as he thought all this. She was intrigued by the young man's face, his warm half-smile. His hunched body which was intimidated by her instead of pursuing her, confused her. She was moved by his intelligent dreaming eyes which dodged away from her instead of chasing her curiously. In that moment she had a revelation, and little by little, with calculated caution, she moved closer to Paco, sliding her body slowly along the sofa. Paco, seeing Ana moving nearer, tensed up involuntarily. Was his imagination playing tricks on him? But this was no fantasy. She was now really close to him, but instead of him reaching out to her, she hugged him tenderly. Her instinct pushed her. A genuine hunch flooded her soul with relief.

In that moment on the sofa, Ana had a premonition that she would feel safe in the arms of this lad, after weeks of incomprehension from her parents who could not understand the depths of her grief. She came to the conclusion that Paco was an emissary from Miguel, who sent him on a mission from heaven. He sent him to validate her pain, so she could have a companion in these difficult times to help her get through her loneliness.

Gathered in Paco's arms, Ana confessed that she already knew her boyfriend was dead. She had learned about it because one of the janitors at the hospital had called her. Miguel had given him her number. The hardest part was hearing that Miguel had spent several days in a bed, almost unable to breath, trying uselessly to gasp for air. On his own. Alone, and with no loved ones around him. Alone, and she had been a bare few hours away from him.

Her only consolation was knowing that Miguel thought of her in his final moments. He called out in dreams, delirious: "Ana, Ana, I promise I will be fine. I promise."

Since then she had lived in darkness. She hid from the world and her parents, who could not bear to hear her crying. She cried every day and all hours for weeks on end, particularly when they did not let her go to the funeral.

"I know it was in Puerto Rico, but I wanted to be there," Ana explained, telling him about other incidents that showed her frustration with her parents.

She ended her monologue assuring him that she already felt a little better.

"I only cry at night now."

After a pause, followed by a sigh, Ana lifted her head which until then had been buried in Paco's chest, and she whispered:

"But I still feel like I didn't get a chance to say goodbye."

Noticing that she was separating from the embrace, Paco lowered his head, and looking her in the eye, wiped the tears from her cheeks. He decided the time had come to give her Miguel's letters.

He produced them one at a time. Ana reread them, although she knew them all by heart. Paco left the last one to the end, the most important one, the one Miguel wrote to say goodbye and which he kept in a sealed envelope that read: "To Ana, my love. You may only open this when your lips can no longer kiss mine." Ana read it aloud in a hushed voice.

Don't suffer, better days will come
and the light of the sun will light up
your days
and the stars your night sky.
The moon will heal your wounds
you will have new dreams,
full of wonderful colors.

Overcome the despondency soon
and find that passion anew
let nothing be impossible in your life
because forever is nothing but a dream
evanescent and without rationale.

*You will embark on beautiful
new aspirations
because a whole world of energy
is waiting for you joyously.
It will be so, you will see,
allow yourself to be carried away.
Allow yourself to be loved again.*

The words burned her on the inside. That was her Miguel: selfless. In life he offered her an unselfish love and now in death she could see just how much he truly loved her. Even in his final hour, Miguel's thoughts did not revolve around his unjust end. He did not write with rage; he did not say goodbye annoyed by how little time he had been allotted. His final wish was focused solely on Ana's happiness. He wanted to make sure she would be alright. He gave her permission to love again, and to forget him.

"How brave you must be to die in peace, begging to be forgotten!"

Ana said this phrase quietly, so quietly that Paco barely heard her. But once he realized what she had said, he pulled her towards him and hugged her and cried with her. They both cried for the same reason: for seeing in Miguel's act the true meaning of love.

After calming down a little and sharing two hours of anecdotes about Miguel, and a few stories from their own lives, they struggled to say goodbye when the taxi driver came to take him back to the hostel. Ana thanked Paco a thousand times for having visited. Paco promised he would come back the next day. But even after having said goodbye several times, neither one moved to separate. The driver was forced to intervene.

"Are you coming, or what?" shouted the man from the car.

"That driver doesn't seem as friendly as the guy who brought me here this morning," smiled Paco.

"You think?" Ana joked. "You'd better call another one then," she said half joking, half serious.

A few more minutes with Paco would be good for her spirits.

"No, I should go. I'll see you tomorrow. Thank your father for the medical examination. I hope I'll feel better tomorrow."

The next day, Paco felt better than he had since beginning his odyssey with MRSA. His body spontaneously recovered its strength. His skin had regained its color. Perhaps Ana's father was right, and yesterday's symptoms were only a twenty-four hour virus. Perhaps the MRSA bug no longer flowed through his veins. Perhaps the constant doses of antibiotics were doing their job. Perhaps.

Before getting out of bed, Paco promised himself not to think of MRSA anymore. He woke up feeling alive. *I am alive and feel free as a fish swimming in the vast ocean*, he thought. No doubt he would overcome the harsh test he had endured for the past few months. He felt happy. But the happiness did not last long. When he arrived at Ana's home, her father was waiting for him at the door.

"You have one minute to turn around and never come back. How dare you put my daughter and my family at risk?" he greeted Paco. "Go to the nearest hospital right now to get treatment. Or wait for me at my office," he concluded, offering him a card identifying his medical offices.

Paco understood immediately. The man knew how Miguel had died, about the deliberate MRSA infection, the reason why he had been pale the previous day, and he closed the door on him to prevent him from doing more harm.

The taxi had already gone, so the boy stood out on the pavement for a while, stunned.

Now what? he said to himself.

His plans only took going to Ana's house into consideration. He had never even thought of anything else. What would his next step be? As he thought about this, he began to wander aimlessly. One step at a time he moved away from the house where he had left his heart.

"Paco!" a voice called him.

Once again his imagination was toying with his feelings. He was fantasizing that he could hear the beautiful Ana calling him. It was not until he felt a hand touching him on the shoulder that he realized he was not in some science fiction tale. Standing in front of him was the gypsy girl.

"What are you doing here!" he exclaimed.

"I came to tell you that I am going to Puerto Rico this afternoon," Ana replied enthusiastically, with irrepressible joy.

But she got no reply from Paco. He was speechless. His eyes asked his question: *how is it possible?*

"I don't have permission," said Ana, outlining her peculiar plan. "Do you want to come with me?" she insisted, when she got no reply.

"Ana, can you travel without your parent's permission?"

"I'm old enough and I have the money."

"How old are you, by the way?" he inquired.

"Eighteen, how about you?"

"The same."

"So, I'll see you at six at the airport?" asked the young woman.

She gave him a paper with the flight information, and began to hurry back to her house, but looking back awaiting a reply.

"See you at six!" called out Paco with an ear to ear smile.

When he was at last able to calm down, cruel reality crushed his plans. He did not have the money to fly to Puerto Rico. His money had evaporated in a month of necessary expenses. He would have to call his parents. If he could contact them in time, they could send him his allowance and a little extra. That was exactly what he did the moment he got back to the hostel. He asked for the money he needed; as usual, he lied to his parents as to his whereabouts, what he was doing, and how he felt, and they in turn did not ask for many details.

The money registered to his bank account two hours later. He paid for his stay at the hostel. He gave Maria Fernanda a big kiss and jumped into the taxi with the euphoria of a boy riding on a rollercoaster for the hundredth time.

Chapter 24

Ana and Paco travelled straight from San Juan airport to the cemetery in a white taxi that welcomed them to Puerto Rico. They were silent for the first time since their flight left Spain. They had spent twelve hours together and they chatted through the night while the rest of the passengers slept. Now jet lag was overtaking them, but before resting at a hotel they wanted to go to the cemetery. They wanted to say goodbye to Miguel and ask for his blessing that it was alright for them to be friends. Neither of them would have confessed this was one of their reasons, but it was obvious. The acid test of their new friendship depended on this moment, and on how they felt once they were facing Miguel's grave.

Unfortunately they did not have the privacy necessary to get in touch with their deepest feelings. On the way to the crypt which housed Miguel's body, they saw a man kneeling in front of the tombstone which was surrounded with yellow, white and pink flowers.

"Excuse me, are you a member of Miguel's family?" asked Paco, curious, even under such unfortunate circumstances, to meet someone close to his Puerto Rican friend.

"Oh, no," the man replied and he nimbly stood up. "Miguel was the nephew of a friend. I came to offer my respects. My name is James Penton."

James offered them both his hand in a surprisingly formal gesture.

"Ana," the girl said her name, and took his hand.
Paco did likewise.

"Ana? Miguel's girlfriend?" asked James intrigued and stunned, his eyes opening wide.

"How do you know that?" replied Ana, also stunned at having been recognized.

Trying to suppress their notion that they were dealing with a lunatic who thought he was clairvoyant, James explained:

"It says so right there," and he pointed to the inscription on the tomb.

They all turned together to read...

Miguel Ramírez
Eighteen years of age,
Loving son of Lourdes
faithful boyfriend to Ana,
friend to all.

The phrase "boyfriend to Ana" engraved on the stone of the tombstone and beneath Miguel's name rocked Paco for a moment. Was Miguel claiming Ana for himself? With that sentence, was he claiming ownership for all eternity?

Ana, on her part, was unable to contain her tears, which came gushing out. She sat down on the ground and hugged herself. She let the lawn and the flowers envelop her. Paco and James instinctively backed away. They moved away from the grave and gave her some space.

While Ana said goodbye to Miguel in private, James peppered a few leading questions into the small talk he maintained with the boy. He did not want to make it look like he was trying to press him for information. But Paco was even more inscrutable than he had expected, so agent Penton was left no choice but to identify himself as such and explain the reason for his visit to the tomb. He was investigating Miguel's death.

Paco grabbed James by both shoulders and put all the weight of his young body against the agent. Almost whispering in his ear, he confessed to agent Penton that he could help him with his investigation. He had all the details of what had happened before his friend Miguel's death. With this act, Paco was releasing the heavy burden he had been carrying.

Ana stood up at that point and slowly came towards them. The agent produced a card from his pocket, and made a note of his hotel and room number. He asked Paco politely to meet him later. And they shook hands to seal the deal.

"What if he's an impostor?" Ana asked Paco three hours later.

They were already in their hotel room in the capital city. It was the same hotel James was staying at.

"We'll call NCIA in London and ask about Agent Penton. But I am telling you now, Ana, I saw his credentials and those things aren't easy to falsify. I think we should trust him."

"After everything that's happened to you, how can you trust anyone?"

"Because in the short time I've been on this odyssey, I have seen both sides of the coin, Ana. Evil people who are ready to kill, and good people who will give their lives for you," Paco replied, thinking of Armand. "If this terrible experience had made me lose my faith in humanity, if I had lost all perspective of the fact that two types of people can coexist with each other, I would not even have tried to meet you."

"Did you believe I would be one of the good people?" asked Ana with a certain shyness which made her seem more coquettish than she intended.

"Of course," he replied, and he almost let on that he already knew her thanks to her letters.

The two youngsters called the NCIA offices and confirmed that Agent James Penton did in fact exist, so they prepared to visit him in his room. Paco thought it was a bad idea for Ana to also join them, but there was no way to convince her otherwise.

She's a stubborn one, Paco concluded, and a small smile appeared on his lips.

"What are you laughing at?" Ana asked when she noticed his smile.

"Nothing. I'm just nervous," he replied as they arrived at James' door.

"You're nervous?" Ana asked sardonically, clicking her tongue trying to get him to admit that his whole body was trembling with anxiety.

"Yes. Because of you. Now I have to worry about you and how to protect you if something bad happens," Paco replied, annoyed.

"Oh, how brave! Just the way I like my men," she said teasing him.

Then she frowned and pointed right at Paco's face, adding:

"You don't have to protect me from anything. I can look after myself."

"Really? You know karate or judo, or you think your aerobics classes will help you fight the bad guys?" Paco mocked her, also pointing at her and imitating her.

"For your information, I am a black belt in karate. Is that something you have on your résumé too?" she asked defiantly.

"No," he admitted, ashamed.

"So shut up then," Ana commanded him seriously.

"Match made in heaven?" James asked sarcastically when he opened the door, admitting that he had heard the whole conversation from the room.

He would get the reply to his question in due time, but for now the answer remains unknown. Could their innocent and nascent union, haunted by death and plots from the very outset, survive the ravages of time without heavenly intervention?

James' room was a typical hotel room: two beds, one table, two chairs, and a television cabinet. However, this room had a spectacular view of the Atlantic Ocean. Observed from the tropics, this ocean had a different color, a different air to what you could appreciate from North America or Europe. The intense reflection of the sun in the Caribbean made its water turn shades of blue and green that you usually only saw in jewels. In some places, the water was so crystal clear that you could see the fish and starfish in plain sight.

Ana had been born in a coastal city and so she appreciated the sea as if it were a second skin, since it had been there for her since her infancy. For this reason she could not imagine living somewhere that was not beside the sea. The Mediterranean of her home country had a different color to the Atlantic Ocean. It was dark blue, deep, containing the imperial secrets of Rome, Greece, Turkey and Africa hidden beneath its waves. The Caribbean Sea was just as old, but was almost childlike in its playfulness. It behaved differently, expressed itself in peculiar terms, and its warm waters seduced and refreshed the body. On the other hand, the Mediterranean could freeze to the bone whoever was not accustomed to its embrace.

Ana could not resist the magnetism of the sea, of any sea, and she was entranced by the view from the window of agent Penton's room, from where she could see the north shore coast with its billions of golden grains of sand. Spellbound, she opened the window and let the wind and brine slip into the room, and she leaned forward to bask in its splendor. It was as if she was making a mental checklist of all the different ways that the waves broke against the shore, and she allowed herself to be drawn in even further.

Meanwhile, James and Paco began to speak about the laboratory in London.

"We were only working for three months," Paco replied to the first question.

"When did you begin?"

"Last November."

"What was the purpose of the laboratory?"

"We were investigating the relationship between the MRSA bug and the different fabrics used in clothes manufacturing."

James abruptly changed the course of his interrogation.

"Were you the one who left the Petri dishes in the air conduits of the lab?"

"You found them?" asked Paco, now with his usual youngster's sing-song voice, instead of the key witness attitude with which he had been answering. "I wasn't sure if someone would find them, but I had to take a chance. I wanted to leave a clue in case we all died at the hospital. When I went to call for the ambulance, I placed the empty Petri dishes there. Sam had already taken away the ones we had been using for the experiments with the live bacteria."

"Sam Cosgrove?" James interrupted.

Although the question triggered an evil feeling in James that devastated him emotionally, for the obvious reason of not scaring his witness, he remained calm and controlled.

"Yes, the man who hired us was called Sam Cosgrove," Paco went on. "And if you want to know my opinion, I think he is to blame for the infection. We were very careful during the experiments."

James could not believe his luck.

"You think it was premeditated? It wasn't an accident?" he asked as he caressed his coarse beard.

"When you spend every day playing with bacteria that can kill you, there is no room for error or accident. I am convinced that someone deliberately caused us to come into contact with the bacteria," Paco stated with the poise and seriousness of a legendary fifty-year old scientist.

"Would you be willing to testify in court?" James asked as if it were a routine question, as if testifying in court were the most common thing in the world.

He deliberately glossed over the fact that facing a courtroom jury was the bane of thousands of people around the world, one of the greatest fears imaginable, although it was a slippery experience for most people. Paco did not even flinch.

"Sure I'll testify! Today if you like. I think it's the only reason I survived. To make those responsible pay for the deaths," he guaranteed with the determination of someone who wants to do what is right.

His firm frown and narrowed eyes demonstrated that he would not back down.

"How come you survived and the others didn't?" James reflected out loud, to distract his attention from the trial towards the question that he had been turning over in his mind since he met him at the cemetery.

"I don't know. I took the antibiotic that we had in the lab and continued taking the prescribed dose until it ran out. That was all I did. I received no medical treatment, and didn't go to a hospital. I don't understand why the others all died. They were young and healthy men. Although that wasn't the case with Miguel..."

He did not say anymore out of courtesy for Ana, who was still at the window but not far from the conversation.

"The other men should have recovered just like I did."

"Why were you all hired? What is the relationship between MRSA and the fabrics?" James asked, and he pressed his young witness to give him all the details.

He was the only survivor. The only one who could answer all his questions. And the agent would ask him every last question even if it took days.

But James did not need to worry. At the current rate, he would get all his answers before sunset. Paco was an exemplary witness. He did not need to be pressed, because he proffered the information in spade-loads. He replied to every question without complaints.

"We were trying to find out in what fabrics MRSA could survive the longest, and in which ones it could not survive at all. Dr. Fowler wanted to find out the types of fabrics in which the cells live longer than twenty-four hours, which is the minimum they will survive on any fabric or plastic."

"And did you get your answers?" asked James, placing his elbows on his knees and interlacing his fingers into a fist beneath his chin.

"Yes. We drew up a comparative table that showed survival times in different fabrics. In most cases, as in cotton, silk, linen, nylon, thermal textiles, the ones you use in exercise clothes to retain heat and reduce moisture, MRSA survives for between one and three days. The winner was polyester with a survival rate of between one and fifty-six days. It was awesome to carry out the experiment, but I preferred the one about the inks," Paco explained enthusiastically because for a moment he forgot about the contagion caused by said experiments and remembered his vibrant passion for scientific investigation.

"And what was that experiment about?" questioned James.

"That study was based on checking to see if MRSA would survive in liquid substances with high levels of colorants, such as inks used in pens and printers. We had inks of all colors and available brands. The technicians also loved that experiment, it was like painting with watercolors. It turns out that MRSA spreads very fast in moist environments, such as the case of bathtubs and showers. That's why it survives in the nose, and that's where doctors look first to see if there are indications that the patient has the bacteria in his body. The bacterium has also been found present in sea water. Last year there were several cases of surfers battling severe infections with the bacteria..."

He lowered his voice for this last explanation, because he had promised Ana they would go swimming and he did not want to scare her. A rough noise suddenly interrupted their conversation.

Someone knocked on the door in a hurried and brusque manner.

"Did you order room service?" asked Paco with his eyes wide open.

James did not show any outward signs, but internally his blood began to pump faster through his veins.

―――――

James slowly stood up from his chair and with a shake of his head told Paco that he had not ordered room service. When he saw that the answer was no, the kid hurriedly stood up, took Ana by her arm, and hid in the bathroom with her.

James laughed cheerfully and told him as calmly as he could:

"You've been watching too much TV, Paco. That's not going to be necessary."

Paco paid him no attention and locked the bathroom door behind him. James then moved to the room door, but stopped at a prudent distance and placed one hand on the gun in his chest holster.

"Yes?" he asked.

A man putting on a voice pretending to be a woman replied:

"Room service."

Paco came out of the bathroom and grabbed James.

"Please don't open the door."

"Take it easy, kid. Besides, who is the special agent here, you or me?"

Paco ran to the open window, but saw he was eight floors up and that there were no parapets nearby to break his fall. Besides, he could not picture throwing Ana out of the window. He locked himself in the bathroom again.

"What do you want?" asked James.

Again the hoarse woman's voice was heard:

"To wipe your ass, Nancy boy."

"Bastard" James shouted as he opened the door and hugged Bakran laughing.

Paco came out of the bathroom still holding Ana in his arms. They both looked at the men and started to laugh themselves. They released all the anxiety they had been feeling just a moment before.

"Why were you so scared? Are the kindergarten cops chasing you for running away from home?" Bakran asked the two youngsters, and both agents laughed stupidly.

"No," Ana spoke over the men's mirth. "The man chasing Paco is already six feet under eating his words and his mockery in company of the devil." She replied furiously, her face contorted with rage; her eyes were two small obsidian pins.

The men stopped laughing at once, and turned at the same time to face Paco. The kid, with an expression of shock before the angry eyes of the agents, said:

"I didn't have time to also tell you that they've been chasing me since the accident at the lab."

The explanation was only directed to James, but both agents began to fire questions at him, for an instant forgetting the familiarity they had so quickly developed:

"Has your life been in danger since the accident? Have you received death threats? Have they contacted or threatened your family? Who was the man chasing you? Do you know who he was working for?"

Once again, Paco went on to explain the persecution in London, just as he had previously explained to Ana, but this time to two English agents who remained long faced from the start of his tale. The jokes and laughter were over. Only the girl laughed inwardly, proud of having put two alpha males in their place. *Now they will listen to Paco the way they should... with respect.*

"You are in serious trouble, mister," Bakran said to Paco when he finished his account of the events.

"Do you have any idea if they're still after you?" asked James.

"Not since I left London, but I keep my guard up just in case. I have no idea if they are on my trail."

"You're right to think they're still after you. Bakran and I will make sure you and Ana get protection," James assured them, offering a hopeful smile.

"Have you been threatened at any point, Ana?" Bakran asked.

"No. But the truth is I haven't left my parent's home since Miguel died."

"Maybe you didn't give them a chance, or maybe they couldn't find you," Bakran said, and he paused for thought, not because he did not have a clear idea of the situation, but because of a sense of sorrow and a bad feeling that overcame him.

"I did get a couple of e-mails asking for personal information to send on some of Miguel's personal effects, but then I discovered they were from Paco when he brought me his letters."

"Not from me! I never sent you any e-mails!"

"It's possible that Sam Cosgrove thinks you know more than you do, Ana. He obviously found your e-mail address in the computer at Paco's flat. Bakran, call the office. These kids definitely need to stay hidden for a little while longer."

"Are we going to stay here in Puerto Rico?" Ana interrupted.

"I don't think so. I think it would be easier to go back to London because we have a lot of agents who can look after you there twenty-four hours a day while we solve this case," James affirmed, placing one hand on the girl's shoulder to show his confidence.

Ana kept looking at Paco.

"London? My father already accepted the idea that I'm in Puerto Rico, but he'll kill me if I don't go back to Spain soon. It took me twenty minutes on the phone to convince him I'm alright and apologize for running away and explain to him why I had to. What reason can I give him now to say it's important I go to London?"

Paco understood her reasoning perfectly.

"We can't go back to Spain, Ana. You'll be safer in London. We can stay at my parents' apartment."

"My father will come after me with his rifle in hand."

"So after all we are going to have to call in the kindergarten cops?" said Bakran, but he stopped himself from offering any other comments or gestures when he received the cold deathly stare from both youngsters who he would have to defend with his own life from now on.

That night Paco and Ana slept in their room under Bakran's protection. The agents were seriously concerned for their safety, but they repressed any expression of their fears. James stayed in his room to make several calls. The investigation of Sam Cosgrove was now becoming tangible and dangerous. He had two survivors to protect, and there was no way of telling how many more people were directly or indirectly involved with what Sam Cosgrove was up to.

His first call was to the central offices of the Department of Health in Richmond House, Whitehall. He needed to get a firm understanding of MRSA and its possible consequences with the help of Sir William Richardson, Medical Chief of the Contagious Diseases Division of the DH, and he needed the knowledge immediately. James would spend the rest of the night taking an intensive course in microbiology. His second call, the one which would unfortunately have to wait until early next morning, would be to the Canabal brothers.

Once Paco and Ana fell asleep, James took the opportunity to call Valeria, hoping she would not already be fast asleep. Apparently she was, as she did not answer the phone. With the chaos ensuing from the new facts in Paco's story and the implications that they had for the investigation of Sam, he missed his usual hour to call Valeria for the first time since he promised to call her every day. Even so, since it was not past midnight, he sent her a text message as evidence that he had called her that day. *To think I have come to this! Reporting daily to a woman. But loving every second of it!*, he concluded and ran a hand across his forehead to shake off his mental urge to touch, feel, kiss, squeeze and hug his Valeria. *One more day...*

"Sweetie, I am in PR on work with Bakran. Clsr to you. Call tmrw when we get to Chi. ORD Flight no. 1821 7:50 pm. Luv."

Chapter 25

Valeria made arrangements for a limousine to pick James and Bakran up from O'Hare at the time indicated in his text message. *It'll be a surprise!* The chauffeur would drive them straight from the airport to the concert that night, and from there to the private box in the AllStar Arena where Valeria would be waiting for him with champagne, strawberries and the music of a Spanish language rock band in the background that would make them feel at least ten years younger. Since the concert started at eight, she would have plenty of time before James arrived to do her job and then wait for him in the box. *It's perfect*, she thought.

"Thirty minutes call to the start of the concert," announced the stage manager from the dressing room door.

The members of *Amuleto Rojo*, the Latin band playing their first gig in Chicago, were praying an Our Father and three Hail Mary's to thank God and ask for His help in winning over the audience one more time. One Our Father and three Hail Mary's, typical of when you ask for absolution of all sins in confession. The medallion of the *Virgen del Carmen* also always travelled with them. The singer would pin it to his lapel, visible to all, the drummer on the sock of his right foot with which he would mercilessly pound the drums, and the guitarist on the elastic of his underwear. "Immaculate Heart of Mary, pray for us. Now and at the hour of our death. Amen," they prayed before taking the stage. It was their good luck amulet, their scapular.

Apparently the divine intervention was already in full swing, since the band attracted thousands of fans. Boys and girls of all ages and creeds, mostly Latinos or of Latino descent, all congregated there. Many spoke Spanish thanks to their parents who still spoke the language at home. But even those who did not have an inkling of Spanish had phonetically learned the lyrics to *Amuleto Rojo*'s songs. The truth was that it did not matter if they knew the lyrics to the songs. The music was so catchy that the lyrics were the least important thing.

Valeria had already forgotten what it meant to go to a concert like this, and she was surprised by the bottleneck of people trying to all enter the same door at once. The lines of spectators, all walking in the same direction. The huge number of cars parking one after another following the order marked by the security staff. The last minute ticket scalpers, the food stalls selling beer and piña coladas...

Piña coladas? Only Latinos... thought Valeria, as she inspected the corridors of the stadium heading towards the merch booths. All the stalls were trying to attract the attention of the kids with their promotional activities.

"Photos, photos... have your picture taken, and then find it on urbanconcerts.com."

"Posters of your favorite band, just ten bucks."

"Free t-shirts!"

"Free t-shirts?" the kids asked the promo team.

"Yeah!" they replied with wide smiles of the kind you saw on toothpaste commercials.

They offered them the t-shirts on a single condition:

"A free t-shirt for anyone who will put it on right now."

The boys would take their shirts off so quickly that fabrics flew through the air and their naked chests awaited the free t-shirt in the middle of the corridor. The girls could not do the same without getting arrested, so the promo teams would hand them out at the doors to the restrooms so that they would change discreetly. With no hesitation, the same girls that a few hours earlier had spent forever picking the perfect shirt for the concert were now scrunching them in their handbags just to win a t-shirt.

"It's a free t-shirt, you have to put it on. It's super-cool. I love the design," the girls would say to each other inside the women's restrooms.

The women's t-shirts were different than the men's. They were tighter fitting, with shorter sleeves and a low-cut neck, just the way they liked it. Besides, the rumor was that the concert was going to be filmed and they would focus on everybody wearing the t-shirt. *You've gotta put it on!*

Valeria watched all the hubbub with excitement. At one of the promotional booths she ran into Mercedes, Gabriela, and a twelve-year old friend of hers, Olivia. They pushed through the crowd to get to the booth. Valeria, Mercedes and Gabriela were already wearing their t-shirts. They put them on at home because they were additional samples that Mercedes had ordered. In fact, they were unique because she ordered them in fuchsia pink as a little private joke with her daughter. The three of them would be "pink ladies" for the night.

Olivia was desperate to get a t-shirt and to be part of the group, even if it was a different color. Her mom let her go to the concert with Gabriela at the last moment because a work commitment came up and she could not take her. Olivia was going to bring her mother's ticket in her pocket to sell it outside the stadium, but with all the excitement she forgot it at home. One hundred and twenty dollars down the drain.

At last they got to the booth, where the promoters were practically having the t-shirts ripped out of their hands by the crowd.

"Not one person is leaving this restroom without the t-shirt on," one of the team, a beautiful young woman, jokingly threatened.

"Bring more t-shirts!" ordered one of her colleagues from the other side of the crowd.

She was six feet tall and stood out from the other girls begging for a t-shirt, amongst them Olivia who was on the verge of getting knocked to the floor. Even so, she struggled on, gritting her teeth in determination and giving her the strength to shoulder barge any girl who tried to push ahead of her. They were all packed together like a rush-hour commuter train, but no one was complaining.

"The restroom is full. Let it empty a little and I'll give you all the t-shirt so you can get changed. There are plenty for all," said one of the promo girls calmly, trying to get people to take it easy and stop pushing.

At last, five minutes later, it was Olivia's turn.

"We'll wait for you here," Mercedes said, and Gabriela's expression changed to relief.

Mercedes was about to identify herself and ask the promotional team to let Olivia straight through. Technically she was paying their salary, so she could in theory ask for that favor. *Thank God it wasn't necessary*, thought Mercedes as she looked at her accomplice Valeria with a joyful expression at the apparently resounding success of the promotional campaign they had developed together.

"I'm going to take a look at how things are going at the other entrance," Valeria said to Mercedes, saying goodbye with a kiss.

"Enjoy the concert!" she said to Gabriela, pinching her cheek.

The girl responded more mischievously than expected for her age:

"You too," and she winked.

She obviously knew about James' return and the plans for the private box.

Meanwhile, James was on the verge of a nervous breakdown. The flight attendants had already asked him to sit down several times because he kept pacing up and down the aisle of the plane, goose stepping like a German storm trooper.

"Sir, you are making the other passengers uncomfortable. Please take your seat," one of the flight attendants told James during the flight back to Chicago.

Unfortunately, sitting down would not solve his problem. James fidgeted in his seat, tried to get comfortable, bumped the seat in front with his feet while his mind ran amok. He lowered his tray table to rest the inflight magazine on it to pass the time with a crossword, but he regretted the decision and put it away again. All of this to the horror of the passenger in front of him who kept flinching every time one of James' abrupt motions bumped his back or rear end.

"Sir, you must calm down. You are making all the other passengers nervous. Is there something I can do for you?" asked the flight attendant.

Bakran replied for him.

"It's nothing a nice girl like you can't solve."

She did not hide her aggrieved expression, but before she could reply, Bakran went on:

"But don't even think about it, this one is practically married. He's on his way to his promised one who he hasn't seen for thirty days. That's what's making him so anxious. He's desperate to see her!"

"That all sounds very nice and everything, but we still haven't arrived to Chicago, so please promise me he will calm down. If not, I will be forced to report him to the Air Marshall," said the flight attendant.

This time she spoke in a firm and direct voice straight at James, and gave Bakran an angry look as she moved away.

"Nothing you can do. We just have to wait until we land to alert Valeria," Bakran assured him firmly.

"Why didn't we open it earlier?" he asked in an attempt to deal with his anguish.

"Because it was delivered late, we almost missed the flight, and we had no choice but to read the results on the plane," replied his companion.

James ran his hand through his hair, and lowered his head to his knees in desperation. Bakran attempted to calm him down.

"We did a lot. We delivered Paco and Ana to the agents who will look after them in London. We asked the Canabal brothers to take the fabric and the ink to a testing lab and to send us the results as soon as possible."

"How many people go to those concerts, Bakran? Ten thousand? Twelve thousand? Twenty-five thousand?" he demanded.

The moment they were given permission to use cell phones inside the cabin, James desperately called Valeria, aware that his time was running out.

"James? Have you arrived darling?" she answered her phone, unable to contain her excitement.

But she could not hear his reply.

Valeria was in the main entrance corridor to the stadium and she was hurrying amongst the crowd. As the concert was about the begin, the young people were all desperate to try to get in, so she was surrounded by thousands of youngsters who had arrived at the last minute and were in a big, big rush.

"I can't hear you James, you're breaking up."

"Sweetie, I need you to cancel the t-shirt promotion."

"What?... Speak up," Valeria yelled in all the racket.

"Don't give out the t-shirts!"

"I can't hear you, my love."

"Vale, listen… there's a problem with the t-shirts."

"Everything has gone really well with the t-shirts, darling. Thanks for asking. Come soon and you can see for yourself."

"The t-shirts are infected! The t-shirts are infected with MRSA!" James screamed, repeating the same sentence over and over again.

Valeria was not sure if she had heard correctly. She was petrified, processing the words when a group of people walking next to her surrounded her due to the bottleneck as they all arrived at the entrance. There, in amongst all the people, Valeria replayed in her mind Josh Cosgrove's insistence on making t-shirts for the campaign; she thought of everything she had read about MRSA and the fact that Latinos and Blacks were most vulnerable to infections; she remembered when Josh suggested starting the series of concerts with a fashionable Latino band and how Mercedes had told her that she knew nothing of a clothes manufacturer in Puerto Rico and that she had never spoken to Josh about it.

She remembered all of those conversations as the wave of people she was caught up in swept her along. The movement was too abrupt and the telephone slipped from her hand. Another push from behind and the people pressed around her prevented her from seeing where the phone had gone. The security guards began blowing their whistles and yelling:

"Don't push, everybody will get in."

Valeria screamed over the noise and voices for the people to give her phone back. She saw it caught between the shoulder of one boy and another girl's back. It was wall to wall with bodies, and in that crowd her cell phone almost seemed to be floating through the air.

"I can't help you, my arm is stuck. Try to reach for it," said the boy right in front of her, who Valeria was involuntarily rubbing her breasts against.

Valeria raised her arm little by little by pressing her body against the boy's back to make some space. When her arm finally reached the boy's shoulder, the phone slipped again and fell. Valeria moved suddenly to try to reach it, but that was the worst thing she could have done.

People were still pushing, and since she was beginning to lean down, she became stuck in that position, with the top of her head touching the waist of the boy in front. Her exposed buttocks raised as if expecting a caning were pressed against the handbag of a girl behind her. Her back was parallel to the floor, as if she were some kind of table. All she could see were the shoes and ankles of everyone around her.

Valeria started to shout and push to make some room to stand up, but she was stuck fast. She was at the mercy of the crowd who were moving her body at will. She screamed louder, but no one did anything to help her up. They kept pushing until she felt sure they would snap her neck at any moment, and she totally lost her sense of direction. She was beginning to struggle for air, and felt like she would pass out, but the only thought in her head was that she would die crushed if she fell to the floor, so she put all her effort into remaining on her feet.

Just when she thought her strength would abandon her and that the pain in her neck was intolerable, a stranger's hand grabbed the back of her shirt and with a firm pull straightened her up. One of the guards at the entrance had seen her predicament as the crowd that had trapped her went past him. He pulled her towards him and against the wall and placed his uniformed body between her and the crowd. He placed his arms around her as a barrier, protecting her from further harm.

"Are you alright?" the guard asked seeing how pale she looked.

Valeria's pulse was racing, she was gulping for air and had broken into a cold sweat as if she were suffering from a drug addict's withdrawal symptoms. She was stunned and did not know what to say, so she simply nodded her head and rubbed her neck.

That was when the concert began. The lights dimmed, the floor began to shake. The cheering began and rose into a cacophony of excited fans that deafened Valeria and the security guard. Thousands of people screaming with pleasure was a wonderful sound when your adrenalin was at their same level, but when you heard it from the outside, the feeling was not the same.

"Everybody!" yelled the singer with his arms outstretched as if he were hanging from a cross, as he encouraged the crowd to sing with him.

Thousands of voices replied "Hey, hey, hey," while they jumped and raised their arms to the sky. The singer swung the mic stand in front of him as if it were a spear and ran from side to side of the stage like a child trying to race to the finishing line before his friends can beat him. The audience responded. Vibration, group ecstasy. Huge doses of Dopamine and Oxytocin were given free range in thousands of young bodies who were feeling the euphoria of music flowing through them, annihilating their inhibitions.

"You… are deadly… mortal," they all sang the first song in chorus. It was the big hit of the moment.

Chapter 26

Valeria snapped out of her stunned state and ran down the corridor of the stadium towards the merch booth.

"How many t-shirts did you give out?"

"All of them," they replied proudly, and waited anxiously for their boss' congratulations.

Valeria ignored them and ran on, this time to the other merch booth.

"How many t-shirts did you hand out here?" she rushed to ask gasping for air.

"All of them," came the reply.

Under other circumstances this answer would have made her jump for joy, but now it was as if she had been hosed down by the fire brigade.

"My God! All those kids!"

Valeria spun around and ran back down the now empty corridors of the stadium, and rushed up the stairs to the private boxes. She had to arrive at the top fast, so she jumped up the stairs two by two.

"Mercedes, lend me your phone," she screamed in her friend's ear when she got to the box reserved for pharmaceutical employees, which was full of some of MagMell staff members with their children, spouses or best friends. Valeria looked around for her client until she located him.

Josh Cosgrove was elegantly dressed in a suit as usual, and enjoying the show in company of his family. His wife looked beautiful in a golden lame pant suit that made her stand out from the rest of the guests.

"How different can two siblings be?" Valeria said to herself for a moment, as she looked at James' sister.

She was only worried about appearances, money and social status. James worried about the world and common welfare.

Dean was also in the box, the only son of the pharmaceutical company's President. The boy had James' eyes, and his uncle doted on him and longed for him to turn out like him. Gabriela, Dean's classmate who had a crush on him, was standing next to him and they were both singing *Amuleto Rojo*'s songs together, which was making the girl immensely happy. Dean was wearing a classic Mötley Crüe t-shirt under his black leather jacket.

Obviously, neither Josh nor his family are wearing the promotional t-shirt, thought Valeria as she headed towards her client. Once she got to him, she slowly came closer to the side of his face and gritting her teeth and trying to seem jovial for the benefit of everyone around them, said:

"Josh, what happened? Didn't the t-shirt look good on you? Why didn't you put on the ones I sent to your office? There were plenty for all, for you and your family."

"I didn't have time to pick them up. You know how it is: do as I say but not as I do. Dean was really upset about not getting one."

The boy grabbed Valeria by the arm to pull her down to his level, and told her in her ear to make sure she heard:

"I'm counting on you to get me one of those t-shirts before the concert ends, because if I wait for my dad to get it…"

Valeria smiled and nodded. But that t-shirt would never get to Dean. Not because she wanted to protect him for his parent's benefit. She wanted to protect him because he was James' nephew. *And, with God's help, soon he will be my nephew too. It isn't the boy's fault that his father is a scumbag.*

Valeria left the box towards the internal passageways of the stadium where the walls would absorb the noise, and she hurriedly called James, who answered on the first ring.

"Mercedes?"

"No, it's Valeria," she replied, but before she could explain why she was on her friend's phone, James asked:

"Why didn't you call me sooner? Did you understand what I said?"

"Yes, but all the kids are already wearing the t-shirts. Are you sure they're infected?"

"Yes. Unfortunately. We sent the fabric and the inks to a test laboratory. They are contaminated with MRSA. We already warned the Canabal brothers, the t-shirt manufacturers. They will send their employees for hospital testing tomorrow.

"But how is this possible?"

"They were deliberately contaminated with the inks," James explained.

"Who would think of such a thing?" screamed Valeria, astonished at the news.

"The Cosgroves. Who else?"

"Do you have definitive proof it was them, James?"

"That's what I'm working on."

When she hung up, Valeria felt confused, she did not know what to do. Should she cancel the concert? Announce over the microphones that everyone should take off the t-shirts immediately? Spark a panic that would kill many instantly if they started to run away as if from a fire?

She decided to wait for James to arrive, because he said he was at the stadium entrance and gave her instructions to go back to the pharmaceutical private box and not lose sight of Josh.

But neither Josh nor his family were where she left them.

"What happened to Josh?" she asked Mercedes when she got back to the box which was heaving with overexcited people dancing and singing.

"I don't know," Mercedes replied, with an expression of confusion.

Both women were screaming to make themselves heard. The thundering sound of the music made conversation impossible.

"Dean said they were taking him backstage," Gabriela informed them, having heard everything since she was clasped to her mother.

Valeria did not think twice, and she rushed towards the backstage door. She had a VIP pass, so would have no trouble getting in.

A black limousine pulled up outside one of the entrances to the stadium. The two agents leapt out of the car from both sides, and ran towards a side door to the building.

"It's closed!" Bakran announced.

"No!" screamed James, and he ran full tilt in the other direction with his partner hot on his heels.

Only one door was still open, manned by two employees who thought their job for the night was done. All the fans were inside except for two men rushing towards them. They asked for their tickets, which the men had in their hands.

"You're very late. There isn't much left until the end of the concert," said one of the employees.

"Yes, we know," said James in annoyance, as he hurried the men to validate his ticket.

"As long as they keep singing, we're in time. They usually play their best songs at the end," said Bakran cheerfully to calm down the other employee who was already calling over the security guards.

He did not like something about James' body language, and when James became aware of it, he added with a forced smile:

"Our wives are going to kill us."

Even with this excuse for their rush, the security search took longer than usual for a concert. Both agents felt like they were back at San Juan airport, where they were forced to remove their shoes and belts and empty their pockets. Here in the Chicago stadium, they were nearly strip-searched, but in the end the staff simply ran a metal detector over them very calmly, leaving no part of their bodies unsearched.

They had nothing in their possession to activate the device. They had left all their things, including their loose change and belts, in the limousine that would wait in the parking lot for them until the end of the concert. Anticipating they would be searched, they even left their side-arms, although reluctantly. They still did not have authorization from their superiors to arrest a UK resident on North American territory. For the moment, that was the FBI's job and until the Home Office informed the American authorities that two English agents would be present on official business, their NCIA agent badges were of no real use.

When at last the stadium staff set them free, James and Bakran ran towards the pharmaceutical company's box following the directions that they were given at the entrance. As they came closer to the private boxes area, they began to run into people in the corridors who were drinking champagne and chatting in groups as if they were at a social gathering instead of a rock concert. They had to ask for permission to go through these groups of people who looked at them with questioning expressions: *who are these people?* James and Bakran really did look worse for wear.

Not allowing themselves to be intimidated by their looks of superiority, James quickly opened the curtains to the private box MagMell Laboratories had booked, but an usher stopped them to check their tickets.

After a few seconds of suspense in which James tried to stare through the curtain to spot Valeria, the usher told them they could go through. At first, he could not see his girlfriend. Not even when he fully entered the place. The box was dark and packed with silhouettes. All he had to go on were the spinning lights from the stage to try to identify faces. Every so often a beam of light would wash over the faces and James could see them all, but none of them were Valeria. Josh was not there either. James could not recognize anybody until he finally saw Mercedes hugging her daughter Gabriela, both singing and jumping up and down.

"Where is Valeria?" he screamed, holding Mercedes by one shoulder to make her stop jumping.

"I don't know. She was here a few moments ago."

James went to the railings and looked down at the crowd. They were ants in a giant hole, all moving together, their only task to move in time to the music. They were faceless delirious bodies. He would never be able to spot Valeria from up here. His frustration made him punch the railing separating him from the fans.

"She must be in the restroom," Mercedes said, this time holding his shoulder to calm him down, and she began to look around for her friend.

"Or backstage… she went looking for Josh," Gabriela informed him.

James planted a kiss on the twelve-year-old girl's mouth, and thanked her with a smile that made older women feel ticklish in their private parts. Gabriela started to scream and jump beside her friend Olivia. Her mother, hearing the noise, turned back to the girls thinking that they were excited about the concert, not realizing that her daughter was celebrating her first kiss.

Bakran and James rushed down the stairs, not missing a beat. They were now planning on showing their NCIA credentials when they got to the backstage door so they would be allowed through. As British agents, this should work in the States, or at least take a bodyguard sufficiently by surprise to let them through to the VIP area, although they were not one hundred percent sure the trick would work.

However, it was not the rock band's bodyguards, nor the stadium security that prevented them getting backstage. It was the TV cameras and the thousands of kids trying to catch their attention and get them to film them wearing the t-shirts. The corridor leading to the backstage entrance was completely packed.

"Fuck. Now what?" James exclaimed.

When it was obvious that they would not be able to get past the barrier of excited bodies, Bakran began to bellow, wave his arms, and jump up and down:

"Take off the t-shirts, take off the t-shirts," he roared, and he began lifting them up on both boys and girls alike.

But he did not get to shout it more than twice, because he was immediately brought down by a man who must have weighed three hundred pounds. He was a security guard, and he squashed Bakran's chest against the ground. Bakran could feel a pain in his chest due to the pressure and not having enough space to breathe, but he continued to struggle with the man who was trying to hold him. A hundred pairs of eyes watched the spectacle.

James took advantage of the tumult to make his way in the spaces that formed when the camera stopped filming the kids and turned its attention to Bakran on the floor. A few seconds later he was at the backstage door. As he spoke to the security guard and showed him his badge, he saw Valeria in the distance. His nerves began to get the better of him with the thought of the MRSA bug touching her skin. He could see she was wearing one of the promotional t-shirts, and he began to panic as his breath came in short gasps.

Suddenly, he felt the need to blink several times. He looked towards the crowd. The band were saying goodbye. The lights on stage were going off and the musicians were leaving their instruments and microphones. "Encore, encore," the audience cried for them to return. They clapped, shouted, whistled. All of this while the call for one more song bounced off the walls and the seats. James went on watching them. Thousands of happy youngsters. All wearing identical t-shirts. All the same color, Chartreuse green, like the ones he had seen at the factory in Puerto Rico.

He turned back to look for Valeria backstage. The t-shirt she was wearing was different. It was a different color. It was pink, not green. James heaved a sigh of relief.

The band reappeared onstage and the kids screamed louder than ever. The guitars began to issue feedback in a great torrent of sound. The last song poured out, fast and furious, to the audience's immense joy.

When James at last reached Valeria, he hugged her as if he had not seen her in a year instead of thirty days, as if she had died and miraculously returned to life. And now that Valeria was safe, he could go on with his mission: confront and arrest the Cosgroves.

"Where is he? Damn him!" was James' next question to Valeria in the backstage area of the concert, after interrogating her with the usual questions about how she was feeling and assuring her how much he had missed her.

"I lost him, James. When I got back to the box he wasn't there anymore. I've looked everywhere," she replied sadly, her expression distorted and blushing.

"Alright. We have to warn all these people. Right now, the moment this song is over," he encouraged her.

A heavy sigh from deep down inside showed that he felt he was fighting a losing battle against evil.

"And what are we going to say? That they have to take off their t-shirts? That the pharmaceutical has tricked them and infected them?" asked Valeria, scandalized.

"Yes, precisely."

"Are you sure they're contaminated?" she insisted.

"I'm certain."

Valeria did not doubt him a second longer, as he answered with devastating conviction.

"Do you know that MRSA can survive for up to ninety days on some surfaces?" Valeria asked him.

James nodded his head and replied:

"In this fabric it can live for hours, days or weeks... until it is washed. The bacteria is caught in the fabric and in the inks. The longer these kids have them on, the likelier it is they will be infected."

"Even so, James, we need to think this through rationally. MRSA does not easily enter the body through the pores in our skin. It's not impossible, but..." said Valeria, and to calm down she concluded. "It needs an open wound."

"Ok. And how many of those kids out there do you think have intact skin like a baby's? One out of ten of them will have some cut, Vale, a scrape on their elbow, a laceration on their hand, a cut from scratching themselves too hard, a pimple which burst on their back. How many will maybe injure themselves tomorrow?" James spoke in an agitated tone.

Valeria did not know what to say, for she understood all of this perfectly. A sudden anxiety washed over her. She imagined all the cuts and bruises on the young bodies. They were common at this age. All of them with open wounds. She visualized the MRSA cells, like golden coins, seeking refuge inside the human body where it could store its treasure and expand its wealth.

"What if one in ten of them die when we induce mass hysteria by telling them?" asked Valeria, imagining a stampede of children trying desperately to get out of the stadium.

"Alright. We don't need to tell them the truth, just that they need to give the t-shirts back as they leave so that the promotion is valid."

"They won't believe us. They were all told they needed the t-shirt to win a prize," explained Valeria, visibly defeated.

"We have to try at least," James implored her as he grabbed Valeria by both arms and firmly held her hands to give her strength to band with him in an effort to do everything possible to reduce the possible harm.

What else could Valeria do, but nod in agreement with that statement. Her nature prevented her from not trying. How could she let these young people be the unsuspecting victims of a deadly infection? It had to be attempted.

Chapter 27

The band said farewell for the last time. Now the concert was definitely over, and the lights came up again. Valeria hurried onto the stage, and took the soaked microphone that the singer had left there. It would not be easy to persuade fifteen thousand kids to return their t-shirts, nor to find a new job once she was done because this action would surely kill her reputation.

"EXCUSE ME EVERYONE," she yelled into the mic. "Hello. How did you like the concert?"

Valeria spoke as cheerfully as she could, making a massive effort to control her trembling voice.

"Yeah!" replied the audience, who had already started to leave, but stopped when they heard Valeria's voice over the loudspeakers.

"How did you like your t-shirts?" Valeria asked at the top of her voice, smiling to hide any concern that could be seen on her face.

"Yeah!" the audience replied again.

Now the hard part.

"Well, for everyone who put the t-shirt on today, and had their picture taken or were on camera, go look on the website for the prizes you could win," said Valeria, in the most cheerful voice she could muster.

"Woooooo," replied the excited spectators.

Valeria could feel her adrenalin carrying her along. She had an out-of-body vision of herself up on that stage.

"And here comes the best part," she went on screaming at the top of her lungs, "For all you truly brave people, the ones who really roll with it, you need to give your t-shirts back to us, and we will give you a free ticket to the next concert where you will get another t-shirt and more chances to participate in our prize draws!"

"Yeah!" screamed the audience, even more euphorically, and some of the boys instantly ripped the shirts off.

When the voices died down a little, Valeria went on:

"Please, stay in your seats so the promotional teams can give you your free tickets in exchange for the t-shirts. Please, all promotional teams, report backstage."

James immediately thought: those promoters are going to need to go to hospital as soon as the concert is over.

But the tickets for t-shirts exchange idea was brilliant. *My Valeria is brilliant*.

Many people sat back down again to wait for the swap, but sadly not everyone. James saw entire groups of people begin to leave the stadium, although the vast majority stayed behind. Some girls ran to the washroom to change, but the rest of the women who wanted to win a free ticket and get more chances at winning prizes stayed in their seats and maneuvered with their arms to take the Chartreuse green t-shirts off at the same time as they put their own t-shirts back on without a slip of bra being spotted. It was a maneuver that men cannot understand, but which girls do perfectly. They had plenty of practice… every time they had to change in the car, maybe to change out of school clothes and into something more comfortable if they were on their way to the movies, or to slip into their favorite sports uniform when going straight from school to a game.

Meanwhile, the promotional teams began arriving at the backstage door along with Mercedes who asked in a trembling voice; as if she were afraid of the answer:

"What's wrong with the t-shirts?" and quickly began to give out the tickets for the next concert. The stadium administrators had delivered them to her before the end of *Amuleto Rojo*'s gig as they had been part of the deal: free tickets for the prize draw, although originally they were going to be awarded in an online competition.

"They're contaminated! I'll explain it to you later" answered Valeria in a rushed tone as she signaled her with wide opened eyes to keep on task. While Mercedes issued instructions to the teams, Valeria slowly headed towards James.

"What next?" she asked him, hugging him.

"We pray that the people who left have no cuts or scratches," James replied, as he hugged her back.

"What about Josh?" Valeria suddenly remembered, pulling away for a moment.

James looked at her. With his eyes, he begged her permission to leave her again, now to arrest a rotten executive.

"Let me worry about that," they heard Bakran's voice coming through the backstage door with a firm step even though he was limping.

"With one crushed leg thanks to the eight-hundred pound man? Nice one!" James said as he remembered the vision of his friend squashed by the bodyguard.

"I think he broke it in several places. I'm serious, James. I'm telling you."

"So then you have to go straight to the hospital with the girls from the promo team," his partner ordered him, pretending he was punishing him.

"Whatever you say, captain," Bakran replied with a smile, saluting like a private would salute his commanding officer.

"What about Josh?" interrupted Mercedes, anxious just with the thought of her boss getting away with it.

Ever since she saw Valeria onstage, and heard with shock what she was proposing to the audience, she instinctively knew that something was wrong and that her boss was involved. When Valeria asked James where Josh was only a few seconds earlier, it confirmed her suspicions. Her friend could tell her the details as soon as they left the stadium. In her mind, she was already planing how they were going to give the news to MagMell's board of directors and how to write the press release to alert the public about the danger and urge them to get rid of the t-shirts or at least wash them.

"Josh has nowhere to go," James explained. "Right now there are several FBI agents waiting near his house, and he doesn't suspect we are on his trail. When he turns up at his house, he won't get out again. He will have to wait for me to arrive so he can hand over the proof I need to arrest him. It is in his house, I'm certain of it."

But he should not have banked on it.

"I'll see you in an hour," he said goodbye to Valeria. "I'm going to pay my dear sister a surprise visit."

"The suspect hasn't returned home," James was told by one of the FBI agents parked two houses away from the Cosgrove mansion in the exclusive area of Lincoln Park.

Since they were on American soil, the English agents had to work with their FBI counterparts to arrest Sam and Josh Cosgrove. It was not the first time that NCIA and the FBI had worked together on a case like this. The English agents cooperated with the Americans when they needed help on the European continent, and vice-versa. They exchanged information, intel and resources. Now they were working together on a case that had started as a simple large scale fraud and had escalated into a crime of bioterrorism spreading an unusual bacterium for this sort of attack; MRSA rather than anthrax, smallpox or contamination of food to cause botulism, all tools used in the past as bioweapons.

"What do you mean he's not home?" James asked the agent, confused and astounded. "He must have come back! He's with his wife and son," he insisted.

Agent Gordon had nothing else to reply, only that the house was still empty and Josh Cosgrove had not returned yet.

"I told you that you needed to have eyes on him at all times. You should have assigned several agents to follow him around the stadium," James told him, and cursed all the missed opportunities.

Gordon folded his arms and remained silent. What was done was done. Nothing could be changed now.

"What about Sam Cosgrove?" James asked impatiently.

"Nothing. I spoke to Patterson and McCormack an hour ago and they said there is no movement in the guest house," the agent replied.

The next time that James asked about agents Patterson and McCormack, the answer was that they had been found hanging from two trees at the rear of the Cosgrove mansion.

Sam had been quite pleased to get a chance to use his favored means of killing again. His initiation in human butchery was at age seventeen when he hanged his then girlfriend in the stairwell of her own home, while the girl's parents slept in the next room. He made it look like suicide. It was the first demonstration of his diabolical talent to pass unnoticed.

Every night since they had been a couple, Sam slipped into her room without being detected by her parents. One of those nights, he prepared the whole scenario. He brought a rope and made sure his girlfriend's prints were all over it. They had played at tying him to the bed before making love. She had not been able to properly tie him up; the rope was too coarse, but even so he allowed her to ride him. When they finished, she fell back exhausted on the bed. He asked for permission to go to the kitchen for some water. She did not notice that he took the rope with him.

When he came back to his girlfriend's room, he woke her up and blindfolded her, saying he had a surprise to give her. He lifted her arms, and covered her nakedness with her pajama. He tenderly took both hands and guided her to the first step of the staircase. He put the rope around her neck, lifted her in his arms and gave her a passionate kiss before throwing her into the void, tearing off the blindfold so she would see what she was up against. He was fascinated by the kicking of her delicate feet in the air as she hung from the rope attached to the chandelier on the ceiling above the stairs.

The only ones who suspected that it had not been a suicide were Sam's parents, but they said nothing to the police when they came to interrogate them. They insisted that he had spent the whole night in his room and that he had no strange vices, even though their son Sam loved to play with ropes and make knots ever since he was small. On several occasions, they had found him with a noose around his neck, pretending that he was hanging himself. They took him to the pediatrician, but he washed his hands of the situation telling the parents not to worry, it was just a phase and that all children went through it. Obviously Sam still had not got over that phase and he was much older now.

How he managed to enter the courtyard of the Cosgrove mansion unseen would forever be a mystery to the agents who were watching the perimeter, and a mistake that cost the lives of two detectives who did not see him coming. Sam not only showed a great talent for getting into places, but also for killing. Now nobody knew where he was. He had slipped from their grasp even now that the moon lit up half the night sky with a faint half-light and it was not the best time for someone pursued by the authorities to wander the streets.

The Cosgrove family mansion was a fort made of strong solid stone. It was enormous and majestic with a tall concrete and iron fence surrounding the grounds. Old trees covered the space with shadows and foliage in the summer. In the winter, it was a white castle in a sinister forest made up of desolate tree trunks that looked like scarecrows. Sam could be hidden anywhere in the grounds. Another possibility was that he had gained access to the house itself without being seen. Or maybe he had already left the property without having been spotted, just as he had entered. Everything was possible at that moment, and that was the part that was making James crazy.

While the agents combed through the nearby streets in search of him, Sam Cosgrove walked slowly through the interior of the mansion in the darkness. He knew the house like the back of his hand. The position of each piece of furniture, the angles of all the walls. He did not need a light to show him the way. Sam had repeated the exercise of walking through the darkness on numerous occasions while Josh, his family and his servants all slept, because he liked to jerk off in the leather armchair of the formal living room. The smell of the seat and the feel of the leather on his skin aroused his member spectacularly, so he never bothered to try to get himself aroused in his guest room when he did not have any female company. He went straight to his friendly armchair, got totally naked, and sat back and enjoyed himself.

Tonight, though, he was not planning on pleasuring himself, but on finding the MRSA hidden in Josh's office to take it to a safe place beyond the police's grasp. He continued his walk through the dark until he was past the living room and got to the hallway outside the room Josh used as his office. He moved quickly forward three steps as there was nothing to bump into in this part of the house. But he was forced to stop in his tracks. A flashlight was shining through the window.

They haven't waited for a search warrant, thought Sam, and he ran to hide in the small restroom behind the kitchen, the servant's restroom. He was counting on having plenty of time while the agents sought permission to enter the property, but clearly it had not gone according to plan.

"At least one of the agents doesn't give a rat's ass about the law. It must be James, for sure. I am going to personally give that bastard what's coming to him," he muttered.

Sam pressed himself to the back wall of the restroom to peer out of the tiny window that looked out on the back garden. The weak light of the waning moon lit part of his face and reflected in the sweat glistening on his skin. A handful of beads of sweat appeared on his brow, but Sam did not notice. He was concentrating on getting used to the moonlight so that he could find a clear path between the skeletal tree trunks that would allow him to exit the property without leaving a trace.

He checked his watch. It was 2:24 in the morning. He looked out of the window again. The neighbors were sleeping peacefully. The empty streets would receive with open arms whoever sought a quiet hiding place. Sam bet he would find refuge the moment he crossed the garden and jumped over the concrete fence.

He grabbed the handle and carefully opened the glass window. He paused for a moment to see if it was possible to use that exit. He was thin, but not that thin. Being so muscular was not an advantage in this situation, and he feared for a second that the window would not let him through, that it would not be wide enough for his hips or worse still, his shoulders. His brute force would come to his rescue, of that he had no doubt, even if he had to rip the window frame from the solid rock with his bare hands. However, this turned out not to be necessary.

He slid like a cornered mouse along the walls, without any problems, until he safely set foot in the garden. From then on, not even the best detective in the world would have been able to spot him. In less than a minute he was two mansions away, in the house of a famous musical producer with four daughters from different marriages. The girls did not live at home anymore, but Sam thought maybe one of them would be paying a visit and would like to do him a little favor. From the front, from behind, however she wanted. Sam Cosgrove was feeling accommodating this early morning.

Inside the Cosgrove mansion, everything was still in order. James went to the windows with his flashlight after ignoring the orders and insults of the agents who were working with him that night. A few minutes earlier he had told them:

"I am only going to take a look around for a second. I'm not going inside," although he knew that stepping one centimeter inside the grounds was in itself a violation.

"Just look the other way. If I get in trouble, deport me on the spot and that way you can get rid of me. Besides, it's my sister's house, I can always say I'm just dropping by," he added, and he jumped over the fence with a flashlight in hand.

He almost got what he came for. In the darkness, he stared intensely into the mansion through the window. He switched on the flashlight just as he pressed his face against the glass. His intention was to catch the man hiding within the walls of the house off-guard. He was sure that Sam was hiding indoors after murdering agents Patterson and McCormack. The only reason to risk killing them was that he needed to get something from inside the mansion.

However, James did not get the results he had hoped for. He did not see anyone running. No body frozen in its tracks. No shadow reflected on the walls of the staircase. Not a single agent saw Sam leave the property.

Half an hour later, frustrated with the stakeout, James called Bakran.

"We have to make sure that they do not leave the country."

Chapter 28

On the following day, Bakran was three-thousand nine-hundred and three miles away from James, at a lowlife bar in London that was probably open twenty-four hours against all the laws of the city and above all, the rules of decorum. It was five-thirty in the morning, and the occupants were still drinking alcohol as if it were their morning coffee.

Bakran had been working the Cosgrove case nonstop for hours since he had returned to British soil. He had not accompanied the promo girls to the hospital, nor had he asked for his leg to be examined after getting squashed by the *Amuleto Rojo* bodyguard. Instead, he boarded a plane at O'Hare, reported to his superior's home in London, who had brought him up to date on the advances of the investigation in the empty laboratory, the MRSA deaths at the hospital, and possible connections to Sam in the whole affair. It was his turn to keep James in the loop, and he called him from the tavern.

"We have a transcript of Sam's calls. The younger Cosgrove brother always made sure that the phones at MagMell and at the Cosgrove mansion weren't bugged. Apparently it was more a habit than precaution, because he always checked every phone and he never used cell phones. However, Sam wasn't as careful in London, where he thought he was safe because he didn't have a fixed residence; he kept moving around, or would stay for one night in other people's apartments. He rented one place for only two days, but he made some phone calls from there which could very well incriminate him in the case against him," Bakran concluded.

James listened in silence. He waited patiently for Bakran to finish his report.

"I called a phone in the United States Sam called on two occasions and it turned out that the guy was expecting my call," Bakran said. "Well, not mine specifically, but someone from the authorities. He alleges he is an FDA employee and that Sam Cosgrove bribed him and paid him huge amounts of money to ensure quick approval of a vaccine against MRSA."

"Does he have any receipt of the deposit, any signature of either of the Cosgrove's, or anything we can use apart from his testimony?" asked James, shocked at the criminal audacity.

"He's an informant and he's scared shitless! He still has the case full of money in his house because he hasn't dared to deposit it. And he doesn't want to testify, we are going to have to subpoena him. However, he alleges that he recorded the first conversation on tape, when Sam approached him with the offer."

"How did he do it?" asked James.

"He used a Dictaphone, one of those you buy in office supply stores. The ones journalists use. When a man, dressed in street clothes instead of exercise clothes, came up to him in a gym, he found it suspicious and the moment he began proposing improper acts regarding his job, he turned the recorder on."

"He happened to have it in his pocket?" he asked skeptically. "Who carries a Dictaphone in his pocket?"

"He had it hidden in a towel. You're not going to believe this, but the guy takes it to the gym to record the grunts the weightlifters make. Make of that what you will," Bakran replied.

"No, no, that is not possible!" was James' reaction, and he heard the mocking laughter of his friend on the other end of the line. "And he told you, just like that?" he asked, trying to learn more details.

"Not necessarily. A little coercion was necessary." Bakran admitted.

"I would think so," James replied, smiling to himself.

"I will be back in the States the day after tomorrow to coordinate the delivery of the recording," Bakran told him, returning to a formal tone of voice.

James had nothing else to say. Somehow doors kept closing while others opened. While Sam and Josh hid from justice, the English agents kept obtaining clues, leads and evidence that were gathering such weight in the Cosgrove case that the brothers would remain in jail for the rest of their lives. At least that's what James hoped. He calmed down with the thought that soon everything would fall into place. He went to sleep for the first time in seventy-two hours in agent Gordon's car, who remained with his arms folded like an army Sergeant, as James gave him instructions to wake him up if there was any news.

While James rested, Bakran allowed himself a luxury that he had not allowed himself all night. He joined the morning drunks in a glass of vodka-lemon on the dirty surface of the dark bar that had acted as his office on this not-so-glorious Saturday morning. In less than forty-eight hours he had crossed the Atlantic Ocean not once but twice, and although he had managed to close his eyes for a couple of hours on the plane, his body felt like it had left its spirit in America. At least a couple of his organs no longer seemed to function, and one of them was his brain. He could not think for one second longer about Sam Cosgrove, Josh, MRSA, the laboratory, the deaths, and the concert with thousands of euphoric youngsters, about… he paused mid-thought. He closed his eyes, let his head fall on the documents on the table, a trickle of drool ran from his mouth, and he began to snore.

An hour later he was awoken by the smash of a glass shattering on the floor after being accidentally knocked by a drunk who had been sitting at Bakran's table for thirty minutes without him noticing. It seems that the man was bored at the bar and in total silence had spent half an hour tying knots in the agent's hair, who had not even realized that his head was being fondled, or if he did realize, he must have thought it was his wife's hands. A nudge had ended the fun when the glass of vodka fell to the floor to the surprise of the drunk and fright of the agent.

"Get out of here, you fool," Bakran screamed at the poor man, who only laughed and touched his greyish hair as he backed away looking at Bakran's hair the whole time.

He was looking at an exact copy of his own hairstyle. Now both men were practically twins. The detective's instinct made Bakran react immediately to the man's expression. He touched his head. There they were, thousands of knots in his hair.

"Damn you, damn you," Bakran threatened the man in a rage, as he stood suddenly with his arms ready to strangle the man as soon as he could grab him.

But the drunk's good fortune saved him from being throttled, as the agent bumped the table with his waist, knocking all the papers, documents and photos of the Cosgrove investigation all over the floor.

"Damn it!" Bakran exclaimed as he collected the papers, and he screamed at the drunk: "Get out of here! Don't help me! Get out of my way! Don't you understand that I don't want you to help me?!" and he tore the papers out of his hands.

The drunk continued to assist him collecting the fallen papers until Bakran completely lost it, pushed him towards the bar and screamed at the top of his lungs:

"Just go drink! Drown yourself in alcohol! Drown in your own piss!"

The man was confused by the last order. He looked down at his fly, opened it and began to pee on the floor, almost on Bakran's papers. One photo was nearly bathed in urine, but the drunk himself saved it from that fate by pointing in another direction while he picked it up from the floor, peeing the whole time. His new aim reached Bakran's shoes and socks, who received the warm stream with the expression of an enraged bull. Now he was definitely going to strangle the guy.

However, as he grabbed the stinking man's collar, instead of protecting himself, the drunk began to signal at the agent to look at the photo in his hands. The man was pointing right at Sam Cosgrove's face in the photo; he was visible in the background dressed as a doctor.

Chapter 29

Bakran's story of what had happened to him at the bar with the peeing drunkard was the joke of the day at NCIA offices in London and FBI offices in Chicago and on the streets beside the Cosgrove mansion. All the agents found out at roughly the same time. James could not stop laughing while Bakran told him over the phone and he in turn told the anecdote to his fellow agents.

"My shoes still stink," said Bakran, concluding his tale of the incident.

"I can imagine. Now they're piss-cured leather. Good thing he didn't aim for your face," James said, bursting into laughter again.

"That's not even the worst part, James. The guy was so, so drunk that he couldn't even tell me his name, much less if he knew the man in the photo. The only thing he kept saying was: 'I took that photo, I took that photo'. So I bathed him to get rid of that stench and gave him gallons of coffee so he could tell me his story."

"Wait, wait, what do you mean bathed him? At the bar?"

"Since when is there a shower room at a bar, Nancy boy?" he replied impatiently and went on. "No, I took him to my place. You can guess the rumors that are going to start going round if anyone saw me with him in my arms. 'This man leads an immoral lifestyle and takes advantage of poor drunks.'"

"They think that even if they didn't see you. We already guessed your romantic inclinations even before knowing you took him back to your place…"

"I couldn't give a rat's ass what you and everyone else say about me. I was doing my job," Bakran interrupted with a defensive bark that James found so amusing that he started to bang on the roof of the car as he laughed at his friend.

When he was able to catch his breath after laughing so hard, he asked his partner who was needled with rage on the other end of the line:

"So were you able to get the information you were after once you had your way with him?"

Bakran's patience was now running as dry as a well during a long drought, and he answered as ironically as he was able:

"Yes, you damned SOB, just before coming between his buttocks, he confessed to me that he had taken the photograph in St. Mary's Hospital the day that Miguel died."

After a stunned silence due to what he had said, Bakran continued, now annoyed by the jokes and the wasted time. James stopped himself from continuing to make fun of him. He realized that lack of sleep had put him in a goofy mood and that it was time to forget about the jokes and get back to business.

"The old guy told me how he had met Miguel. He explained that he was a janitor in the hospital, and that Miguel asked him to take his picture, so he took his daughter's digital camera, but since he didn't know how to use it, he started to take pictures in the corridors to see how they came out."

James listened in total silence, his senses at last all focused on the explanation.

"I pointed at Sam in the picture and asked him if he knew that man. He said no, but that at the time he assumed he was a new doctor because he saw him that afternoon in room 1221 injecting medications in the patient's drip. James, you do realize that the other lab employees died in rooms 1221 and 1222?"

"Yes, I read it in the report you sent me," James replied and immediately followed up as his mind was full of questions. "Was this man sure that the doctor who was injecting stuff in their drips is the man in the photo? How can we trust the testimony of a drunkard?"

"That's exactly what I asked him, Nancy boy, and he told me that he had not always been a drunk. He simply explained that after Miguel and the others died, he felt terribly guilty because Miguel kept saying that they were trying to kill him, but he hadn't believed him. When he tried to warn the hospital management and he showed them the photos as evidence of his suspicions of the man in the white coat, they fired him for trying to create a scandal and damage the hospital's reputation. Of course, that wasn't the reason they gave him for firing him, but he knew full well. So with the guilt and the depression over not having a job or feeling useful, he started drinking in his apartment until he lost control. He hadn't known where he was or where he was going for days until our chance meeting at the bar."

"Did he apologize for pissing on you?" asked James, who could not help himself from going back to the jokes.

"No, can you believe it? He said it was my fault, because drunks are very obedient and he was simply doing what I had told him."

When they finished discussing the janitor's testimony, James and Bakran spoke for several minutes more trying to clarify each other's doubts and plan their next move in the investigation. James asked his partner to go and interrogate the hospital administrators to see if they had analyzed the drips. The security camera tapes were already in police custody. They had to find images of Sam Cosgrove amongst all the doctors. James said goodbye:

"Bakran, we cannot lose sight of this witness. I guess you already told him not to leave your side for a single instant?" alluding to the new star witness' comment on the obedience of drunks.

"Do you have a crystal ball or something? That was exactly what I told him before calling you."

After hanging up, James felt a sudden anxiety. All these loose ends were annoying him. So many inconclusive leads. He needed definitive proof that

Josh and Sam were directly related to the lab accident and the infected t-shirts. He also needed a motive. His mind could not come to grips with a single obvious reason for exposing the innocent public to deadly bacteria except for greed. And the notion of money being the sole motive turned his stomach. *How many lives were at the mercy of these selfish egomaniacs?*

He decided it was time to spring into action, to get an immediate answer, but luck was not on his side. There was nothing he could do but wait to directly confront the responsible party. Until then, he had an innocent population to worry about, as well as real victims as he read in the press a few days later.

Five youngsters die of MRSA infections at a Chicago Hospital
The fifth victim was a twelve-year-old girl

Chicago – Olivia Robinson, a twelve-year-old resident of Highland died last night, the latest victim of an MRSA superbug infection (Methicillin-Resistant Staphylococcus Aureus) at the Children's Memorial. The same bacteria took the life of four other adolescents earlier this week. Prior to infection, the girl appeared to be in excellent health. She began to exhibit symptoms such as a high fever and irritation of the skin, just like the other four victims suffered. It is still not known how and where these patients contracted the infection. It is suspected that these are isolated cases and they may have come into contact with the bacteria at their schools or homes. None of the victims had been in a hospital or attended a medical office recently, so the authorities have ruled out MRSA-HA, which is common in hospitals and greatly feared in surgical procedures.

"This is a clear case of MRSA-CA, or in the community. They contracted it outside a medical facility, in their own communities. Usually, in cases like these, as long as the patients do not have a preexisting immunological deficiency, they can be effectively treated. However, it appears that the MRSA bacteria that attacked these youngsters has undergone a mutation allowing it to resist all the aggressive treatments that we employed", explained Dr. Brian McAfee, clinical director of the Children's Hospital, who avoided the question regarding how many MRSA cases are treated at the hospital on a monthly basis.

Hospitals are not required to give information of the number of patients who die of a bacterial infection during hospitalization. Some states have implemented voluntary programs by which hospitals provide this information, but this is not a requirement in the state of Illinois. Some hospitals also require routine MRSA testing of both patients and staff, but this is not common practice yet in hospitals across the United States.

"Testing to see if a patient who is admitted to the hospital has been infected with MRSA is very simple", explained Dr. Jane Phillips, epidemiologist. "All that is required is to run a cotton swab inside the mouth or nose of the patient and analyze these secretions in the lab. In this way, we may prevent the spread of infections to the rest of the population and protect patients who visit our hospitals", Phillips concludes.

Given MRSA's current resistance to antibiotics and the mutations it has undergone, it has become an extremely potent bacterium which is difficult to eradicate from the body once it has entered through cuts, bruises or open skin. The earliest symptoms include a sore or welt on the skin, similar to an insect bite. Approximately 18,000 people die every year due to infections with this bacterium, many more than those who die of AIDS.

The news was read by all the inhabitants of Chicago. The fact that they were such young victims moved the whole city. The expressions of indignation and concern were so intense that it forced the Centers for Disease Control (CDC) and the Government to launch a very aggressive prevention campaign and forced them to issue a press release asking for the population to remain calm as a number of demonstrations took place outside the schools demanding that they be fully sterilized. Twenty-five schools closed voluntarily for cleaning, including Gabriela and Dean's school. Neither of the children would have attended school anyway. She was devastated by the death of her best friend Olivia, the fifth victim, and he had not returned home since the *Amuleto Rojo* concert.

"For several years now there have been sporadic reports about MRSA related deaths, the most shocking one about the athletes from the same school who all caught it and one of them died. Do you remember?" asked Mercedes.

"But every single time, people only talk about it for a few days after rushing to pharmacies and supermarkets to buy hand sanitizer. In spite of the momentary hysteria, people forget about these precautions as soon as the news stops being fresh," Valeria concluded.

"The news comes out, people get hysterical, buy antiseptics, medicines and a week later they've already forgotten their precautions and even the possibility that they could get infected themselves," agreed Mercedes.

"It's an endless vicious cycle," concluded Valeria. "No one wants to think about illness all the time, Merci, that's why they forget about it."

"But no one wants to lose a son, or see their children cry," Mercedes interrupted, wondering how many people had missed the news about the contaminated t-shirts at the concert.

She then looked at her daughter Gabriela from afar, who was in the kitchen with several of her school friends. Their eyes were all red, and with a far-off teary look. They had all gone to the funeral. Twelve-year-olds, all holding hands and hugging each other, crying disconsolately at Olivia's death. It had been a heartbreaking moment.

"First Miguel and now Olivia. How can you console these young spirits who still see the world through rose-tinted glasses, who haven't had their souls corrupted by evil and malice, who don't understand the daily worries and deaths and why things happen. Some of them even blindly believe that adults always have the power to do the right thing, be they doctors, politicians, police officers or the chief executives of large companies. They haven't experienced greed in person, some of them may have felt envy, but not to the point of harming another person. So, Valeria, please tell me, is it fair to burst their bubble at that age?" Mercedes ended her monologue.

Valeria had no idea how to reply to this. She thought of her childhood and how when she grew up she realized, a drop at a time, that as things happened she had been protected from evil by magnificent parents who dressed her in an invisible protective cape so that she would not see the harsh reality. Maybe that's why now she was so cynical about anything to do with social welfare. Maybe she should ask her parents to give her protective cape back again, to see if the love she now felt for James and the hopes to start a family, could make her see the world in a new light.

As they were surrounded by young people, it was inevitable that Mercedes and Valeria would remember their youths and chat a long time about it and how their parents had protected them from the daily concerns. They remembered their own innocence and how they had dreamed, because life was a dream back then: all goals were achievable; there was no violence or abuse. It was a perfect world for two indomitable damsels.

It was clear that the fantasy world they created in their minds for a few hours was the bubble that allowed them to go on living as adults.

The day after Olivia's death, they had no choice but to face reality. The Board of Directors of the Pharmaceutical company had to face the press. Until then, the t-shirt contamination had caused a generalized paralysis amongst the directors, who all shirked responsibility for the affair. First they aggressively threatened litigation and taking Valeria and Mercedes to court according to the provisions of their contract, which prevented them from divulging any information they could have of the incident. Then they called dozens of consultants, lawyers and PR companies to discuss the situation and arrive at an agreement about how to weather the storm and notify the general public about the contamination. Should they say it was accidental? Should they blame the supplier? With their endless meetings and lack of agreement, they left the population unprotected until Mercedes and Valeria took the initiative of going over the Director's head and they drafted a more agressive press release for people to take action against the MRSA infection.

The press release instructed all those people who had attended the concert to take all necessary precautions and visit the city hospitals for a mouth-swab MRSA test. The hospitals had already received warning that they would receive a large number of patients requesting the test and the reason for which they needed to be treated urgently.

After sending the written notice to all the print, TV, radio and online media outlets, Valeria and Mercedes waited in the MagMell Laboratories offices for the journalists to start calling, and thought of the consequences that said press release would have on their professional careers. They did not regret having sent it, on the contrary, as they were saving lives. Even so, a bitter aftertaste remained in their mouths. The idea of losing their jobs was really devastating to them. Just as they were discussing ways of rebuilding their lives if they lost their jobs, such as hiding out in a beach house in Puerto Rico or opening their own Marketing and PR agency, a call from James interrupted them.

"Oh, James," a mortified Valeria blurted out. "Last year a woman died taking part in a competition to win a videogame console, I don't remember if it was a Wii or a PlayStation, one of the two. The thing is that the participants had to drink enormous quantities of water without going to the bathroom, and the woman died of water intoxication. Can you believe it? We laughed and laughed about that in the agency for a whole week, about the poor idiot who had come up with that campaign. Now we are guilty of doing the same thing. We've killed the participants of our own campaign," said Valeria, cruelly mocking herself.

She was tortured by the irony and cruelty of the situation. She tried to lighten the tone so that the rage would not eat her whole. She did not want these abominable events to make her life a living hell.

"You are not to blame," James stated.

"That's not what the agencies will say," Valeria replied impulsively.

"They can say what they like, Vale. When we catch the real criminals, these baseless claims will be forgotten," he said, convinced that his words would relieve his girlfriend's anxieties, at least for five minutes.

Until the Cosgrove brothers were in jail, Valeria and Mercedes' sense of guilt would chase them unremittingly. It would always be lying in wait, less so in the mornings, but by evening it would stalk them mercilessly. They blamed themselves, just like he did in his lonely moments, about not figuring out the evil master plan in time, and not realizing that many of the Cosgrove brother's actions and requests would lead to this catasthophe. It simply did not occur to them.

The moment Valeria hung up, Mercedes said:

"Until now we were thinking about the awful effects of the promotion on our careers, but this runs even deeper, Vale. We have to remember that the campaign was thought up to promote a vaccine. And the vaccine is real, effective and safe. The question is: do I still try to issue the positive message that there is a vaccine against MRSA? As an employee of MagMell, am I part of the cure or the disease? We have an effective vaccine to sell, but our campaign deliberately infected adolescents…"

Valeria interrupted her:

"Merci, we have to set all that aside. What are people going to do? Not get the vaccine? When it comes down to it, people will want to make sure that they won't die, that they won't run the same risk as the children at the concert. They will get the vaccine."

"That's because for now we are the only ones with the product, but at least two other pharmaceutical companies will begin to develop MRSA vaccines. And then what? Which would you pick? The one made by the Pharmaceutical company that killed people? And what about our other medications? This whole situation adversely affects the company's reputation, end of story."

They both fell silent for a moment, thoughtful. Mercedes looked into her mug of coffee. When she looked up she saw that her friend's eyebrows were furrowed.

"I know!" Valeria almost shouted as she jumped up and clapped her hands.

Valeria stood up and began to pace quickly around the office, and her hands began to wave like fans as she said:

"What we need to do is meet with the Board again, and convince them that they can't keep waiting for Josh Cosgrove. They have to begin the damage control campaign without fail. This should include a press release announcing Josh Cosgrove has been fired as President of MagMell. We also need to prepare a full page ad in which the pharmaceutical company takes full responsibility for what happened, and exonerates itself by explaining that these were the actions of an individual and not the company. In other words, distance Josh Cosgrove from the company."

She took a deep breath before going on:

"We need to discredit him and destroy him to the point that when this goes to court, no jury in the world will believe a word that comes out of his mouth."

"I would like to see Josh Cosgrove's face when he sees in the news that he has been fired," Mercedes approved the idea.

"To the first phase of his punishment," said Valeria, as they toasted with their coffee mugs.

That afternoon, Valeria paced around her apartment, still unable to understand why all this had happened. She walked from the kitchen to the living room, from the living room to the bedroom, and from the bedroom back to the kitchen. One single question worried her: what if it hadn't been Josh Cosgrove? What if Sam was to blame for everything and Josh had no idea what his brother was up to?

She called James, who at that moment was paying for a jug of hot chocolate, another jug of coffee, and a whole load of Krispy Kreme doughnuts. He was preparing for a long night outside the Cosgrove mansion. The FBI agents had already searched it. The judge had issued the search warrant, and the servants helpfully opened the doors. However, six agents searched for eleven consecutive hours and came up with nothing. Nothing was found to back up the case. James carried out his own search. He went in saying he was the wife's brother and that he had left something there the last time he had visited. The servants told him that the Cosgrove family was on holiday in Europe, but James knew that was a lie. They had not left the country. They were nearby.

"Sweetie? Is something wrong?" he replied, intrigued by Valeria's call, as they had said goodnight only a few minutes earlier, and he had not expected to speak to her again until the next day.

"James, I'm worried. What if Josh isn't to blame? You do realize that if you're wrong we will be staining an innocent man's extraordinary career. Besides, it will forever affect your relationship with your sister, and you will never see Dean again."

"I've thought of that. A thousand times, believe me, and that's why I'm stationed outside his house. I have plenty of proof against Sam, but only speculations regarding Josh. But I am sure he's involved... I don't have the slightest doubts of that, and the evidence is in his house."

"How can you be so sure?"

"Ah, that's an official state secret," he said laughing to try to ease her frayed nerves. "I have my contacts."

And he certainly did. The perfect contact, he just did not know it yet.

Chapter 30

James' words did not calm Valeria. She continued to pace around the apartment. She pondered the situation. She explored theories in her head as if she was the English secret service agent, instead of her brave lover. In her mind, she interrogated Josh Cosgrove, with extraordinary authority. She insulted him. She said to him: you are a miserable, wretched swine.

Back in the real world, all this mental and physical exercise was causing her a great deal of anxiety and an awful sense of powerlessness until she finally surrendered to sleep. Her internal exhaustion made her blood run cold and quickly paralyzed her limbs. Unfortunately the storms that assailed her once she was in a deep sleep were not wondrous, and they transported Valeria to nightmareland instead, where unlikely fantasies were the order of business and the hours seemed interminable.

In a fluffy world of silk cushions, Valeria saw a woman in the distance dressed in white from head to toe who was jumping from hill to hill and coming closer at an extremely fast pace.

She was a nurse. Valeria realized when she was so close that she barely noticed that the woman had tossed her into a blue lake, but instead of splashing into it, the waters of the lake parted like a huge cliff. Valeria instinctively closed her eyes to avoid feeling vertigo, but opened them again when she felt that her body was hanging suspended in midair like a trapeze artist. She laughed at her new powers, until she noticed she was inside a hospice, where people were waiting for death to come for them.

An ashen body covered in sheets was what told her she was in such a dreadful place. The dying person asked for her help as soon as he spotted her.

He spoke directly to her with a deathly voice, making a terrible effort to hold on to the remnants of mortality. It was Josh Cosgrove, who was resting on a hospital gurney with his chest open, but still conscious and alive. Valeria could barely recognize him with his shipwrecked appearance of a decrepit beggar. She could see the bacteria jumping in and out of his body as if it were at a party. Throbbing music danced in his veins. The bacteria danced mercilessly.

Suddenly Valeria noticed he was surrounded by nurses and doctors who were laughing and mocking him. They pointed at the open wound and prided themselves on having started this party in the dying man's body.

Another nurse arrived.

"Doctor, aren't you going to do anything for him?" asked the new girl seeing the horde of bacteria bouncing on Mr. Cosgrove's open chest.

The doctor she spoke to picked up a syringe and repeatedly stabbed one of the bacteria. After injecting the medications in the first bacteria, he claimed:

"Nothing to be done. It's resistant," and he laughed along with his fellow doctors. "Let's see this one..."

He needled another playful bacterium, but the medication just seemed to tickle it.

"Nope. Also resistant."

The thundering mockery of all present deeply disturbed Valeria, who moved away from the scene. However, even in the distance she could clearly see how the bacteria continued their dance of death and how the doctor tried to catch them and weaken them with a useless antibiotic. The other doctors and nurses jumped and celebrated all the failed attempts.

Behind padded walls, Valeria could hear the hysterical voices of the next of kin of all the patients located at the hospital, each body full of bacteria. Amongst the multitude, Valeria recognized the voices of Josh's wife and her son Dean.

"How can you possibly be allowing him to die? We only brought him to the hospital with indigestion!"

Not a single doctor or nurse responded to their imploring questions. The sober voice of an older woman answered with pity:

"Be strong, beautiful lady, I already lost my husband who came in for a heart operation, and my daughter who had a drop in insulin, and now I lost my ten-year-old grandson who I brought here with a cut on his finger he got while he was riding on his bike. All three now rest in peace because of those deadly bacteria."

In the midst of this cataclysm, Valeria heard a distant voice. She picked it out amongst the chaos. It was Josh Cosgrove, in a begging voice:

"Help me, Valeria."

She was still balancing on the tightrope and instinctively offered her frozen panic-stricken hand. One of the doctors suddenly grabbed her hand before she could touch the nearly deceased man, and said in an accusatory tone:

"Are you going to help him? Make up your mind. Didn't you want this man to pay for his sins? Well, there you have it. We are giving him a dose of his own medicine... time to get even."

The libertine laughter of the doctors and nurses exploded all around her. The impact of the hand and the savage words blurred Valeria's vision for a moment. The entire scene disappeared. She shook her head, and when she was able to refocus she could see that it was James, her dear James, who was now on the gurney and the doctor had become an elegantly dressed Sam Cosgrove with a syringe in hand.

"Close him up," Sam ordered the other doctors. "The bacteria can take care of him now."

Then he turned to her:

"You won't mind being on your own, will you Valeria? You can always hire me to keep you company."

Rage swelled up in her. She wanted to tear apart this insolent man who was capable of such atrocities and prided himself on his ability to pronounce death. She felt the torrent of blood rising and one of the doctors followed his deadly orders and began to sew up James' chest, who was paler with every passing second and seemed to be having hallucinations of eating fish and chips. Valeria prayed heart and soul to Divine Providence to give her the strength to save James.

But her trapeze-artist body was tied to the rope, and she could not free herself however much she struggled against the knots.

"It's unavoidable. Inevitable." said one of the doctors.

"No. It's unbelievable!" replied Valeria.

She watched the doctor's shocking discussion in confusion.

"Wouldn't it be better to leave him open a while longer to let the bacteria continue to have their fun? They're having so much fun," observed one of the younger doctors.

"It's just that my wife is expecting me, and I want to go play golf later. I can't waste any more time," replied the eldest doctor.

From up in the air, Valeria screamed out a question at the top of her lungs:

"Can't you do anything to stop the bacteria from entering the human body? Isn't air conditioning set to a low temperature supposed to contain its spread and that's why hospitals are so cold?"

The older doctor replied that this was only possible in theory.

"The truth is that the only thing that can stop bacteria is sterilization and you can't expect us to be disinfecting all the instruments, beds, tubes, machines, walls, extractor fans every five minutes... imagine that. The janitors would earn more than the doctors! A ridiculous suggestion, don't you think?"

"Well, if the janitors are the ones who will save patient's lives, I can understand that they deserve better pay," replied Valeria still struggling against the restraints holding her arms and legs.

"Very funny!" replied all the doctors and nurses at once.

They mocked her rudely. They laughed until they could laugh no more...

"Very funny!"

"Very funny!"

The echoed repetition of her favorite phrase tore Valeria's soul apart, but when she tried to scream "It's not funny, it's not funny...", her words did not match the movement of her lips and they left her mouth in an unintelligible noise until they were no longer heard.

Seeing she was immobilized in body and word, Valeria began to hurl insults at the nurses and doctors which shocked them, not because of what she said which could not be understood, but because of the vulgarity of her gestures. Then, they turned their backs on her to direct their final attention to James. They closed his eyes and covered his lifeless body with a white sheet that fell from the ceiling like a parachute.

Right then, the hospital administrator entered the hospice dressed as a priest and he absolved the doctors and nurses.

"I purge you of all blame," he said to each one, as he made the sign of the cross on all their foreheads.

Valeria could feel she was plunging into a mirage of unacceptable revelations and she struggled again with the rope holding her feet, at last freeing herself. She fell hard against the floor of her apartment. She woke up with her eyes shot with tiredness and her speech impaired. She remained awake with her eyes closed thinking of the meaning of her dream and a strange sensation of having witnessed a harsh reality.

As soon as the light of dawn peeked through the curtains, Valeria returned to Mercedes' home and spent several days with her to have some company to help clear her head of all those negative thoughts.

Chapter 31

Just as James was finishing his first coffee of the day, the call came in from Agent Gordon which forced him to redirect his thoughts away from the mortification he had felt all night regarding Valeria's claim of Josh Cosgrove's possible innocence.

"Agent Penton. Several trucks are arriving. They are delivering champagne, catering, and so on. It's as if they were preparing for a party," informed Agent Gordon, who had returned to his surveillance post facing the Cosgrove mansion after taking several hours' rest.

"Is Mr. Cosgrove or his family there?" asked James, stunned.

"No, sir, we have not located them. We have clearly seen each member of the delivery staff entering the house, but none of them are Mr. Cosgrove or his wife."

Hours later, James received another call as he was watching the rear of the house while Gordon and two other agents waited at the main entrance.

"Twenty limousines have just pulled up. All at once, one after another in a cavalcade. Each one is carrying six to eight people in evening gowns and tuxedos. One of the limousines was carrying the Cosgrove family. Josh and Sam Cosgrove are now in the house, along with about two-hundred guests.

"Damn them!" he shouted and threw the phone on the floor.

The last thing James was expecting was for them to throw a party. When they arrived with two-hundred guests, in other words hostages blissfully unaware of the danger they were in, they had the perfect human shield to allow the Cosgrove's to search for what they needed.

"Damn them a thousand times over! Get me a tuxedo. Now!" James ordered, and he jumped in the car to head towards the main entrance to the mansion.

Nothing is going to stop me from entering that house, he thought, although the tuxedo never arrived, or at least James was not patient enough to wait for it.

Because of his curly hair, his intense brown eyes and his six-foot physique, James Penton was not a man who went unnoticed. However, that night, amongst men dressed in tuxedos and looking like penguins and their partners with glittering sequins even on the heels of their shoes, it was his clothes that gave him away. He entered the Cosgrove family party dressed in ordinary clothes, with his casual pants, loafers and long sleeve shirt. He left his gloves and coat at the entrance with the butler, and entered the party as if he were modeling for Armani.

His sister greeted him after only ten paces.

"This is a private party, my dear brother," she explained through gritted teeth so that no one else would hear her, and she led him to the kitchen. A pleasant aroma of spices perfumed the air, while the cooks and busboys mingled in a seductive dance amongst the pots and pans and the shining trays, knives, wine glasses and beers.

One of the cooks, with knife in hand, looked up and examined James up and down. James moved amongst the service staff, barely giving any of them a second glance, but still looking at all of them. Instinctively he made sure that his gun was unnoticeable so that no one could take it, in case one of the cooks was more than just a master chef but also a disguised bodyguard.

When they reached the other side of the kitchen, he told his sister:

"I have a meeting with Josh. He's expecting me. Can you tell him I am here?"

The elegant woman's expression morphed dramatically from an expression of surprise to concern. The erratic behavior of her husband over the past few days had alerted her that something strange was going on, and her brother's tone of voice indicated to her that this was not exactly a friendly conversation with his brother-in-law.

She moved closer to James, and hugged him tight. She had not hugged him like that since she had left home to marry Josh. James expected the worst. His sister was going to beg, to plead for him to leave, to not get involved in their lives, to leave them alone. The same thing she had yelled at him when he tried to intervene to stop her from marrying so young, persuaded by empty promises of love.

"Destroy him, James, and his brother too," she whispered in his ear, and she pushed away as violently as she had hugged him a few seconds earlier.

She turned her back on him, grabbed a glass of champagne from one of the trays, made a huge effort to appear to be having fun, and made a beeline straight back to the party.

It was not that he needed her permission, but having his sister as his ally made the agent feel like he was in control of the situation. He pushed hard on the kitchen door, and looked at each and every guest at the surprise party. They were all important people pretending to have important conversations. Politicians, the Presidents of companies, businessmen, admirers of Josh Cosgrove's work... marionettes dressed up in elegant disguises.

Their eyes met at the same time. Josh and James, brothers-in-law, looked at each other across the room. Josh and James, enemies, walked slowly closing the distance between them. Josh and James, criminal and cop, about to face off in a war of words. Their glacial mutual examination froze the blood of all who noticed the situation.

Josh was a powerful and elegant presence in his perfectly tailored dark jacket and his five-hundred dollar Italian shoes. Not a care in the world. Calm. Arrogant. Explosive. His body seemed to inflate, the veins in his neck became visible, and his shoulder muscles seemed to broaden.

Seeing his airs of grandeur, James felt shivers running up and down his spine. He had been meditating for a week on what he would say to the Cosgrove brothers when he finally had them. He fantasized with burying a knife into the younger brother's neck to make the pharmaceutical company's president confess his crime. But he could not see Sam anywhere, even though he was examining the room with great care.

Josh continued to advance into the room, and as he arrived at a column he turned away, looking at James the whole time and inviting him to follow him. They arrived almost at the same time in front of great oak double doors, with eccentrically carved wood panels. Beyond the doors was an office, library and bar, all in one room. On a table between two sofas were several books, amongst them Racing Style – A tribute to Goodwood, the legendary English racing venue, which rested in a case made of authentic Michelin rubber. To one side of the room stood a retractable screen and digital projector, and small noise-cancelling Bose loudspeakers were strategically placed near the sofa. It would have been a perfect bachelor pad for any wealthy young man if it had been in a downtown building. Here, in the Cosgrove mansion, it was the owner's man cave.

This was the first place that James had searched days earlier when he went into the house seeking the evidence he so desperately needed. The agents also spent a long time looking in the office, as if to refute the theory that the police never search in the most obvious place. Now James was back within the elegant walls of the office.

Josh sat down at the monumental writing desk. It dominated the rear of the room, and two French doors from floor to ceiling flanked his position. He leaned forward in the chair and placed his elbows on the desk. His palms remained open, extended, as if stroking the polished wood. In that posture, Josh looked like the President of the United States talking to the White House Chief of Staff. James felt a repugnance and indignation irritating the walls of his stomach.

"I have several questions for you," he began the battle before allowing his repulsion to make him lose his cool.

He remained standing at a certain distance, in the middle of the room. His brother-in-law had not invited him to sit down, although James would have refused the offer in any case. He was not there to socialize. He was not there on family business, and Josh knew this well.

"Go ahead. I hope your questions are important enough for you to have come here without showering, eating and virtually without sleeping," Josh replied, placing particular emphasis on James' appearance and alluding to the fact that he knew he had been parked outside his house for days.

The agent's first impulse was to say: "You are under arrest for being a son of a bitch, for being a bad father and husband, for making my girlfriend and her best friend have nightmares, but above all because you're guilty of an indefinite number of suspicious deaths related to a microscopic bacteria you used as a deadly weapon."

But he could not say that. He could not arrest Josh, just ask him to go to the police headquarters for questioning. If he were in England he could arrest him without a warrant. But in the US, he needed an arrest warrant, and he expected Agent Gordon to come in with one any minute. In the meantime, James needed validation that Josh was involved in the crime, since all the evidence that he had was circumstantial. And he was too impatient to wait for the warrant so he could take Josh in and try to extract a confession. He wanted to do it here and now, so he did. Afterwards Gordon could repeat all his questions at the police precinct, read to him his Miranda Rights and get his confession on tape. For now, he would consider it just an informal conversation between brothers in law.

"Where do you keep Dr. Francis Fowler's lab results, and the Petri dishes with MRSA?" asked James unhesitatingly.

He did not have time to beat about the bush. It was best to go straight for the jugular, no bluffs.

Josh shook his head and laughed out so loud that if the oak doors had not been so thick, it would have been heard throughout the house.

"James, James," Josh began to say as he stood up and walked towards the bar. "Something to drink? Whiskey? Wine?"

"No, thanks," he replied, and added. "Just in case, it was not a joke. Answer the question."

"I could have answered that question at the office, or any director of the board could have told you. MagMell does not have, nor has it ever had, any link to Dr. Francis Fowler's studies," Josh said.

Before James could reply, he walked to the middle of the room, poked him in the chest with his index finger and asked:

"Why have you interrupted a private party at my house? I am speaking to you because I thought you had a personal question to ask me, maybe about how to please a woman in bed."

If James could have seen himself in a mirror, he would have seen himself turn bright red for a second, after which his face slowly mottled and drained of all color, turning an ashen gray. He could not believe the arrogance of the man standing before him.

While he changed color, Josh took his seat again, and sipped his drink, not looking away from James' chest for a moment. He seemed to be inspecting a target, measuring the distance he needed to finish him off with a single bullet. James experienced a moment of concern: could he respond to an attack if Josh decided to produce a weapon?

He knew that Josh Cosgrove did not have a weapons license, but this had never prevented the bad guys from using them without the slightest qualms, so James could not be sure that his brother-in-law did not indeed have a gun close at hand. A few days ago there was nothing in the desk, but that had been a few days ago. Now, today, in this very moment, Josh could have a gun strapped to his leg and he would have no way of telling until it was too late.

James trusted his training, his years of experience and pushed all worries aside. There was no way Josh would be quicker than him unless he was practicing daily at a shooting range.

"Any other questions?" Josh Cosgrove fired off as he took another sip.

"Why did you contaminate the t-shirts at the concert?" James countered pitilessly.

Josh put his glass on the desk. His expression gave away the fun he was having, and after a pause that felt like it was several days long, he said:

"Every so often there needs to be an epidemic. Something to wipe out a great proportion of the population. If it's not war, then it's disease. This is the way the world balances itself out. It has been like that throughout history. Medicine and technological advances in this sense have dramatically altered that balance. There are too many people out there. Soon there will not be enough resources for all of them. The Earth was not made for such large and demanding populations. Extermination is necessary… so the Pharmaceutical companies are basically doing you a favor. We kill off a few people here and there. We cure others here and there. In any case, we can't protect the whole world. For us, they are bodies without faces, just numbers, just dollar signs. Who's turn was it this time? Oops, bad luck… it's a roulette."

James could not believe his ears. With one single question, Josh Cosgrove had gone off on a monologue of global domination. Of absolute superiority. *This self-indulgent man is playing at being God*, thought James, and he said "God" out loud.

"Even God destroys every once in a while to make sure we don't forget about Him," Josh explained with a victorious expression, although he had not been asked anything.

James' fury was unparalleled, and he initiated a massive attack against his enemy, whom he now considered the devil incarnate.

"Are you making fun of me, or are you for real? Are you trying to tell me that this is a conspiracy, just like that theory that AIDS was created in a US Government lab? Are you trying to tell me that Pharmaceutical companies deliberately kill their clients? That there is a consortium that meets every year to agree on what disease can better balance the world population for the next few months? Do you seriously expect me to believe that?"

"We are all free to believe in whatever we choose," said Josh parsimoniously, and he did not wait for his brother-in-law's reply before going on. "My dear James, do you think that what happened with medication production in China two years ago, when they discovered they were producing sugar pills instead of medications, was just a bunch of little China men trying to make money? Who do you think financed that, James? How do you think they could copy the packaging, the labels, and duplicate the pills in such a short period of time. Less than two months after a new medication was on the market, the Chinese operation had its placebo counterpart. Do you think that's a coincidence? That the Chinese are just cleverer than everybody else?"

"Obviously not, but…"

"Of course not, my dear friend," Josh went on, drowning him out. "It's all just business, the law of the jungle. People die every day even though they're religiously taking their pills. Why do you think that happens? With all the research labs working around the clock all over the world with hundreds of scientists and doctors working for them, don't you think that in the past fifty years we shouldn't have been able to achieve much more, unless you think our generation of scientists are morons? All of that progress in medicine from 1900 to 1950, with new vaccines, medications. Why don't we have a cure for AIDS yet? Or for cancer? We discovered cancer over fifty years ago. Do you think we just get stupider with each passing year? Don't you think fifty years is long enough for scientists to find more cures?"

"Are you telling me that all scientists are part of a conspiracy?" interrupted James, more to stop his head from spinning than to get a reply.

So many questions fluttered around his mind and were driving him mad. In a fraction of a second Josh had disarmed him, made him doubt the system and cancelled out his values and beliefs. His confusion was written all over his face, a detail that Josh had well noted and he had taken advantage of James' moment of uncertainty to go on with his dissertation.

"What I'm telling you, James, is that certain people in positions of power and responsibility are able to silence the efforts of the scientific community. All you need is an informant in every laboratory carrying out small acts of sabotage. We call them the Special Unit, the same way the FBI has its special forces working on secret or complex cases. We have one of those units too."

All of this sounded highly unlikely to James. *It couldn't be true, or could it?* He had to clear this up once and for all, so he said:

"Are you telling me that the Pharmaceutical companies are part of this alleged consortium to prevent scientists from finding cures?"

"No, James, I am telling you what you want to hear…"

A long and bitter pause stopped the conversation for a few seconds.

"You want me to tell you I am guilty. That the Pharmaceutical companies are to blame for those people's deaths. That is what the whole world wants to hear. To find a scapegoat for all the ills and injustices of the world, and so the Pharmaceutical companies must be to blame. They are so powerful, they must be to blame, right? Isn't that what you want to hear, James?" Josh asked, fascinated by the expression of perplexity that crossed James' face, who could not help but turn away from him to avoid facing him.

However, James figured it out at once. Josh had played him with doubts and guesses. He had challenged him to believe all the conspiracy theories he had heard hundreds of times in offices, on TV or anywhere that people spoke about the causes and reasons for the daily deaths of loved ones. His mind wanted to believe, because it was easier to pretend that it was all the work of a malevolent entity rather than a natural event.

When James did not reply, Josh went on:

"I know why you came here tonight. You want me to tell you that MagMell Labs, and therefore by extension, I am guilty of the deaths of those poor children who trusted us and ended up contaminated with a deadly bacteria."

"Are you denying any participation in the matter? Are you denying that your plan consisted of creating an epidemic so that the government would have no choice but to change their minds and move to make MagMell's MRSA vaccine mandatory in the shortest possible time?" James asked, this time coming over to the desk and facing his brother-in-law head on.

Slowly and inexplicably, he saw the hostility in Josh's face vanish. The iron curtain came down.

"No, James. In truth I am still responsible for those deaths. I was the one who requested the t-shirt campaign. But from that to being guilty of contaminating them are two different matters."

The tiniest shadow of a doubt overcame James, and left him speechless for a few minutes after Josh' confession that he had not known about the MRSA contamination prior to the concert. Before entering the Cosgrove mansion that night, James had been certain that his brother-in-law was the mastermind behind the plan to infect the audience with the t-shirts. His hypothesis was clear. If he had written the justification, it would have gone as follows:

"In the past decades, the pharmaceutical market has been diluted to such an extent that their managers have had to search for ways to reinvent their business model. Given that they have lost their market since they no longer have the backing of patents, now they seek other ways to use medications. If medicines were previously only prescribed for children, they are also sold today for adults and vice-versa. Instead of targeting the adult market, other companies return to discontinued markets such as vaccines. This is the case of MagMell Laboratories and their President Mr. Josh Cosgrove, who arrived at the conclusion that he had to provoke mass hysteria and cause deaths by MRSA bacterium to increase demand for the vaccine they had developed and force the government to take immediate action to classify it as mandatory."

Before his conversation with Josh, James had no doubt that this was the truth of the matter. His theory indicated that Cosgrove had deliberately infected the t-shirts so that demand for the MRSA vaccine would be so great that in one fell swoop he would rescue his company's ailing finances.

"Why did you go to Cairo to buy the fabric?" he went on with his interrogation.

"Because I had an argument with your sister that week and I decided to go with Sam as a last minute thing. And I don't regret it, I must admit. After disappearing off to Cairo for several days, your sister was as gentle as a kitten when I got back."

"What about Puerto Rico?" he went on implacably, ignoring the reference to his sister.

The mere idea of her lying beneath Josh Cosgrove made him sick.

"I love going to Puerto Rico. I go every chance I get. I go to the factories, I eat an *alcapurria* at Piñones, I come back with a tan. Your sister hates it. She says the humidity makes her clothes stick to her skin. She only came with me once," said Josh between sips of his whiskey, as if he were chatting with a best friend about his favorite vacation spot.

"How do you think the MRSA got into the t-shirts?" James pressed him to capitulate and take the conversation seriously.

"Either the ink or the fabric," said his brother-in-law, certain that he had hit the nail over the head. He went on: "One of the two must have been contaminated. There is no other possible explanation."

"Josh, you delivered the ink... and the fabric," James reminded him, raising his left eyebrow and firing an accusation between the lines.

The glass of whiskey remained on the desk, out of Josh's reach who no longer seemed interested in the alcohol.

"Yes, but I didn't test it for MRSA before delivering it. Who would do that?" he answered at last, after a long pause.

"You, and your brother. You prepared the inks at the Leinster Place laboratory in London. I have a witness. A survivor."

James tried to push Paco and Ana out of his mind. He did not want to make the mistake of giving their names away, nor tell him that they were safely hidden in a little hotel in London waiting for news of the arrest of the Cosgrove brothers. He did not want to run the risk that Josh's malice would take over his thoughts and extricate the information as to Paco and Ana's whereabouts. Josh's reply, however, left him stunned.

"We don't have any labs at that address, James. We have four offices in England, and many laboratories around Europe, but none of them are in Leinster Place in London. Isn't that a residential area?"

James looked Josh in the eye and tried to tell if he could spot the shadow of a lie in his pupils. The only thing he could see was the color draining from his cheeks and a lump forming in his throat and travelling slowly along his trachea. Josh was nervous for the first time in the conversation. It was the moment to bring him down.

"You had to do it, didn't you Josh? It was your responsibility, you had to respond to your investors. Everything depended on you and the success of this new MRSA vaccine. Your future, your family's future, your employee's future. Were you that desperate?"

"We live in desperate times. People do what is necessary to survive," replied Josh, now as tame as a pigeon incubating its eggs.

His gaze fixed on the middle distance, towards the door to the office behind his interrogator.

James managed to stop himself from swearing at him. He remained in silence and tried to control his rage. But he was unable to do it. He slammed his fist on the table and screamed at Josh:

"Coins!"

Both men remained still, staring fixedly at each other's serious expressions. James calmed down a little and said:

"Under a microscope the MRSA bacterium looks a little like gold coins. Don't you think that's marvelous? Like a metaphor for your greed. All for money."

Silence enveloped the room again. Only one question remained in the air: *"Were you that desperate?"*

"I am neither desperate nor guilty of the greed you accuse me of," Josh replied to the invisible question. "I took action. I have put my company in order. I have revised priorities. I have restructured the company. Moreover, the mere announcement that we had developed an MRSA vaccine made our shares go up fifty percent. And I repeat and I insist: I gave no instructions to open a lab in London, much less in Paddington. Someone is yanking your chain, and it isn't me."

There was no time to go on chatting. Sam Cosgrove's unmistakable voice floated into the room from the oak doors.

"How come I wasn't invited to this little party?"

The man had intervened in the conversation just as the lump had formed in Josh's throat: in fact, he was the reason for it. But James had not noticed the connection, thinking that he simply had his prey cornered.

Now Sam was inside the office, dressed in a tuxedo similar to Josh's, and a demented smile on his lips. Both men were petrified, as happened in ancient times, in the intense minutes before duel. Unfortunately only Sam was holding a weapon.

Josh broke the ice:

"I invited you, but you disappeared."

"I followed your suggestion to have some fun, relax, and that's what I've been doing this whole time with McGovern's wife," said Sam, smiling like a buffoon.

"You're an animal, Sam," said his brother, ignoring James' presence.

"This time I obeyed all the rules of etiquette, and I asked Mrs. McGovern straight out if she wanted to taste my balls. She accepted the invitation, so I really don't see what the problem is."

The exchange between brothers had turned embarrassing, and James felt like he was in the middle of a couple's argument. Sam proceeded with his cascade of improper revelations, intimate details of his maniacal love for the perineum, while Josh tried to silence him with the discretion that governors use when one of their special advisors is about to give a political secret away. James decided that this was the moment to leave the room. He forced himself to forget that Sam was holding a gun.

But Sam had not lost track of the situation. He poked the gun into James' ribs the moment he tried to leave the room through the same door that was now beginning to swing open from outside. The three men looked at the open gap to the outside, and heard the music and voices from the adjoining room. A young hand appeared around the door, and gently kept pushing it open. Simultaneously, the men in the office held their breaths. All the voices from the party next door faded out in their ears. This allowed them to clearly hear Dean's voice when he asked:

"Dad?"

"How many times have I told you not to come into my office?" said Josh in the annoyed and cruel tone that James thought he would use when replying to his interrogation, but to his surprise had not. Josh had avoided showing his true self during the interrogation, but the interruption of his son as a reminder of daily life had made him drop his guard and show his other self fully. James could not help but judge him with suspicion, and Sam could not control his impulse to squeeze the gun against his ribs.

Dean did not seem to notice the severity of his father's tone of voice, and went on speaking.

"Dad, I'm sorry. Senator Howse wants to talk to you."

A seventy year old man of respectable and venerable appearance poked his head around the door, which was now completely open thanks to young Dean's friendliness.

"Forgive me, Mr. Cosgrove. I did not know you were busy. Your son assured me that I wouldn't be interrupting."

"No, that's quite alright Senator. I had already finished this conversation a few minutes ago. We were just saying goodbye, weren't we James? This is my brother-in-law: James Penton, Senator Howse."

Josh introduced both men, hiding his discomfort as well as he possibly could, even though he felt like a sardine trapped in a can. When the formal presentations were over, he lightly pushed Dean and James, forcing them out of the office. Over his shoulder, he could see his brother Sam putting the gun away in his pocket. Josh then sighed deeply, as if the can of sardines had suddenly burst and he had been set free. For the moment he could breathe easy, until he would be in danger again when someone tried to eat him alive. That was the destiny of the common sardine.

PART 8
The Resistance

Chapter 32

Dean was pale and trembling as he left his father's office. James noticed at once. His nephew was terrified of his father.

"Dean, I want you to come with me," he said when they reached the internal staircase of the house, the one that led up to the private rooms where the Cosgrove family slept, not always peacefully.

The staircase reminded Dean of the last beating Josh had given him. He had been asleep for two hours, when Josh forced him out of bed by the hair. He pushed him into the bathroom, took off all his clothes, turned on the shower, and under the stream of water he belted him and badly bruised his skin. The water burned in his wounds. However, that same water alleviated the feeling of bleeding out as the blood turned an innocent rosy color that made him momentarily forget that it was his own blood flowing from his body. He awoke soaked in the bathtub, in the same position that he fell asleep after his father turned off the water that was falling on his prone body. He never found out what the reason for the beating was. His father never gave him explanations.

Dean did not go to school either that day or the next. The two days of the weekend gave him precisely four days for his body to recover. Only a bruise remained visible on his left cheek by Monday morning. It was a blow with the belt that missed his back and had struck his face and scratched open his skin like a cat's claws. That was exactly what he told one of his seventh grade friends. "The cat scratched me." Fortunately, no one knew he did not have a cat, nor did his teachers.

From that day on he decided to spy on his father. He wanted revenge. He wanted to slit his throat as he slept. It would have to be one of those days that his mother was uncontrollably drunk. He did not want her to be a witness.

Two nights later he clearly heard his mother stumbling from side to side, bumping against the walls. Right then, Dean decided that his father would not live a day longer. The noises against the walls were not due to his mother's drunken state, but when she rebounded after her husband punched her or slapped her face. The drinking would begin later. It would be the anesthetic that would help her to forget the pain and sleep like a baby the whole night through.

After beating his wife and leaving her on the bed, Josh went down to the kitchen to put some ice on his hand. Dean was careful not to make any noise as he went down the stairs, and he waited on the last step before his father entered his office. He tiptoed over and saw how Josh went straight to his liquor bar with bottles from around the world, as he made a phone call.

Josh spoke animatedly. His voice was incredibly calm. After a while, he pressed a button on the inside of the bar and all of a sudden a row of bottles disappeared as if a shelf had come loose. He finished his call, and walked to the door. Dean barely had time to make it to the kitchen and hide behind one of the central island cabinets. Between his agitated gasps for air, Dean heard the slight creaking of the wooden staircase. His father was going upstairs.

Once he felt safe and alone on the first floor of the house, Dean silently entered his father's office. He walked straight to the wooden bar that decorated one of the flanks of the office. It was not a particularly large piece of furniture, but enough to store bottles of liquor from around the world. Josh's favorite drink and the one he had enjoyed during James' interrogation was a Linkwood 15 Year Old 50.4% whiskey, which he bought regularly from Demijohn, a unique liquor store in Edinburgh, Scotland. The Scotch whiskey was individually bottled in an Italian glass bottle called 'cubana', which was sealed with Portuguese cork. Four countries represented in a single glass container.

Dean felt a great admiration for his father's Demijohn bottles because when he was seven years old, Josh sat him down to talk to him for the first time in his life, and the subject of the conversation was the concept of the Demijohn store. He explained how you could go in and taste the liquors before selecting the one you liked the most, and how they poured it into the bottle you wanted in the actual store and manually carved into the glass the name of the liquor. His father promised him that when he was older he would take him to Edinburgh to see the store. Another broken promise.

Dean's other favorite collection of bottles was the one that vanished when his father pressed a button. That night, try as he might, he could not find the hidden bottles nor could he make the shelf return to its position. He went over the whole piece of furniture, front and sides. He opened a compartment that revealed a row made of stainless steel and a drawer with space for sixteen bottles of wine. He searched in all the drawers. He pressed the same button he had seen his father press to make the shelf disappear, to no effect. He even searched for a screwdriver his mother kept in the kitchen and removed the bottoms of several drawers. Nothing. That night he could find no trace of the bottles… that night at least. He also did not take his revenge on his father… that night at least.

"Let me grab a change of clothes and my backpack," Dean told his uncle James when he received his invitation to leave the mansion party.

"Alright. I'll tell your mother that you will sleep with me tonight."

James would have to lie to his sister. Dean could not sleep with him because James did not plan on sleeping. He would have an urgent meeting with the FBI to tell them that he did not extract a confession from Josh Cosgrove, but that they could arrest Sam for threatening an agent with a weapon —they already had an arrest warrant in his name for the next morning. Then he would make an emergency call to the London headquarters to receive further instructions from his boss, he would talk to Paco and Ana and he would agree with Bakran in terms of the witness testimony. After all that, he would close his eyes for a couple of hours on some FBI office desk until the cruel light of the new day would force him into a cold shower and a fresh coat of deodorant and after-shave.

Dean would not accompany him on these tasks because he would leave him with Mercedes and in Valeria's care. He was counting on them to keep his nephew safe.

———

Valeria had not slept in her own apartment for the last two nights. She had temporarily taken residence in a spare room in Mercedes' house from the day she dreamed that the bacteria were eating the bodies of patients in a hospital room. The stillness of her home made her anxious and awful thoughts would come to her mind. She would stir impatiently as the case against the Cosgrove brothers slowly arrived at a conclusion. Sitting alone in her apartment, the wait seemed interminable.

In the ample incense saturated rooms of her friend's home, Valeria forgot all about the assaults of invisible bacteria, but not the events that took place at the *Amuleto Rojo* concert. The friends calmed each other down when they thought of everything they did to try to save the audience. They consoled each other mutually for the tragic death of Olivia and the other kids. Mercedes worried incessantly about the psychological impact that this would have on her daughter, and Valeria desperately missed James.

Carrying on like this was not healthy for either of them, so to distract themselves they bought a bottle of wine and chatted endlessly. As the hours flew by, they began to remember their past. Valeria went all the way back to the famous sleepovers that they had as girls every weekend. One night they would meet at Mercedes' house, the next at her best friend's house. That night, as they waited for news of the arrest of Sam and Josh Cosgrove, they were little girls in long pajamas of somber tones instead of the pastel colors that their mothers used to buy for them.

Valeria sat on the kitchen counter while Mercedes told her an anecdote about how a University Professor had once given her an F in class to force her to go and speak to him in his office and take advantage of the opportunity to ask her out. He was a young professor, single and handsome, but even so. *What balls!* thought Valeria as she listened to her friend's story.

Just then the doorbell rang.

"It must be James," said Mercedes, but Valeria arrived at that conclusion quicker and she was the first one to the door.

Dean was standing there, but not James. Another agent was with the boy, offering profuse apologies from James for not bringing the boy himself and why he could not come in and have a hot cocoa, and why it was impossible for him to explain what was going on with the Cosgrove brothers. A thousand apologies.

After saying goodbye to the agent, they offered Dean a seat and explained that Gabriela had already gone to sleep before knowing he was coming over. Valeria and Mercedes sat down with the boy facing the switched off TV. Dean had never felt so uncomfortable in his life. The women stared at him, asked him questions and raised their eyebrows. They waited for his replies. But Dean did not find their questions the least bit coherent, at least not for him.

"Can I use the computer?" he asked in the middle of one question, cutting the interrogation short and thereby asking for permission to do something other than continue with the torture he was being subjected to.

"Of course you can, Dean," Mercedes replied, instructing her friend to be quiet with a look. "The computer is on the second floor. Here, I'll show you."

It would be a long night for the friends, because they were too wired to get any sleep. Knowing that the Cosgrove brothers had returned was generating an enormous expectation in them. It seems that Dean was also startled, because he refused to accept their suggestions that maybe he should get some sleep.

At about midnight, Gabriela got up to go to the bathroom and had the surprise of her life. Dean Cosgrove was sitting in front of her computer. Was this a dream?

"Hello," said the boy in a very low voice and with a slight hand gesture and an expression of terrible embarrassment.

"What are you doing here?" Gabriela asked in a sleepy voice.

"My uncle brought me. I'm spending the night," and he lowered his eyes to show his discomfort.

"Oh, I didn't know," said Gabriela and she rubbed her eyes to wake herself up a bit.

"You were already asleep when my uncle called," Dean explained, and frowned as if to concentrate on what he was writing on the keyboard.

"What about your parents?"

"They're having a house party?" said Dean, feeling that his face was burning all of a sudden.

"Oh, I didn't know."

Silence.

"Are you on Tumblr?" Gabriela interrupted.

"No."

"Facebook?"

"No."

"YouTube?"

"No, eBay," Dean finally answered to get Gabriela to stop asking questions. But Gabriela ignored the intention, and impertinently went on.

"eBay? What are you bidding on?"
"I'm selling."
"What are you selling?"
"Bottles."

Dean did not look at her at any point as he answered in short sentences in the hope that Gabriela would tire of asking. He had no idea just how insistent some girls can be.

"You collect bottles?" went on Gabriela.
"No. My dad does."
"And he gave them to you to sell?"
"No. I stole them."

Dean was expecting this revelation to stun her.

"Oh, I didn't know," said Gabriela, unfazed.

She did not even stir from her position on the chair. Dean found this unbelievable and tried to alarm her a second time.

"I want revenge for something he did to me."

It did not work either. Gabriela was still there, asking away.

"What did he do to you?"
"I won't tell you," Dean snorted, as if to indicate the conversation was over.

"Ok," concluded Gabriela

Silence.

Ten seconds later:
"Can I see the bottles?"
"No!" Dean virtually screamed.
"How did you steal them?" Gabriela persisted.
"Do you think you're some kind of reporter or something?" Dean mumbled.

However, to Dean, Gabriela's last question felt like the gates of heaven opening. He was desperate to tell someone about his exploits, but his uncle James was in no mood when they left the mansion, and he was in a big rush to get him to Mercedes' house. He would not have dreamed of breathing a word of it to Valeria and Mercedes, but Gabriela... maybe Gabriela would be fascinated by this. At least she was as curious as he was.

Dean told Gabriela about how he found the bottles in the basement of his house. The night he spied on his father, as he tried in vain to get to sleep, he remembered a documentary he had seen about the dry law, when bars in New York, Chicago and other major cities had false doors installed to hide the liquor and the bars were rigged to pour all the bottles into the sewers via secret tunnels under the building. He had witnessed the bottles disappear from his father's bar and he had gone to the basement that night to confirm his suspicions. He found that the Prohibition era idea had been copied. Apparently a similar system was installed in his father's bar, but instead of dropping them into the sewers, the bottles fell to the basement and into a padded box.

As he finished his tale, Dean answered Gabriela's question regarding why his father would want to hide the bottles.

"My Dad's old bottles are very valuable because they are collectors' items. They are medicine bottles manufactured in the 1800's. One of them in particular, the oldest one, for Turlington Life Salve, was manufactured in England in 1723. They are very small and fit in anyone's pocket, so maybe he was hiding them from thieves", he explained.

Dean's revenge would be to sell them at a ridiculous price on eBay and deny his father his precious bottles.

"My father will have a heart attack when he realizes..." Dean concluded, and invited Gabriela to take a look. "Would you like to see them?"

Gabriela hesitated for a few seconds before asking:

"I don't suppose they could be where your father hid the MRSA?"

"Whaaaaat?" asked Dean, alarmed. "What are you talking about?"

Gabriela had listened to the adult conversations, as most kids her age tend to do. During one of James' phone calls, Gabriela turned down the volume on her iPod and heard Valeria ask if he thought he would find the proof for the MRSA infection in Josh's house. She tied the loose ends of several conversations together, some between James and Valeria and others between Valeria and Mercedes, and she had no doubt that they suspected Josh was to blame for Olivia's death as well as other kids at the concert. She heard her mother mumbling in self-pity that they should have got a pink t-shirt for Olivia too, and Valeria wracked with the guilt of not having realized the t-shirts were contaminated in time.

Gabriela told Dean about the conversations in all manner of detail. When she finished, neither of the kids had to say another word: they knew what they had to do.

They left the room with the computer, and in Gabriela's room they dressed up in ski masks, coats and winter gloves. Dean put on Gabriela's violet colored ski jacket, although he could barely squeeze into it, and waited for the mockery from the girl which never came. Gabriela was deadly serious. Her eyes and expression showed her concern.

"Did you touch the bottles in your house?" Gabriela asked at last, expressing her deepest fear.

"No. They were in a box, and I put them in my bag just as they were," he replied, and he indicated with gestures how he had put the bottles in his bag.

"Thank God!" she said, relieved.

They returned to the computer, and just as they had learned in science class, they produced the medicine bottles from the bag, holding them by the sides with two fingers, as if they were Petri dishes, although really there was no need for them to handle them that way.

Gabriela carefully put the bottles in a tote bag her mother had given her a few years ago and which she used to keep one of her porcelain dolls in. Dean placed the others in a plastic bag he took from the trash can in the room, and then they both put their bags inside the video game console box that Gabriela kept because her mother insisted she had to in case they had to return the digital device.

As Dean closed the box, Gabriela went down to the kitchen to find thick adhesive tape, not expecting to run into Mercedes.

"Gabriela, what are you doing up? And why are you dressed like that?" Mercedes asked on seeing her dressed for skiing from head to toe.

"Nothing," the girl replied, and she went on with her plan as if her mother had not seen her.

She took advantage of the fact that her mother was saying goodnight to Valeria and that they were turning off the lights to rush upstairs. Dean was waiting anxiously. He tore the tape from her hands and began to wrap the box up. One strip from left to right... snip, cut the tape. One strip from side to side, snip, cut the tape. One strip from top to bottom... snip, he cut the tape again. He repeated each movement. When he was on his sixth strip, Gabriela desperately growled at him:

"How much more tape are you going to use?"

Dean looked at the box. The whole thing was covered in tape.

"Ok. I think that's enough."

They had no idea if the MRSA in the medicine bottles was alive or dead. If it could harm them or not. What they did know was that they were possibly holding the only evidence that the bacteria was in Josh Cosgrove's house and more importantly, the testimony of his own son that he had attempted to hide it.

"If he hadn't tried to hide the bottles, we would have never suspected a thing," said Dean.

A collection of medicinal bottles on display on the bar of his own home was not something the FBI could have used against him. That was how Dean turned into James' perfect contact. Another star witness, just as soon as the presence of MRSA could be confirmed within the bottles.

"The day he gave me a terrible beating for poking around some 'dangerous' Petri dishes was probably the day he moved the contents to the medicinal bottles. He must have used those special syringes that you see on CSI when they study DNA," said Dean, as he sat beside Gabriela on the small sofa next to the computer desk.

Gabriela had only heard 'he gave me a terrible beating…' With that sentence, unwittingly, Dean had told her why he wanted revenge on his father. Gabriela would have asked more questions, but this time she controlled her curiosity. This time she fell silent and rested her head on Dean's shoulder.

"Why would your father want to keep the MRSA? Can MRSA survive for a long time in a liquid?" Gabriela asked.

"I have no clue," replied Dean.

Chapter 33

Bakran set Paco and Ana up in a discreet little hotel in a London suburb. He picked an area that was frequented by people of dubious habits, meaning that it was under constant surveillance by the police and narcotics department. That way the young Spaniards would have twice the security: that offered by the agents Bakran had assigned to the task, and about half a dozen police officers who were constantly patrolling the area in search of their favorite bad guys.

"You'll be safer in this cockroach nest than in a five star hotel where no one suspects anyone and the residents are less frequent," he told them as he gave them the keys to the room and asked them to never stick their heads out of the door.

Agent Bakran said goodbye on a Monday and three days later, Paco and Ana were climbing up the walls. From the start they sensed their imprisonment had enchained their hearts, as they felt it was not fair to spend their youth pent up between four walls. The first day, they complained incessantly. They did the same thing on the second day. At the end of the third day, they decided it was better to make the best of a bad situation. On the fourth day, trying to kill time, they asked the agents protecting them for food at all hours of the day, they played cards, they listened to music, they told each other jokes, they talked about the past, they talked about the future. They talked. And they had no choice but to hear the moans of passion of their room neighbors. They bit their nails. It was a slow and pitiless torture. They adopted the same habits of people who are locked up against their will.

On the fifth night, their restlessness turned malignant and became a full blown anxiety attack. Both of them became silent and impatient, to the point that instead of sharing their evening meal, they sat at opposite ends of the room with their backs to each other, not speaking, not moving, barely breathing.

The infernal silence lasted for over an hour, until it was banished by Ana who suddenly said:

"I always thought I would be ready for his death," she said, referring to Miguel. "I was so wrong!"

It had been five days since the girl had mentioned Miguel, and Paco had taken it as an indication that her heart was healing. However, there it was again, a stab to his feelings. Paco remained silent, but he turned to look at Ana's stoical profile.

"I started getting ready for his death from the first day we spoke about the possibility of a lung transplant, the last resort when you have cystic fibrosis. There are all kinds of complications; there is a high probability that the body will reject the organs, not to even mention the possibility of contracting a bacterial infection during the operation or recovery. Anyway, I knew that Miguel would never leave the hospital alive," she said with the authority of a woman of sixty years of age, until her breaking voice made it necessary for her to stop.

Paco came over and sat beside her on the edge of the bed.

"I'm sorry," he said.

Ana was about to cry. Seeing her suffer, Paco felt dreadful, and he shuddered to think that Ana could only see him as someone who was just there to console her. Even so, he gave her permission to cry and to express the language of her pain with tears.

She nodded, and endless tears fell from her almond eyes until her swollen eyelids and blocked nose forced her to stop. As she made an effort to control herself, she noticed her chest relaxing after the pressure of the tears which for a few moments had hurt her ribs and hunched her shoulders. With a sharp sigh, she finished the expression of sadness she felt in her soul. She straightened up and wiped her face.

"Nothing makes you feel better than a good cry," she said in a toneless voice as she rubbed her eyes. "Thanks for listening to me," she added, smiling shyly.

"You're welcome. Anytime," he replied.

Right then, Ana decided never to think sad thoughts again. This would be the last time that she openly cried over Miguel.

An hour later, worn out from so much talking, they both fell asleep on the same bed.

Paco woke up startled in the middle of the night. He found Ana in his arms, and he could not get back to sleep. Without realizing, Ana had curled up like a little girl in his arms and legs, and she was to blame for his lack of concentration and his inability to get back to sleep.

Paco tried to close his eyes again, but he could feel the warmth of the feminine body moving near him like a burning flame that was impossible to resist. When he tried to move her away, he noticed the shadow of her nipples under the nightie. Instinctively he pulled away a little, because her floral print pajamas was almost touching his naked chest and was brushing his skin which was feeling exceedingly sensitive at that point.

Now that she was further away, he let his desires take hold and he stared long and hard at the dark shadow beneath the fabric. He tried to draw the shape of her breast with his eyes as if the fabric were tracing paper and he were a small boy outlining his favorite shape. And he sighed. He covered his mouth so that she would not hear him, and with this moan he admitted to himself that a struggle for power was going on inside him. One part of him would do anything to see those naked breasts right now, and another part was desperately resisting the impulse. He shook away his bad thoughts and noticed something amazing that made him feel proud of himself. His hands were behaving. They were close to his body and not caressing Ana's body. That was the way it should be, because he did not want to be accused of a disloyal act.

But his hands were one thing and the swelling in his trousers was quite another. That part of his body was not behaving decently, tormented with the chaos of instinct. So, before he could weaken, and with the firm intention of defending his and Ana's honor, Paco decided that he would leap out of bed to enjoy solitary affections in the bathroom.

However, just as he was about to unzip his trousers, he heard Miguel's voice so clearly as if he were there in the bathroom with him. *Don't you dare think about her while you're going at it!* He stopped himself. He stood still for fifteen minutes during which, by controlling his breathing, he managed to get things under control. It was an old trick and it worked once again. The calm slowly returned, although for a moment Paco thought he would not be able to. As the odyssey ended, he thanked God.

When he got out of the bathroom, Ana was peacefully wrapped in the sheets and pillows, and thus she remained in her placid dreams until dawn came. The same could not be said for Paco, who slept uneasily tossing like a wild horse in the adjacent bed, and only at the very end of the night.

Several days went by since the incident where he locked himself in the bathroom, which fortunately did not happen again. Since then, Paco acquired new mental powers that allowed him to pass the time without worrying about the needs of his groin area taking over his whole body. *I'm maturing*, he told himself every night before going to sleep.

Fortunately, the tension of the first days gave way to a restorative calm, which they both enjoyed morning, noon and night.

"We're lucky to do whatever we want, except leave this room," they told each other.

So they began to become more extravagant with their ideas of how to pass the time. They asked the agents to bring them food from exotic restaurants, they rented foreign movies in languages they had never heard before but which thanks to the magic of subtitles they could enjoy as if they were sitting in a movie theater. They each asked for a notebook to keep a diary, an idea they stole from the 1959 movie version of "The Diary of Anne Frank". But most of all, they asked for fanciful items from their home country. All paid for by the UK government.

The day the box arrived from Spain, they celebrated like birds in a nest. Ana had requested castanets, flamenco shoes and a dress and two gypsy hair combs. Paco received some old school flamenco music: Tomatito, Diego el Cigala, Paco de Lucía and the master of the masters, the legendary Camarón de la Isla.

Before the heat of the moment could pass, Ana grabbed one of the combs and made a bun of her hair just at the back of her neck, with her hair parted in the middle and pulled back tight, except for a lock of hair at each ear. She threw the flamenco dress over her head and let it settle on her waist, where she adjusted it as she stroked her hips. She slipped her naked feet into the shoes and began to dance to the rhythm of Tomatito's guitar, striking an imposing figure each time she waved the dress towards the front as she turned. Her arms curved and marked the beat, one on her hips as if holding an invisible vase and the other in front of her pert breasts. Her neck was always stretched. She resembled a gazelle. She was slight and agile. She laughed with each move she made, with an expression of joy which came from deep within her.

After a few minutes, Paco joined in the fun. With a surprising fluidity, like a professional dance couple and each moving on their own way, their bodies accompanied the striking rhythm of the castanets, the percussion and the handclaps in the background. They were used to this sensual Spanish dance, because for many years they had attended family reunions with their Andalusian relations, and they had been forced to dance *coplas sevillanas* so that they would not lose their customs and forget their heritage.

Today, Paco and Ana, using as an excuse the urge to relive their patriotism in a London hotel room which had been their home for precisely two weeks, joined and separated their bodies and faces as their folded arms waved near their heads, almost touching each other's necks, without losing sight of each other's eyes except at the moment that they turned quickly with great emphasis to then end up facing each other.

When they finished their fourth *copla*, they looked deep into each other's eyes breathing heavily and they stood still for a few minutes, as if an invisible bar were going through their bodies, not allowing them to move. Ana finally looked down, trying to hide from the first phases of love.

The sight disturbed Paco immensely, and lowering his voice to a whisper he said:

"You are so beautiful."

As he said it, he regretted it.

Ana returned the compliment with a shy smile, and she quickly reached out for one of the chairs in the room and collapsed into it saying she was absolutely exhausted. She watched Paco from there. She tried to understand him in silence, and this scrutiny made him even more uncomfortable. Ana was looking at him fixedly and seemed to analyze all of his motives. He looked for signs in her body language from afar; the girl was cutting through his soul and for a moment he even thought she was in his brain and reading his thoughts.

It was impossible to stop her if she was intending to read his mind. The only thing Paco could do was hope that she did not have the power to really do it and that the sweat dripping down his face would be attributed to his efforts during the dance and not as a sign of how uncomfortable he was.

A few more seconds went by, and just as Ana was about to ask him about his intentions toward her, the alarm clock in the room let them cruelly know that it was time to go and visit Bakran at the NCIA offices. Paco had a mission that day: he had to identify the vials of ink that were delivered to the agent as trash coming from the laboratory.

The version he had been told was that one of the sanitary employees kept the vials for no apparent reason except to use them in his room. When he read in the papers about the MRSA cases and their apparent connection to a clandestine lab located in the sector that he worked in, he was immediately consumed with panic and he handed the vials over to the authorities.

Paco confirmed the sanitary employee's suspicions and affirmatively identified them as the vials of ink used throughout the studies of the MRSA bacteria and he was present when one of Dr. Fowler's prints was lifted from one of the vials. After his participation in the investigation, he returned with Bakran and Ana to the hotel room which already felt like a prison.

Just as the girl entered the room, Paco grabbed the agent by the arm and held him in the dingy corridor of the hotel. He whispered in his ear:

"Is there any way we can have separate rooms?"

Before Bakran could answer, Ana opened the door and announced:

"I'm going to take a bath. Do you have the key?"

When she got her answer, the girl closed the door to the room, and a few seconds later the bathroom door.

"Not being able to touch her is driving me crazy. This is worse than running away from Sam Cosgrove," Paco admitted to Bakran with heart rending intensity.

"Are you in love with the dead boy's girlfriend?" asked the agent suspiciously.

"Thanks for putting it so unpleasantly," he replied, internally regretting having confessed his heartache.

"The only cure for what you've got kid, is…" Bakran paused, before ending frivolously, "a fatal injection of MRSA. Shall I get one for you? I've got all the MRSA I could possibly want at my disposal."

"No thanks, I've had enough of that damned bacteria," Paco replied testily, ignoring Bakran's intention of lightening the mood with a joke.

"Relax, kid. If you survived that, you can survive some heartache."

He then opened the door to the room, pushed Paco in, and walked off down the corridor, shaking his head and smiling.

Chapter 34

The morning was as cruel as James had expected it to be the night before. He only slept for two hours after he forced out of bed the lab technician who had been assigned to the investigation. He wanted immediate confirmation of the contents of the medicinal bottles that Mercedes had sent to him at one in the morning. How they had come to be in his nephew Dean's possession was still a mystery to him.

"If I use a chromogenic method, it will take at least eighteen hours of incubation to be able to identify the MRSA cultures in the sample," the technician explained to him. "Go and get some sleep and we'll talk later."

"There aren't any faster processes?"

"I could use the molecular method to analyze the presence of the mecA gene, which is what gives the staphylococcus resistance to antibiotics…"

"How long would that take?"

"Much less, but even so it'll take a few hours."

"A few hours could be ten, fifteen. Can you be more specific? Because I don't have a few hours."

"I don't know exactly how many hours," he declared, and he gave James an empty stare.

"Wrong answer! Try again," James said, imitating the voice of a quiz show host.

"There is a new test, but it's designed to be used with damp nasal samples for patients suspected of having contracted MRSA. I could use that test and see if it works."

"Good thinking!" James explained, biting his tongue because what he really wanted to do was insult him for speaking to him in technical terms and punch him for not thinking of the quickest alternative sooner.

"I'm still half-asleep..." added the man, as if he had guessed his thoughts.

James could still feel the ache in every inch of his body from the hard desk he had used as his bed as he waited for the lab results. *To think that as a youngster I could sleep perfectly comfortable on the floor, without a pillow or blanket, and always woke up fresh as a daisy! Brand new.* Now the exact opposite was true. He awoke as if he were a mimosa, drooping with the weight of nights without sleep, the same way that the weight of the branches slowly bend this curious plant which goes to sleep when you touch it.

Fortunately, even with the passage of time, a shower in cold water had the same old effect. It restored his muscles. The only thing was that it took him longer now. His musculature used to be revitalized with the first touch of the water on his back. Now he woke up little by little and slowly... slowly... so slowly.

"What's up?" James asked the man who knocked on the door and interrupted his bath time.

"You have a call from agent Gordon."

Ah, the shower had not finished doing its job.

"Hi, Gordon," said James as he dried his hair with a navy blue towel that Valeria had bought him for Christmas, together with a full set of bath accessories he could use on his travels.

"The suspects are on the move," said Gordon.

"Both of them? Arrest them! Don't let them leave," he gave his instructions and with the phone to his ear he began to dress even though the blue towel had not yet touched an inch of his body.

"Too late," said Gordon, "We are in pursuit."

"Intercept them," James demanded.

However, before he could continue to issue instructions to stop the car Sam and Josh were riding in, he thought it through carefully. His superior's orders were that they should arrest them for interrogation. James and Gordon were going to do so that morning, together with two other FBI agents, but Josh and Sam had got ahead of them.

"What are they wearing?" he asked Gordon.

"Work suits and ties."

"Are they headed downtown?"

"Yes," Gordon confirmed over the phone.

"Don't lose sight of them," James ordered and then asked: "Are there other agents in pursuit?"

"Yes, we are in radio contact."

James finished putting on his shoes and said:

"Perfect. I'll meet you at the MagMell offices."

"How do you know that's where they're going?" asked Gordon, to which James replied:

"Because Josh is playing at being an innocent man, and we are going to let him play a little longer."

James stood in front of Josh Cosgrove with his hair uncombed and still a little wet, but his expression was calm and even. He leaned in the doorframe of the President's office at MagMell Laboratories, and unconcernedly crossed his legs. His upper lip could not help but rise a little in a failed attempt to repress a smile, because he was met by a visibly older Josh, who looked bitter and beaten. His bloodshot eyes and listless expression gave him the look of a UN refugee.

Before he could say a word, Josh spoke first:

"James? Have you come to help me clear out my office?" and he turned his back on him to collect his briefcase from the floor and place it on his writing desk.

"Are you moving?"

"Not necessarily. I'm leaving," he replied as he took down a reproduction of the painting "Diana and Endymion" which had decorated the wall behind his desk.

"They kicked you out?" asked James, with a smooth expression of satisfaction on his face.

"As if you didn't already know that," replied Josh vaguely, not looking at him.

He was busy opening and closing drawers on his desk. He was looking for all his personal effects.

"You couldn't convince them you're innocent?" asked James suspiciously, folding his arms across his chest.

"Innocent or not, the damage is done. The company cannot survive if I stay on," he said in a calm and tired voice.

"From President to Scapegoat," James went on with a cruel smile.

"Precisely."

Josh looked up for the first time in the conversation and stared hard into his brother-in-law's smiling eyes.

"I'm so sorry about all this," James went on with sharp cynicism.

"No, you're not, James."

For a second he looked inexpressively to the front, showing no interest in continuing with the conversation, and he looked down again. He placed a paperweight and a folder on the corner of the desk.

"You're right, I'm not sorry," James confirmed. "Where's Sam? Your shadow, your accomplice," now he persisted in a more aggressive and threatening tone.

"He's looking for empty boxes in the HR department," Josh replied, acting as if he did not have a moral conflict raging in his head, as far as the agent could tell.

"Rubbish!" James cried out, with the unpleasant sensation of his blood boiling watching Josh playing the fool in his idiotic attempts to protect Sam. "Do you know I have come to arrest him for unlawful possession of a firearm?"

James asked not knowing that he could also accuse Sam of destroying evidence in the homicide case. The younger of the two Cosgroves shredded the receipts for the purchase of fabric, ink and laboratory materials. In addition, he made Dr. Francis Fowler's reports disappear, as well as the confidentiality agreements signed by Paco and his lab mates, the newspaper clippings about Miguel's death, and Miguel's original letter to the papers.

"Sam is a little temperamental. He always has been. I don't know why he felt the need to protect me from you with a gun, but what I do know is that he has a permit for the weapon. How could he be head of security without one?" asked Josh, with a stunned expression.

His eyes narrowed, and revealed a certain discomfort.

"Are you aware of all his movements and actions?" James asked, in an effort to incriminate his brother-in-law.

Soon he would finish him off, but he would patiently await the confession. Meanwhile, he didn't mind if Josh continued to underestimate him.

"No, not everything. Sam never wanted to follow in my footsteps. I hired him this year in a final effort to get him to do something decent with his life," explained Josh, taking responsibility for his brother.

"Why are you defending him, Josh? You know full well he is involved in the t-shirt contamination."

Josh could have killed James with the expression he shot at him as he placed some papers in his leather briefcase. He did not reply, but his face was clearly asking... Are you going to persist on this course?

James kept going:

"Where is the HR department?" he asked inexorably, desperate to put an end to the charade.

"On the seventh floor," Josh answered hesitating.

His voice was weak, almost a whisper.

"Thanks," said James, and he turned on his heel making no farewell gesture.

"I'll come with you," said Josh, and he hurried after James, who turned to face him.

"That won't be necessary, Josh. That's what my new friend Gordon is here for."

He put his hand on the FBI agent's shoulder, who at that moment made his presence known for the first time.

"And Gordon's friends too who are waiting in the lobby for my instructions in case Sam tries to resist arrest."

Josh insisted on following James and agent Gordon. The three men arrived at the elevator lobby at the same time.

"What is your evidence against Sam?" Josh asked in a loud voice.

James repressed his satisfaction to avoid betraying his intentions. *He is falling into the trap. I'm reeling him like a fish*, and he whirled around to reply.

"You think I'm going to tell you that?"

He stood there for a few seconds, blinking, not looking away from Josh's face, trying to force him to move his lips and let go of the secret he kept deep inside him: the truth. Until he noticed the smoke coming through the elevator doors.

"What's that?" asked Gordon.

The smell of burnt cardboard and other flammable materials you usually find in office buildings filled the air in a few seconds. Instinctively both agents searched the walls for the fire alarm while the elevator doors began to open.

Several people got out of the elevator, coughing in the clear smoke, and one of them was Sam Cosgrove, but neither agent saw him as they were too busy searching for a fire alarm to give warning that there was a fire in progress to the early birds who had already come in for work that morning.

"Use the stairs, quick, quick," James shouted, and he headed towards a dozen people who were hurrying in and filling the corridor in seconds.

"Sam... are you responsible for this?", Josh mumbled to his brother.

"No," and he grabbed his arm. "But we have to get out of here," and he pulled his brother away from Penton and Gordon.

"Did you destroy everything?" Josh asked again, coughing a little from the smoke.

"Yes," said Sam.

"Good job," he said proudly, patting his brother on the back.

They both smiled, sharing a secret message.

Their smile was wiped away by the sound of the fire alarm in the building, and the security department announcement ordering an evacuation. Both brothers hurried away from the elevators. But before they got away, James was able to spot them amongst the mass of bodies.

They could only exchange looks instead of bullets. There were too many people in the corridors, too much distance between them. Even so, it was not enough for James not to notice Josh and Sam leaving with a half-smile on their faces. They headed into the East stairwell. Two rams getting away. Guilty men saved by the bell.

The sound of the fire alarm resounded throughout the Financial Place fire station. One of the fire fighters ran for the fire truck with the dispatch order.

"Isn't that the bank there was a fire at a few years ago?" asked one of the younger fire fighters.

"No," replied his commander, yelling over the wailing of the sirens. "But it's on the same block."

The younger man clearly remembered the fire at LaSalle Bank, one of Chicago's historical buildings. Twenty-five people were hospitalized due to a fire that broke out on the twenty-ninth floor and could not be stopped in time because there were no sprinklers installed.

There were still dozens of Downtown buildings in the same conditions. They were old buildings, many of them historic monuments of the city and not in compliance with current construction requirements. This had forced legislators to push for an ordinance that all historical buildings in the city install sprinklers before the decade was out. Unfortunately, this had still not come into the effect, and the forty-five floor building where James was had absolutely no fire-protection safeties, except for the two stairwells for emergency evacuation, one at either end of the building. The building was at the mercy of the flames.

The fire truck driver hit the siren and the scream warned pedestrians that they were on their way to a fire. The flashing light was reflected along the street and the thundering alarm rebounded against the walls of the buildings generating a deafening echo that made people on the sidewalks hunch their shoulders a little, as if with that gesture they could turn off the sound in their ears.

Inside the building, the flames were gathering strength on several floors just minutes after the smoke was first noticed. Suddenly the smoke turned dark and menacing, and had a single purpose: to announce the destruction that was to come. In the distance, James could hear the voices of people begging for help and the windows shattering from the impact of chairs thrown against them. The walls began to whistle around him, and the smoke crackled as the fire became a relentless beast that navigated its way along the ceiling towards the end of the corridor.

All of these sounds bombarded and paralyzed James. The noises seemed to be getting closer because his hearing became extraordinarily sensitive. His hands began to shake like those of an old man with Parkinson's. He looked around, and all he could see was Gordon hyperventilating, meaning that the oxygen could not do its job and he was in danger of passing out at any moment. James saw the terror fill Gordon's eyes, and he saw himself reflected in them. He was looking death in the eye.

"Gordon, Gordon. React…" he screamed at him, but his words seemed to stand still and not reach the other end of the corridor.

G O R D O N … R E A C T… The series of letters just floated in the air and did not reach the agent's ears. Gordon was frozen, as if he were in a freezer rather than a burning building.

James went over to him and tried to maneuver him towards the stairs. But it was in vain. He was sitting there, like an iceberg in the middle of the ocean, heavy like a submerged rock. In the deafening noise and with Gordon's unexpected reaction, James could not decide what he should do, and he feared for his life.

The fire engulfed the office floor.

Chapter 35

The billowing smoke and the huge amount of people piling down the same stairs that the Cosgrove brothers were using, made progress slow and hard for them to keep together. Sam was at least ten steps below Josh, who could see his brother's back as he went past slow moving people and cheered his brother on:

"Keep moving, Josh, it isn't far now."

But suddenly, Josh could not see him anymore.

The door to one of the floors flew open, bashing him in the face as three terrified women ran through. After the blow, Josh was stunned, and he waited for the people around him to move past. Without his realizing, they all left him behind. He seemed to be alone among the noises of the fire that was melting the walls several floors above, and the thunder of the marching steps descending several floors below. That was where Josh found himself. At a standstill.

When he at last realized he should keep moving, he gave a hesitant step forward, tripped on the edge of the step, and rolled down. He came to a halt on a landing, and at that same moment his vision started to blur and life seemed to escape him. Just a few seconds passed, when suddenly an extreme pressure built in his chest and made him recover consciousness, only to give way to a sensation of suffocation and of his lungs bursting. His throat was in considerable pain, he felt a terrible stabbing agony in his head which was lost in a riot of intermittent and passing sensations that he was unable to fully process. To die asphyxiated in a burning office building was not the end that Josh Cosgrove had foreseen for his career or his life.

This is ridiculous! was the thought that ran through his mind.

He felt such indignation and disbelief that the internal and external sense of vertigo grew in his body, and Josh recovered some control over his body. His mind focused on better times.

This morning I was drinking mimosas and reading Fortune. This will not end like this.

He made an effort to spot a way out through the thick smoke that enveloped him. In the gaps forming between the grey and white walls of smoke, he saw the door at the end of the stairs, but his brain did not give his body the instruction to stand up. He breathed in deeply the searing air. He felt his throat burning. His heart began to lose strength; it seemed to be fluttering weakly.

He thought he could hear other people descending the stairs. They came across his body slumped on the floor and they took his pulse. But they could not feel anything. They continued on their way. Meanwhile the smoke was getting darker and filling every molecule of space, consuming all the oxygen, so people no longer had to trip over Josh to fall beside him. One woman fell on top of him, and put her hands on his face. They were trembling, just as Josh's had been a few minutes earlier. The stranger whispered to him to remain calm, that she could hear the fire truck sirens. They would soon be rescued. And she rested her long curly hair on Josh's weak heart.

Josh's subconscious started to scream at him. He pushed the woman aside, and quickly stood up gasping for air. He went up the stairs quickly, and ran for the door. But when he tried to tug it open, he could not budge it a millimeter because it was locked. He began to beat on the small glass window, desperately screaming to be let out. For someone to open the door. When he did not receive an answer, he slid back to the floor. But his body was not beside the door. He was still stretched beneath the weight of the lifeless woman who was on top of him, both surrounded by other unknown bodies.

Several floors above Josh, near the West staircase – the other of the two emergency stairs in the skyscraper– James knelt beside Gordon. The man was gasping, frozen with terror, and James was trying to shake him out of his condition. The problem was that Gordon was trapped in a different fire. The one that ravaged his childhood home. His four-year old sister had woken him up. She was scared. Gordon noticed the strange smell when he left his room. Just then his parents came running out of the main bedroom, half-naked and sleepy. The fire was blocking the escape route downstairs, where it had begun and was leaping around like an adolescent organizing a party when his parents are out.

Gordon was reliving the sight of his father sliding out of the bedroom window and jumping to the ground. The effort broke his right leg. But he stood up as if nothing had happened and instructed Gordon to jump, that he would catch him, to not be afraid. In midair, on the way to his father's arms, he saw the expression of terror of his father as he screamed the names of his wife and small daughter in desperation. They never saw them again.

Meanwhile, the fire in MagMell Laboratories was getting dangerously near and the screams of those trapped in the rear offices were no longer heard. Instead, the snap, crackle and whistling of the fire had intensified. The sound of cell phones ringing constantly filled the air. The TV must have broken the news that a fire had started in the building. Families were calling their loved ones incessantly in the hope that they would reply and tell them they were already safe.

What most disconcerted James were the office phones which were also ringing nonstop. *That can't be family. That's not a phone call they would want to be answered*, he thought. *Perhaps it's journalists, thinking that someone can describe to them what's going on. Or maybe it is a family member making sure that their children, parents, partners and lovers know that there is a fire and they have to get out.*

However, all James wanted at that moment was for them to stop ringing. They could all talk later. The priority was to get out of there. So, what was he doing there waiting for the smoke to get to him? *Waiting for Gordon*, he answered his own question and looked at Gordon who was still in a catatonic state until his lips began to pout like those of a two year old, and one hand went up to point.

James jumped at what Gordon was indicating. A man enveloped in flames and screaming in horror was moving down the corridor towards the elevators. His hair, face, glasses and clothes were all melting as he ran, and sticking to his burning skin. James broke a fire extinguisher case and doused the man as quickly as he could to quench the flames. But it was too late. The man gibbered incoherently, collapsed and was dead before he touched the floor, landing between the luxurious double doors which announced the name of Josh Cosgrove, President.

James instinctively produced his gun and began to fire at the name etched in the glass doors, shattering it with several shots. He went on firing at the ceiling, the walls, the smoke. With his Glock 17 in hand, as if it were a hose, and standing like a valiant firefighter challenging the great orange beast, he shot several rounds into the air and shouted at the distant fire:

"Come and get me, if you dare."

He went on in this maddened state until Gordon grabbed his hand to stop him from shooting, and pushed him towards the stairs. Agent Gordon was himself again. The shots had snapped him out of his panic attack, and he immediately knew what he had to do: run down the stairs. Both agents did so, chasing one another down the steps as if they were each other's shadow. Rhythmically, together, one, two, three, forty... they leaped down the stairs two-by-two. Every so often they dodged high heel shoes they encountered on their way which had been left behind by their owners.

Out on the street they ran into the TV cameras, and Gordon pushed the journalists aside with all his strength to get through. He needed to get as far away from the building as he could. James stopped on the sidewalk, with the cameras tracking his every slow movement. First he looked up at the rectangle of sky he could see amongst the skyscrapers, and then he leaned forward and grabbed his knees with both hands, resting in that position, gulping down air, coughing, until he was able to stand up and run his blackened hands across his forehead to push the hair out of his eyes.

Then he walked to the side of the building and threw his guts up in private. Right there in the alleyway, with one hand resting on the cement wall of the burning building and hunched forward, he got rid of all the bile. That was his reaction to the pure terror he had experienced in some of the longest minutes of his life.

"I'm getting too old for this," he told himself out loud.

"If Bakran could see us, he'd get back at us for mocking him over the drunk pissing guy," he heard a voice say behind him.

That was when James noticed he was not alone. Gordon was nearby, sitting on the floor, trying to dry the sweat from his face with his shirt sleeve. Both men looked each other in the eye, and their eyes locked almost at once. It was the equivalent of a handshake. They ended the conversation with that gesture. There was no need to verbalize their thanks.

At the other side of the building, where all the ambulances were parked, a six foot tall man in a grey three piece suit and black leather shoes was being hauled along on the shoulders of a policeman. He wore a thin gauze mask on his face, of the kind used for skin burns. Apparently, his face had been badly burnt, but his hands had miraculously escaped unscathed.

"I don't know what's worse, but losing your face has got to be awful," said one of the FBI agents in a low voice as he went by.

The FBI agents were fruitlessly waiting for Sam and Josh Cosgrove to appear amongst the survivors. They were waiting for them to appear alive. They were waiting.

While they held position, Sam allowed himself to be dragged along by the police officer to the paramedics and the ambulances, where he confused himself in the crowd of patients and passersby. The officer who had helped him to reach the area, handed him over to the paramedics who rested him on a gurney while they examined a more seriously injured patient. After a few seconds, Sam stood up as if surprised to find himself there, and walked into the crowd. The white gauze mask with breathing holes that he had stolen from the paramedics equipment in the building lobby and which allowed him to remain anonymous while he made his escape, was found two hours later discarded on the street.

Chapter 36

"For the time being, eleven people have been confirmed dead in the mysterious fire that broke out at the MagMell Laboratories office tower. The firefighters' official version of events indicates that the fire broke out on the twenty-eighth floor in an office that had been undergoing remodeling. The documents and old papers contained in the office were stored in temporary boxes for their removal to a warehouse. The fire chief explained that any dry material, such as paper, may act as a flammable agent. 'All that is required is a simple spark to cause a terrible accident of large-scale proportions such as this', indicated the Fire Chief, Adam Palusky. Amongst the first people reported deceased is Mr. Josh Cosgrove, president of MagMell Labs and a well-known philanthropist and humanist."

Valeria listened to the news report in shock at Mercedes' house. Minutes before she had been pacing impatiently waiting until eight a.m. for Mercedes' press conference at MagMell Laboratories to begin, announcing the dismissal of Josh Cosgrove as president of the company. For that reason she had turned on the TV, and to her surprise she had instead seen the news of the fire.

Now she was sitting on the sofa with her knees huddled together up to her chest, and her hands clasped between her legs. She watched the images on the TV dumbfounded, the windows shattering and glass falling through the air down to the street, the jets of water from the fire trucks coming in different directions, the side of the building tinged in black and the flames... flames that cruelly tore out the interior of the offices and showed their malice glimpsing through open windows. The reporter went on:

"At this time, while we are reporting, there are possibly still people trapped inside the offices or in the stairwells on the upper floors."

Valeria interlaced her fingers like a clamp. Her knuckles went white as milk. Her teeth chewed on a piece of ice in her mouth. The rest of the ice cubes were melting in a glass of orange juice that was left untouched on the side table beside the sofa since she turned the set on and heard the bad news.

Three thousand people work in that building. How many managed to get out?, she thought as she watched the fire in action, not blinking. Suddenly her mind screamed out.

"Mercedes? Where is Mercedes?" and in the precise instant that she picked up the phone, her friend's call came in to allay her fears.

"I never even made it into the building. The fire alarm had already been activated when I got here," Mercedes explained to Valeria, who nervously asked her about the incident.

"Do you know Josh is dead?" asked Valeria.

"Yes. I saw the firefighters come out with his body. He was one of the first."

Valeria heard the journalist talking about Josh Cosgrove and his premature, untimely and unfortunate death.

"A pillar of our community has passed away in the ravages of the fire that has gutted the central offices of MagMell Laboratories."

The report took great cares to gloss over the man's defects and to exalt his greatness. Valeria and Mercedes listened in silence, both feeling that they were losing all sense of justice. Josh was being glorified, a memorable death that allowed him to hide his guilt and deny his involvement in the MRSA contamination.

If the fire had not happened, it would have been a different story. If Mercedes had her chance, she would have explained to the public by means of the press conference planned for that morning, MagMell Labs' position concerning the t-shirt infection and Mr. Cosgrove's role in the whole affair. If it had not been for the legal restraints, she would have even shown the medicine bottles found in the mansion basement and which the lab had now confirmed contained MRSA exhibiting different mutations and resistances to antibiotics. She also would have revealed that some of the medicine bottles contained two types of ink contaminated with the same bacteria. Mercedes would have abstained from explaining how the bottles had arrived in her hands; when she had gone into her computer room at home, Dean and Gabriela finally confessed why they were dressed up for skiing in the dead of the night.

Valeria remained perplexed in the middle of the room until the TV cameras showed two men leaving the building... One an FBI agent who pushed the cameras aside to make way for himself, and another who could not be seen clearly because he was leaning forward gasping for air. *It's James...* Valeria could clearly see him when he stood up straight and walked away from the building.

Afflicted by the fact that Josh Cosgrove would go unpunished for his crimes in life, and that James had almost perished in the same fire, Valeria turned off the TV and allowed a new thought to enter her mind. It occurred to her that there was still something she could do to remedy the situation. She had to respond, to react, to make something up to fix what had happened with the MRSA, or at least improve matters. *Something to make the charred body of Josh*

Cosgrove spin in that hell where he can go on burning for all eternity. He will pay for his crimes in death.

It took her an arduous four day campaign to persuade the Board of MagMell Laboratories that her strategy was the right one. Weeks later, a notice appeared in the papers:

> "MagMell Labs is initiating its FREE campaign for preventive vaccination against MRSA across all the major cities of the United States. This is a never before seen effort on the part of a Pharmaceutical company. Thousands and thousands of patients attended the vaccination centers on the first day. Millions of dollars went into the Pharmaceutical giant's bank accounts, not from sales of the new MRSA vaccine, but from sale of its patent. Mercedes Mojena, vice-president of MagMell Labs explained during a press conference that the proceeds from the sale of the patent of the new vaccine will be reinvested into a series of aggressive studies for combatting Cystic Fibrosis, a condition that afflicts over seventy thousand children and young adults around the world..."

While news of the free campaign flooded the papers, mass media websites and the social media, Mercedes took part in a meeting of the Chicago Local Council. Approximately one-hundred people attended said meeting to hear a report of conditions at hospitals around the city.

> "All patients are undergoing mandatory testing for MRSA prior to hospitalization in

both public and private centers and community clinics in a major effort to contain the spread of the bacteria. Automatic hand disinfectant dispensers have also been installed at hospital entrances so that patients and visitors can wash their hands before coming into contact with other patients or hospital personnel. Mandatory tests to rule out the presence of MRSA both before and after operations have also been implemented at major hospitals, and community clinics will soon be required to do the same for any invasive procedures, including dental hygiene."

Before coming up with this whole campaign against MRSA and right after recognizing James emerging from the building in flames, Valeria received a call that changed her way of seeing things.

"Sweetie?"

"James? James? Are you alright? I just saw you on TV when you came out of the building. Your face... your face was black with soot. I thought I saw you limping..."

"I'm fine, Vale. I'm on my way over," he reassured her over the phone, gently and with aplomb.

He was longing to see her.

"No... Don't come."

Valeria surprised herself hearing no hint of alarm or warning in her voice that something was wrong, no expression of dissatisfaction or regret. Nothing.

"Why?" asked James, uncomfortable.

"I don't want to see you. I can't see you anymore."

This time when she replied, her voice was precise, sad and bereft, and her face reflected in the dead TV screen showed her anxiety, but she remained firm. Firm in her decision.

"Vale, meet me at Oak Street Beach in one hour," he replied with the same determination, and hung up.

Chapter 37

That year, the cold in Chicago persisted well into Spring, and for that reason many of the trees took longer to turn green again. Even so, that morning the day dawned bright and sunny, with clear skies. Spring at last took hold of the weather. When Valeria got up that day, she could feel that something incredible would happen. However, she never thought that the deadly fire at MagMell Labs would be the high point of the drama she had experienced in those last few months.

"There's no place in this city to have this conversation," she lamented herself as she took off her pajamas which had been her clothing for the whole time she had been glued to the TV set watching the news about the fire unfold. Now she had to get dressed to meet James and tell him something that neither of them wanted to hear, and for that she would have preferred to be surrounded by nature to feel better about her decision.

She would rather speak to him somewhere they could hear the breeze brush through the first leaves of springtime, the hesitant first songs of the birds perched in the trees, the beating wings of insects carried by the perfume of flowers and the toads chatting in the thick undergrowth; it would make the conversation less unpleasant. However, the city still did not have enough sunshine and there was nowhere that felt like a meadow in March, unless she went to the roof of City Hall which although it imitated a meadow and was frequented by the birds and the bees in Spring, was not the perfect place for two lovers to reunite after not seeing each other for so long.

James had told Valeria to go to Oak Street Beach facing Lake Michigan, knowing it was her favorite location in the city.

Valeria was the first to arrive. The soft murmur of the wind caressed the surface of the lake. Her long hair drifted fearlessly while her eyes observed the magnificent landscape of a borderless lake, with no coast on the horizon to limit its greatness. A sea. The passage of the wind around her body made her shiver. She hugged herself seeking warmth, and at that moment perceived James arriving in the distance. She could feel his presence although she did not turn to greet him. The anticipation pumped through her blood like a frenzied drumming.

He drew closer slowly. Valeria could hear his footsteps sinking into the sand. As he arrived, James ran his knuckles down her arm, and delicately ran his fingers over her feminine shoulder. While he caressed her, he walked alongside her and stopped in front of her, a living obstacle between Valeria and the lake. But she felt no discomfort due to the interruption. The landscape became more real, more accessible, because she could not wrap her arms around the majesty of the lake, but she could wrap them around the man she loved and hold him close.

They remained silent for a time, holding each other, intertwined, not allowing the passage of time to rush their feelings. Their hearts were beating fast, Valeria's much faster than James'. She thought she was going to lose him. He always knew he would return. Even so, seeing her in such a delicate state turned his heart upside down. He only knew Valeria's strong side. She was like a rock, so sure and confident. Now he could see what love was doing to her: her defenses were crumbling and she was setting them aside just for him. Valeria betrayed her true self, and for a moment showed her vulnerability. Only James would have the privilege of knowing her completely, and he took this responsibility very seriously. Forever. Valeria and James.

"I'm fine, Valeria, I swear to you," he said at last when the emotions gave way to calmness.

"James, I can't. Your job is going to kill you and so it's going to kill me. I can't bear it."

She preferred to keep her distance, so she pushed his chest away, opening a space between their bodies.

"I know, Sweetie. It isn't fair…"

However, for a change he did not finish his sentence. Valeria slipped back into the conversation. She stole his turn.

"I'm not a woman who can sit back and wait for the bad news, James. I admire the wives of police officers and firefighters. They are my heroines. But I was not born with that gene. I need peace. I need an open mind to remain creative. If I had to wait on you, I would become obsolete," she said stunned by the opportunity that she was allowing to slip away.

James knew full well that everything Valeria was confessing to him was true. He could recognize that it was a turning point in their relationship, and for that reason, to prevent her from throwing him overboard, he covered his girlfriend's mouth with his right hand, put his other hand behind her neck, and made a kind of gag as if she were a hostage.

"I have a plan that you are going to love, Vale. You are going to open your own marketing and PR firm. I am going to obtain, once and for all, a photojournalist license. I'm also a photographer, did you know that? I wasn't lying when I said that. You can give me a few jobs so I can get established. And we live happily ever after."

Even when he released her, Valeria remained mute and she looked at him incredulously, with a head full of a single doubt: *Is he serious?* But she did not make any gestures to formulate the question, so James took advantage of this and went on.

"Would you lend me some money to buy a couple of cameras? They stole mine in Cairo," he finished with a Machiavellian smile.

Valeria hit him with her handbag, and asked irrepressibly, but with a new ray of hope:

"You would do that for me?"

"No. No, I wouldn't do that for you," he said, making a short pause that felt like an eternity before explaining himself. "I would do that for myself," James at last replied, and he stared deep into her eyes.

Valeria's trembling lips parted.

"What about James Bond?"

"I shot him three times in the MagMell offices."

And he remembered his frustration engulfed in the fire.

"Seriously, Vale, I will hand in my resignation tomorrow morning," he replied, sure that it was time to cut ties with his old life. He was removing the weight of the world from his shoulders. Now, other discreet heroes would take his place.

Two weeks later, on another continent and in another language, a boy and a girl were also expressing themselves, but with serious tones and not much emotion in their words. They were talking about day-to-day things, and not even openly. Ana and Paco were the speakers.

They were talking in their native tongue about the events that had taken place in the States regarding MRSA. On the terrace of a rooftop restaurant overlooking the Plaza Santo Domingo in the four star hotel they were staying at in Madrid, they were eating churros and hot chocolate. Bakran had moved them to a different hotel, and returned them to their home country.

"Everything is about to come to a conclusion," he assured them, and admitted that they would soon catch Sam and the youngsters would soon be set free.

A similar mask to the one that had hidden Sam Cosgrove's identity during the fire unfortunately also gave him the perfect route out of the United States, so the masked man was still the most wanted man in the world. Bakran took several days to track down a clue. A solitary clue that led him to another clue, and so on. Until he was able to receive confirmation from a forty-eight year-old American nurse, who he found destitute in a London alley, that Sam had returned to the English capital. The nurse had helped him escape Chicago. She had shaved his head, cured the burn wounds on his neck which were self-inflicted so that he would seem to be a patient with severe burns, she obtained a new gauze mask for him, travelled with him as his personal nurse, and all in exchange for promises of marriage and safe sex.

"The burn victim story won't last him very long. We are already on his trail, and the scarring on his neck will make him easier to identify," Bakran told Ana and Paco as he said goodbye. "So, kids, have fun within the limits of the hotel. As soon as we have him, I will come and get you so you can go back to your lives. Just another couple of days, give me another couple of days."

Paco and Ana dreamed of that day being today, so that this odyssey could end and Ana could go back to her plans of enrolling in University and Paco could make serious plans for himself for the first time. Neither one of them was sure of their future, only that they would become independent of their parents.

So they spent two hours of small talk admiring the view of Madrid, with neither one of them expressing what was really going through their minds. In the meantime, they ordered another two mugs of hot chocolate with churros to kill some time. Paco knew that what he really wanted to do did not depend on him, and so he was silent. How could he impose that he wanted to remain forever beside Ana? She would have to tell him, let him know. So the minutes went by and neither one of them took the initiative. The wall between them would simply not fall.

When the time drew close to say goodbye, Ana going to her room and Paco to his, he produced a cloth bag which he had kept hidden the whole time, containing a white box with a yellow ribbon and he gave it to Ana, his hands trembling. She looked in his eyes, but did not ask anything. She delicately pulled on the yellow ribbon, and the knot vanished. Inside the box there was gift wrapping paper hiding the contents.

Ana explored excitedly until her fingers felt a small notepad decorated with rose petals. She took it in her hands, admiring its beauty, and asked what it was. But Paco, in silence, told her with a gesture to open it. There was a dedication on the first page, telling her what it was.

"This is a collection of my jokes so you can laugh first thing in the morning. You can add your own, the ones that Miguel told you, and the ones you pick up along the way. So that you will always be happy. Paco."

Ana did not waste a single second, and she began to read them out, one by one. Their laughter could be heard down the corridors and internal windows of the hotel. One of the waiters, amazed by the sudden change in mood of the customers at table two, looked out onto the terrace and what he saw stunned him. The two youngsters could not stop laughing, and joyful tears poured from her eyes. A wonderful sparkle could be seen in his eyes as he admired her magnificent smile. Suddenly he could not contain himself, and he kissed her. He kissed her passionately. He kissed her tenderly. He kissed her as he ran the tip of his fingers along the delicate contours of her body.

With that kiss, Paco reached Ana's soul. She went red with touches of sunflower yellow glowing in her feminine features. Overwhelmed and amazed, Ana was briefly tormented by the grief over Miguel's death, but she locked it away behind iron bars in her past memories, where Miguel had told her to hide her pain so she could go on living. After that, she hid her gypsy features in the boy's young chest, the boy who was offering her a new beginning, and she smiled. She trembled in his arms. In that instant, their calm turned into a hurricane when Ana returned the gesture of love and initiated their second kiss.

"Samuel, Samuel, you have customers waiting at table seven!" ordered the head waiter in a loud bark.

On hearing his instructions, Sam Cosgrove lifted the collar of his shirt to hide the scar still healing on his neck to head towards table seven to continue working. With a subtle turn he stopped spying between the curtains on the two young guests on the terrace, who were wearing out their lips with kisses.

Author's Notes:

This book is dedicated to the Lopez family, especially their beloved daughter Sarah, God rest her soul, for being the inspiration and motivation for this story. Part of the proceeds from its sale will be donated to the Cystic Fibrosis Foundation, commemorating Sarah's fight against this disease. To read more about this brave girl's admirable life, you can visit www.padmorepublishing.com/goldenplague

I began writing Golden Plague just after a deadly incident occurred in the United States, where several students at a high school were affected by an infection caused by the MRSA bacteria. Apparently the spread of the bacteria occurred in the lockers of the school's sports facilities. All affected students were football players. Many things have changed since then. More studies and measures are being carried out to try to minimize MRSA infections. However, bacteria remains a mystery to the scientific community, because they seem to have a mind of their own and they mutate from time to time to prevent being destroyed. It is for this important reason that humans must never lose sight of them, because at any time, they regain strength and attack mercilessly.

All the data provided on MRSA and its proliferation is accurate, at least upon completion of the book. However, the story is completely fictional. Any similarity to any event in real life is purely coincidental. At press time there was no vaccine to prevent contagion with the bacteria. Therefore, let your family and friends know the importance of preventing MRSA infections.

If you or one of your loved ones has suffered from a bacterial infection and wants to share the experience, we have dedicated a space for you on our website www.padmorepublishing.com/goldenplague We'd love to hear your story.

I hope this book has helped you understand the problem of MRSA infections in an entertaining way. If you enjoyed reading it, let others know. And if you fancy to write a short review on social networks or on the online store where you purchased it, so that other people can also get excited to read it, I will be forever grateful for your support.

Book Discussion:

1. How did you feel when you found out what happens to Miguel?

2. Did you know the disease Cystic Fibrosis and its characteristics before reading this book?

3. If you were Valeria, would you have been able to accept not knowing James' occupation early in the relationship?

4. Were you able to relate to Paco's dilemma once he has to escape from the hospital?

5. Do you know someone who has cought a bacterial infection while in a hospital? How did the news make you feel?

6. What did you think about Valeria's reaction to the challenge of marketing a pharmaceutical product and work with such a demanding customer?

7. Is it vital for pharmaceutical companies to aggressively promote their products?

8. Do you think pharmaceutical companies manipulate the market for medications to increase their consumption?

9. Do you think the FDA (Food and Drug Administration) is too lenient when approving new medical products?

10. What is your opinion about the work of the CDC (Center for Disease Control) to prevent epidemics?

11. What would you have done if you had found yourself in the same situation as Valeria in the concert?

12. Do you think that Paco was wrong to fall in love with his roommate's girlfriend? Will the love affair between Paco and Ana last?

13. How did you like Valeria's dream in the hospital moratorium? Do you think that dreams are the subliminal way our mind face reality?

14. Should hospitals report cases of bacterial infection in their facilities and make this information available to the public?

15. Do you think that Josh was guilty of contaminating the T-shirts or it was only Sam's plan?

16. After she saw him on the TV news, was Valeria right to want to end her relationship with James?

17. Do you think James is really going to quit the NCIA?

18. What is your opinion about Sam's juxtaposition between being handsome and elegant in appearance, but with a perverse mind and attitude?

19. What is your favorite scene from the book?

20. Discuss the title of the book and its meaning.

Acknowledgements:

To all the people who shared their stories of grief after losing a loved one in a hospital due to a bacterial infection. I personally know of several patients who have died for the same reason and the impact of knowing that it was not the operation nor the disease that ultimately provoked their death, but a bacteria lodged in their body during the same procedure that was done in order to save their lives, is a difficult fact to accept. I greatly appreciate the courage of all of whom agreed to express their feelings.

To the doctors and pharmaceutical employees who, under promise of anonymity, discussed their recommendations, voiced their concerns and shared their knowledge on this subject. Without their help, this story would not have been possible.

To all my friends and former colleagues, because when they learned that I had written a book, without having read a single word or knowing the plot, told me with surprising enthusiasm: "I want it! Is it already in bookstores? ". I hope you enjoy reading this book, and by doing so you are rewarded for the trust that you blindly bestowed upon me. I hope I have been able to repay the belief you had in me and for the emotional investment made in my writings. Kisses.

To Gloria Maristany, my first victim, who read the manuscript in two days, said it was ready for publication after sending me a list of everything she didn't like (and what she liked too) and then scolded me because now she has to wait for the sequel.

To Manolo Oliveras, with whom I discussed pharmaceutical confidences, character names, his apathy towards a character because he consider it too tragic until he understood his heroic role, and his suggestion that I used Lab Rats as a title which I assigned to one of the chapters. As an incorrigible bachelor, his dream was for me to write a heroine with an irresistible character, because he is eager to ask out one of my protagonists. I listened, I wrote Valeria, but introduced her to James. Sorry, Manolo. Next time.

To Ana Mercier, for your support, your notes and your text messages in the middle of reading to say you were on the beach crying inconsolably because I killed one of your favorite characters. But the best of your comments proved to be the most desired by a writer, when you confessed that from a certain point on you could not put the book down and you even read it up in the bathroom. Thanks Anita for giving a wonderful touch of humor to the tedious task of editing a book.

To Natalia Galindo for your relentless corrections and revisions and extensive knowledge of grammar, which you selflessly shared with me along the entire initial editing process. I will be forever grateful.

To my dear Ingrid Rivera, for her encouragement and assurance that this book would be published. Thank you for being my partner in the first phase of this incredible adventure.

To Maricarmen Carbonell and Alina SanGiovanni, for their reviews, suggestions, discussions, some late at night and others for long hours at a restaurant table, but above all, for their sincere friendship.

To my husband, to whom I owe the impetus to continue when everything seemed too overwhelming. Thanks for being my life and great romance. And to my children for being so understanding, especially when they had to wait to tell their stories of the day because I was writing last words in a hurry so they did not escape me. I love you guys. Thank you for being my greatest fans.

To my mother and my sister for showing me unconditional love. Thanks for always giving me a boost, but most of all for listening. To my brother-in-law for his insightful suggestions that helped me phrase everything related to advertising. To my brother and my sister-in-law for always be happily surprised when I tell them what I am up to.

And finally, to my father for giving me the love of reading. Without that, I would not be what I am today.

Author's Biography:

Ila Monroe became the editor of a respected health magazine at twenty-five years of age - the youngest editor ever at her employer's offices: a woman's magazine, business newspaper and general interest publishing house. She won the Excellence Award for Journalism from the American Medical Association, and also received recognition for her ability to write healthcare news in a provocative yet accessible style. She is also the winner of the Innovation Award for her interactive educational series: "Heroes from our History", in which Monroe demonstrates her ability to be a versatile producer and writer. By means of her editorial career, Monroe has also written a publication on pregnancy (which is still number one in sales lists for books at her publishing house), several short stories, essays, and children's books. Her new collection of historical books for children will be published in autumn 2013, by Padmore Publishing Group. **Golden Plague** is her first novel, informing readers, in an entertaining style, about several medical enigmas that plague our modern world. Monroe currently resides in Florida with her husband and two children.

Printed by Libri Plureos GmbH in Hamburg, Germany